Stealing a bride was a miserable business, Connor decided.

And wrapping this one like a Christmas pudding was not sufficient. He should have gagged her mouth as well as her flailing limbs, for he needed both hands to handle a horse galloping with two riders. The girl shrieked like a kestrel, and as he pressed his hand over her mouth again, her breath warmed his palm through the wool. Mercifully, she quieted.

"Hush," he soothed. He settled his arm across her chest, his fingers on her jaw, while his other hand gripped the reins.

He had no taste for bullying women, and his patience was easily tested. His promise to Duncrieff obligated him to carry out this regrettable snatching. Take her, her brother had said, see it done, explain later.

When the time came tonight to consummate the marriage, Connor wondered how he could possibly take her, see it done, and explain later.

Other **AVON ROMANCES**

Coming Soon

And Don't Miss These
ROMANTIC TREASURES
from Avon Books

SARAH GABRIEL

Stealing Sophie

AVON BOOKS

An Imprint of HarperCollins*Publishers*

Permission has been granted to reprint lyrics from the song "She Will Find Me"—Music and Lyrics by Dougie MacLean, published by Limetree Arts and Music (PRS & MCPS UK). First recorded on the album "Riof" 1997, Dunkeld Records DUNCD021. For more info visit *www.dougiemaclean.com.*

AVON BOOKS
An Imprint of HarperCollins*Publishers*
10 East 53rd Street
New York, New York 10022-5299

Copyright © 2005 by Sarah Gabriel
ISBN: 0-06-073609-7
www.avonromance.com

First Avon Books paperback printing: February 2005

Avon Trademark Reg. U.S. Pat. Off. and in Other Countries, Marca Registrada, Hecho en U.S.A.
HarperCollins® is a registered trademark of HarperCollins Publishers Inc.

Printed in the U.S.A.

10 9 8 7 6 5 4 3 2 1

To good friends, here and elsewhere, who listened, advised, brainstormed, hugged, healed, sang, fiddled, shared, and saw me through this so graciously. I am forever grateful.

I know that she will find me
I know that she will find me
Even if I vanish without trace
O and though I'm running blindly
I know that she will find me
Hiding with the shadows that I chase

Dougie MacLean, "She Will Find Me"

Chapter 1

Love makes its own magic.

Inscription on the Fairy Cup of Duncrieff

Scotland, Perthshire
Spring 1728

Connor MacPherson heard their approach long
before they appeared. Thick fog and darkness
obscured the glen and the hills, and sounds were
distorted. But the jangle of bridles, the creak of
leather, the thud of hoofbeats on the old drover's
track signaled the approach of the escort party.

His heart slammed suddenly, the long wait over.
His left hand clenched the basket hilt of his sheathed
sword. Katherine Sophia MacCarran—Kate—would

soon be his bride, snatched away without warning, married swiftly. The marriage must be made this way, whether either of them wanted it. The folded paper tucked inside his shirt contained her name and his, a note signed by her brother, laird of Duncrieff and chief of Clan Carran.

He would honor Duncrieff's request. After all, Connor had caused the MacCarran to be captured and imprisoned—and rumor now said that he had died a few days ago.

The pain of that cut deeper than he wanted to admit.

Striding ahead, footsteps silently crushing brown grass and old heather, he glanced back at his two companions, who followed like graceless bears. Their belted plaids, pale shirts, and faces were blurred in the shadows and mist, but he saw the gleam of pistols and swords. Weapons were illegal for Highlanders to carry now. He and his men carried them nonetheless.

Slipping behind the shelter of a cluster of tall, ancient stones, Connor waited for his comrades. He bent to pick up the folded extra plaid that he had earlier stored in this same spot in anticipation of this night's work. Tucking the tartan cloth into the pocket formed by the folds of his own plaid, he turned.

"All is set?" he murmured in Gaelic.

"The ropes are in place," his ghillie, Neill Murray, replied. "And the priest is waiting at the old chapel in the hills."

Connor MacPherson nodded, watching as ghostly veils moved over the glen. Poised to spring like a wild cat, he could not even see his prey. He scowled, placed a hand on cool stone.

"This is a mere prank," his cousin, Andrew MacPherson, said. "We can do worse."

"No worse," Connor said. "We're inviting trouble enough."

"There are other ways to get a bride," Neill growled.

"None so fast as this," Connor replied quietly.

The chink and creak of saddles and the thud of hooves sounded closer now. As the milky veils drifted apart, he saw the ribbon of the drover's track for only a moment.

But he knew the course of the moorland road like his own hand, knew the placement of the two burns that poured down from the mountains to cross the moor. Even in obscuring mist he could gauge just where those bridges were, and how long it would take the escort to reach them.

"Horses," Neill murmured as the sound grew louder. "Two Highlanders on foot and two dragoons escorted the lass and her maid when they left the magistrate's house."

"Aye," Andrew confirmed. "We saw them earlier. After they dined there, Sir Henry sent her home with a military escort."

"Courteous of him," Connor drawled. "Sink the men and spare the ladies. Then slip away. If I'm caught for bride-stealing, I'll hang alone."

"We're at your back as always, Kinnoull," Neill said.

Connor ignored the bitter tug in his heart. *Kinnoull.* He had the title still, but not the property. The fact that Sir Henry Campbell inhabited his house now seared like fire in his belly.

Motioning to his companions, he strode forward cautiously. He would not crouch—he was too tall a man for it, and too proud. He slipped behind another cluster of rocks and tilted his head to listen, hearing wind, water, the approaching escort. He could almost hear the hammer of his own heart.

He could still walk away, he told himself, and escape this madness. Kate MacCarran was a fine, bold lass, and though he had seen her but once, he knew she had fire and spit in her. Her brother had confirmed that she was involved in Jacobite espionage—she would be a good match for an outlaw, though some might say that Connor MacPherson was no fit husband for a bride.

Foolishness, he told himself. He should not be here. On such a night, he should be sitting beside a fireside with a dram and his fiddle, alone with his music and his lost dreams. But the urge to proceed felt like a deep core hunger within, stronger even than his own unyielding pride.

The escort party came closer. Peering through the fog, Connor could just see the faint shapes of two Highlanders walking, followed by the cloaked women riding, and finally the dragoons mounted behind them.

He did not want a bride—not yet, not this way. But that note bound him to an ill-omened promise, and he always kept his word. Always, though the man who had exacted this promise from him likely was dead. All the more reason that Connor felt he owed him, and his clan, this favor. Duncrieff had said that the girl must be stolen away and made a bride before others could interfere.

Easing around the cluster of stones, Connor narrowed his eyes. Not far ahead, to either side of the patch of ground where he stood, two burns crossed the glen, spanned by two wooden bridges. Through the fog he could see the escort party coming closer to the first bridge.

Turning to his comrades, he motioned. Neill and Andrew ran ahead, then dropped to lay flat, grabbing hold of a pair of stout ropes that snaked through grass and heather to end at each of the bridges.

Connor watched as the two Highlanders in the escort crossed the first bridge. The women followed, recognizable by the long drape of their gowns and cloaks. One of the women shone like a star, her bright gown reflecting the scant light. A good distance behind them came the dragoons, their white breeches and cross halters pale blurs in the mist.

As they came closer, Connor heard the thud of hoofbeats on the planks. He heard voices now, too—a Highlander speaking, a female complaining. Another female answered, light and sweet.

His heart bounded. Her soft voice had magic in it.

His bride. He felt the certainty of it like a physical blow, and nearly lost his guard for an instant. He would hear that lovely voice in his own house—upon his own pillow, God save him, and in his dreams.

The MacCarrans of Duncrieff were said to have fairy blood, with magical abilities passed down through generations. Connor did not believe in such things, but the girl's voice had an enchanting quality, fey and alluring. A shiver went through him.

Just a trick of the mist, he told himself.

Scowling, he turned his attention to the task. Wrapped in mist, he stepped forward, intent on timing. The women's horses cleared the planking of the bridge and struck out over the moorland toward the second watercourse. Ahead, the two Highlanders reached the next bridge. At the same time, the dragoons' horses stepped onto the first bridge.

When the women were isolated in the middle ground between the burns, Connor gave a low owl's hoot. His comrades whipped the ropes taut in the grass.

Both bridges groaned and collapsed in unison, planks crashing into the water. Men shouted, horses neighed, and the women cried out, their horses sidestepping wildly.

Connor surged forward through the darkness.

Sophie MacCarran pulled on the reins as her horse whirled. The men in her escort had fallen into both burns—somehow the bridges had collapsed. In the confusion, unsure whether her companions were safe or hurt, all she could do was try to calm her horse. Beside her, Mrs. Evans, her companion, shrieked loudly, her advanced age and nervous disposition making it difficult for her to control her sidestepping mount.

"Mrs. Evans—hold tight!" Sophie called out, unable to turn her horse to help the other woman.

Gripping her own horse's reins, Sophie tried to look around. Able to see little through the gauzy vapor, she heard her cousins, Allan and Donald Mac-Carran, crashing about in the water and swearing in Gaelic. Behind her the two English dragoons splashed and shouted, while their horses whinnied as the men struggled to help them.

Her horse whirled again, and Sophie lost her sense of direction. The commotion seemed to come from all sides now. Where were the two burns? She could not risk her horse stumbling down a bank. Her riding skills were basic at best, and currently rusty after six years spent in a convent.

Her efforts to control the animal took all her strength and concentration. She pulled on the reins, tilting back with the effort, nearly sliding off as the horse turned again.

"Steady, lass." She felt a hard, firm grasp on her waist as a man reached up to help her regain her seat. At the same time, he flashed out a hand to grab her horse's bridle, stilling the animal with a gentle murmur.

Through milky fog she glimpsed a broad shoulder draped in plaid, saw long dark hair and the side of an unshaven jaw. He reached through mist and darkness to soothe her frenzied horse.

"Allan? Donald?" Relieved, Sophie wondered which of her Highland cousins had climbed out of the water to safety.

Her savior turned his head, and Sophie saw a stranger.

As he pulled her horse forward, she assumed that he must be a nearby tenant farmer who had come to help. "Thank you, sir," she called.

He looked at her, then turned back without a word. All she saw was a piercing glance, a sweep of dark hair, a plaid.

"My horse is fine now," she went on. "My companion needs assistance, and so do the men in the water."

He did not answer her, pulling on the bridle to lead her horse away. Did he speak only Gaelic? She had known the language in childhood, but could not recall much now under duress.

"Tapadh leat," she managed. "Thank you—but my companions need help," she went on in English.

The Highlander ran now, drawing her cantering horse deep into swirling fog, putting distance between her and the watercourses where her escort floundered. Behind her, Mrs. Evans shrieked and moaned, her horse still not under control.

Alarmed now, Sophie leaned back in the saddle to try to stall her horse. The animal whickered and sidestepped, uncertain.

"Let go," she called to the Highlander. "Stop!"

Not even a backward look. Only that strong fist wrapped around the leather bridle, only that muscular arm draped in a linen shirt, the broad shoulders and dark head turned away from her. Silently, steadily, he moved forward.

She saw the gleam of the weapons in his belt.

Dear God. A brigand! Returning to Scotland only days ago, she had already heard tales of the rebels and outlaws who lived in these hills, some renegade Jacobites, some lawless men entirely. Sir Henry Campbell, the magistrate who had hosted dinner for her at Kinnoull House, had warned her not to cross the length of the glen that night.

But she had felt safe in the company of her Highland cousins and the two soldiers assigned by the magistrate. And she and Mrs. Evans, weary from their travels, had been anxious to return to Duncrieff Castle that night. Sophie herself had been more than ready to depart Sir Henry's company. Her father, before his death, had promised her to Campbell in marriage, no matter his daughter's protests. Finishing her education in a Flemish convent, she had been sent back to Scotland by her widowed mother to keep her father's promise, and marry a man she despised.

Now she wished she had stayed at Kinnoull House when Sir Henry had extended the invitation. The magistrate's dire warning about brigands and the like had proven true.

This Highlander was clearly no well-meaning local. He led her horse deeper into the mist instead of turning back to help her escort.

Heart slamming, Sophie dug in her knees, leaned back again. The horse obeyed the man. She tried to scream, but the sound stuck in her throat. She glanced back wildly.

Through the obscuring fog she heard Mrs. Evans's banshee shrieks, heard men shouting and horses whinnying. None of her companions realized that she was being abducted.

"Turn back," she gasped frantically. "Oh, God, let me go!" Gathering breath again, she managed a sundering scream.

The Highlander whirled, set his foot upon the stirrup, and vaulted into the saddle behind her. He moved so fast that she had no chance to shout again, or even to shove him away before he snatched the reins from her and closed one hand over her mouth.

With his right hand he guided the horse, stopping her mouth with his left. His arms, hard with muscle, pinned her own arms to her sides as he leaned to his task. Signaling the horse, he plunged them forward into billowing fog and darkness.

Twisting, Sophie realized that her gown and cloak were caught beneath the stranger's legs, her thighs trapped by the grip of his own. His arms surrounded her, his torso pressed to her back, unyielding and warm. He urged the horse to a gallop, leaning so that she had to bend low. The horse launched ahead under the man's unhesitating command.

Writhing, unable to shout with his hand pressing her face, Sophie freed an arm enough to elbow him.

"Be still," he said, his voice firm but quiet, deep as darkness. "You'll come with me." His voice had an unexpected mellow richness, both soothing and thrilling.

Feeling his hand on her shoulder, she tried to shrug him off. His iron-hard arm only pulled her tighter against him, preventing movement. She gasped, flailed.

He loosened his hand from her mouth. "Can you breathe?"

"You stole me away," she blurted. "You attacked my escort. Why? Have you taken my companion as well? She's elderly, you must not harm her! Why are you doing this?"

"Breathing fine, I see," he said.

He did not speak broad Scots, but rather the perfect English of a native Gael, with a softening of the words, a whisper of a lilt. The tone was deep and rich, as if cream and whiskey had turned to sound.

She gathered her wits. "You should have helped the others!"

"They will be fine. I came for you, lass, not them." His breath warmed her cheek, his hands tightened on her arms.

"But why?" she asked breathlessly.

He did not answer, pressing her back against him, his fingers spreading on her arm. Sophie forced herself out of the spell he seemed to cast, for his very touch, his presence, calmed her somehow.

But he had snatched her like a thief. "Do not touch me!" she snapped.

He let go abruptly. Sophie tilted and slid sideways, unable to grab hold to save herself from falling. Her captor righted her then, and when his strength closed around her this time, she felt sheepishly glad of his support.

"Where are we going?" she asked as the horse bounded forward. "Why did you steal me away? Are you sure no one was hurt? What of the men? And my maid? I know you broke those bridges on purpose! How did you do it? What do you want with me?"

"So many questions," he said, and answered none.

She drew breath again, a prelude to a scream that never emerged, for a length of plaid descended over her head, swathing her in blackness.

She felt the hard strength of his arm encircle her again, pinning her. Wool rasped her cheeks, and she inhaled the mingled odors of smoke, pine, and man. Struggling under the blanket, she felt as if she might smother. The brigand's chest pressed her back, his legs trapping hers.

"Be still now," he murmured. "All will be well."

She rode in stiff silence, hot tears pricking her eyes. Breaths heaving, she felt anger and indignation stir hot, and sought courage to quell them, to think, to do what she could to save herself.

Fuming under the plaid, she remembered her Highland cousins at Duncrieff talking about a local renegade whom they called the Highland Ghost. He stole cattle, they said, attacked parties of English soldiers, even sabotaged the new stone roads that the English troops were building through the Highlands. He had never been seen in daylight but was said to be a fierce man, violent and clever by turns, striking when and where he pleased. A beast of a man, one of the Duncrieff maids had told her. A savage, said the housekeeper. A rebel and a brigand, said her cousins.

He was said to lurk in this very glen. Sophie shuddered. She should have listened to Sir Henry and stayed at Kinnoull. Her own cousins seemed to suspect that the Ghost was involved in her brother's arrest. She should have asked more about that.

Was this Highland thief the Ghost himself? Perhaps he had somehow broken those bridges to bring down her Highland cousins and the dragoons. Why would he snatch one woman?

Oh God. She did not want to think about that.

She found the voice to scream, though it was muffled under the plaid. His hand closed over her mouth again.

"Hush, you," he said quietly at her ear.

Her head spun. She felt strange, as if she hurtled through thunderclouds, as if she rode in the arms of a demon with no sure ground beneath her and hell awaiting her.

Chapter 2

Stealing a bride was a miserable business, Connor decided.

And wrapping this one like a Christmas pudding was not sufficient. He should have gagged her mouth as well as her flailing limbs, for he needed both hands to handle a horse galloping with two riders. The girl shrieked like a kestrel, and as he pressed his hand over her mouth again, her breath warmed his palm through the wool. Mercifully, she quieted.

"Hush," he soothed. He settled his arm across her chest, his fingers on her jaw, while his other hand gripped the reins.

He had no taste for bullying women, and his patience was easily tested. His promise to Duncrieff obligated him to carry out this regrettable snatching. Take her, her brother had said, see it done, explain later.

When the time came tonight to consummate the marriage, Connor wondered how he could possibly take her, see it done, and explain later. He was not a brute to force a woman to that. He savored and enjoyed the act of love, especially when his partner enjoyed it, too. And Kate MacCarran would be one to savor the pleasure of that with him, he judged, from what he had heard of Duncrieff's bold sister.

A frisson of lust slipped through him at the thought of touching her perfect womanly shape, evident through layers of clothing. But how the devil he was to convince her to bed her new husband so that he could carry out the rest of this marriage business was beyond him.

He had planned carefully, or so he thought. But now that the snatching was done and Duncrieff's sister Kate writhed inside the plaid, the chapel where the priest waited seemed a very long distance away. This accursed adventure had just begun.

The MacCarran had been adamant that his sister be fully and legally married. Connor knew that his right and ability to protect his bride must be unquestionable should legal disputes arise later. His sister was promised in marriage to Sir Henry Campbell, Duncrieff had explained just before he was arrested. But Rob had been weak from the wound he had taken and gave few details. Connor understood that she must not be allowed to marry Campbell.

More than willing to seek some vengeance against the magistrate himself, Connor had given his word to snatch Kate MacCarran and make her his own.

He sighed, hard and long. She bit him then, nipping through cloth. Wincing, he tightened his fingers over her jaw just enough to convey his disapproval. Under the plaid, she thrust her elbow in his stomach.

Even her own brother admitted that Kate MacCarran was known for her hellion ways. Katie Hell, some called her, and Connor knew that she had acted as a Jacobite spy. The MacCarran had mentioned another sister in a convent somewhere. Undoubtedly she was the opposite of Kate the hellcat.

The wee nun would have been easier to steal than this wild monkey, Connor thought sourly.

He knew nothing about MacCarran's pious sister, but it was a fair bet that she would never endanger herself, or others, with reckless actions and Jacobite involvement. No wonder the MacCarran had exacted his promise to marry Katie Hell. Only a rebel husband, a rogue himself, could keep a capable watch over her in her brother's absence.

He sighed again.

As they left the moor and climbed the first upward swell of the hillside, Connor knew that he and the girl could not share the horse for long riding uphill, particularly through darkness and fog. On foot, they would be safer and have more advantage—though he had a sudden image of carrying a thrashing, protesting girl into the chapel.

Glancing around, he saw little enough, but listened past the sound of hooves for any sound of pursuit. He urged the horse up the slope cautiously, balancing the girl in front of him.

Hearing shouts down on the moor, he judged that the men would be out of the water by now and in hot pursuit once they realized the girl was gone. The arrival of her riderless horse would add to the confusion and perhaps buy a bit more time.

Pulling on the reins, he slid downward, then lifted the girl down with him and set her on her feet. She stumbled, entangled in the plaid, and Connor steadied her.

She pummeled at him, crying out, a whirlwind of fists and sharp-toed shoes and flapping blanket. Then she thrust her knee upward. He angled away in time but felt the glancing, dull blow.

Swearing under his breath, he yanked on her plaid, wrapping her as snugly as he could. Then he slapped the rump of her horse, which turned to trot down the slope. Since he could still hear the faint echoes of shouting down on the moor, Connor knew the animal would find its way back to the escort.

His would-be bride was twisting, the plaid peeling like an apple curl. Pulling the plaid over her head, Connor lifted and shouldered her. Though she bucked, he held her firm with one arm, glad that her squealing protests were well muffled.

"Be still," he warned her, then headed up the hillside with his squirming, kicking bundle.

"Put me down! I thought you meant to save us back there!"

"I *am* saving you. Stop squirming and let me do that."

"You're a madman!" she gasped through the swath of wool.

"So they say," he agreed affably, and took the hill with long strides.

She was not much of a weight, and he was accustomed to carrying game home from the hunt—but this catch was wrestling like a kelpie. Somehow he managed the climb and the carry, slowing his steps as the hill grew steeper. He would not admit weakness, or defeat, by setting her down.

"Stop," she said. "Please, stop! Let me go! Why did you steal me away from my escort?"

"I am your escort now," he said.

"You don't intend to see me home. I do not know what you want, but if you plan to—to disgrace me, I will never submit to it! *Never!*" She blurted the last on a sob.

He set her down, fast and sure, tore the plaid from her head, grasped her chin in his hand. "I am not that sort of beast," he said angrily.

"Beast . . ." She stared at him, eyes wide, breath heaving. "You're the one they call the Highland Ghost!"

"What do you know of that fellow?" Connor lowered his hands to grasp her shoulders, keeping her close so she could not hobble away or kick him.

"I hear he is a cattle thief and a murderer, that he strikes where he wills and does as he pleases. Is it you?"

He cocked a brow. "Do I look like a ghost?"

"You're not a bear of a man, as they say he is," she said, scrutinizing him through mist and darkness. "My maid heard that he is dark and very large, said to be a giant—and you are tall and have dark hair. With your whiskers and long hair, and your Highland gear, you do look the savage . . . but you seem rather pleasing in countenance beneath it all."

He inclined his head in wry acknowledgment.

"But pretty looks can mask a lunatic nature," she added.

"Shall I beware of you, then, mistress?" he murmured.

Pulling her brows together, she glared up at him.

"I hope there is something kind said of this Ghost," he muttered. Frankly, he did not want to discuss this—and certainly did not intend to give her more detail than she had already heard from castle gossip. Taking her arm, he turned, and she took short steps to keep up, the plaid still in a loose tangle around her.

"To be fair, one of my cousins did tell me that the Ghost can be generous to unfortunates, according to his whim, and has helped tenants and farmers who have been dispossessed by the English. When cattle are stolen from poor widows and such, he replaces them. And they say he regrets each life he takes."

"Ah. How reassuring." Allan and Donald MacCarran had always been good comrades, and Connor was glad to hear that they spoke well of his antics as the so-called Highland Ghost—though he felt a qualm, again, for the rumored death of their chief, which apparently had not been shared with the family. He was not about to tell any of them until he had confirmed that himself.

As for the Ghost, he was less involved in stealing cattle and protecting widows than in undermining General Wade's efforts to construct military roads through the Highlands. Duncrieff himself had joined some of those raids—resulting in disaster, and the hurried promise he had extracted from Connor.

"I suppose there is good in everyone." Duncrieff's sister looked at him with an earnest, clear gaze, though her shoulders tensed under his hands and he sensed a fine trembling in her.

He frowned. "What else do you know of this Highland Ghost?"

"I was told that he betrayed the chief of the Mac-Carrans," she said bluntly. Anger flashed in her bright, lovely eyes.

Brave girl, Connor thought, to confront him when it might be a risk to do so. But Kate MacCarran's boldness was well known.

"Perhaps," he growled. "Perhaps not."

"Will you deny it?"

"If I were this Ghost, I would."

"I would know that from you, now or later."

"We have more immediate concerns," he said, taking her arm to guide her along, though she stumbled to keep up. He would have to carry her again, or find another way to subdue her so they could make quicker progress over the hills.

She stopped, and he stopped with her. "If you are the Highland Ghost, then I have serious grievances with you."

Holding her arm, he could still feel her shaking. She was courageous, but genuinely frightened. That realization disturbed him. He hated what he had done—what he still must do.

"I know your grievance," he said grimly.

She drew herself to her full height, just to his shoulder. Her face was a pale oval, her eyes wide and silvery. He wondered what their color would be in sunlight. "For now, I will ask for mercy, sir. I believe you have an honorable conscience, despite all. Let me go, and prove it."

Gazing down, Connor saw more than fragile courage in her demeanor. He saw a compassion that he did not deserve. His breath stopped in his throat.

She watched him earnestly, caught in his grip. "Release me unharmed and I will tell my kinsmen that you treated me well. That you . . . saved me down on the moor. That is not such a lie. And I . . . promise that I will forgive you."

Connor huffed in plain astonishment. She bargained kindness for freedom. He had not expected anything of the sort. He had planned to subdue a struggling woman and haul her off to be married—but he did not know how to answer this. Katherine MacCarran was not known for virtue, but apparently the notorious Katie Hell had her saintly side, too.

Either that or she was very clever.

The damnable thing was that she was right. He was a decent man who followed an inner code of honor, though he broke laws to do that.

But he had neither time nor inclination to explain or apologize. The marriage must be made quickly. If force accomplished that, so be it.

"We are in a hurry here, Miss MacCarran."

"You know my name!"

"I did not abduct you on a whim."

"Then all this was planned?"

"Quick-witted as well as bonny," he murmured.

"But I do not know you!" She paused. "Are you that Ghost?"

He shrugged. "We must go, Miss MacCarran."

"Did you betray my brother, or have a hand in his arrest? They say you did. Please—I must know."

"We have no time for this," he said fiercely.

She frowned up at him, tilted her head. "At least answer me this," she murmured. "Why did you take me away from my escort? Were you waiting for us as we crossed the moor?"

"I was," he nearly whispered, bending lower. His breath swept her cheek; and her breath, coming in small, frosted clouds, touched his lips. "I think I would have waited for you forever."

Why the devil had he said that? He sounded like a besotted fool, or a damned poet. She had a strange effect on him, a lure that he could not quite resist. Not only did her lovely voice, even raised and tense, affect him—her beautiful eyes and lush form had their influence on him as well. He scowled at her.

Her gaze searched his. "And now you must let me go," she whispered.

He could not. Would not. His nose brushed the delicate tip of her own. As he held her arms, he felt her slump a little, sensed her surrender for a moment, soften expectantly, as if the same power that rushed through him affected her. Suddenly he wanted to kiss her, to take her into his arms and bury himself, lose his senses in her, fill her as the demand filled him.

Bending toward her, heart thudding, he very nearly did kiss her, forgetting for that moment the urgency of his promise to her brother. All he could think about was touching her—though he did not know how she had affected him so quickly, so intensely. He was not generally an impulsive man. But now, as his mouth hovered near hers, he struggled to resist temptation.

Her head tilted, her eyes drifted shut. Her loveliness only increased his desire. He leaned closer, drawn toward her.

She stiffened and pulled back. "Do not give my kinsmen even more cause for revenge. They will find me, and you."

He touched a finger to her alluring lower lip, as if that would drain off the passion rising in him. "Your kin will not find us. But we cannot linger here. Come ahead."

Once again he pulled the plaid over her head, lifted and shouldered her. Her protests were muffled as he strode ahead.

Soon Connor saw movement in the fog. He stepped behind a cluster of gorse and rock and crouched down, setting the girl on her knees to face him. Taking her in his arms, he pulled her into his arms, holding tight to keep her still and quiet.

"Hush," he whispered. "There are lawless rogues out in these hills." He knew the irony of that, but she stilled nonetheless, without comment.

Likely only Neill and Andrew crashed about in the heather out there, Connor thought. But the escort party might have extracted themselves and their horses from the water by now, and collected enough wits to search the hills—providing they could find their way in the fog.

The girl rested her head on his shoulder—probably for lack of a better spot, he guessed. She felt so warm, so damn good against him, that he felt his body stir. Closing his eyes, he let himself savor the feel of a woman in his arms. It had been so long . . . not so long since he had eased his desires with a woman, but since he had just held one.

He lifted his head and watched as two figures appeared through the mist. Recognizing Neill and Andrew by their shapes and their familiar strides, Connor waved.

Andrew approached and looked down at the plaid-draped girl. "Is this the one?"

Connor rose to his feet, helping the girl to stand. Wound inside the plaid, she stomped hard on his foot, then began to shriek. He clapped a hand over her mouth. She twisted.

"Aye, she's the one," Neill drawled.

"Hellish, is that what they call her?" Andrew spoke in Gaelic, as had Neill.

"Something like that," Connor responded, holding fast.

Andrew leaned toward the girl. "Do not misbehave, lassie," he said in English, "or the Ghost will see you pay dear for it. He's a braw man and a daft one, and it's best to give him no more trouble."

"It's he who is giving me trouble," she snapped from under her plaid covering.

"Daft, is it," Connor growled. Andrew and Neill grinned as they watched his wrestling effort with the writhing, stomping girl. "Have you two anything to report, or are you standing about in the mist for your health?" he asked irritably.

"The men came out of the water complaining like bairns but only soaked," Neill said. "Now they're searching for the lass, thinking she fell in, for her horse came back to them. The other lady is howling like a wounded pig."

"And the priest is waiting," Andrew said. "We left Roderick and Padraig with him."

"Those two!" Connor huffed. "The priest would escape from their watch if he had but one leg. Sorry, Neill," he added.

"*Ach*, it's true, though they're my sons and I love them well. Andrew, go back to the church and guard the priest yourself. I'll travel with Connor and watch his back."

Connor nodded. "Send the lads to Castle Glendoon. We'll be going there after we take care of the matter with the priest."

"Aye, then." Andrew nodded.

"What are you talking about?" The MacCarran girl swiveled her head under the plaid.

"Does she not have the Gaelic?" Andrew asked.

"I do have the Gaelic," she said in that language, her words stilted but her accent good. "Please say it again."

"Enough," Connor barked when Andrew began to recount the conversation. He hoisted the girl over his shoulder again and headed across the hill. Neill followed, while Andrew ran off over the hills toward the old church where the others waited.

She seemed heavier suddenly, and he realized that she deliberately made herself a more awkward burden by going totally limp. He gave her a tap on her firm bottom to let her know he was not fooled by her antics nor would he slow.

Aye, he told himself, he'd far rather be seated beside his hearth with his fiddle on his shoulder just now, alone and cozy. Solitude and music always eased, for a while, life's grievances.

Instead he packed an unwilling bride through murk and mist on the strength of a promise. He did not know where this night would lead him, but with every step he took, he knew that he shouldered far more than a stubborn wee lass.

What did he have to offer a bride, after all? A rundown tower, a barren plot, a few cows, a scattering of sheep. A little music if she pleased, a few dreams to share, a passionate touch to give. Would any of it be worth a damn to such a fine and fiery lass, the sister of a chief? She would want a husband to make her proud. A husband to love.

Love. Once he would have welcomed that.

He plodded on, and she calmed, probably exhausted by her efforts. She seemed lighter in his arms as he walked onward.

Strangely, he felt as if he carried his own destiny.

Chapter 3

~~~~~~~~~~~~~~~~~~~~~~

She felt ill. Folded over the brigand's hard, wide shoulder, her head hanging down, Sophie sucked in a breath to quell the feeling, but that did not help, and she feared losing her extravagant supper altogether. She needed fresh, cold air desperately.

"Stop," she begged. "Please stop."

His step did not lag.

Sophie tried to calm herself and master her roiling stomach, but it remained uneasy. Not only had she been carried off by force, but she now bounced along nearly upside down after too much food and wine taken at Sir Henry's house earlier that evening. The snug stays beneath her gown did not improve matters, either.

When she left the convent in Flanders weeks ago to journey home to Scotland, she had craved adventure after six years of such a quiet life. The prospect of marrying Sir Henry did not promise excitement, or even happiness. She had wanted to be free of that, and even wished that something daring, something wild and wonderful, would happen to her.

Now she had more adventure than she could want in a lifetime. Be careful what you wish for, Sister Berthe had always said—if your wish is sincere, it will come to you, and you had better know what to do with it.

Sophie closed her eyes, thinking of the elderly nun who had been the gardener at the English Convent in Bruges. The little French nun had often advised her, and the other students, to learn wisdom from the flowers. Cultivate grace, gentleness, sweetness, and beauty, Sister Berthe had said; display a sunny nature, and bloom with kindness and compassion. Flowers teach forgiveness and happiness, Sister Berthe had said; flowers teach love, comfort, and peace.

Well and good in the convent gardens, Sophie thought. Sister Berthe had spent her adult life as a nun, never living in the secular world. She had no idea what it was to be stolen away by a Highland outlaw, flung over his shoulder like a sack of meal, and threatened with dire consequences.

Her younger sister, Kate, would have known what to do. Kate, who had gone to London for a few weeks, would never have allowed herself to be carried off by madmen. Had any attempted, there might have been Highlanders lying on the misty moor groaning when she was done with them. Kate had a natural charm that brought men to their knees—and when they did not fall adoringly around her, she knew weaponry, and the sharp side of her tongue was a marvel.

But Sophie knew she had no such courage or fire in her. She and Kate had both inherited what was called the Fairy's Gift, a touch of natural magic inherent to MacCarrans, but both girls had the fairy's temper, too. Sophie had spent years learning to subdue hers, and she had taken well to the peacefulness of convent living, putting her innate abilities into flower gardening.

All that stood her in little stead now. Besides, she had already tried forgiveness and tolerance. The outlaw had been uninterested in either. And she found it nearly impossible to meditate upon cheerfulness or gentleness with her head smothered in a smelly old plaid.

"Please," she croaked. "Mr. Ghost—Sir Ghost! I need air."

He paused, then set her on her feet, steadying her while he loosened the plaid that covered her head and face.

Gasping in the cool, damp air, Sophie felt a hideous wave of sickness overtake her. Dropping to her knees, she retched helplessly into a heather clump at the Highlander's feet.

He sank to one knee beside her and took her shoulders. Dimly, she felt his hand pass over her hair, pulling it back from her face while her stomach cleared itself.

"Water," he snapped in Gaelic to his comrade. "Now!"

Head spinning, Sophie sat back while her captor unwrapped the bulky plaid from around her, freeing her arms. She shoved at her tousled hair, which was sliding out of its braiding, and found her lace cap, a flat pinner, barely clinging by a silver pin to her hair. Using it as a handkerchief for her mouth, she grimaced and threw it into the bracken.

All the while, she could not look at the Highlander. How embarrassing to be vilely sick in front of him, she thought. He would think her a weakling when she needed to appear strong.

She had tried valiantly to fight and resist him, to face up to him—and her finicky stomach had undone all of it. The sumptuous dinner and wine she had consumed at Sir Henry Campbell's table that night had been far too rich for her, but perhaps she would feel better, clearer, now.

His comrade brought a dripping cloth, which her captor used to wipe her lips. She sucked at the wetness.

"Thank you," she whispered. "Thirsty . . . I need a drink."

"Not yet. Can you stand?" He helped her to her feet and rested his arm around her shoulders while he spoke in rapid, quiet Gaelic to the other Highlander.

The pressure of his arm felt good, somehow, a shield and a comfort. She allowed herself to lean against him while he conversed with the men.

She glanced around. They stood on the slope of a high hill. The fog was thinner here, filtering the moonlight that spilled over the slopes and flowed over the misty glen. The Highlander had climbed higher than she had realized.

Turning, she saw that the moonlight was strong enough to show her captor in better detail, even in darkness. Looming over her was a warrior angel. Or was that a trick of mist and moonlight? she wondered. He was tall and broadly built, his face handsome by virtue of natural symmetry: strong cheek-bones, a square jaw shadowed with whiskers, straight dark brows over deep-set eyes that in daylight might be blue or green. His long dark hair waved loose to brush the collar of his shirt. He frowned down at her, his expression somber.

She tilted her head and studied him. He radiated a quiet, earthy power, although she saw an unexpectedly impish quirk in the shape of his lips. Pride and inner strength showed in that face. She saw, too, keen intelligence and a hint of surprising gentleness in his eyes and mouth.

Then she realized that he had been studying her while she was looking at him. She looked away.

"If I do not wrap you in the plaid," he said, "will you walk where I take you?"

"I'll walk home," she snapped, and stepped away from him.

He caught her arm. "You'll come with me."

She glared at him. "Why?"

He did not reply. Taking her arm, he led her down an incline to a fast-flowing runnel. He knelt beside it, rinsed his hands, and scooped water in his cupped palm, rising to offer it to her.

"You said you were thirsty," he explained. "I have no cup."

She blinked at him in surprise. Then she tentatively touched his hand, bringing his palm close to her mouth, and sipped.

The water was cold and refreshing, and his skin carried an earthy, manly scent. Standing so close to him, her lips touching his flesh in a strangely intimate way, she did not feel awkward or embarrassed this time. She felt that surprising sense of being in his protection she had experienced earlier.

But this man did not want to protect her. He clearly had another intention by snatching her. Her cheeks flamed, and she remembered the moment when he had seemed ready to kiss her. And she had nearly responded—not to her captor, but to the man she sensed existed beneath the surly Highland brute.

But she could not allow that to happen again.

Swallowing, lifting her face, she stepped back hastily.

"Thank you," she murmured.

He bent slightly and scooped her into his arms. She gasped as he began to carry her again.

"Oh please, no," she said.

He stopped. "Will you be ill again?"

"I do not think so. But I will not be carried. It makes me feel sick. And all that carrying could hurt you."

"I stole you away, lass, and you care about the state of my back?" Sounding bemused, he set her down. "If you will not be carried, we can conduct our business here. Neill!" he barked, looking over his shoulder. "Fetch the priest. We'll wait here."

He spoke the last in Gaelic, but she understood what he said. "No." She stepped away. "I'll walk." She was tempted to ask him why he wanted a priest.

"If you'll walk, you must keep step with me."

"I can do that." She lifted her chin.

"We'll see. Whoa—come back here," he said as she moved away. He grabbed her arm, then drew a length of rope from inside the pouched folds of his belted plaid.

"Rope?" she asked, stunned. "Rope?"

"I brought it along in case you did not want to come with me earlier."

"I didn't then, and I don't now," she said pragmatically. "Stop that!" He wrapped the rope snugly around one of her wrists, then knotted the other end around his own wrist.

"My apologies," he said quietly.

"You are truly mad," she said, outraged by the makeshift leash. When she pulled, it only tightened further. "This is not necessary!"

"I cannot risk you running off over the hills at night. You might get lost or be injured."

"Oh, and you will not injure me, I suppose."

"I will not." His answer was calm, even soothing.

She could hate him for that mellow voice alone, she thought.

That deep, true-pitched tone belonged to a king or a bard. It was too good for a rogue like him.

"Come ahead. We've a distance to go yet."

"Where are you taking me?"

He gave the rope a tug and stepped away. Sophie had no choice but to follow or fall to her knees. She stumbled along, glaring at his back. The leash was less than a yard long, but as she moved with him, mist drifted between her and the outlaw.

"My kinsmen will find me," she said, "if you have not murdered them all."

"I do not do murder," he snapped.

"You steal women and drown men. You betray your friends."

"I never," he growled, "betray friends."

She was too angry herself to care. "You will have no chance to betray anyone else. Allan!" she called impulsively. "Donald! Help me—I'm up here!" Her words rang out.

The Highlander spun, pressed his hand over her mouth and snatched her close. His comrade hurried toward them, speaking rapid Gaelic. Her captor snapped out an answer, then drew from his sporran the damp cloth that he had earlier used to comfort her. Now he gagged her mouth with it, tying the ends at the back of her head.

Sophie glared at him in outrage.

He inclined his head and turned away, holding fast to the rope looped around her wrist.

The other Highlander, a sinewy older man with a shock of iron-gray hair and scruffy beard to match, spoke sharply, clearly disapproving of the rope. Her own Highlander—she thought of him that way now—snapped a reply that quelled all protest. The men murmured in Gaelic, while Sophie strained to listen.

She had learned Gaelic in childhood from relatives and servants in the family household at Duncrieff Castle, but she had heard it infrequently during her years on the Continent after her father's exile from Scotland. Now she could grasp only some of their words, unable to follow their pace, but she was certain that they mentioned a priest once again.

A cold frisson of alarm slipped through her. Priests and mass were sometimes hidden even in the Highlands, where there was tolerance for the small proportion of Catholics like her own family. A pack of brigands, were they of the Roman faith, would not plan to confess their sins or attend mass in the middle of the night.

The Highlander meant to marry her that night—

or else intended to deliver her to another man who schemed to become her husband. Had Sir Henry Campbell ordered this? Her heart quickened with dread.

At Kinnoull House earlier she had been so concerned for her brother's welfare that she dared not reveal how much she hated the idea of marrying Sir Henry, but he might easily have deduced it from her avoidance of his advances. Her clan needed the local magistrate's cooperation to help their chief, who had been arrested two weeks earlier on charges that remained vague. Espionage, Sir Henry had hinted. Although in her heart Sophie did not doubt it, she kept her suspicions and fears to herself.

Perhaps the magistrate had sensed her reluctance—and her repulsion—toward the idea of being his wife, and decided to force the marriage on his own terms.

"Please," she gasped around the gag. "No priest!"

The Highlanders stopped to stare at her. Her captor reached out to loosen her gag for a moment. "What?"

"No priest!" she repeated.

"You have more Gaelic than I thought," he said.

"Then be careful what you say," she snapped.

He pulled the gag up again and continued to speak with the other man, their discussion so fast that Sophie could follow only words and phrases here and there.

She thought again of the magistrate's cold, fishy hand on hers, of his tight smile and gimlet eyes. Had he arranged the abduction, sending for these Highland ruffians as soon as she and her party left Kinnoull House?

If not, then the Highlander himself planned this, and she could not imagine why. Since he knew who she was, he at least knew of her brother. Did he think her wealthy, as the sister of a chief? Did he want to be associated with the MacCarran name? But Duncrieff was only of modest means these days, and Robert sat in jail in Perth with a threat of treason over his head. Forfeiture was more likely for Duncrieff than wealth now.

She reached up a hand to touch the small pendant at her throat, a sparkling bit of smoky crystal set in a tiny silver cage on a silver chain. The ancient stone had been given to her ancestors by a fairy, long ago, and embodied the family legends for Sophie. Its power and protection would carry through her life if she used it well, or so said tradition.

The little crystal, and the touch of fairy blood in her veins, bound her to an unspoken promise. She could marry only for true love. If that was not honored, so said the legend of Duncrieff, bad fortune would come not only to her, but to her clan. The well-being and the future of Clan Carran could depend on the wise use of the small fairy stone by its wearer.

And it was said that the tiny crystal could effect a miracle—just one—should true love be in jeopardy. Otherwise, its fairy power could wreak havoc for its wearer, and for those around her.

Sophie knew she could not marry Sir Henry Campbell, although her own father had promised her to him before his death to meet some obligation. Nor could she marry the Highland stranger who had stolen her on some whim.

She touched the cool stone, seeking comfort in its familiarity. Beneath her fingers it felt different somehow, as if it shimmered under her touch. Surely that was her imagination, for the stones of Duncrieff only came to life in the presence of love, or so the old legend said.

The two Highlanders murmured on, and her captor turned to look at her with clarity and intensity, suddenly, as if he knew all her thoughts.

Choking back a sob of frustration and temper, Sophie tugged on the rope to annoy him, if nothing else. He tautened the rope as he spoke with the older man, bringing her closer.

Sophie had no choice but to go with the stranger who had snatched her away from all she held dear, and who, by turns this night, had been both tolerant and cruel.

But she had no idea what he intended for her—and she did not know what fate would bring if she married against her will.

"What are you talking about?" she asked irritably. "Why did you mention a priest and a chapel?"

"Priest?" The Highlander smiled a little. "I feel an urge to pray, Miss MacCarran."

"*Tcha,*" Neill said with a derisive snort. "She is a wee bonny thing to be tying like a cow." He looked at Connor from under his frowning brows. "Sick as well, poor lass."

"I like this no better than you," Connor replied tersely. "If I let her loose, we will be all night chasing her over the hills, believe me. I just want this over with."

"As soon as they discover her gone, there will be men searching the hills for her," Neill said. "Best if

she's wed by the time Campbell finds out she's
missing."

"Exactly. Go ahead to the chapel, and wait with
Andrew and the priest until we come. I'll bring her
through the hills to the north. It's not the easiest
route, but no pursuers will take that way. Follow the
drover's track over the hills to the chapel and make
sure we have not been followed."

"Where will you take her later tonight? The search
will be in earnest, Kinnoull, until she's found."

"They'll learn where she is when I am ready for
them to know it. By then, she'll be a contented bride.
Or so we'll hope."

"If any man could please a woman, lad, they say
that you—"

"*Truis*—be off with you," Connor said curtly.

Neill grinned, then turned and ran into the
shadows.

Connor glanced at the girl. Under her long, lightweight dark cloak, her satin gown was the color of
bright embers. With her blond hair slipping loose
about her face and shoulders, she glowed in the mist
and moonlight like a fairy queen.

For a moment he wished that he could make her
happy as his bride. He was not off to a good start.

But life's recent lessons had taught him that he was
not destined for happiness, beyond what scraps he
could claim for himself—his music, his books, a few
peaceful hours now and then for dreaming of a future that might never be.

Broken man, laird, unrepentant Jacobite, and ded-
icated cattle thief, Connor had become a dark legend
in these hills. Once he would have been a suitable

husband for the sister of a clan chief. He had been rightful heir to a fine holding, the son of a viscount, educated in France.

In the last three years he had seen his father arrested and taken to his execution, had lost his home and his mother, had seen the inside of a jail cell himself. He had looked through the loop of a noose straight into the face of death.

As for home and family, as for love—aye, he wanted that. Always had, and always would. How long would Kate MacCarran stay with him, he wondered, once she learned about her husband's role in her brother's troubles—and perhaps in his death? She would hate him for it, Connor thought. Either way, she would not care to play Lady Kinnoull to his landless Lord Kinnoull.

Well, he would do his best to keep her safe for a little while, and guard her from whatever threat Duncrieff had perceived. He would keep her long enough to fulfill his promise. That would have to be enough. A lifetime of contentment and love was a daft expectation.

And this night's work was not going to net that dream for him.

Chapter 4

Holding the rope taut to assist the girl, Connor led her over the crest of another hill. The route was rough with rock, exposed to wind, and so steep in places that they had to follow the shoulders of the slopes. But it was the safest track, for he knew that no one would pursue them here.

The girl struggled behind him, so uncomplaining that he had to admire her spirit. He had removed her gag, worried that it compromised her breathing. Since then she had stayed quiet. No doubt she had little air to expend on words.

Frankly, he was concerned for her. "How are you faring?" he asked, stopping to allow her a chance to catch her breath.

She shot him a sour glance. "I'm on my feet and following along—what more do you expect?"

"Well, you sicked up earlier," he said. "I'm not heartless, though I know you may think it."

"I do think it," she retorted.

Connor grunted in wordless reply and turned, tugging on the rope to lead her along.

The mist had nearly dissipated here, though it filled the glen below. Overhead, the moon drifted in and out of clouds. There would be rain soon, Connor thought, glancing up.

He turned and walked backward for a bit to guard her progress, going slowly to set a comfortable pace for her sake.

She looked like a Renaissance angel in that fancy gear, he thought, the dark cloak fanning like wings, that red-gold gown with its snug bodice and billowy skirts shining like flame. The silver chain and pendant at her throat sparked like a star.

She was delicately made, her shoulders, arms, and hands slim and pale, her feet small in a pair of pointed shoes that must be beastly uncomfortable. Soft flaxen curls haloed her head and slipped down to frame her face with its perfectly shaped features, her beautiful eyes, the exquisite swell of her lips, the lovely but stubborn line of her chin.

He had not expected Katherine MacCarran to be a beauty.

Well, he had simply not thought about it. Having never met her in person, he had seen her from a distance and thought her bonny. But he had avoided encounters with her to safeguard his involvement, and hers, in Jacobite activities. He remembered her across the market square one afternoon—a pretty thing, slight and nicely made, with golden hair.

But he had not expected such heart-stopping

beauty. In that spectacular gown, she was no less than a living flame. Looking at her stirred desire in his body like a spark from an ember.

Frowning, he reminded himself that he was here because she was a hellion and her brother wanted her married off for her own protection.

But she had offered him forgiveness. Sincerely offered it.

If she was a glittering angel, then he was a demon to do this to her.

At the top of another hill, Connor reached out his hand to her, stopping on the peak. Her breaths sounded rapid and wheezy.

Frowning, he took her shoulder and turned her around.

"Take off your stays," he ordered.

She wrapped her free arm around herself and tried to whirl away. "For love of God, what about the priest?"

"He will not care whether or not you wear stays," he said, deliberately misunderstanding her question. "Take them off." His fingers searched at the back of her waist for ties, ribbons, hooks of some kind.

"I will not," she said haughtily.

"How d'you loosen these damn things," he muttered, groping at the overlap between the stiffer bodice and the wide, soft gathers of the skirt and finding them joined. He snatched next at the tiny hooks that fastened up the back of the dress.

She gasped, and he realized that she was frightened. "Stop—this is a savage thing to do to me!"

He sighed harshly. "Then you take the stays off, or at least loosen them. You cannot breathe, my girl.

Here," he said, drawing his dirk from its sheath at his belt.

"No!" She squirmed as he held her by the waist.

"Keep still. I am not threatening your virtue," he barked.

"You have a knife!"

"Every Highland man has a knife, madam." He ripped through the lower stitches. A knot broke and the lacings loosened. He pulled at them. "Officially, we have only the dull knives that King George allows us to use for eating our peas. Or so the English think," he added, yanking.

"Let me do that—you will ruin it," she said, reaching back with one hand, the other still roped to Connor. She worked the seams and lacings in some mysterious feminine way, Connor saw, and a gap opened at the back. She drew a deep breath. Another.

He glimpsed the pale, smooth skin at the small of her back. A hot lightning strike of desire sank through him.

"Fasten the back of the dress again," she said, pulling at the sleeves of the gown, which slipped down over on her creamy shoulders. She glanced at him. "Please, Sir Ghost. I cannot manage the rest of this beastly climb with my gown hanging off of me, though I must thank you for allowing me to loosen it."

"Well, you need to breathe," he muttered, oddly discomfited by her expression of gratitude. Frowning, he joined the hooks and eyes as best he could near the top, leaving a gap at her waist where her stays were now open.

When he saw the slender curve of her lower back, the sight went straight to his groin like an arrow. He tugged her cloak over her and stepped away, glad for the blast of cool air under his plaid. Tugging on the rope, he moved ahead.

"Hurry," he said gruffly. "Now you can go faster. We have little time."

"You truly are a beast," she muttered behind him, her gratitude apparently forgotten.

"If you're bothered about the dress, I'll buy you another."

"You'd have to steal a lot of cows to pay for it." Temper colored her voice.

"Cattle," he corrected coldly. "I'd have to steal a lot of cattle."

He led her around the shoulder of another hill, sparing her the steeper climb over it. For a while they walked in silence, though inwardly he steamed.

Beast—aye, he thought. He was the worst of rogues to drag her over the hills and force her into marriage. His behavior was savage, his treatment of her inexcusable. As a husband, he had little to offer a wife, and he did not like the reminder of it.

"Where are we going?" she asked.

"Not far."

Behind him, she stumbled over a rock, nearly lost her balance. He reached back and caught her safe, then took her hand with its bracelet of rope and led her along beside him.

She accepted his grasp. "Thank you."

He scowled. He deserved no thanks after what he had done, what he planned to do. "For a hellion, you're a polite wee thing," he said.

"Hellion?" she asked. "Not me."

He huffed a doubtful laugh and kept her hand tightly in his, the rope swinging between them.

* * *

His unflagging stamina was beginning to annoy her. "Slow down," Sophie said. "My feet hurt."

"It's not far now. You seem to be doing fine."

"You are not climbing mountains in corsets and skirts and dancing shoes. I wish I had a simple plaid and a pair of tough brogans."

He glanced back at her. "Aye, you'd look fine in those. But you can take off the corsets if you like. And the skirt, too, if you please. Best leave the dancing shoes on for now. Your feet are not toughened up to manage Highland hills."

"I have no intention of running about in my delicates. And none of me is tough enough for these hills. Slow down," she said. "Stop. Let me go, and I will find my way home, and we shall forget this night ever happened."

He stopped, turned. "Miss MacCarran," he said slowly. "I cannot let you go. And we have only a little farther to walk. I promise. And I always keep my promises," he added.

Instead of leading her onward by the rope, he set his arm about her shoulders to lend her his support. At first she resisted, but his strength felt like a shield, and a calmness exuded from him that strangely reassured her.

In the moonlight, he reminded her of a dark angel, his face handsome and compelling, his size imposing, for he was tall and robust. Moving with the graceful power of a stag on a rill, he was clearly at ease with the natural world around him.

Though he was a savage Highlander by appearance, and his behavior was ruthless, there were intriguing layers in her Highland captor's character. He spoke like an educated man, and showed her small courtesies, taking her hand to help her over rocks or runnels of water, slipping an arm around her shoulders when she tottered on a slope. For that, she was grateful. For the rest, she was puzzled more than frightened.

As they walked, she relished the cool, fresh wind that rippled through her hair, and savored the scents and the raw strength in the hills. All the years she had been on the Continent, she had desperately missed Scotland. Now she felt as if she had truly come home—even in the company of this Highland stranger.

For a moment Sophie felt like his equal, not his captive. Power and passion flowed through her like water pouring down a mountainside. The Fairy's Gift seemed to stir in her, the power that gave her the talent to bring flowers to life in gardens, the talent she had otherwise suppressed. She had been longing for adventure in her sheltered life, and this Highlander challenged her to find her courage, to fight for her freedom. Something stirred within her, awakened, in his presence.

She touched the fairy crystal on its chain at her throat, a constant reminder of her secret obligation. To protect her gift, she had hidden in the convent, burying her innermost yearnings, learning to cultivate peace. But she had not found true peace or fulfillment. She had always yearned for something more in life.

The Highlander held out his hand to assist her over a cluster of rocks. Sophie stumbled as she came down to the ground, and he caught her against him, preventing her from falling.

Her arms looped naturally around his neck and

her body slid against his. Feeling his hard torso pressed to hers, she looked up at him, stunned by the warm thrill of that sensation. His fingers, cupped at her back waist, slipped a little inside the gap in her stays.

The shock of that warm contact, skin to skin, caught her by surprise. She gasped. He did not let her go, looking down at her.

"Just what," she said a little breathlessly, "do you intend to do with me, sir?"

He did not answer. His grip on her waist tightened. Slowly, he leaned down, brushed his nose against hers, while her heartbeat slammed. Then his lips touched hers.

The kiss was tender and warm, and so quickly done that she found herself wanting more—when she should have been insulted, or alarmed. When he pulled back, she only stared, stunned.

He took her hand and the rope, and turned to lead her through a pocket of mist in a dip between two hills. Sophie walked in silence, her heart pounding fiercely.

After a few moments he slowed his pace and looked down at her. "I beg your pardon, Miss Mac-Carran," he murmured.

She glanced up at him. "Wh—What?"

"I beg your pardon," he repeated, and then lengthened his stride, forcing her to nearly run, her gown rustling like a whipping wind.

Bewildered, her head still spinning, she wondered if he apologized for that swift, searing kiss or for setting a pace she was hard pressed to match.

Abducted, dragged about, kissed by a man whose name she did not even know, Sophie felt a glimmer of irritation begin again. He told her little, rarely answered her questions. Her entire world had gone topsy-turvy in the space of a few hours, and all he did was murmur an apology.

Bunching her skirts with one hand, she did her best to keep step with him. When he halted on the ridge of the next hill, she closed her eyes, lifted her face, and drank in the cool, brisk mountain air.

The Highlander touched her arm. Sophie opened her eyes.

Ahead she saw a chapel.

Chapter 5

The rectangular medieval building was roofless, its peaked end walls jutting upward into the misty night sky. A door in the side wall gapped open, and two arched windows pierced a far wall. A stone cross with a center roundel thrust upward in the yard.

"I know this place," Sophie said slowly. "It's Saint Fillan's chapel. This land is owned by the MacCarrans—by my brother," she added, looking up at him.

He took her arm and moved forward. "Aye. Come ahead."

Panic rose within her. "I will not—I know what you want."

He stopped. "Aye, and what is that?"

She lifted her chin. "I refuse to be married in there.

Is the groom waiting inside? Did Sir Henry pay you to steal me?"

"I would not take a penny from Campbell." His fingers tightened and he leaned down, his gaze intense. "You and I are to be married in there, Miss MacCarran."

"What!" Although he had said as much before, it suddenly became far too real. Her heart slammed. "You steal me away, tie me like a criminal, and now you want to force me to marry you?" Her voice nearly broke. "Here, on MacCarran property, as if this were sanctioned by my kin and my clan? I will not do it." She yanked back on the rope.

"You have no choice. I have the right."

"The right? I do not even know your name! What gives you the mad idea that you have a right to force me to do this?"

He moved ahead. "You're one for questioning a man."

"You're one who deserves questions," she snapped.

He huffed in grudging agreement and pulled her along with him. Although he exerted little pressure, his iron will was a compelling force. Summoning dignity, Sophie walked beside him over the windblown grass. But when he led her onto the stone porch step, she hung back.

"Enough," he said impatiently. Lifting her, he carried her over the threshold and set her on her feet inside the ruin.

Terror and excitement swirled in her gut. The eerie church was cluttered with stones and weeds. Roofless, its walls broken, it held nothing inside but a single cracked altar stone. Candles glowed there, and three men stood waiting.

She gasped, pulled back. The Highlander dragged her toward the flickering light at the far end of the nave.

Sophie recognized the two Gaels from earlier. Between them stood a priest in a black frock and pale shawl. His thin hair wisped about his head like a dandelion puff. In the play of mist and darkness, he seemed to waver slightly.

"No," she whispered frantically. "Please—no. Listen to me. I do not want this."

The Highlander set his hands on her upper arms. "We will be married here tonight. I've given my word to do this."

She stared at him. "Well, I did not set *my* troth upon it!"

Without reply, he leaned down and pulled her hard against him, touching his mouth to hers. The kiss was thorough this time, his lips warm and incredible upon hers. A sensation spilled through her body like warm honey or sunshine, and she yielded, melted, in his arms.

Years ago she had been kissed by a suitor, often enough to know how to respond. But she had never been kissed like this. Never, but by this one man.

Her limbs faltered, so that she welcomed his strong support. Her hands found his chest, her fingers twisted at cloth. Meaning to push him away, she somehow drew him closer.

Once it began, she did not want the kiss to end. She wanted to melt like this in his arms—her body demanded more, craved it. She sighed, sought another kiss.

He drew back. "Now you've given your troth."

Turning, he took her arm and pulled her deeper into the church.

Gossamer streams of mist and moonlight spilled downward, and Sophie walked ahead, simply stunned.

"The priest is drunk," Connor hissed as Andrew and Neill approached him. The girl had begun to twist out of his grasp again. She had gone still and silent after the kiss, but his heart still slammed, and every fiber in him vibrated like a fiddle string. Pulling her close, Connor frowned at the priest.

The old man did not waver from infirmity, as Connor had at first thought, but from a more temporary influence that he could smell from several feet away.

"The man can barely stand," he muttered to Neill.

"Roderick and Padraig gave him a flask of my wife's best whiskey while they were waiting. It put him under quick," Neill whispered. "He would not do this without payment immediately, and it was all we had. I did not know he was a *misgear*."

"A flask of your wife's best whiskey could put anyone under—even a drunkard—damn quick," Connor said between his teeth.

"He was the only priest we could find," Andrew said. "You insisted on a Catholic ceremony, and you wanted it to be held up here. We did what we could."

The bride had begun to breathe in great steaming gulps, glaring at all of them. Andrew sidled away from her.

Connor swore under his breath. The old priest smiled and waved them forward.

"Good evening, Father," Connor said.

"Father Henderson of the Small Glen parish—this is the groom. And his bride." Neill smiled pleasantly.

The priest smiled, too. "And what a bonny bride."

The bonny bride tried to twist free, but Connor held tight. He motioned for Andrew to buttress her on the other side.

"Here, mistress." Andrew spoke in English and held out his hand to her, his tone shy. A small bunch of flowers drooped in his large fist.

"Oh!" She reached out. "They're beautiful." She took the bouquet and admired it. "Snowdrops and crocuses! And you found a daffodil, too." She sniffed the flowers and smiled up at Andrew, who blushed to the roots of his fair hair.

Seeing that smile, Connor felt thunderstruck. Lovely and unexpectedly impish, with a hint of a dimple, her smile was like a candle flaring.

Then she glanced at him and the light vanished.

"I don't see why you smile at Andrew," Connor said, though he knew he sounded petulant. "He helped snatch you, too."

"But he brought me flowers," she said, her face still half hidden in the petals. "I love flowers."

Connor scowled. "I did not notice any flowers."

"You would not have picked them if you had," she retorted.

That was probably true, but he was not going to admit it. Nodding curt thanks to Andrew, Connor wished he could have earned that enchanting smile for himself. All it had taken had been a few limp flowers. Still frowning, he turned his bride's shoulders so she faced the priest.

Father Henderson wavered where he stood. Neill propped him up with a beefy hand on his shoulder.

"What is wrong with him?" The bride leaned toward Connor.

"Drunk," he answered succinctly.

"I will not be married by a sodden priest!"

"Aye, you will, and so will I." He tightened his grip on her shoulders.

She leaned toward the priest. "I'm so pleased to meet you, Father Henderson," she said in a sweet tone. "I'm sorry, but there will be no wedding tonight. These Highland men will take you home now." She shot Connor a searing glance.

Andrew edged backward. Connor reached out to hold him in his sentinel position. "No one's going anywhere."

"No wedding? But I was promised a keg," the priest said.

"What?" Connor looked at Neill.

"A keg and a cow," Neill said. "For his parish."

"You will not pay for my wedding with stolen cattle and whiskey!" The girl had followed their Gaelic, Connor noted. Then she leaned back in that damnable way she had, like a donkey on a country road.

"At least we're paying something for it," Connor said, dragging her close again. "Being outlaws and all."

"But old Saint Fillan's is haunted," she argued. "We should leave this place—"

"We'll chance the bogles in the night," Connor said. "No more excuses. Father, proceed."

"Dearly beloved—" the priest began.

The bride suddenly looked at Connor. "You said you had given your word. To whom?"

"I'll explain later." He held her shoulder so tightly now that he feared she would bruise.

"We are gathered here—" the priest went on.

"You'll explain this *now*," she insisted.

The priest looked startled. Neill and Andrew exchanged uneasy glances.

Connor sighed. "Gentlemen, please excuse us for a moment," he said, then took her arm and dragged her around to the other side of the altar.

"Who paid you to steal me?" she demanded.

"No one." He lifted his palm for peace. "Stolen brides are commonplace in the Highlands. My own parents had just such a beginning."

She flapped her flowers in the air, their sweet fragrance strong. "And look at their son! Tell me about this promise. *Now*. Please," she added hastily.

Connor smiled a little—she was such a contradiction of wild cat and kitten. He leaned down, choosing his words carefully. "I have your brother's permission to marry you."

She gaped. "I do not believe it."

"Read this, then." Reaching into his plaid, he drew out the folded paper.

She opened the crumpled, stained page warily. Light from the altar candles spilled over the page as she read the message. Connor could smell the sweet fragrance from her limp posy of flowers. Frowning, she caught her breath as she read, then glanced up. Connor saw that her face had gone pale.

"Is this note . . . stained with blood?"

"It is," he said gruffly. "His own."

She swallowed hard. " 'I, Robert MacCarran of Duncrieff,' " she read in a near whisper, " 'do request and grant permission to Connor MacPherson of' . . . what is that word? Something is crossed out, replaced by 'Glendoon.' "

"Glendoon will do." He would not tell her that the words Robert had scratched out had been "Lord Kinnoull."

"Connor MacPherson—that is your name?" She glanced at him.

He nodded. "Read the rest."

" '—to wed my sister, Katherine Sophia MacCarran. Signed, Robert MacCarran of Duncrieff—' "

" 'Chief of Clan Carran,' " he finished for her. "It's dated two weeks ago. I've been waiting for you to return to Duncrieff Castle, Katherine."

"This looks like his signature, but he would never—"

"He did."

"But my father promised me to Sir Henry Campbell."

"That engagement is broken as of now," Connor said fiercely. "Your brother told me that he wanted that marriage prevented. I was happy to oblige."

"By stealing me away? By intoxicating the priest so he would not remember who he married this night?"

"That," Connor said, "was unintentional."

"Sir Henry will kill you for this."

Connor narrowed his gaze. "I'll take that chance."

She drew her slender brows together. "If this was agreed between you and Robert, why is his blood on the page?"

"He had the note in his shirt when we were attacked in the hills. He was pistol-shot, bleeding freely. He gave me the paper and insisted on my promise."

"Insisted," she repeated. "I do not believe it."

"Regardless, it will be done."

"If you were with him the night he was arrested, why did you not prevent his capture?"

His heart slammed. "I did what I could."

"They say that you betrayed him."

"I did not. Trust me—or not. We have no time to discuss it now." Nor was he ready to tell her the rest—that Rob had been near death, that he had done all he could to save him.

Nor would he tell her that it had lately been rumored that Rob MacCarran had died in prison only days before. If so, news of his death might be kept secret to avoid an outburst of further rebellion among Perthshire Highlanders loyal to the Stuart cause.

Katie Hell had espionage ties herself, and he would have expected her to know some of this already, but she seemed unaware. "This cannot be his blood," she whispered.

"It is." Connor had not wanted to show her the note because it was stained with her brother's blood. But she had the right—and he knew now she had the fortitude—to see that paper.

Tears welled in her eyes and she touched the handwriting, her fingers graceful and trembling upon the page. "How can you claim to be Robert's friend?"

"I am. And I did not betray him. All I want to do is keep my promise to him and do what he wanted done. What *he* wanted," he added. "Not me. You wanted the truth. Now you have it."

"He would never expect me to marry an outlaw willingly. It would take force."

His nostrils flared and pride and hurt turned within him. "Your brother knew you would not be willing. He suggested that you be stolen. He meant only to protect you by doing so."

"I think you forced him to agree. You attacked him and demanded this, thinking you would get a wealthy bride—and then you betrayed him to the English."

The words cut like a knife. "Why would I do that? I have no need of a bride right now. And the man had no time to pen a wee missive, Miss MacCarran—believe me. He had it on his person when I met him. He planned this, and I gave him my word. And I will keep it."

"You cannot keep it if the bride refuses."

"Lass," he said impatiently, "we are done with pretty speeches." He led her back around the altar to stand before the priest. He circled his arm around his bride.

"Two cows, Father, and two kegs, if you get on with it," Connor said.

The devil himself held her fast at the altar while the priest droned the wedding Latin. Trapped in her groom's encircling arm, Sophie glanced up at Connor MacPherson.

The warrior angel had vanished, replaced by the handsome villain whose scheme she could not fathom. She leaned away, but he pressed her close. She felt the warmth of his body, smelled wood smoke and the tang of sweat, felt his dirk handle jutting into her ribs. His fingers gripped her shoulder. She knew if she tried to scream or protest, those fingers would clamp over her mouth.

But her protests would not stop this wedding, she

knew that now. Had MacPherson told the truth about Robert's bloodied note? She shuddered, uncertain why her brother would promise her to a Highland fugitive. It made no sense at all.

The signature was Rob's, she was sure, but the Highlander might have forced his decision and his hand. But if her brother did want this marriage, perhaps he needed her compliance to help him somehow.

"Answer him," her groom said.

The priest repeated his request for her name.

She glanced around, delayed the moment, thinking frantically. Saint Fillan's was the ancient chapel of her clan. Suddenly there was something she had to know, a sort of proof.

"Why did you bring me up into the hills for this wedding? You could have found a church closer," she whispered.

"Your brother wanted it done here, though I do not know what difference it makes. A church is a church. Say your name, lass, for God's sake," he said between his teeth.

She frowned. His answer confirmed that Robert may truly have wanted their marriage. Long ago, wedding unions in the MacCarran chief's family had always been performed at Saint Fillan's, and she and Robert, and their sister Kate, had always vowed they would hold their own weddings here, too.

Keeping silent, delaying while her would-be groom glared down at her and the others stared, she realized that marrying Robert's choice for her—brigand or not—meant that she did not have to marry Sir Henry Campbell.

Bless Robert, she thought, for an ill-guided attempt to help her escape the burden of her future. Drawing a deep breath, she took the greatest chance of her life.

"Sophia," she whispered hoarsely. "Katherine Sophia MacCarran." Her brother had used her proper birth name in his note of permission—another bit of proof.

The priest intoned on, and woodenly she repeated her vows. Connor MacPherson said his own vows, and the priest pronounced them man and wife.

Married. Her heart slammed, the world spun around her.

Connor MacPherson leaned down and kissed her. His lips were warm and gentle on hers, and though she did not return his quick kiss, her limbs trembled and her heart thumped like a drum.

The shadowy chapel seemed to collapse around her. Sighing, she sank downward, and felt her Highlander grab her waist. She batted at him and fought against fainting while he held her up, pulled her against him. She could not appear weak, not now. Courage—she had to find it, keep it.

He led her outside, pushing her down to sit on a broken block of stone. "Breathe," he said. "Slowly." He kept his hand on her shoulder.

Her breathing was rapid, panicked, and she struggled to suck in enough air. MacPherson's hand on her shoulder was calming rather than entrapping, as if he lent her his own control.

Turning, he spoke to the older Highlander—Neill, the man was called—who handed over a silver flask. MacPherson opened it, handed it to Sophie.

"Drink," he said. She caught a waft of strong whiskey.

"I do not imbibe hard spirits." She pushed it away.

"It will revive you. I won't have you fainting away. This night is not yet over."

She glanced at him, her heart pounding at the clear implication. In silence, she took the flask, touching it warily to her lips. Swallowing, she felt the first harsh burn in her throat and coughed. A mellow taste and a bloom of inner heat followed, surprisingly pleasant. She swallowed again. Another cough, another wave of warmth. Relaxing a bit, she inhaled, breathed out fully.

"I do feel better. Thank you," she said.

"Go easy," he murmured when she raised the flask to her lips a third time. He took it, drank some himself, and tucked the flask in the folds of his plaid. Then he held out his hand.

Refusing his support, she stood shakily. The whiskey had sparked a little strength in her. "What now?" she asked dully.

"Come with me," he said, taking her elbow.

Chapter 6

His bride hung back on the rope, jerking it to catch his attention. Connor slowed his stride, turned. He had set a hard, fast pace toward Castle Glendoon, and she had kept up with him, though she was likely taxed beyond endurance. He did not feel good about that, but he wanted to get her to safety quickly.

"I'm cold," she said. "I'm tired. My shoes hurt, my skirts are damp, I am hungry. And I do not know where you are taking me. I do not even really know who you are!" She blurted the last bit in an irritated tone.

With his left hand resting on his sword hilt, he held the rope taut in his right. "I suppose you want to rest for a bit."

"I want to go *home*."

"That cannot be arranged."

"Then take me to your home, so that I can rest. *Alone*," she added. She sent him a dark glare in the moonlight.

"I do not have a home." He did not know why he said that. Customarily he kept his life and his feelings private—few needed to know his business, his thoughts, his heart.

"None?" She looked astonished. "Even brigands and thieves have homes. Surely you have a house— even a hut or a cave."

"There is a place where I stay. I do not call it home."

"If it has walls and a hearth, it will do," she said peevishly. "I just want somewhere to sleep. Somewhere safe. And I want a cup of tea."

Tea? Did she expect him to brew tea for her, rub her feet, sing her a bedtime lullaby? He extracted the flask from his plaid. "For now, another sip of *uisge beatha* will have to do for both of us."

She took the flask readily, tipped it to her lips.

"Just a bit," he warned, then retrieved it from her to take a long swallow himself, wiping his mouth on the back of his hand.

He resumed walking, as she did. Then she hastened to catch up to him, rope swaying between them. "I beg your pardon, Mr. MacPherson," she said. "I try not to surrender to my temper."

"You seem quite at ease with your temper," he replied dryly.

She glanced at him, her hair slipping loose of its braiding, her eyes wide. Connor glanced away, feeling guilty enough without that fey and beautiful gaze fixed on him.

"Nonetheless, please forgive me. You have shown some kindness in this situation, and I do appreciate it."

Connor blinked, looked at her. Her apology seemed sincere. Not sure how to answer, he said nothing, acutely aware that he held her tether in his hand.

"We don't have far to go now," he said, in lieu of accepting her apology. "Less than two miles."

She sighed, shoved back her hair, trudged onward. She looked spent and bedraggled, yet she had an elusive, luminous quality that he found fascinating. "Mr. MacPherson, I must rest soon, or you will have to drag me the rest of the way by this horrid rope, or carry me like a sack of wool."

He paused. "If you need to stop, there are some bushes over there—see the flowered ones? They will give you some privacy."

"I did not mean—oh, very well. But not with you holding this rope. Untie me, please." She held out her wrist.

He hesitated, then reached out to work at the knots. "For a moment only. If you think to run—"

"I know very well what you would do. Thank you," she murmured, as the rope loosened. "It's kind of you."

He glanced at her warily, his hands stilling on hers. "You are quick with thanks where it is not necessary."

"I was raised to be polite—and my convent education taught me to express my appreciation for all things. It is a habit now."

"I see. Convent?" he asked curiously.

"My father was exiled from Scotland years ago. My siblings and I were all educated in France and Flanders. My sister and I went to a convent school."

"Ah." Kate and Robert MacCarran had returned to Scotland a couple of years ago, he knew. The other sister had stayed in the convent, he recalled. "I spent some time in France myself. Many Scots with Jacobite leanings have found their way there, or even to James Stuart's court in Rome, at one time or another," he added.

"That's true—our family certainly did," she murmured while he worked the knots. "Where is your home, sir?"

His fingers released the knot, but a gate closed within him. He did not want to tell her that he had grown up at Kinnoull House as the privileged heir to a viscount. And he was not about to admit that his father's forfeited lands now belonged to Sir Henry Campbell—who would have made her mistress of Kinnoull.

All Connor had was the empty title now. He had married her partly to spite that other suitor, but he had no fine home to give her. He stood over her, feeling cumbersome and shabby in her refined presence. But he was proud—he had that. He did not want to hear her appreciation or her sympathy for his sad tale.

Her skin was smooth beneath his fingers, so soft it made his breath catch. Pulling the rope free, he stuffed the hempen curl inside his plaid, then rubbed her wrist where it was chafed.

"My home is gone, and my family is gone, too," he finally answered. "I rest my head where I will and do what I please. But I will spare you a cozy nest of plaid and heather on a hillside tonight."

"Thank you." She gave him a shy hint of a smile. "But I'm so tired I could fall asleep anywhere, and count myself fortunate to have a place to lay my head."

"I'm sure you would." He stepped back. "There, you're free—for now, at least. Best be careful. That bush is prickly gorse, and full of thorns."

She shot him an eloquent look and walked like a queen around the other side of the cluster of gorse dropping out of sight.

"Do not think to run off now that the rope is gone, Mrs. MacPherson," he called amiably.

"Mr. MacPherson," she called back, "that is not my name."

He laughed to himself. He could not help it.

A mile or so on, the sound of the falls grew louder, and he felt its moisture in the atmosphere. Connor took his bride's hand to help her once more, and met her gaze in the moonlight. She smiled at him, bright and beautiful and quick, the smile she had bestowed upon Andrew for the gift of a few flowers.

Now Connor suspected that her brilliant eyes and happy expression were not due to the thrill of his presence, but rather to the contents of the flask he carried.

She had emptied at least a third of it, though she coughed each time she swallowed. He had taken some himself to warm and revive him—but he had stopped, for it made him too relaxed, too eager to think about kissing her, touching her, when he should think only of getting her safely to shelter.

She stumbled a bit and sighed. "I'm very tired. It's a long way, this thieves' den of yours."

"It's not far now, I promise."

"And you always keep your promises," she reminded him. "If my brother will hold you to a promise, I will hold you to this one. It had better not be far."

"Trust me. Careful, Katherine." He assisted her in crossing the slippery stones that bridged a small stream.

"Do not call me that. No one calls me that. We were married tonight, but we are not familiar enough to use christening names."

"Mrs. MacPherson, then, or even Mrs. MacCarran by Scottish custom."

"Miss MacCarran," she corrected primly. "Scottish women do often keep their own names after they wed. But I do not know how long we shall be married, you and I," she added coyly.

"If you expect to be widowed courtesy of your kinsmen, I assure you that will not happen."

"My cousins have a justifiable grievance with you. But I am not so wicked as to wish murder upon you, despite what has happened tonight . . . and what you intend to do later."

Halting, he looked down at her. "Just what do you think I intend to do?" he asked in a deathly quiet tone.

She did not answer, but her keen glance showed her thoughts.

He drew her toward him slowly. Her breath quickened and shadows curved between her breasts. "I suppose you think I have a wicked turn of mind," he murmured.

Her pulse beat at the base of her throat. "I am aware of what will happen soon enough." She lifted her chin.

She was the loveliest creature he had ever seen,

and he did not want to frighten her—though it might be too late for that. But he could not resist leaning closer.

"If I was as wicked as you think, madam," he intoned softly, "I would have done that to you already, with the heather for a bed. Why wait to bring you to my devil's nest, hey?"

She did not flinch, her chest rising and falling with rapid breaths, nor did she move away. She only watched him. Her courage and will seemed as fine as good steel.

With his free hand, he touched her hair, smoothing the gossamer strands that fluttered in the breeze. He traced his knuckles over her cheek and cupped the side of her face in his hand. He let his fingers slide into the thickness of her hair, so soft and cool to the touch that he took in his breath sharply.

"Tell me what you think should happen," he whispered as he rubbed his thumb over her cheek. He lowered his head and felt her breath gentle upon his lips. "What you want to happen."

She tilted her head in his hand, closed her eyes, and did not speak. But he knew what she thought, as if the thought were his own. He felt her heart beat in tandem with his.

Her eyes drifted shut. "If you were to kiss me again," she whispered, "perhaps we would see . . . what would come of that."

Desire swept through him like a crashing wave. Slipping his arms around her, he lowered his head and kissed her, his heart leaping like wildfire.

Another kiss followed that, a chain of kisses, and he could not seem to stop. Each felt deeper, more exhilarating than the last. She tasted of flowers and mountain air, with a hint of whiskey. As she gasped and pressed closer, Connor forgot all else but kissing her. No barriers existed between them, no danger, no doubt, neither of them a stranger to the other.

She tilted her head and sighed, lifted her hands to cup his shoulders, opened her mouth slightly under his, and he let the kiss intensify, parting her lips with his own, tasting the moistness within. He felt himself harden and fill, wanted desperately to sink into the luscious sensation of her.

The feel of her firm body against his inflamed him further, and the heavy pulsing need began, a craving that could not be satisfied with kisses. He traced his fingers along her neck, smoothed over her shoulder, brushed lower, so that his fingers shaped the creamy curve of her upper breast and the stiff roundness of the bodice beneath. He slid farther down, to the small, taut span of her waist confined in stays and satin. Moving his hand under her cloak, he found the spot at the small of her back where he had earlier torn the stitches of her dress to loosen her stays.

He did not know what was happening to him—he could not take her here, now, like the brute she believed him to be. He would not surrender to the desire that skewered his mind away from logical, reasonable purpose.

Heart pounding, he felt her lips quiver against his, questing for more. He summoned inner strength and broke away.

For a moment he tipped his brow to hers and held her by the waist, catching his breath. She touched his jaw, her fingers gentle as butterflies. Her touch was poignant, and forgiving as well. Connor squeezed his eyes shut.

He did not deserve her forgiveness, her gratitude. He did not deserve to kiss her as he had done.

"I do not even know you, Connor MacPherson," she said softly. "And you should not be touching me at all . . . but when you do, it feels . . . right, somehow."

He exhaled a rueful laugh. Inside, he agreed. Lovemaking with her would be magnificent, he realized, beyond any dream or hope he could ever have. Each time they kissed, he sensed her passion rising hot to meet his own.

Silent, he could think of no good reply to her words. He had not anticipated the desire he felt for her, which went beyond simple lusty urge. Hellions and temper fits he could understand and handle, but he had not expected sweetness and thankfulness in his stolen bride. Nor had he been prepared for his own strong feelings and reactions.

Marrying an impetuous virago to protect her was one thing, but he felt a new sort of quicksand beneath him.

"I want you to know," she said, "that I am not frightened of what may happen next." Yet her voice quavered. "If my brother intended us to marry, he had his reasons. Likely he wanted to help me escape my father's promise to Campbell of Kinnoull."

"Sir Henry," he snarled, "is not of Kinnoull. He rents the damn place. And he has no right to you."

"Not now. Though Sir Henry is a decent man, I'm sure, I did not want to marry him. I tried to bring up that subject when I dined with him this evening, but he would not give me a chance to talk about it, and scarcely listened to me on other topics."

"Because he is not a decent man, madam," Connor growled.

"Every man has his strong suit, Mr. MacPherson. Sir Henry expressed genuine concern and distress for my clan's troubles. But I am grateful to you for rescuing me from marriage to him."

How had she managed to put such a shine on it? He frowned. "I am no hero. Do not think it."

She tipped her head. "I confess, Mr. MacPherson, that I am rather enjoying being stolen away."

"Enjoying it?" He stared at her.

"It is . . . rather thrilling." A coy sparkle danced in her eyes. "I have a deplorable craving, sir, that has never been satisfied."

Connor wished she had not said that. Somehow her words shot straight to his groin. He waited.

"I have a taste for adventure. It is a lamentable quality, along with my temper. And my craving has never been met until tonight."

Adventure? The girl had acted as a Jacobite spy for a year or more, or so her brother had hinted—what more excitement could she possibly want? Connor scratched his head, bewildered.

"We all need backbone in life, and you have your share, lass, believe me."

She shook her head. "Not me. But I will apologize for my impulsive temper. I cannot always control it. But I still disagree with you regarding this night's work."

"Aye so, we have differing views on that," he acknowledged.

She could turn with the wind, and he was hard pressed to keep up with the changes. Feisty but grateful, timid yet brave, prim yet passionate . . . she was both hellion and angel. Turnabout witch, he thought, frowning.

He took her hand, striding onward. "Come ahead, madam."

"Where are we going? To an outlaw's hideaway? A cave, perhaps? Might we have a fire, and some food?"

"Luxuries. Next you'll be asking for a bath and a lady's maid. Or would you rather have a musket and a powder horn of your very own?" He cocked a brow at her. "How far does that taste for adventure run?"

"I should never have mentioned it—a silly fantasy. I don't have the courage of a midge."

He looked sideways at her. "Several midges, I'd say."

"All I want now is a bed . . . alone. You will give me that tonight, sir, if you please. That is, if you have a bed."

Every part of him tightened with deep, dark excitement. "A heathery nest for a Highland thief."

"No real bed, no hearth, no home—you are a true fugitive. A genuine brigand."

"Fierce as wolves, I am. Now hush it." He rather liked the sound of her voice, so lovely upon the night breeze. He had to admit he even liked her chatter. A little of it, at least.

"I will not stay in a filthy outlaw cave for long, I warn you. I am more content in a house, where I can putter about."

"Putter as much as you like later. For now—shhh!" He reached out with his free hand to cover her mouth, not with haste and strength as before, but gently this time. So gently.

Touching her like that was a mistake. Her lips under his fingertips were moist, luscious, felt nearly as good as kissing her had felt.

Not yet, he told himself. Go easy, until he had puzzled out the situation and knew where he stood in it. He lifted his hand.

"You're talking as much as I am," she pointed out.

He cast her a quelling look.

She did not seem quelled. But then she sneezed delicately, and coughed. Connor drew out the flask and offered her a little more of its contents, against his better judgment. After she swallowed two or three times, he took it from her and sipped some of its clean burn himself.

They resumed walking, and his bride leaped the next runnel without his help. She giggled and threw her arms wide.

"Be silent," he hissed, drawing her close with one hand.

"Or you shall gag me?"

"I shall."

"Tie me up?" She tipped her head.

"Aye," he growled. She was enjoying this now. "That whiskey did more than warm and restore you, I think."

"Aye, it's relieved my fear of brigands."

"And your fear of almost anything," he drawled. Little wildcat, he thought. What the devil had he taken on tonight?

Grabbing her wrist, he stomped onward.

"A man without a hearth needs no wife."

He turned. "What?"

"Why did you steal yourself a bride if you do not have a home and do not seem to care about that? This is not the Middle Ages. You did not need to steal yourself a wife. A man does not always need a wife, but for . . ." She shrugged.

"But for what?"

"Love," she answered. "A commitment of hearts and minds under the bevol . . . benevolent guidance of heaven."

He huffed. "Be quiet, or you'll find out quicklike one reason that a man needs a wife."

"A man does not always need a wife for that. There are women available in most towns who will—" She stopped.

He glared down at her. "Who will what?"

"Take care of his needs," she answered. "In fact, I have heard that some men prefer to take care of their own needs."

"Jesu, madam!" He stared in sheer astonishment. "You're an outspoken wench. Where did you learn such nonsense?"

"In the convent school. The other girls knew a good deal about men."

"So they claimed. Now hush it." He glanced around warily, but likely they had not been followed this way.

"It may be the spirits. I am not used to imbibing."

"So I see," he muttered, and pulled her onward.

Chapter 7

$\sim\infty\sim$

Emerging from a cluster of evergreen trees that fringed a steep slope, Sophie heard the thunder of a waterfall. She followed MacPherson, pine needles pungently crushing underfoot. Peering ahead in the darkness, she saw white water streaming down like liquid moonlight over a shelf of rock.

Closer, she saw a black gash in the earth where the water poured into a frothy burn. The Highlander's grip on her hand gave her a solid sense of safety as she looked around.

"Oh," she said, raising her voice over the sound of the water. "It's so wild and beautiful here!"

Without reply, he tugged on her hand and led her along the edge of the gap toward the falls. She followed his guidance. If she trusted him in no other way, she knew by now he would keep her safe out here.

Sophie watched his broad-shouldered back swathed in plaid. His legs were powerful, his climbing step longer and brisker than hers. He exuded raw strength and animal grace in every movement.

As she thought about where he was taking her, dread and something deeper, something exciting, turned in her stomach.

He carried his secrets easily. All she knew about him beyond his name was that he preferred to avoid soldiers and the fact that he knew her brother, for good or evil. Her mind was left to conjure the rest.

He led her past the roar of the falls—a white horse's tail spilling over steep black rocks—and above it, so that the roar receded behind them. Making their way uphill, they followed the track of the wide, rushing burn, walking so close to the banks that her slippers and the hem of her gown grew wet.

In the misty darkness, Sophie could see little more than the lacy swirl of the burn, the rugged contour of the slopes. She was sure they were still on MacCarran property, which extended miles past the chapel. In all, the Duncrieff MacCarrans held twelve thousand acres, encompassing much of the glen and its hills. A modest estate by some standards, but vast enough.

Stepping in a pool of cold water, she yelped. Her shoes, impractical heeled slippers with thin soles and silver buckles, were unsuitable to rugged walking. Her toes were chilled through, and blisters were forming on her heels.

The whiskey that warmed her earlier had faded from her blood. She felt near exhaustion and grateful for MacPherson's assistance. His strong, capable hands were always there to pull her along, to lift her, to support her.

At the peak of the long hill, the wind whipped cold and the burn gurgled in its gorge, which had grown quite deep. Sophie stopped when MacPherson did. He pointed.

Across the burn's gap and over a long meadow, a castle perched on the rise of another hill. Washed in moonlight and mist, its dark silhouette rose against a black sky.

The broken bones of the structure thrust into the night, a jumble of cracked walls and jagged half towers. Its windows gaped empty, without a glimmer of light, and a crumbling wall ringed the yard. Thin mist swirled around its base.

A soulless place, desolate and bleak. Sophie shivered.

"Is that your home?" she whispered.

"It's where I stay," he replied. He took her hand and walked along the burnside. They came closer, keeping the burn and the meadow between them and the castle. The angle of the old ruin changed, and Sophie gasped.

"I know that place! Glendoon . . . aye, I thought it sounded familiar to me. I have not heard the name since childhood. It was once the seat of my clan. No one has lived there for centuries."

"Your ancestors deserted it long ago, after rock slides turned this area into a devil's tub."

"I used to hear stories. . . . They say it is haunted."

"The ghosts won't harm you."

She caught her breath. "Have you seen them?"

"No, I'm too practical for it, I suppose. But those ghosts have saved my life a few times."

"How can that be?"

"No one ventures up here unless they have to, because of the long, hard climb, and because of the legends—it is not a good place. No blessings of home and happiness here," he said.

"There used to be, long ago."

"Perhaps. But if visitors come too close, the Glendoon ghosts keep them away with their unearthly moans and shrieks."

"Shrieks?" She gulped.

"It's proven a benefit to the outlaws who hide here."

She wondered, suddenly, if he was teasing her. She hung back on his hand when he tugged her forward.

"Come along. There's nothing to fear. They're MacCarran ghosts. They'll be delighted to welcome a kinswoman."

Sophie looked behind her. "I . . . please, you must let me go—"

"What happened to your appetite for adventure?"

"It does not extend to screeching ghosts. This was all a terrible mistake, Mr. MacPherson. We should never—I should not have agreed. Outlaws are one thing, but ghosts . . . I do not think I can face them." She leaned back. As a child, she had suffered nightmares about ghosts and bogles. Even as an adult she was not keen on the dark. And she had heard long ago that ghosts inhabited Castle Glendoon, though no one she knew had seen them.

She tried to free her arm, twisting to face the long hill. She would have fled down it had MacPherson let her go.

"That way," he said, leaning close, his voice low in her ear, "lies a treacherous descent, as you know. Would you make it safely, alone in the dark? And this way," he continued, turning her toward the castle again, "lie ghosts and outlaws. Which will you choose, my lass?"

She stared at the castle's black silhouette, feeling the outlaw's hands warm upon her shoulders. Then she glanced again at the dangerous incline, shuddering.

"Call upon your courage, lass," he whispered. "There's an adventure in either direction."

Drawing a breath, heart racing, Sophie closed her eyes. She felt as if she stood on a cliff, about to step out into open air. For a moment she reached up to clutch the silver and crystal pendant at her throat, wishing its dormant, rumored magic could impart some guidance. She breathed slowly, then knew. Just knew.

She must go to Glendoon, with him.

"Wherever I can find a hearth and a pillow, and a cup of hot tea," she said, lifting her chin, "that way will I go."

Wherever I will find love, she had wanted to say, *I will go there*—but she kept that thought to herself. If her fairy stone urged her toward love, she was not likely to find it here.

"Aye then." He took her arm. "Come with me."

Heart pounding, she walked beside him, warily eyeing the castle that loomed on its black hill.

She glanced at the gorge that held the burn, which served as a natural moat for the castle grounds. Its walls were too steep to climb down. "Where is the bridge?"

"If we had a bridge, anyone could come up here." MacPherson pointed across the gap. "We'll have to jump."

She gaped at him. "Jump!"

"Or we can walk all the way down the hill again and find a cave for the night."

She paused, sure that he was challenging her again, for his tone had a wry twist to it that signaled humor or testing. Though she felt tired and miserable, she would prove to him that she could take each new hurdle he showed her with grace and some courage. Sophie had her pride, as she sensed he had his.

Letting go of her, MacPherson stepped back a few feet, then ran forward and leaped the gorge, straddling the air like a dancer, to land easily on the other side.

"It's not so bad," he said. "Come over."

"No." She backed away, turned, thinking to run while he was separated from her—but she stopped, looking down that dark and treacherous hill.

The Highlander leaped back again, landing beside her, taking her arm before she could move. "The jump is not far. It just seems so because of the deep gorge. I think you can do it."

"You *think*?" She gave him a scathing look. Then she yanked away from his hold and turned to walk along the edge of the bank. "Surely there is some other way to get across. Not everyone leaps this place—or did, when there were living people and not ghosts inside Glendoon," she snapped.

"Well actually, there is," he admitted.

"You could have told me that!" she fumed.

"The leap is faster, and I thought you were anxious for your tea . . . and your bed."

"Hateful man," she said. "You just wanted to see if I would jump after you. I will not. I am tired and I have no more patience. I want to rest. Where is the crossing?"

"Two miles up this slope. Keep climbing and you'll find an easy place to cross."

"Leap across here if you want, sir. I'll take the safer route. But I will have tea for my trouble." She picked up her skirts and walked away. He did not follow. Was he really letting her go so readily? She glanced around, wondering suddenly if she could risk trying to escape from up here.

"Watch out for wildcats," he called after her.

Though her heart quailed at that, she did not turn. A moment or two later she glanced back to see him not far behind her. Sophie felt relieved, but she would not ask about wildcats, or wolves, either, though she glanced about uneasily.

Raising her skirt hems, she picked her way along the side of the gash. Farther up the slope, less than a quarter mile, the gorge lessened considerably, cut up a steep incline, and the burn became a shallow slice through rough grass. Smooth stones offered a secure crossing not far ahead.

At that spot, Sophie sat on the grass beside the bank, her amber satin gown, with its laces and frills, billowing around her. The dress had been a gift, made in Paris, from her widowed mother, who now lived there after remarrying. Sophie treasured the gown, and tonight was the first time she had worn it. After the evening's escapades, she feared that the irreplaceable dress and its underskirt were ruined. Frowning, she pulled off her shoes and stockings, and did not glance up when the Highlander strode toward her.

She stood, lifted her skirts, and stepped onto the

first stone. Squealing involuntarily at the shock of cold water sloshing over her feet, she sought her balance and proceeded to cross to the next stone.

"Aha," MacPherson called. "You've discovered my secret."

"What," she said, stepping forward again, wobbling slightly, "that your guests must cross the River Styx before they are permitted to reach your portal, Sir Cerberus?"

"Something like that." He sloshed into the burn and strode from rock to rock, sliding past her with a hand at her waist. She felt a quick thrill as he touched her briefly.

Reaching the opposite bank first, he turned and extended his hand. "Are you prepared to pass into the underworld, Persephone?"

His fingers were long, his palm large and flat. She saw strength in that hand, and mysteries untold. Another thrill shivered through her. This man had some sort of magic over her, she thought. She should be angry with him, resentful, anxious to escape. Instead she felt full of anticipation, as if her body, her spirit, thrummed with excitement. In a way, she was relishing this extraordinary night.

Or was that whiskey, exhaustion, and shock? What would she think tomorrow?

She gathered her wits. "So long as there is a cup of tea in it, and a place to rest, I'll come over to your world, sir," she replied with dignity.

Stepping on the bank, she whisked past him without taking his hand. He chuckled behind her and turned with her as she walked onward. She smiled a little to herself.

For a moment she thought of her sister, Kate, who

had lately gone to Edinburgh to fight for their brother's rights in the Court of Sessions. Kate was reputed to be the hellion in the family, doing what she pleased with boldness, bravery, and charm, so different from her, since she kept to herself, preferring the convent instead of returning to Scotland with her siblings after their father's death and mother's remarriage. Now she understood a little of Kate's courage and confidence, and it felt very much like freedom.

Freedom—even though she walked into the unknown with her captor, her new husband, beside her.

Pausing to shove her feet into her shoes, carrying her stockings, Sophie crossed the grass toward the castle. MacPherson moved ahead of her, his legs long and powerful. She admired the way he walked, she thought then, with animal grace and the confidence of a king.

The castle loomed over the meadow like a dark and silent beast, its black shell mysterious and eerie. She slowed her step. All of a sudden she was reluctant to go inside, even with rest and hot tea in the offing. The place was a harbor for thieves and ghosts. Her sense of adventure and freedom were fragile dreams, after all. She lacked the courage for this. She stopped, stared.

Then she heard barking—the low monotone of a large old dog, the yelps and higher barks of other dogs. She hesitated. The Highlander looked back at her, held out his hand.

The sound was not ghostly, but comforting somehow. In her childhood, dogs barking excitedly at the gates had been the herald of a beloved master returning home. Her father kept loyal, friendly dogs, and she had loved them. As the barking continued, she heard delight in it, not a threat.

She glanced curiously at the outlaw who had insisted that this was not his home. Refusing his hand, she walked toward the front gate set in the ruinous curtain wall.

He reached the gate first, which was comprised of two immense iron-studded wooden doors set into the stone wall. He pulled it open, the hinges creaking as he shoved. The barking quieted expectantly, but for a few throaty woofs.

"Welcome to Castle Glendoon," Connor MacPherson said with a bow. "Or what is left of it."

Chapter 8

Shutting and barring the gate behind them, Connor took his bride's arm and guided her into the shadowy yard. The dogs ran toward him, the two cairn terriers reaching him first. They leaped up, paws waving, tails going like mad. Behind them came the brown and white spaniel, more dignified in his demeanor than the terriers, who were always ecstatic to see him—or anyone, Connor thought wryly. Two sets of small, muddy paws batted at his legs as Connor bent to greet them.

"Hey, Una! Scota! Bonny wee girls." He rubbed each terrier in turn, then gave his attention to the quieter spaniel. He glanced up to see his bride bend tentatively to greet Una and Scota when they scampered over to her. The spaniel was already sniffing her hand, and within moments she was murmuring to his dogs, smiling, charmed and wholly charming.

The last of the dogs, a shaggy dark wolfhound, hung back from the others, watching them with customary wariness. He had spent his bark and waited with dignity for Connor to walk toward him and ruffle his fine old head, which he did. "Hello, Colla," he murmured.

He turned to look at Katherine Sophia. "The dogs will not harm you. The wee cairns are Una and Scota," he explained as she patted them. "The spaniel is Tam, and this is Colla." He stroked the tall wolfhound's shoulders. "He's deaf and very old, but he's still a fine sentinel. He can bark like a hound of hell when he wants to. Come ahead, madam." He reached out and took the girl's arm, leading her across the yard. The dogs followed.

A crumbling curtain wall encircled the castle grounds, the whole dominated by the massive keep, a four-story tower, partly ruined yet still strong. As they walked, Connor sensed her fatigue, and something more—a tremor of dread or excitement. He felt something like that himself, for his own heart pounded too quickly.

"This way." He led her up stone steps to the second story tower entrance. "Easy, the steps are cracked in places," he warned. The dogs scrambled up with them to wait by the door.

Connor opened it. Remembering that this was the girl's wedding night, after all, he lifted her in his arms to carry her over the threshold into the dark foyer. She gasped and circled her arms around his neck in surprise.

He nearly tripped on the terriers in the foyer, then set down his bride and walked toward the scarred oak and iron door that led to the great hall, shoving it open.

"Go on," he told the dogs sternly. "Go inside, the lot of you. Stay," he warned, when little Una gazed at him, trusting and hopeful, tail and ears erect. "You'll sleep by the fire tonight."

When they went inside, he closed the door only partway, knowing the dogs would set up a reliable ruckus if anyone came to the gate. He would have invited Duncrieff's sister into the great hall, but he knew she was tired and would not want a tour of the dubious wonders of his ruined castle. She needed to rest.

Taking her hand, he led her up the narrow spiraling steps. The dark stairwell was relieved by thin moonlight through arrow-slit windows. When they reached the next level, with its narrow stone landing, he opened a wooden door.

The room glowed with faint light. Connor lifted his bride again, carrying her over that threshold into his private room.

When he set her on her feet, she sagged with weariness. He guided her to a tapestry-covered chair beside the fireplace. In the hearth, peat embers licked with blue flames gave off a musty, cozy fragrance.

Mary Murray, Neill's wife, had been here earlier, he realized. She had freshened the fire with peat bricks and left food and drink on a table near the hearth. Lifting a cloth from a pewter trencher, he saw oatcakes, cheese, a few slices of cold mutton. A crockery pitcher contained lemonade, which he knew would be made from the precious store of lemons and loaf sugar which Mary sometimes bought at the Crieff market.

A wedding gift, he realized. Mary was particular about sharing her loaf sugar.

No one else was in the castle with them. Connor knew the feel of the place, knew it was empty but for the animals out in the byre and the ghostly sense that lingered throughout the place. No one would return until morning.

He and his bride were alone.

A powerful sensation stirred deep in his belly. He crossed the room, hands trembling as he removed his sword and pistol and laid them on an oaken table beside the door. Then he went to the window to tug on the velvet drapes, making sure they were drawn, so that cold air did not leak in and light did not filter out.

The girl leaned her head against the high back of the chair and closed her eyes in silence. He heard her sigh.

He turned. His four-poster bed dominated the room, its green embroidered curtains drawn back. The forest green coverlet, stitched with flowers by his grandmother's hand, had been drawn down to reveal fresh white linens and plumped pillows. Mary's careful touch again, he thought.

His footsteps were muted by a thick Flemish carpet as he returned to the fireplace to pull a willow stick from a tall box. Lighting that, he used it to flare the wicks of a few candles stuck in brass and pewter holders.

The room leaped to life, gleaming wood and glittering fabrics. He loved this room for its comforts and its privacy, and the familiar pieces reminded him of the home he had lost.

His bride sat straighter in her chair. She stared

around the room, and he saw her wide-eyed astonishment.

"This is no outlaw's cave," she said.

He shrugged. "It's cozy."

"It's like a jewel box," she went on. "A treasure room."

He shrugged again, but inwardly agreed. The furnishings were of polished cherry and oak, the handsome bed was imposing, the rugs underfoot were rich with color. The candlelight brought out the glitter of brass, pewter, silver, even the gilt threads in the tapestry chairs. A small black japonaise cabinet gleamed, as did a small tabletop inlaid with mother-of-pearl, where a glass decanter glowed with pale gold whiskey.

"Where did you—" She hesitated. "Did you steal these things?"

Connor gave a rueful laugh. "These belonged to my family." His mother's treasures, his father's pride—things from Kinnoull House filled a few rooms in Glendoon. Connor had removed whatever he could from the house before Sir Henry Campbell had taken it over two years earlier, leaving the rest behind out of necessity. No doubt Campbell now made good use of those things.

What he stored here at Glendoon reminded him of a gracious home, a happy family. His close kin were gone now, some scattered to France, some dead. Of the old, proud line of the MacPhersons of Kinnoull, he was the only one left in Scotland.

"What a beautiful vase," his bride said, looking up at a blue and white vase on the mantel. "Is it Chinese?"

"Aye. My mother used to fill it with roses every

summer." Why had he told her that? He rarely shared the details of his life with anyone, and he had known this girl only hours. Yet though he preferred to keep his secrets, he felt strangely at ease with her.

"It is a lovely home," she said.

"It is a storage place," he replied. "That is all." Connor fought the urge to tell her any more about these things or about his past. With her luminous eyes and gentle ways, she would listen and understand—and he might reveal too much, and crack the shell he had formed around himself.

His bride gazed thoughtfully at the elegant furnishings and the ruined walls that held them. Then she looked at him.

He knew what she saw. A savage in a gentleman's room, a rough Highland man clad in a worn plaid and threadbare shirt. Like the ruined castle, he did not suit these costly things.

His plaid, in dark greens and blues, was faded, his linen shirt rumpled, but clean. His brogans were worn, too, his muscled calves wrapped in tartan stockings and leather thongs. A few days' growth of whiskers shaded his jaw, and his dark hair was long, unkempt, its thick waves not controlled in a queue.

Aye, savage. He waited for the awareness, the disappointment, in her lovely eyes. Their color, he could see now, was somewhere between seagreen and sky blue—magical and fairy-like. He kept himself still, feeling awkward when he should be taking charge, acting the brigand who had stolen the bride. But he waited.

She smiled a little. "Mr. MacPherson, thank you."

Not expecting that, he narrowed his eyes. "What for?"

"For bringing me here. I thought your outlaw's lair would be . . . different. A nasty dark ruin. But your home is beautiful."

He frowned. "Most of the rooms are uninhabitable."

"But you live here very comfortably." She waved her hand.

"I keep some things here."

"Where is your family?"

"Gone. Exiled, some of them."

"I understand. The same happened in my family. We have that in common, sir, and more. We are both of Jacobite stock, or so it seems."

"We are," he said.

She stood and stretched, her torso and arms gracefully slim, her hair slipping down in tousled golden knots. Even bedraggled and exhausted, she was lovely. She belonged among beautiful things, he thought. He had been raised with privilege, but he was rough-edged and somber now.

"Are we . . . alone?" She looked around.

"But for the mice and the ghosts. Neill's wife, Mary Murray, comes here now and then to do some cooking and laundry, and her sons help with the chores. But no one is here now."

"So you live here alone, then? I thought your band of merry outlaws would be here, too, plotting cattle thievery and more bride stealing." She slid him a glance.

"I do not have a merry band. Neill Murray and my cousin, Andrew MacPherson, and a few others, are tenants of Glendoon. They have homes nearby, but they come here as often as they please. I am alone here otherwise, but for the dogs. Until now."

"I expected a group of desperate brigands."

"They'll be here tomorrow," he replied lightly.

"None of this is a jest, Mr. MacPherson."

"I'm aware, Mrs. MacPherson." He looked at her intently.

Then he dropped to one knee to take up a poker and jab at the embers in the fireplace. The peat was glowing nicely and needed no tending. But Connor needed an excuse to turn away from his bride's beautiful, curious gaze.

Now that she was here in his private chamber, there was one part of the obligation left to fulfill. She had handled the shock of her abduction, marriage, and wedding journey well so far. He admired her for it. Would she accept the rest so readily?

He must make her his own. If she came with child quickly, the marriage would be irrefutable. Duncrieff had counted on that, Connor knew. Although he owed more to the MacCarran than he could say, and would keep his promise, the price was high.

He had not planned on a wife and family so soon. First he had meant to regain his rightful lands before considering the future. He had little to offer a bride otherwise.

As he stabbed at the peat bricks, blue flames licked upward and the sweet, earthy, chocolatelike smell of the peat wafted toward him. That fragrance always evoked a sense of home for him, even more so than the furnishings. The family possessions were a constant reminder that he was not at Kinnoull House and that his family was gone. They sometimes evoked loneliness, memories.

But the sweet smell of burning peat gave him a pure sense of home and comfort no matter where he was.

His bride stepped closer, her bright gown rustling beside him. He glanced up. Amber satin and golden hair, creamy skin and extraordinary eyes. God, he thought, she was beautiful, like a blessing in this gloomy place. She glowed like a hearth fire, and the sight of her curving figure made his own body surge.

He jabbed at the embers again, yearning for something deep, something missing, that he did not want to name.

Light illumined his face as Sophie gazed down at him, feeling as if she saw him clearly for the first time. As he worked at the fire, she was free to study him.

His face had the natural symmetry of true beauty, a harmony of elegant shape and proportion, the strong, firm jawline, the slight arch of his nose, the curve and quirk of his lips, the long, powerful throat. His eyes were satiny green framed in black lashes, his dark brows straight.

As he twisted the poker, she saw how strong and nimble his hands were, his forearms supple where muscle shifted beneath the skin. Wide shoulders worked smoothly beneath his shirt, and his long legs were tucked beneath him as he knelt.

He was a beautiful man, she thought, despite the scruff of dark beard, the overlong hair—a glossy dark brown, unkempt just now. The marks of sun and wind and laughter framed his eyes. In her mind she put him around thirty years of age, her brother's age, several years older than her own twenty-two.

His body was tall, broad, hard, his Highland garments faded but well-kept. He carried an air of wildness, strength, of something untamable, a man who knew his mind and his heart and his needs, who would be fierce about loyalty and honor.

Beyond his physical beauty and imposing presence, she sensed a code of honor in him. And yet he was an outlaw, at the very least a rogue and a rebel.

In this modern age of knowledge and discovery and social sophistication, she thought, he was something timeless, a warrior with the courage of a lion, and the heart of one, too.

Was it the whiskey, she thought, or fatigue, or did she indeed sense honorable magic in this man? He had stolen her away, had taken her future and her hopes. Yet there was an intriguing nobility about him.

She glanced away, feeling the burn of her secrets. She was familiar with what a man and woman would do together, how their bodies fit like hand and glove, how passion could both rule and delight them. She had lost her virginity at the age of fifteen, and in return had experienced only a faint shadow of what love and passion might be like, initiated in a clumsy encounter with a boy scarcely older than she had been. She had let her own wild passions lead her down a merry road to a dreadful mistake. Love had not been waiting there, but disgrace.

Fate had thrown her into this sudden marriage and this strange wedding night, but it was perhaps the single situation where she would not have to explain why she was not a virgin. A brigand stealing a bride had no cause to complain about the state of the goods, she thought sourly.

And that was one more advantage to this marriage arrangement—she would not have to marry Campbell, and she would not have to explain herself the next morning.

Her heart pounded hard and fast. Glancing at the handsome four-poster bed, she imagined what might happen there with this strong and stunning man. A warm velvet ripple of excitement stirred within her. The wild fairy blood that flowed in her veins began to stir.

Her Highlander looked up at her then, but she looked away, unable to meet his gaze.

She fingered her necklace, the crystal cool and delicate to the touch. The Fairy's Gift prevalent among the MacCarrans of Duncrieff had blessed Katherine Sophia MacCarran, too.

With her fairy blood came a passionate nature, a touch of natural magic, and a powerful urge to give and receive love in any form. Years ago, when her family had spent a summer at the Scottish court at the Muti Palace in Rome, Sophie had been so eager to find true love that she became infatuated with a boy of her own age. Imagining herself completely in love, she trusted too quickly and delighted too well in kisses and arousing caresses. In the palace garden, she had given herself to her beloved friend with enthusiasm and curiosity.

She had only been disappointed, slightly sore, and in dire trouble once her mother found her slipping away one night. Unaware that the deed was already done, Sophie's parents had sent Sophie to the convent in Bruges for protection, and to finish her education. Kate had been packed off with her, for the younger girl's nature promised to be even more troublesome.

Both Sophie and her sister bore the Fairy's Gift of the Duncrieff MacCarrans, unusual abilities that ran in generations of the family. Both wore around their necks small crystals that were taken from the Fairy Cup of Duncrieff, a golden goblet studded with a band of semiprecious stones. The cup, and the fairy blood, had been given to the family by a fairy ancestress centuries earlier.

Their eyes were a clue to their power—fairy eyes, as the MacCarrans called them. Some were born with pale eyes of extraordinary clarity, blue or green or silver, like translucent slices of sky or sea or crystal. The gift that came with that marker was natural magic—a gift for healing, for growing things, for evoking feelings of love, a charm of voice or music or beauty. In each generation it took on a new form where it appeared.

The tiny crystal focused the power, and reminded the wearer to seek true love for the sake of the lovers, and for the sake of the clan. Love—true, abiding love—nourished and protected Clan Carran and had helped keep it safe and prosperous over the centuries. This was the protective spell of the fairy ancestor who had left the stones, and the cup, with the early MacCarrans.

But Sophie had tapped her magical nature too early, frightening herself with her passionate urges, inviting chaos rather than harmony. She had the gift of growth, for plants and living things flourished around her. She had learned to channel that magical touch into the flowers and plants she had nurtured in the convent gardens.

But to properly use the gift, she had to find true love. Now fate, and this beautiful rogue of a Highlander, had decided who she would marry. The decision that Connor MacPherson—and her own brother, who knew the legends—had inexplicably made about her life could alter the nature of the Fairy's Gift irrevocably.

"Look at me, Katherine Sophia," MacPherson said quietly. He rose to his feet. "You seem deep in your thoughts. Are you frightened, lass?"

Averting her eyes, she shook her head. What she feared was her own heart and the power of her innermost passions. The nuns had taught her that physical passion was sinful, although other passions were perfectly acceptable—prayer and devotion, poetry, music, art, gardening, cooking, even lacemaking—but the powerful, mysterious urges of the body were to be suppressed.

She looked at Connor MacPherson again. She felt his undeniable power, sensed the river of life that ran through him. It was present in his piercing gaze, in his deep, rich voice, in the tender strength of his hands. He had a natural charisma, a kind of magic. She felt her own body answer the force that came from him, responding with a quickening of heart and loins, a stirring of the soul. Something within her wanted desperately to unleash and experience what had been denied for so long.

In a way she *was* afraid. Oh, she was.

Chapter 9

❦

"**M**ary left some food for us," Connor said, glad for a distraction. He lifted the cloth from the pewter plate to reveal cheese and oatcakes. "There's lemonade if you'd like some. Mary guards her sugar carefully, so this is a treat." He smiled a little, and poured the drink into a pewter tankard, handing it to his bride.

She drank a bit and set it down. He offered her oatcakes and cheese, which she accepted, and mutton slices, which she refused with a shake of her head. He rolled those up and ate them himself.

The girl ate demurely, he noticed, though with good appetite, before rinsing her hands in the little bowl of rosewater that Mary had included on the tray. Wiping her hands on the linen napkin, she sat back in the tapestry chair, while he continued to stand. The fire felt hot and good at his back.

He rinsed his fingers, too. "They say," he began as he dried his hands, "that finger bowls are no longer placed on the king's banquet table in London."

She looked up. "Why not?"

"Because," he told her, lifting the tankard of lemonade to wave it over the water bowl, "when a toast to the king is made, those who are loyal to the Stuart cause will be sure to drink to the king . . . over the water." He smiled.

She laughed, the sound like the chiming of silver bells. He laughed, too, more from delight in her pretty laughter than for his own small joke.

"And you drink to the king over the water?"

"Always." He looked at her, puzzled. Surely Kate MacCarran would know where Connor MacPherson stood on that issue. "Duncrieff may have told you of my staunch Jacobite leanings, madam."

"He has never mentioned you to me, Mr. MacPherson."

"Never? Odd," he murmured. "I thought he would have said something."

"Not that I recall." She stood, draping her cloak on the chair, her gown shimmering like flame as she moved.

Connor noted her lush shape, her breasts full above the smoothly contoured bodice that tapered to her small waist. Her graceful fingers brushed sensually over the billows of her gown.

God, he thought, she was a vision, brilliant amber and gold, a dazzling jewel dropped into his life. His body surged, demanding that he take her, match her fire to his own. His nostrils flared. The heat in his blood went beyond whiskey, beyond intense physical lust, toward a less definable urge, as if he starved for something he could not name.

She crossed her arms and shivered. "It's chill in here. Are you not cold, Mr. MacPherson?"

He shook his head, not about to mention the degree of intimate heat he was feeling. "Cold rarely bothers me. I am accustomed to it in the way of a Highlander, I suppose. Plaids are reliably warm most of the time, and a dram or two of whiskey always helps. But if you are uncomfortable, we can build up the fire. And I'll go down to the kitchen and see if there's a tin of tea. I promised you that, after all." He stepped away.

She whirled. "Don't leave me. Please."

Her plaintive tone tugged at his heartstrings. "The ghosts will not come knocking while I'm gone," he said. "I promise. You're protected here."

Her quick blush was rosy in the low light. "Perhaps a bit more whiskey will do to warm me for now," she nodded toward the crystal decanter. "Just a bit."

He hesitated, certain she had taken enough already. But he poured a little golden whiskey into each of two glasses beside the decanter and handed one to her.

Swirling the liquid in his own glass, he frowned as he thought of the deed yet to be faced. His bride did not love him, nor he her. A consummation would be awkward at best, yet the marriage must be indisputably sealed. There was only one way to ensure that.

He downed another long gulp, the liquid burn sliding down his throat, and set down the glass. He did not seek false courage so much as a blunting of thought and reason.

His bride sipped demurely, coughed, sipped again, coughed so hard that Connor tapped her on the back. He understood how she felt—both of them were girding themselves, he realized.

"Highland whiskey must be approached with respect, madam," he murmured.

She wrinkled her nose. "It's quite wretched at first, isn't it. But then it gives a most lovely warmth."

"Aye. This is Mrs. Murray's Highland brew. She cannot make it fast enough to meet the demand in England and France. Her kinsmen smuggle it out as fast as they can manage."

"You're a free trader as well as a brigand?"

"No, Mary's kinsmen are involved in the trading business. Neill Murray, whom you met tonight, is her husband, but he takes no hand in the whiskey trade." Rebellion, but not smuggling, he almost said.

She sipped, coughed again, and sat so abruptly that Connor moved forward to shove the chair securely beneath her bottom, swathed in yards of gleaming satin.

"Oh!" She fanned herself. "I do feel much warmer."

He removed the glass. "Any more of that, lass, and you'll go down like an oak."

She shook her head. "I'm fine. I needed a little . . . um, forti-fortifying, I think." Her words were gently slurred.

He needed some fortifying himself. The whiskey had been just enough to warm his blood and nicely blur the edges of reason, but not enough to diminish passion. The hot stirring inside him craved release. Gazing at her, watching her breasts rise inside the shell of that fetching and fiery gown, he felt himself ripen further.

"We've both had enough." He capped the decanter. "You were sick earlier—you don't want to repeat it."

"That was before I had any whiskey. I have a finicky stomach."

"Then we do not want to agitate it. How are you feeling now?"

"Fine. Very fine. I like Mary Murray's whiskey."

"Wait till morning." He cocked a brow.

She looked away. "How is it that you live . . . stay at Glendoon?"

"I rent the property from your brother."

"You're a tenant of Duncrieff? Do you have your own tenants here on this land?"

"A few. I act as a small laird, renting the castle and the land with it."

"Why would you rent a ruin?"

She did love to question him. "It's better than a damp outlaw cave, and I can afford it. Your brother asks almost nothing from me in return."

"In coin," she said, sending him a quick, keen look.

"In coin," he acknowledged.

He knelt as he spoke, needlessly rousing the peat embers with the poker. She stepped closer to the fire, her skirts brushing his shoulder.

"My gown is nearly ruined." She sounded dismayed as she lifted the soggy hems to peer at her feet. "And my shoes. Had I known I was to spend the night hill-walking, I would have worn sturdier shoes."

He twisted his mouth to suppress a smile. "If you had known, lass, you would have stayed inside Duncrieff Castle, and I would have had to climb up and come in your window."

She gasped. "Would you have done that?"

"If I had to. But my comrades saw you ride out with your escort. It was still light then, or we would have snatched you before you went to . . . see Campbell."

"I should have accepted Sir Henry's invitation to stay the night at Kinnoull House. I would have been safe there."

"No," he growled. "You would not be safe with him, believe me."

"And I suppose I am safe with you," she snapped.

"You are." With the poker, he worked at the embers, which sparked and gave off more heat. "You may want to borrow some clean garments," he went on, changing the topic to something more neutral.

"I will want my own things . . . if I stay here."

He noted the wording. "You're my wife, madam, not a prisoner, though we'll keep you safe at Glendoon for a while, according to your brother's wishes. The chest over there has women's things in it, though they may be too large for you." He glanced at her slender form.

"I refuse to wear things that have been used by . . . other women you have brought here."

He fixed her with a stern glare. "They belonged to my mother."

She blinked. "Oh! Where is she?"

"She died a few years ago. You may use her things. No one else does."

"Thank you." She was silent for a moment. "But I will need my own possessions. I do not have many things, but I would feel more comfortable if I had them with me."

"Certainly. I will fetch your trunk from Duncrieff, but not just yet. The local Highland watch and your kinsmen will be searching for you, and best to keep clear of them. But I will get word to your kinsmen that you are safe. Allan MacCarran knows me."

She nodded. "I should see my cousins myself so they will know I am safe. Then I can gather my own things at Duncrieff."

"Oh ho," he said, "you will not. I'll fetch them. Just tell me what you need."

"I am not going to list my intimate garments for you to steal from my home."

"I'm not a thief. And I've seen some of your intimate garments already. Very pretty," he said, as he jabbed the peat bricks with the poker.

"You would be caught and arrested if you went to Duncrieff. I should think you'd rather hang for stealing a bride than for stealing her undergarments."

"Hang for a penny, hang for a pound," he said lightly.

"A pound of laces," she said, slurring the sounds.

"Even better," he said. "I will bring your necessary things back for you."

"H-How?" She hiccuped.

"I have my ways. You'll need just one trunk, I hope. It's a long way up this hill."

"That will do for now. Oh, and we must do something about my potted bulbs."

He quirked a brow. "Your what?"

"My tulip bulbs, already started. I planted them in pots during the winter to start them early. The leaves are up, though tight, and they will flower soon. I was going to plant them in the garden at Duncrieff."

"I'll find a way to snatch your garments, but I'm not going to plant flowers before I leave Duncrieff."

"Then bring them here and I'll put them in your flower beds."

"Flower beds? There are no fancy gardens here."

"But Mrs. Evans—my maid—may not remember to water them and plant them. She will be too distraught over my disappearance to think of it."

"No doubt. Your potted bulbs must take their chances, madam."

"They'll die unless I plant them there, or here."

"They'll definitely die if you plant them here. Nothing grows at Glendoon."

"That's silly. Everything grows. Surely you have a kitchen garden or a flower garden."

"Do you not know your own family legends?"

She touched the silver pendant at her throat that winked like a star. "Le-legends?"

"They say that Castle Glendoon is cursed, that nothing will survive up here, not a weed, not a flower, nor even the castle's inhabitants, madam." He shot her a dark look.

"I remember something—but it's nonsense. There are grasses and buttercups in the meadow outside the castle. And you live here," she pointed out. "How long have you survived at Glendoon?"

"A little more than a year."

"Well, then," she said.

"Nonetheless, there may be some truth to it. The ground up here is barren—mostly rock covered by poor, thin soil. Nothing grows but the toughest heather and gorse." He stabbed at the fire and made a shower of sparks. "At any rate, I'll fetch laces but not tulips. And you may borrow whatever you need in the meantime from that trunk over there."

She nodded wearily, then stretched her arms to

warm her hands before the fire. Kicking off her shoes, stumbling a bit, she lifted her skirts to expose her feet and ankles to the warmth.

He watched her, heated by the sheer sight of her. Keen excitement coursed through him. If he allowed his body to dictate events, very shortly his marriage to Kate MacCarran would be indisputable.

His bride combed her fingers through her tangled hair and raised her arms to sweep the skein over her shoulder in a shower of gold and honey.

Desire shot through him, crown to root. He wanted to touch her hair, her creamy skin, wanted to remove every stitch of her damp clothing and warm her, body and soul, against him. The very thought of loving her made the blood steam in his veins. But he was not a brute, he told himself, though she felt the need to fortify herself with whiskey.

Studying the lovely slender profile of her waist and bodice, he saw her waver where she stood. The girl had a better head for whiskey than he thought, but she was showing the effects of it now. She was drunk, and no doubt. He wished he was a bit more sodden himself.

"Is this your bedchamber?" she asked. "Will you sleep here . . . or elsewhere?"

He sighed, then stood. He reached out and took her arm to draw her toward him. She watched him like a lamb regarding a wolf. He brushed back the golden curls that edged her brow.

Turning her around by the shoulders, he began to work the fastenings at the back of her dress. It was time, he told himself. His heart thumped like a drum.

Earlier he had ripped through the back waist with

the tip of his knife, ignoring in the darkness the small hooks that closed the back seams. Now he carefully eased each hook from its tiny loop and pushed the gown off her shoulders. He would give her a few moments, this way, to think. To accept.

She said nothing, made no protest, only ducked her head, resting her hands at her waist. The splendid satiny thing was in one piece, bodice and skirt, he saw, as he slid it down farther, over her slender arms to her waist.

Beneath it she wore boned stays over a long chemise, and over that a quilted petticoat and another of dark embroidered fabric that showed between the front panels of the skirt. With the bodice dropped away, her back and shoulders emerged, the skin like cream and honey in the firelight. Her tousled hair, a mass of waves and golden curls, slipped over one shoulder. Her neck, small and exposed, had a touching vulnerability somehow.

He leaned down to kiss the back of her neck softly, felt the warmth of her beneath his lips, felt her shiver slightly. She wavered again, and he felt her lean a little against the support of his hand on her waist.

Aye, he thought, she was a bit sodden, and it was his doing, for he had given her the whiskey with half the thought in mind that it would not only warm and revive her when she needed it, but lessen the shock of what was to come. Stolen away, wedded and bedded in one night—not easy for any woman, or for her abductor and groom, though he would not let on. A little whiskey in her blood was a good thing just now, though he would not force her if she refused. But her behavior told him that she would allow him to touch her, to do what he would.

His heart slammed. He was a cad to proceed, but he had been a cad to take her away and marry her without her consent. And she knew, as well as he did, that this must be done if the marriage was to stand.

She said nothing, nor did he. She waited, allowed, and his head spun with the anticipation, with the freedom she gave him. His fingers trembled a little as he unhooked the last fastening on the skirt and pushed the dress over her petticoats.

Her sensuously curved hips moved until the gown and petticoats dropped away to pool at her feet. She stood only in stays and chemise, her face turned away from him, her silence eloquent.

Connor already knew that her stays did not lace at the front, as some did. The lacings were damp, and the tied bows at the back, three of them, would not come loose.

She brought her hands behind her to help ease the lacings free, and wriggled out of the stays, still without a word—and without hesitation. He helped her draw the corset away, set it aside. Her chemise was a plain linen garment touched with a little froth of lace along the low neckline.

"Come here," he said gruffly, and turned her to face him. She tilted her face to his, and her eyes drifted half shut, her hands resting on his forearms.

He bent to brush his lips over her cheek, then he touched his mouth to the satiny skin along her neck, over her shoulder. She sighed, seemed to melt against him.

Feeling desire strike through him, he covered her lips with his own, tasting whiskey on her lips. He sensed her trembling throughout like a bowstring. Tentative at first, her mouth softened beneath his, her sigh releasing tension, both hers and his own. When she looped her arms around his neck and arched a little against him, he felt a spark sizzle through him. He felt it catch in her, too, for she gasped softly. Then she opened her lips for him, inclined her head, came deeper into his embrace. Her breasts pushed against his chest and he felt the warmth of her through linen and wool.

Connor broke the kiss for a moment and looked down at her silently. As she returned his gaze, the question was asked, and answered. Aye, she would allow this.

Whiskey and desire blurred thought and logic, erased any need to question why she had accepted this. He needed her now with every fiber in his body, and thought she felt that craving, too. That in itself was enough reason now, and the sanctity of marriage smoothed the way.

He was done with explanations, with questions. He was fulfilling his solemn promises. Connor swept her up into his arms and carried her to the big bed. Her surrender was clear in her silence and in the way she rounded her arm over his shoulders and nestled her face against his neck.

Chapter 10

~~◦◦◦~~

Her heart quickened, the darkness whirled when she closed her eyes, and the lingering fire of the whiskey melted resistance. She loved the feel of his hands upon her, loved how he had disrobed her and carried her to his bed. Glad to be free of the damp, heavy gown, she felt warm and sensual now, her body pulsing with excitement. Whether this was folly or fate, she wanted it to happen.

As she sank into pillows that were aromatic with lavender, she glanced at him, saw the dark warrior angel again, his face perfect, his touch tender as he stroked her arms. Even his hands were beautiful, strong and knowing. Her own hands trembled on his forearms, the muscles warm iron beneath her fingers.

She sighed, closed her eyes, felt the bed rock beneath

her as he lowered himself beside her. He nuzzled her cheek, his lips found hers, and she sighed, sinking into the mattress, into the kiss, into the moment.

Her head spun and she felt dizzy. She knew she was a little drunk, just enough.

"I'm sorry," she whispered fuzzily, thinking of the unladylike amount of whiskey she had swallowed.

"Hush," he said. "Hush. Don't be. We are married, you and I." His fingers traced eloquently along her arm. "But if you want this to stop, Katherine Sophia . . . you must tell me—"

"Hush you . . . do not call me Katherine—" He kissed her before she could add that she preferred Sophie.

Married, she thought in a fog—married to a strong and fascinating man. She felt caught in a dream. The beginning had been a dark nightmare, but now it was thrilling. As he kissed her, she felt herself dissolving, and let herself sink deeper into the spell.

His hand traced the line of her jaw, slipped downward, his palm warming her upper breast. Her heart pounded. He paused his fingers, encountering her little necklace.

True love, she remembered. As a bearer of the fairy crystal, she was bound by the legend and her fairy ancestry to seek true love, only true love. Sacrifices would be made for love, said the old legend. She had made that mistake before—and the sacrifice had been her dreams.

Now, in this moment, she hovered on the verge of fate and desire. Whatever stirred within her, fairy blood or physical passion, dissolved rational thought.

His kisses, his touch, were magic, and she felt willingly swept away.

Love makes its own magic. The words came suddenly to her. Love could not exist here—how could it happen, so soon, under such conditions—but she wanted to take a risk. She wanted to surrender to intense passions that had been held in far too long. If this was wrong—what choice did she have? He had stolen her away, but she had repeated the wedding vows of her own volition.

Then he moved his hand downward, grazing her breast, tracing past it so that her heart leaped within her and she could scarcely think. She was giddy with whiskey and desire.

His mouth traced along her throat, and she felt the deliciously warm sweep of his tongue upon her lips. She swept her own over his, slid her hands up his arms to his back, where he was muscled and strong beneath the rasp of wool and linen.

He touched the curve of her hip then, her skin swathed only in thin, soft cotton. His hand felt warm, and her breasts tingled as he cupped her breast. She drew in her breath, moaned, wanting him to touch her there, and wherever he pleased. He kissed her more wildly now, fast and hard and hungrily, and he rolled her to her back. There was deep purpose in his kisses now, determination underscoring his hands wherever they touched her.

He compelled her with a touch, a kiss, and she stretched back in his embrace, opening for more of his kisses. With his mouth, he traced a sensual ribbon of kisses down her throat to her upper breast, pulling aside the cotton there. One hand spanned her waist, slipped upward. Her skin tingled, her nipples ruched. He feathered kisses over her breast, touching her nipple, and she felt herself pearl for him. Moaning, she felt overwhelmed by the wonderful sensation.

Warm and sure, his fingers caged her breast gently, so that her breath caught. He shifted and his mouth found the other nipple. She leaned back her head, dizzy, so dizzy, her head whirling, body pulsing.

She closed her eyes and felt the delicate chain pull again around her neck. The fairy crystal held her to a promise of her own. True love must be sought. If it was found, there would come a moment of choice, when a sacrifice of the heart must be made.

She had avoided it all these years—afraid she would lose love if she ever found it. Now she had jumped into a maelstrom, and did not know what would become of the choices she had made tonight.

Head whirling, Sophie could think no longer, felt as if she grew more drunk on kisses and caresses, adding to the liquor warming her veins. Her body urged her to continue, and she could not think any longer, wanted only to feel.

His fingers slipped along her abdomen, traced down over her thighs, began to push her thin cotton shift aside. She placed her hand over his as his fingers slipped down. "Connor . . ." she whispered, his name coming so naturally to her lips that she gasped at the sound in her mouth, at the strength and intimacy it evoked. "Connor . . ."

"Aye," he answered, kissing her mouth. His hand warmed her in a place no one had ever touched, and she felt her body pulsing, her head spinning madly. "Aye . . . tell me," he whispered.

His fingers eased over her, paused, waiting and tender, and she caught her breath at the divine pulsing she felt.

She rolled in his arms, tucked herself close against him, so tightly that she felt his body stiffen against hers—that male hardness she had learned about from another male, years ago, the same young lad who had taught her something about kissing, the year she had lived with her parents in France, the same year her father died and she went to the convent and her life changed utterly.

But not nearly as much as it was about to change.

Now, as she parted her thighs a little, so naturally, to accept his shape and contour as she lay in his arms, she felt that rigid part of him against her, like velvet over warm steel. She felt him pulsing with the same blood-borne rhythm that pounded in her own body.

"Connor," she whispered.

"Aye . . ." His mouth traced over her cheek, his hands tender and warm where he traced her back, her hips. "What?" he breathed against her ear, sending another small thrill through her body.

She sighed, tipped her head back, felt his mouth upon her cheek. She hardly dared to talk, did not want sound to intrude upon the eloquent silent language of touch and caress that prevailed inside the great curtained bed. But though her body throbbed and demanded more, her head whirled like a top, so that the bed seemed to sway when she moved.

"My head is spinning," she finally whispered.

"Aye, mine too." His fingers stroked through her hair, sending a tingle through her.

"Everything is moving . . . oh, but you feel so

steady," she breathed. She wanted him tightly against her, wanted to feel him inside of her so much that it threatened to overtake her. "Don't let me go," she whispered.

"I will not. I promise." He wrapped her tight in his embrace, nuzzled her cheek and throat.

"Mmm . . . and do you keep all your promises?"

"That I do," he murmured. "Now hush."

She sighed against him, felt his hands soothe over her while her head spun with dizziness. After a moment she lifted her hands to his jaw, lifted her face to seek his lips again. She wanted more, wanted it with such power now that she could not stop.

His kiss was infinitely tender, and somehow, with that kiss and the next, while his hands wove a sensual pattern over her breasts, he wove deeply into her dream. . . .

She floated upon a dark river, its surface strewn with flowers. He was there, too, holding her, caressing her. The glorious scent of rose petals and lavender was everywhere as she whispered his name, heard her name upon his lips.

Only it was not quite her name that he whispered, and she could not find the voice or the wit to tell him so.

Chapter 11

❧

Waking, Connor was startled for a moment, his heart leaping when he saw her still there beside him. So he had not dreamed it. Her back was turned and she slept peacefully on her side, golden hair spilling over the pillow. Reaching out, he stroked her from shoulder to hip above the blanket. She was a quiet, still sleeper. He played with her hair, twirling its silk around his fingers thoughtfully.

Last night had been filled with a rousing passion that astonished him with its intimate power—he was sure of that. Frowning, he realized that he was not so sure of the rest of the evening's details.

He rolled away and sat up. The coverlet slid down over his lean stomach as he propped his arms on his knees. Sighing, he shoved his fingers through his hair.

The whiskey had done its work too well, he thought. His head ached dully. Fresh air would clear that adequately, he knew, but would not help the rest. The details of his wedding tryst in this bed was as misty as the glen from which he had snatched his bride.

Had he fulfilled the final part of his promise?

He recalled the gorgeous terrain of her body, and he knew he had touched and pleasured her—and he had the feeling that she had boldly explored his body as well. But he was not entirely certain.

Groaning low, he shut his eyes, feeling even more a cad than if he had forced the girl in the bed. Had they brought their passion to a conclusion? They must have. When she awoke, he would find out from her, without disclosing his own uncertainty.

Exhaling, he tipped his head to his arms. Then he shoved back the covers and sat on the edge of the bed, naked in the dark.

His bride would know—women knew these things. And the telltale signs of a deflowered virgin would be obvious enough. If events had not followed to their natural conclusion, he told himself, it would definitely be a pleasure to broach the subject with her again.

Standing, he snatched up his discarded shirt and plaid—he had still been clad when he brought her to that bed, so that was a clue, at least. He dressed, grabbed his shoes, and left the room quietly, heading up the dark stairs to the roof. Not only did he need some fresh air, isolated beneath the starry sky he could think clearly.

The air was chilly and still misted when Connor climbed the stair to the roof level. Here, the highest remaining section of the central tower jutted upward, surrounded by a partial parapet, once walked by sentries. He went to a favorite spot—a broken corner wall that exposed a small guardroom. Its missing outer wall provided shelter and a convenient lookout position.

From that angle, in day- or moonlight, the glen and the hills were visible for miles. Rumpled hills, long runnels of water spilling to the valley floor; grassy moorland and drover's tracks, the narrow blue loch at the far end of the glen, the white dots of wandering sheep—all could be seen from here. He could even glimpse Duncrieff Castle, a block of golden stone set on a green hill.

A river wound its way through the northeast part of the glen between two hills. Sometimes, when the skies were very clear, he could see through that pass to the lands of Kinnoull. The glen itself, Glen Carran, belonged to Duncrieff. His rightful lands of Kinnoull, a gift to Connor's ancestors from their MacPherson chief, lay on the other side of the glen.

Now the glen was filled with mist like vapor in a cup. When it burned away during the day, he would be able to see the road.

General Wade's crews of soldiers had cut a straight military passageway through Glen Carran. It followed a drover's track over the moor past Duncrieff Castle. Over months, the crew gradually advanced the road southward, paralleling the river through the pass.

Connor and his Highland companions had done everything they could to delay the advance of the construction. As long as he lived in these Highland hills, the English would not have an easy time of their road building efforts.

But he had not come up here to study the lay of the road. He wanted to clear the fog and befuddlement of the previous night from his mind and his heart.

He drew a flat wooden case toward him, snapped the brass latches and opened the lid. Lifting his polished fiddle from its blue velvet wrapping, he took up the horsehair bow, and after tightening the bow and tuning his instrument, stood up. Setting the fiddle to his shoulder, he tipped his chin down, raised the bow, and began to play.

The first quavering note flowed outward, followed by another and another. Notes rang out as his fingers and the bow met the strings to pattern the melody, and the fiddle released it into the air. The instrument was true-pitched and gracefully made, crafted by a renowned luthier in Edinburgh. The fiddle had been a gift from Connor's parents years ago when he was a boy, when there were funds for fine things, and a supportive family to encourage his talent.

The lament he played now was a stirring weep of a tune. The sounds resonated in the fiddle, and within Connor, too—healing tones, soothing and expressive. His left hand danced over the fingerboard in familiar patterns and his bow hand moved loosely, without conscious effort. He knew this melody so well that it had become natural to him. As the song was born into time and space again, he stopped thinking altogether and let the music work its cleansing magic upon him.

The plaintive whisper of a ghost awoke her from her dreams.

Sophie opened her eyes, found herself curled warm in the big bed. Listening for the strange ghostly sound—what exactly had she heard?—she realized that it had vanished. It must have been part of a lost dream.

After a moment she rolled over carefully and moaned a little. Her head ached terribly and she winced as she moved. Another moment passed before she realized she was alone. Connor MacPherson was gone.

She did not even know if he had slept the night beside her. Between whiskey, the newness of loving, and sheer exhaustion, she had slept deeply.

Oh God, she thought. She did not quite know what had happened last night, beyond a delicious blur of kisses and caresses, of his lips and hands upon her in ways that made her blush now, and she remembered her hands upon his strong, hard—

She gasped, sat up quickly, wincing as her head slammed and her stomach lurched. Groaning, she covered her face in her hands, her hair slipping down in tangles.

What had they done last night, what had she allowed him to do? She could scarcely remember—but whatever had happened, she knew it felt wonderful at the time. That much she was sure of, though the particulars were fuzzy.

Moving a little, she discovered that her back and legs were stiff from hours of walking and climbing the previous evening. And she felt slightly, definitely, tender in secret places as well. She was not a virgin—but her first experience had been so long ago, and so disappointing, that she had forgotten what it felt like.

But oh, she wanted to know what it had been like with Connor MacPherson—sensing that the encounter must have been extraordinary, she felt almost cheated—a disappointment of a very different nature this time.

Burying her head in her arms, she groaned to herself. The warm strength of his arms wrapped around her, the depth of his kisses, his soothing, rousing touch—all that came back to her. But the rest had vanished like a dream.

But the sensations in her body hinted at what had happened. And she was nude when she pushed back the covers. She had not dreamed it at all. A sense of guilt, the training of the nuns, tapped at her, but she resisted. She had always inherently felt that there was no shame in what could happen between a man and a woman.

Rising from the bed, shivering, she pulled on her discarded chemise and took up her cloak from the tapestried chair where she had left it. At the window, she opened the drapes, noting that the pewter-colored sky was moving toward dawn.

The sound came again, soft and eerie. Sophie went to the door and opened it to listen, then stepped into the corridor. The music was faint and haunting, as if made by a violin or fiddle. Sophie moved toward the stairwell, entranced by the heartbreaking melody that seemed to pour from somewhere inside the castle.

She had the chilling thought that one of the castle ghosts was luring her onward.

Common sense told her to return to the bedchamber. The castle was dangerously ruined in places, and she did not know her way in the dark. And she had no desire to confront a ghost or a spirit. But the mysterious music was irresistible as it floated outward from its source.

Climbing the steps slowly, she made her way upward, aided by the dim light that leaked through the arrow slits in the outer wall. On the next level she saw three doorways, none of which had an intact door. The music had ceased again. Sophie stood still in the shadows, waiting, her heart pounding.

Cautiously, she peeked into the rooms on that level, finding only empty stone chambers with partially broken walls, open to cold drafts of wind. A steep stairway led to the roof, a common feature in tower houses and castles. But she could not summon the nerve to follow those steps upward. The castle was in poor condition, and she knew it would be foolish to go up.

She turned around and went back to the bedroom. Shivering, she hurried to the hearth and added some peat bricks from a stack, then took up the poker to build more warmth in the fire.

By the time the embers snapped with sparks, Sophie heard the door latch click. Startled, she looked up to see Connor MacPherson entering the room and leaped to her feet, heart slamming.

"*Latha math dhut fhèin,*" he murmured.

"Good morning to you, too, Mr. MacPherson," Sophie answered.

He carried a tray with a cup and a pretty china pot, setting it down on the little inlaid table. "I brought the hot tea that you wanted last night," he said. "A bit late, but I thought it best to keep that promise." He smiled a little.

"Thank you, that's lovely," she said gratefully, and

went to the table to pour a cup of the steaming amber liquid. When she offered some to him, he shook his head.

"Did I hear you walking through the castle a little while ago?" he asked.

"I heard a sound, so I went out, wondering what it might be." She sipped the tea, a good China blend. She closed her eyes for a moment, savoring it.

"Be careful where you wander at Glendoon—some of the floors and steps are unstable. What did you hear?"

"Music. Strange, beautiful music."

"Perhaps it was our ghost."

She shuddered. "Did you hear it? Where were you just now?"

"Patrolling the castle, as I often do. And I went down to the kitchen for the tea. I did not see any ghosts, though." He moved back to close the door, and she watched him warily, then rubbed her brow.

"Headache?" he asked softly.

She nodded. "The tea should help. And it will warm me. It's bitter cold this morning."

"Early spring," he said. "The castle is falling apart, with some walls missing entirely, so the place is nearly impossible to warm. Staying in bed is sometimes the only method for keeping warm. Get under the covers," he suggested. "Enjoy your tea there. No need to be up and about anyway."

"And you?" Heart quickening, she wondered if he thought to come into the bed with her. Last night was one matter—but now she did not quite know what she wanted to happen.

"I do not sleep much, by habit. Besides, I have matters to see to this morning."

"Matters of thieving and bride-stealing?"

He huffed. "You're the only bride I'll ever steal, madam."

"Well, I hope so," she said somberly, though she knew he teased her.

"I must go out, but Mary Murray and her son will be here with you. I'll remind you that you are not to leave the castle grounds. Mrs. Murray will see to your comfort. If you want anything, just ask her."

She tipped her head. "For the key to the gate? Or a horse?"

He came closer, his size imposing, his gaze keen. "More tea, or something to eat. Fresh clothing. A bath."

Sighing, she relented. "Any of those would be lovely, thank you."

"No need to thank me for every small thing. I've done nothing to earn your gratitude."

"You've shown me courtesy, even if you are a—a brigand." She shivered again, and her teacup rattled in its saucer.

He frowned. "You're cold, lass." Waving her toward the bed, he picked up the tray. "I'll set this over there. Go on, back to bed with you, Kate."

A strange chill went down her spine. "I am not Kate."

He halted, tray in his hands, and stared at her.

Chapter 12

御〜〜〜〜〜〜

"Katherine, then," Connor said calmly, though her tone gave him an uneasy feeling. "Or Katherine Sophia, if you prefer."

Huddled inside her cloak, she watched him, her eyes large and colored like the sea, her bare toes peeking out, her golden hair gloriously mussed about her shoulders. She clutched the fine china cup, one of a set from Kinnoull, until he thought it might break. "Do you think I am Kate?" The words were clipped, brittle.

Connor felt as if his stomach sank like a stone. He set down the tray, then turned to study her in the pale light that now leaked between the curtains. Months ago he had seen Kate MacCarran in the market square at Crieff. Her hair, he remembered, was strawberry gold.

Not this bright flaxen color.

She was not Kate MacCarran.

"Your hair," he blurted, though he sounded like a dimwit. "Is it powdered? Bleached?" Knowing the answer, he dreaded it.

"It has always been this color." She sounded impatient. "Did you think I was Kate MacCarran when you stole me away?"

He frowned, gazing at her. "Aye," he said. "I did."

She drew a fast breath, another. "And last night?"

"Aye," he murmured. Feeling dumbstruck, he stayed outwardly calm.

The cup rattled in her hands. She sucked in another breath, then suddenly, swiftly, threw the cup. It smashed against the fireplace, and tea dripped down the stone facing.

His bride gave a half sob, her eyes brilliant with anger—and hurt, too. He said nothing, made no move. She went to the hearth and knelt to pick up the shards, placing them in the saucer, her fingers shaking. His own heart was pounding, but he stood still and silent. Resisting the urge to help her, to hold her, he let her do the work, gave her that moment of distraction.

Finally she set the saucer down and stood again to glare at him. "I am not Kate," she said again.

"Who are you, then?" He almost snapped it out.

"My name is Katherine Sophia. I am Kate's sister. Sophie."

Dear God. He shook his head, staving off a moment of panic. "Duncrieff wrote that name in his letter—but I took it to mean his sister Kate. He never corrected me on it."

"He knows the difference. I am Katherine Sophia,"

she repeated. "And Kate is Marie Katherine." She lifted her chin.

Connor blew out a breath, spun away. At a loss for words, he pressed thumb and fingers against his eyelids.

What the devil was he to do now? Find the priest and demand an annulment? Throw this one back like a small fish and search out the bride he wanted? He swore under his breath, then turned.

"Why in blazes are you both named Katherine?"

"You need not swear. Our grandmothers were both called Katherine. So we each have the name, but we use our other names. Kate and Sophie. It has been easy—until now."

"Jesu." Duncrieff had misled him. Had that been a mistake, or intentional?

"So you meant to steal Kate and marry her?"

He nodded, frowning and silent.

"Oh, God," she whispered.

"Your brother said nothing about the similarity in the names. Nor would I have recognized either of you. I've never seen you until tonight, and I've seen Kate once, from a distance."

"Am I expected to believe that this is a simple mistake?" Her voice rose on the last word.

"You are," he snapped, vexed.

She folded her arms and whirled away. Connor raked fingers through his hair, rubbed his face, thinking swiftly.

He had seen Kate last summer, when he and Duncrieff and Neill Murray had brought a few cattle—stolen from the Kinnoull pastures—to the marketplace at Crieff to sell them. Duncrieff had pointed out his sister, who was with other MacCarran kinsmen. Rob went to greet them, while Connor stayed with the cattle, keeping his distance, maintaining his ruse as a Highland drover in a tattered plaid and a scruffy beard.

Knowing something of Kate MacCarran's secret Jacobite activities, he felt it was safest for all concerned, considering his own rebel leanings, if she was not seen with him. Someday he expected to work with her, but the time had not arrived.

He recalled a lovely young woman, slender and neatly made, in a hooded cloak and blue gown. A lacy cap had perched on her glossy hair, which was gold. Ruddy gold.

Not Sophie's glorious sunlit color. But he had not seen that in fog and darkness. And he had no reason to ask if she was the correct Katherine MacCarran.

"Where is your sister?" he asked. "The MacCarran told me that she would return to Duncrieff Castle this week. I knew that Kate had gone to Edinburgh, so I thought you were she. But where is Kate?" How was he supposed to resolve this? His mind whirled.

"She was in Edinburgh last week. She met me when the ship I was traveling on landed at Leith harbor."

He raised a brow. "You sailed to Scotland but a week ago?"

"I sailed from France with Mrs. Evans, my mother's lady in waiting—the lady who was shrieking when you sank my escort."

"I see. So Kate is in Edinburgh now?"

She shook her head. "She went to London to see family there. Her arrangements were made before word came of Robert's imprisonment, just as I returned. Kate urged me to go on to Duncrieff with

Mrs. Evans to see what could be done for our brother. He already knew that Kate intended to meet me in Edinburgh and then go on to London. Robert was planning to come to Edinburgh, too," she added softly.

Connor reached into his sporran and drew out Duncrieff's folded note. "I wonder who the devil your brother intended me to marry," he muttered as he looked at the page.

"He wrote my name." She extended her hand for the note, which Connor gave to her. "Look . . . part of your name is scratched out. It says . . . Kin–Kinell—"

"Kinnoull," he supplied.

"Then I wonder who the devil Robert intended *me* to marry," she snapped with equal ire. "Campbell of Kinnoull? Perhaps you did force my brother's hand on this page after all."

"Blast it," he said. "I am sometimes called Kinnoull."

"How? Were you Sir Henry's tenant?"

He dismissed that with a wave. "Later. Are you sure your brother knows your full name?"

"Of course! I cannot help it if you thought he meant Kate." She fisted a hand at her waist.

Her tiny waist, which he had measured with his hands. That lovely bosom, now heaving in irritation, which he had shaped with his fingers, tasted with his mouth. Oh God, he thought.

What had Duncrieff wanted? Rob must have known that he would assume the bride was Kate. As a Jacobite sympathizer and rebel capable of looking out for her, he would make her an ideal husband. But he knew of no reason to wed Duncrieff's other sister, leaving Kate unprotected when she needed it most.

All he knew about Sophie was that she was a lovely fairylike creature—as well as mule stubborn, nimble as a fox, and so damned polite at times that it drove him mad. He also knew that liquor loosened her tongue and gave her the heart of a lioness.

And he knew she tasted like clear mountain water and felt like heaven in his arms. He turned back toward her.

"Sophia," he said gruffly, trying out the name.

"Sophie. Or Miss MacCarran," she added in a spicy tone.

He blew out a breath, rubbed his brow. "Sophie . . . I owe you an apology for last night." He had never found it easy to admit any sort of mistake, but this was particularly important, and somehow the words came.

"Thank you," she said stiffly. "But we are married now. And last night we—" She stopped, looked away.

He sighed. He was not even certain if the marriage had been consummated. "Duncrieff mentioned both of his sisters months ago. I knew he called one the hellion—Katie Hell. And the other . . . ah," he went on, remembering, "Saint Sophia."

She scowled. "He used to tease me with that name because I went to a convent school."

"Convent." In the confusion, he had forgotten that the other sister was a nun. He nearly groaned aloud.

"I spent six years in the English Convent in Bruges." She stood before him, shoulders squared, hair glowing. Her breasts, full and luscious, rose and sank beneath the translucent gathers of her thin cotton shift. He remembered the smoothness, the warmth and weight, of her breasts in his hands. He thought of touching her. Kissing her.

"You do not look like a nun," he finally managed.

"Because I am not a nun."

"Novice, then."

"I did not take vows. I was educated there."

"Close enough to a nun." He felt bitter, angry with himself over this colossal error. "It is a good thing I am halfway to hell already, since I am surely damned for last night," he drawled. "Saint Sophia . . . what will I do with you now?"

Her mouth tightened. "Last night you were more than willing to act the bridegroom, and to relieve me of my obligation to marry Sir Henry Campbell."

"Relieve you of your virginity," he clarified. Had he? An instinctual certainty in his body, a constriction and a knowingness, made him dread the answer.

She flared her nostrils. "I am sorry that you got me instead of my younger sister. I can understand that you are disappointed."

Hardly, but he would not elaborate. "What I got was a wee convent nun masquerading as a hellcat." He glared, and she returned it fearlessly.

"I played the hellcat to survive, sir," she snapped. "I was stolen away by a rogue and mishandled against my will."

"Not all of it was against your will," he said meaningfully. "You rather liked some of that mishandling, as I recall."

"What about the rope?" she reminded him.

"I apologized for that. It was necessary at the time." His mind was still whirling. "I can understand if you are angry—you were snatched away.

You have a rogue for a bridegroom, a ruin for a house, and not much of a future now," he said in a deadly calm voice. "But you will never be mistreated in my keeping."

"I suppose I will thank you for that at least."

Inclining his head, he smiled flatly. But he admired her boldness and strength, and he liked her contrasts—soft in nature but tough in spirit. Saint and sinner, he thought, remembering her in his arms, in his bed—

A deep inner hunger stirred in him, grew hot. Kate or Sophie or turnabout witch, he wanted this small golden-haired woman as he had never wanted another. She was divinely desirable, had already matched him for passion.

But no matter how much he desired her, he could not touch her again until he understood this situation. He had married the wrong lass, and he needed to solve that somehow.

He leaned toward her. "I am a rascal, Sophie MacCarran, and you are a nun, or the closest to one that I shall ever meet. Perhaps we should annul this marriage as fast as we made it, and forget what has happened between us."

"Forget—how can I—" She stopped. "But I would be free to marry Sir Henry if we did that."

He lifted a brow. "Tell him you are a nun. That should discourage him."

"It is discouraging you," she said.

"As it should. I would think you'd be pleased about that."

She glowered at him but did not reply.

"I mean to find out what your brother intended," he said.

"Did you truly want her?" she asked. "Kate?"

He paused. She might be further hurt to know that he had indeed accepted the idea of marriage to Kate. Closer to the truth now was that he wanted Sophie—something she would never believe. Nor did he understand it himself.

"I keep my word when I give it," he finally answered.

"What now? Can we . . . even annul this? Is it possible?"

He narrowed his eyes. "Do you not know?"

"I . . . am not certain."

"Did the nuns teach their students nothing about Adam and Eve?" But even as he spiraled into sarcasm and anger, he knew he could blame only himself for a good part of this dilemma.

"I know perfectly well what happens between a man and a woman," she said, hoisting her chin. "I just do not remember if you and I did that!"

"It must have been a memorable evening for you indeed, Mrs. MacPherson." Could a woman truly not know?

"The whiskey . . . I do not quite recall. Tell me. Please."

He felt a muscle jump in his cheek as he looked down at her. Thanks to Mary's whiskey, he had no good answer for her. But he had a clear suspicion.

"I told you I am damned to hell," he said. "Make of that what you will."

He whirled on his heel and went to the door, slamming it shut behind him.

Cold rain pattered over Connor's head and shoulders as he strode down the hill that led away from

Glendoon. Thinking of his bride's revelation—Sophie, he reminded himself, her name was Sophie—he reached the narrow place in the gorge and leaped the gap with scarcely a change in his pace. Landing on the opposite bank, he headed down the slope toward the lower hills that formed the bowl of the glen.

Though it was well past dawn now, the steely sky threatened rain. But work would not stop on the military road, Connor knew, and so his own work of rebellion must continue—no matter the distraction of his pretty bride.

Sophie did not remember what had happened between them last night, either, he thought, thanks to Mary's whiskey. He had promised Duncrieff to make sure that the marriage was indisputable. Repeating the wedding night was no sorry turn of events, but now that he knew she was a nun—or near enough—and not Katie Hell, he felt some genuine misgivings. His bride was an innocent, and he was a cad. He shook his head and swore, then swore again, louder, as he stomped down the slopes.

He could only conclude that Duncrieff had tricked him into this marriage for unknown reasons. And nothing could be done about it short of annulment or divorce.

Duncrieff was dead, or so the guards at the Tolbooth in Perth had told him the previous week when he had gone there to see the prisoner. Died of his wounds days before, they said, and the news had hit Connor like a gut blow. The death of a Highland chief was a tragedy for any clan, but the death of a friend felt worse—particularly when he had an indirect hand in it.

Although Connor was a kinsman of Cluny MacPherson, chief of that clan, he was a tenant and friend of MacCarran of Duncrieff. Therefore his clan loyalties were twofold, and a strong sense of guilt and obligation bound him to Clan Carran. Now that he had married the deceased chief's sister, he was kin to her kin.

Connor missed his friend greatly—Rob had been a strong and clever comrade, loyal to clan and kin, to the Highlands, and to James Stuart. Kinnoull House and Duncrieff Castle were twelve miles apart, but Connor and Rob had not met until they both attended a Jesuit school outside of Paris, when their fathers had been exiled to France. They met again during the two years Connor spent at Edinburgh University. By the time Connor joined the newly formed Black Watch regiment assigned to police the Highlands, they were fast friends and rebel sympathizers.

Connor had joined the military regiment only because his father hoped it would protect him from the rebel affiliation of his kin. Later, he and his father were both arrested for Jacobite activities, and Duncrieff had hired Edinburgh solicitors to help them. Connor gained a release, but nothing could be done for his father.

In Duncrieff, Connor had a true friend. He would never forget MacCarran's generosity, his capable strength and intelligence, his weakness for red-haired women, or his love of a good jest.

Jest indeed. The MacCarran would have chuckled over this mistake. Connor sensed a touch of his friend's ironic sense of humor in the agreement they had made—and sensed a deeper purpose to it as well. He meant to find out what it was.

Scowling as he walked, Connor looked up to see a young Highland man standing among the pine trees, intently watching the glen below. He slowed his step and moved toward him.

"Good morning, Roderick Dhu," Connor said.

Roderick Murray whirled quickly, his hand going to the sword hilt at his belt. The tall, black-haired lad always had a ready blush in his fair, unbearded cheeks, but now his cheeks turned hot red in the thin and rainy light.

"*Latha math*, Kinnoull. I did not hear you."

"Watching so carefully for red soldiers in the glen that you did not think to look behind you, hey?" Connor grinned.

Roderick laughed sheepishly.

"Ah, there's your father coming up the hill. We were to meet here just after dawn."

Roderick turned as Connor pointed toward the older man who climbed the hill toward them. "He and Andrew went down to the glen while it was still dark to watch the road."

"Kinnoull!" Neill waved as he came near. "I am bringing some news."

"Aye?" Connor waited.

"General Wade's crews are making quick progress on their construction despite the weather. That road is coming this way faster than we thought."

Connor nodded, not surprised. "General Wade is a determined and disciplined fellow. He would expect the same from his road crews, no matter what the conditions."

"You ought to know, having been part of the Black Watch yourself."

"That was long past." Connor frowned at the reference.

"We've had some success delaying Wade's progress on the roads," Roderick said.

"A delay is not a true success," Connor said. "Though it helps."

"My news today is that the red soldiers are taking their straight stone road deep into the pass between here and the lands of Kinnoull," Neill said. "I do not know where they intend to take the road, straight or turning east for Perth, but either way they are invading your lands."

"Those are Campbell's lands now," Roderick added.

"Whoever owns the deed, they remain Connor's lands," Neill told his son. "His tenants are loyal to him, and still pay him rent, though he is no longer their laird. Twenty-eight households, is it, Kinnoull?"

Connor nodded. "I have asked them not to pay me, but they insist on scraping funds together through what little means they have to give me the customary rental fee, although they now pay Campbell the same amount. They cannot afford it."

"Some of them borrow from Campbell's herds, as we do, and pay Campbell with proceeds from his own livestock," Neill pointed out. "But if you wish it to change, then the best thing you can do is gain back your rightful lands."

"I wish I could," Connor murmured. "Come ahead, we'll go look at the Kinnoull road."

Neill glanced toward the castle perched on the hill above them. "Your bride—you will not want to spend the day away—"

"It's fine," Connor answered brusquely. "She is exhausted after last night."

"Exhausted?" Roderick lifted a brow.

"From the journey," Connor growled. "She'll rest and stay the day with Mary there. And we'll be back before long."

"Roderick, take up your post by the house until we come back," Neill told his son. "And do not let Kinnoull's bride get away. Kate MacCarran is a clever lass."

"She is not Kate MacCarran," Connor said. The Murrays turned to stare at him. "Though she is just as clever, if not more so."

"Not Kate?" Neill looked dumbfounded.

"As it turns out," Connor said, "I've married her sister Sophie."

"What!" Neill exploded, while Roderick gaped silently.

"Duncrieff's other sister," he explained. "She just came out of a convent in Bruges."

"A nun?" Neill's brows rose high. Roderick laughed, until Connor shot him a dark glare.

"Not quite, but close enough. To be fair, Sophie looks like Kate—enough to fool me."

"Kate's a bonny lass. Is Sophie fine, too?" Roderick asked.

"Very fine," Connor said, and saw Neill glance at him.

"Well, then," Roderick said, "what's the problem?"

"I would not have thought the lass to be a nun," Neill muttered. "Though she did cow Andrew with just a look. They have a way about them, nuns do."

"It's all that praying," Roderick remarked. "All that holiness. It's frightening."

"Andrew is easily cowed," Connor pointed out, "and Sophie is not a nun. Exactly," he added, frowning. He had not asked about the details of her convent life. The fact that she was Sophie, and not Kate, was more than enough detail for now, he thought.

"*Ach*, we'll hope for your sake a wee nun enjoys something at bedtime other than praying." Neill winked and Roderick chuckled.

"None of this is amusing," Connor snapped.

"How could you marry the wrong lass?" Roderick asked.

"I was told she would be at Duncrieff this week, and their names are similar—she is Katherine Sophia." Connor shrugged. "I thought she was Kate."

"*Tcha*," Neill said. "Why did Duncrieff not make it clear?"

"Perhaps he thought I would refuse to marry a nun."

"He would be right," Neill observed. "So where is Kate now?"

"London. Her sister came from the Continent only days ago."

"Duncrieff must have known their plans," Neill said thoughtfully. "He gambled that you would marry the wee nun and realize the truth when it was too late."

"That seems so," Connor agreed.

"He set a trap for you, Kinnoull," Roderick said. "Does your bride know the reason?"

"She does not. But perhaps her brother confided in his kinsmen. Allan MacCarran might know. I'll seek him out."

"You will not be in the MacCarran's good graces

with Duncrieff's arrest and the stealing of their kinswoman," Neill warned. "When they learn about their chief's death . . . it could go badly for you in this glen."

"I know. Roderick," Connor directed, "go back to Glendoon and stand guard there. Make certain the lady does not leave. Sit with her until I return."

"You might have to sit on her," Neill advised. "And have some rope to hand. We'll send Padraig to help you when we see him. Your mother's gone up already."

Connor nodded. "I let Mary in the gate myself, and she bolted it behind me."

"Come, Kinnoull, I'll show you where I spied the English working the road this morning," Neill said after Roderick ran off toward the slopes of Glendoon.

Connor turned with Neill to walk over the hills in another direction. His ghillie bounded ahead of him, despite being nearly twice his age, his legs lean and wiry from years of running over the hills and moors. Connor proceeded slowly, thoughtfully.

He glanced back toward the ruined castle on its forbidding hill. His beautiful, desirable bride waited there. But for now he had best keep his distance from her, at least until he knew more about their wedding arrangement.

Neill spoke to him then and pointed ahead. Connor peered through drizzling rain, searching for the newest section of the military road.

Chapter 13

Brushing dried mud from her gown, Sophie frowned over the torn hems. Her mother had given her the dress in celebration of a bright future. But she would not marry a Highland magistrate, Sophie now thought grimly. Instead she was a rogue's bride.

And the rogue did not even want her now that he had stolen and seduced her.

She had to get away, she told herself, and return to Duncrieff. Her brother needed aid, and her sister was still away. No one was left but Sophie to fight for Robert's welfare—Mrs. Evans, a stranger to Duncrieff Castle and Glen Carran, would not know what to do, and she was of a nervous disposition anyway.

And Sophie knew of no reason MacPherson should keep her here now—she was not the bride he wanted. A desperate feeling of need and loneliness went through her. She had to go home. No matter what her foolish heart—or her body—tried to tell her, she could not stay at Glendoon.

But if she left . . . She thought of Sir Henry and shuddered. This hasty marriage offered her protection from the magistrate's interest in her, and in her clan. But she would have to trade that risk for the privilege, and the need, to be home again.

She had been gone for years, she thought, and home only a few days before this had happened. MacPherson would not be able to keep her here easily—especially now.

She would explore the castle that morning and find some way out of Glendoon. Connor MacPherson would be gone for a while. And since she was not the bride he had intended to marry, perhaps he would make no strong effort to keep her here.

Wriggling into her stays and petticoats, she dressed, fastening the gown as best as she could without help, and then braided her hair and tucked it up with silver pins from her pocket, though she lacked a pinner or lace cap to cover her hair as would have been proper.

Leaving the bedchamber, she took the stairs down. She could smell something heavenly wafting from the kitchens as she approached, and her stomach rumbled. The last full meal she had eaten, but for some cheese and oatcakes, had been at Sir Henry's generous table—a meal she had lost all over Connor's Highland brogans.

Well, he had only deserved that, she told herself.

She entered a shadowy corridor and found the wide arch of the kitchen entrance there. Sophie saw no one about as she entered the large room. Under a vaulted stone ceiling an enormous hearth held a cheerfully blazing fire. A wooden table, scrubbed clean, held stacked wooden bowls and a few vegetables scattered about on the surface, as if someone had been working there. A covered kettle hung from an iron chain inside the hearth, and its simmering contents smelled heavenly, promising a good soup or stew. Her stomach growled again.

The large table also held a plate of stacked oatcakes and a bowl of winter apples. Sophie gave in to her hunger and took an oatcake, biting into it and sighing with pleasure, for it was crisp and still warm.

Elsewhere in the room she saw iron pans, utensils, and knives, and two sagging shelves held bowls, cups, pewter trenchers, and pewter tankards. There were even several wineglasses of etched green glass.

An aumbry cupboard set in the wall held food stores: a sack each of oats and barley; wooden boxes holding carrots, onions, potatoes, and apples, withered from the winter months; along with jars of seasonings, spices, honey, and butter. The supplies were not abundant, but adequate.

She left the kitchen and saw an exterior door that led to a small path and a tangled garden. Stepping out into the rainswept air, she heard the dogs barking and saw them running toward her from the back of the bailey yard, where a cluster of dilapidated outbuildings leaned against the curtain wall.

Everywhere she looked she saw broken walls and stones collapsed in heaps, and hopeless tangles of undergrowth, ivy, and briars. Although in poor condition, Castle Glendoon had once been a proud medieval tower. The crumbling keep dominated the center of the bailey, surrounded by a partly intact curtain wall sound enough to offer some protection. The front gate overlooked a steep hillside and a forbidding gorge, and the castle's back and sides were buttressed by forested slopes.

The terriers ran toward her, followed by the brown and white spaniel. She stooped to greet them, and noticed the tall wolfhound ambling toward her, too. She petted his grizzled head, and shared bits of her oatcake with each dog.

They trotted with her as she walked through the courtyard. When the wolfhound gave a loud woof, she whirled.

A young man approached her, wearing a plaid of red and dark colors, his hair long black and glossy as it floated about his shoulders. He had very wide shoulders and a muscular build and moved with an easy spring in his step.

"Good morning, mistress. I'm Roderick Murray." He smiled, his cheeks stained pink, his eyes sparkling blue. His smile was a beautiful thing indeed, she thought, charming and impish.

"Mr. Murray. I'm Sophie MacCarran of Duncrieff." She held out her hand and touched his fingers briefly. "Did Mr. MacPherson tell you to keep me here?"

"Aye, until he returns." He grinned sheepishly. "Come away from the gate, mistress."

"I was not intending to leave. I was only exploring. Where is the laird?"

"Out and about, tending to his business."

She tipped her head. "What business might that be?"

"He does what he does." Roderick's eyes danced. "And it is not so fine a morning to walk about the castle yard, mistress. There are broken stones and uneven ground, and the rain will make more mud." He glanced up. "You should stay inside the castle today. And be careful wherever you go at Glendoon."

"I hoped to meet Mrs. Murray, too. Mr. MacPherson said she would be here."

"My mother was here earlier, and then she took some of the cattle out to pasture and said she would go home to tend to some chores there. She left a vegetable broth in the kettle and some oatbread. I was to tell you about it."

"Thank you. Do you keep cattle here?" Sophie looked past him toward the back of the bailey, realizing that she had heard some animal sounds there. A few chickens scampered in front of what she now assumed was the cattle byre.

"Aye, the laird keeps livestock—some cattle, a goat, a few chickens. He has a flock of sheep, too, but they stay out in the hills most of the year."

"Ah." Likely all the beasts were stolen, Sophie thought.

The spaniel, Tam, came over to them then, nosing at her hand. Sophie rubbed his head, and when the terriers bounded toward them, Roderick leaned over to them.

"Here, you dogs," he said. "Go on, all of you. You're wet and dirty and should be leaving the lady alone. Mistress, it will be raining any moment now. Come inside. You will be spoiling that bonny gown." He shooed the dogs toward the back courtyard and waved his hand to beckon Sophie along.

"It's spoiled already—Oh!" Fat raindrops plopped

on her head, and she laughed, picking up her skirts to run back toward the kitchen door. The terriers raced past her, while the wolfhound reached the doorway and waited inside like a sentinel as she entered.

She glanced back and saw Roderick Murray running for the outbuildings with the brown spaniel dashing ahead. Whooping in delight as the rain soaked him, he ducked into a ramshackle wooden building that was either a stable or a byre.

Rain spattered over grass and stones, and Sophie watched the downpour, standing in the doorway. Finally she turned away, intent savoring some of Mrs. Murray's soup.

After that she took her time exploring the levels of the castle, finding one empty room after another, some of them crumbling and open to the elements. Only four rooms were furnished—the kitchen, a large great hall, the bedchamber, and a room that appeared to be a study or library.

The great hall was huge and drafty and contained only a table, a few chairs, and a spinet decorated with painted scenes. Gray daylight filled the high, curtained windows.

Next to that room, a small study in an angle of the old keep housed bookshelves crammed with a collection of volumes. A writing table and upholstered armchair took up the center. Like the other rooms, this one was also filled with fine possessions. Delighted to find books—she had always loved to read—Sophie hoped for a chance to explore those shelves later.

If she could not leave, guarded as she was, and Connor MacPherson meant to keep her here for a day, a week, or longer, she would need something to occupy her time. In the convent she had always kept busy. She had to find something to do at Glendoon, unless she managed to claim back her freedom somehow.

Crossing the study, she looked out the small window covered with red velvet drapes slung from a rope nailed into the wall. She gazed out at the hills and rainy sky.

Far in the distance she could make out the slopes of Glen Carran and the river that ribboned through the glen. Although she could not see Duncrieff Castle from here, she could imagine it well enough. Suddenly she felt a stab of homesickness, and tears pooled in her eyes.

Feeling lost and alone, she ached to be home, to be far away from this old castle and the mysterious, compelling laird who hid his broken dreams in this ruined place.

Her gaze dropped to the yard below. She noticed the contour of the curtain wall that surrounded the castle. One part of it curved outward to contain a tangle of growth that, from above, took on a meaningful shape as she studied it.

She saw botanical chaos—a mass of bushes, ferns, ivy, and other indistinguishable plants, all wildly overgrown. Trees thrust up like sentries at the back. She saw traces of another wall, enclosing the whole section with a gate.

A garden. She gasped in delight, recognizing the remnants of a large old garden, blurred by time and neglect. It must have been planted long ago—perhaps hundreds of years ago, she thought, for it had the old-fashioned layout of a hortus conclusus, an enclosed medieval garden.

Her curiosity was engaged. Glendoon was hardly the outlaw's hideaway she had expected. She felt strongly that the old castle could be a beautiful, proud home again if someone would take care and effort with it, and give it the love and attention it needed. Its laird refused to see that.

Nor would she stay to see if the place could flourish, either.

"They are laying their road down alongside the river," Neill said, pointing northward, "and bringing in more stone by cart. Padraig and another ran a long way along the drover's track toward Perth and came back to report that they are bringing at least a dozen ox-drawn carts that way, each filled with stones. See, there comes another now, with a few of the red soldiers."

Connor nodded, watching as a wagon pulled by a huge ox rumbled along the drover's track that crossed the moor. Three dragoons in red coats and white breeches rode alongside the cart. Beyond, Connor could see the straight stretch of the military road in the distance, like a stone ruler laid upon the moorland.

He lay on his stomach beside Neill, hidden by long grass and old heather on the crest of a low hill overlooking the glen. From that vantage point he could see much of the northern end of Glen Carran. Opposite their hill, across the valley, higher mountains rose to meet a glum sky. Fast clouds had scudded overhead all morning, sending rain down in spurts and showers, so that the ground was damp and even boggy in places. Just now, as he lay there, rain spattered his head and back.

Pulling part of his plaid over his head like a hood, he continued to watch, while Neill plucked a long strand of grass and chewed on it.

"Stone roads," the ghillie muttered. "Bah. We do not need stone roads in the Highlands."

"The English need them for transporting troops, supplies, and cannon."

Neill spat again in clear commentary. "We should do to this wee road what we did to that road in the Great Glen, when we were up there last year."

"Blow it by force of black powder?" Connor asked. "That did not stop Wade from building his military highway, if you recall."

"But it delayed him, and annoyed the government. And Wade chose another route for that road, away from the places we wanted to protect. We can do that here, too."

"I have no doubt we can discourage them again."

"Unless the Highland Ghost is too distracted by his pretty bride to do his work properly," Neill drawled.

"He's certainly distracted," Connor muttered. In truth, he had scarcely had a clear thought all day that did not involve a golden-haired girl.

Neill huffed a laugh. "The stone in that cart is gray fieldstone, did you notice? Dressed fieldstone. Interesting."

"Aye. What sort of stone was in the other cartloads?"

"Padraig mentioned three loads of graveled stone, two of smooth cobbles, another of smaller stones," Neill recounted. "He said there were three or four wagons of the big gray stones, like those down there. And more to come, Padraig said. Near a hundred tons of it is expected."

"They are planning to bring it along the track to this part of the glen?"

"Aye, and through the pass between the glen and Kinnoull. Padraig and Andrew saw them this morning, moving between the hills, alongside the river."

Connor rolled to his back and looked up at the sky, resting his forearm over his eyes. His head still hurt from last night's indulgence. And now his heart ached, too, in a strange way that was not physical, but rather from a burden of dread.

"What else did they see?" Connor tried not to take routes through Kinnoull's territory, but for the times he and his men went to the Kinnoull fields at night to snatch a beast or two.

"They are using the gray stones to build abutments on the river banks. Not far from the house, and below the old wooden bridge that has always served Kinnoull."

"But that narrow bridge would not support troops and cannon." Connor groaned low. "They're building a new bridge."

"Aye, so we figured. They use the smaller stones to cover long stretches of the road, before they lay down the cobble and gravel. But the larger fieldstones . . . aye, it is a bridge."

"Once they can cross the river near Kinnoull, they will bring more troops into the area. They might establish a garrison there, or even in the house itself. Damn," he swore low, his forearm still shielding his eyes. "*Damn.*"

"By the devil . . . Campbell holds Kinnoull House now. You will not want red soldiers on your lands or in your house. But what can we do about it?"

"Something," Connor muttered. "I do not know

what. But something, by God." He rolled, rose to his feet. Neill stood with him, and they set off over the heathery hill.

"We could blow the thing up," Neill suggested.

"Aye," Connor said slowly. "If we had the black powder for such a thing, and the plan to carry it out." He frowned. "But it would take the sort of gunpowder used for cannon, rather than small shot. Larger grains. More explosive force."

"I would not be worrying about that, Kinnoull. Just steal the black powder that Wade and his crews use to blow their merry way through the hills of Scotland," Neill drawled. "They have it on their wee carts down there. Padraig saw it. Kegs of it."

"Aye so. Let's take a look, then. Hide that pistol, lad," he said, seeing the gleam from Neill's firearm.

Murray pulled at the upper folds of his plaid. "You know they're searching for the lass and will be suspicious of every Highlander they see out here."

"Then we won't be seen," Connor replied, and strode ahead.

Later that evening, when Connor MacPherson did not return for supper, Sophie ate more of Mary's soup with Roderick Murray. All the while she wondered how she could manage to leave the castle. While she cleaned up the dishes afterward, Roderick yawned widely and went outside to see to the livestock kept in the back byre. Noticing the twilight growing darker, Sophie was sure that she genuinely had a chance. Roderick was busy with chores, and Connor still had not come home.

Not home, Sophie corrected herself. Just to Castle Glendoon.

She stood at the kitchen entrance to the tower, watching Roderick walk through the shadows toward the back buildings. The terriers followed him, while the spaniel and the wolfhound curled up on the warm kitchen hearth.

When he was well out of sight and she heard the lowing of a cow and the flat bleat of a goat, Sophie left the tower. Taking the narrow path through the kitchen garden, a jumble of old, weary plants, she headed around the tower toward the front gate.

Opening it now might attract attention, she thought, remembering how it had creaked when Connor first brought her to Glendoon. Casting her gaze about, she saw a collapsed section of the curtain wall, midway between the front gate and the first outbuilding. The stone foundation of a small building—the old medieval bakehouse, she realized, for ovens honeycombed its interior—hid that section of the curtain wall.

Sophie hurried there, looking cautiously behind her as she went. Roderick had still not appeared, and she was sure he had not seen her. Since the terriers had gone with him and the other two dogs slept by the fire, the timing seemed perfect.

Gathering up the folds of her gown, its bright satin flashing like fire in the twilight, she carefully made her way up the wedge of broken stones where the wall had collapsed long ago. A patch of wooden slats filled the gap at the top, but it looked loose enough for her to shift it aside and slip through.

Shielded by the bulk of the bakehouse, she

reached the top of the stone pile. Crouching ten feet off the ground, she peered down the other side and saw the hills that fronted Glendoon. The drop was not considerable here, for the collapsed stones formed rough ramps on both sides of the wall.

No wonder someone had closed the gap with a wooden barrier, she thought. Fortunately, she was able to pry it loose on one side, where iron nails were loosely embedded in the stone. She broke two fingernails shoving at the planks and picked up a large splinter that she had to pull out, but it was little enough to pay for freedom.

Within minutes she scrambled to the ground, brushing stone dust from her hands and her gown, the satin newly torn. Glancing behind her, she heard no outcry, saw no sign of being followed.

Picking up her skirts, she ran across the meadow that led to the burn. She knew where to cross the water, and from there she could find her way through the hills to old Saint Fillan's chapel, a distance of a few miles. Once she found that spot, her childhood memories would supply the proper way home.

Unlike the previous night, she was rested and alert, made good time as she headed down the steep hill, keeping close to the trees in case she should be seen.

At the crest of a hill she paused. The whole of the glen spread below the hill in a breathtaking panorama of dark hills and sweeping moorlands, here and there sparkling with water and dotted with wandering sheep. Above the line of hills the dark twilight sky was streaked with saturated pink and gold, like the painterly strokes of an artist's brush.

Scotland, and beloved Glen Carran—how she had missed this place all those years away. But she had no time to linger. As she crested another hill, she saw the old chapel in the distance. Slowing her step, she thought about the last time she had been up here.

And she thought about the Highlander who had brought her, who had challenged her and kissed her and married her inside those ruined walls. He was not only her captor, he was her husband now—and that gave him the indisputable right to bring her back.

But MacPherson did not want his stolen bride now that he had discovered her true identity, she thought. Possibly he would not even care that she had slipped away from Glendoon—except for his stubborn insistence that he keep his inexplicable promise to her brother.

Turning, she gazed into the glen and recognized the contours of the hills above Duncrieff. The distance was only a few miles down the hills and across the glen, and she knew the way now.

Raising her skirt hems, she hurried onward. A mile or so farther she felt a sense of exhilaration—she had succeeded in escaping. But she felt a twinge of remorse for Roderick, who might reap trouble because of her actions.

Connor MacPherson would be angry and frustrated, which would only serve him right, she thought. Yet she realized how much she would miss him—far more than she wanted to admit. His rich voice, his strong hands, his satin green eyes, his stirring kisses were unforgettable. She scarcely knew anything about him—yet she suspected that she had lost a little of her heart to him already.

And that, she realized, was another reason why she ran.

With one hand she covered the little pendant that bounced and sparkled at her throat as she walked. That token demanded that she settle for nothing less than extraordinary love, rare and true. If not, she would never fulfill her small but essential role in the Duncrieff legend.

Whenever a MacCarran with the true fairy gift fell in love, the rest of the clan drew benefit from it. Fortunes improved for others, love and healing came their way, too. Every Duncrieff MacCarran had a trace of fairy blood, but only a few had the gift, that touch of natural magic that Sophie had avoided facing.

Just as she avoided Connor MacPherson now, she thought. On a half sob, she fought the sudden, strong urge to turn back and find him. A wild need rose in her to give that passion a chance, and discover if what seared within her heart was real—the sort of love that could be touched by magic.

But he did not want her, and she had made a stupid mistake years ago misjudging love. She would rather go her entire life without love than repeat that—although it might be too late.

Stumbling a little, she continued to run, picking up her skirts and hastening down a rough slope, hardly looking where she went. Tears started in her eyes, though her gut told her to turn back for the ruined castle and the laird of Glendoon.

Blinded by tears and by doubts as well, paying no attention to her surroundings, Sophie skimmed the shoulder of a rock-studded hill where dark pines thrust upward.

And too late, ran directly toward the man who stepped out of the shadow of the trees.

Chapter 14

The flash fire of a satin gown and a stream of golden hair caught Connor's attention as he made his way down the slope. At first he thought he imagined her—she had been in his thoughts all day—but he had definitely glimpsed a woman running across the hillside.

Stepping out of the trees for a better look, he saw a graceful form, billowing amber skirts . . .

Connor swore. His heart nearly jumped up his throat when he saw his bride crossing the shoulder of the hill a little below where he stood. Lengthening his stride, he approached, while she halted to stare up at him.

"Sophie," he growled low.

She hesitated, then picked up her skirts and came toward him rather than running away. Bless her for the boldness she did not even know she possessed, he thought. She looked gloriously defiant. The blend of stubborn strength and grace he saw in her was irresistible.

"Where's Roderick Murray?" he asked, determined to hide his thoughts. "Picking flowers?"

She blinked. "Flowers?"

"I'm assuming the only reason you're out here is that you convinced your escort to go with you to search for flowers, or some such nonsense. Otherwise," he said in clipped tones, "you could not be so utterly mad as to leave Glendoon tonight."

"I don't need an escort, or a guard. I've had enough of being locked away, so I decided to go home."

He took her arm, though she flinched away. "Believe me, it's safer for you at Glendoon, in my safekeeping."

"In your keeping? You left me alone for the day. And I'd rather have my freedom," she retorted.

He pulled her along. "Are you longing for more adventure? If you wander these hills at night alone, I guarantee you'll find more than you could possibly want."

"I've had my fill of adventure, thank you." She yanked away. Connor let go of her arm but rested his hand firmly on her shoulder, turning her to lead her along beside him.

"Duncrieff is that way," she insisted, pointing behind her.

"Glendoon is this way," he said easily.

"There is no reason for me to stay at Glendoon now." She spoke breathlessly as he set a hurried pace. "You married the wrong sister. You don't want me for a bride."

"I haven't made up my mind yet. Watch those stones in the ground," he warned.

She avoided them. "I need to go home. My sister is away, and only I can help my brother now—I cannot stay at Glendoon twiddling my thumbs while you decide what you want. Let me go."

"There is nothing to be done for your brother now," he said. Too late, he realized what he implied. "Let me look into it. If there is new information about him, I'll find it out." He was determined to discover whether Duncrieff was alive or dead.

"But I cannot stay at Glendoon—I do not want to," she said, jerking her arm away from him. He gripped her shoulder again. "You do not understand."

"But you must understand that it is not safe for you to wander the hills, or even stay at Duncrieff without a guard. Your brother was adamant that you stay with me, and I gave him my word on it."

"There is no threat to me. But if you feel so strongly about it, then guard me at Duncrieff Castle, and let me go home."

"I cannot go to Duncrieff openly just now," he growled.

"My sister is the one who needs a watchdog," she said.

"I am aware. But your brother suspected Sir Henry of planning to undermine Clan Carran with this marriage—which means that he felt the need to put you in safekeeping, and I will do that as I see fit." He was growing impatient with this, and knew it showed in his tone and his grip on her shoulder.

She sent him a little glare but did not answer.

"I'll fetch your trunk from Duncrieff," he said. "So you need not go there yourself."

"What about my tulips— Oh!" She nearly stumbled. Connor caught her with a hand to her waist. Glancing around, he searched the hills, the trees, always wary.

"There are more than soldiers searching for you out here," he said. "There are renegades in these hills as well. We'd better hurry back to Glendoon."

"You have no right to keep me there, or anywhere."

"Marriage vows, marriage lines, and a wee note from your brother," he explained. "And besides, I would not like to see you encounter caterans or brigands on your own. Hurry."

"Oh, but it was fine for me to encounter you last night."

"I am the exception. And do not forget that the glen is crawling with soldiers searching for you, madam."

"Good—perhaps I can get a ride to Duncrieff."

"Not the sort of ride you'd want," he said crudely. "There is no guarantee that they would treat you well if they found you. Most soldiers have manners and morals—but some do not."

"And I suppose you know a great deal about soldiers."

"I was in their ranks for two years."

"You?" She gave a hollow laugh.

"Captain MacPherson of the Am Freiceadan Dubh," he said, inclining his head.

"The what?"

"Black Watch. A fairly new regiment formed of local Highlanders to police the Highlands. General Wade, who is busy building the new road you may have noticed cutting through your wee glen, formed the first company two years ago. It has grown quite a bit since then."

"It is hard to imagine you among those ranks—a rebel and a bride stealer."

"I know, but it is true. I promised my father I would join a regiment, and so I did."

"You always keep your word, don't you," she commented.

"No matter how much trouble it may bring me." He glanced pointedly toward her.

"Perhaps you should stop making promises, then."

"Perhaps. Hush, now." He scanned the area as he pulled her along, heading for a stand of trees that would offer them better shelter than the open side of the hill.

"Why do they call it the Black Watch?" she asked.

"For the plaids they wear, hues of blue and green so deep they look black. I still wear mine on occasion, it's a fine plaidie, though I do without the red coat these days."

"You joined to please your father?"

"And to help out my fellow Gaels. It seemed to me that if the government was bent on policing the Highlands, I could do my part to help those who deserved to escape unfair punishment."

"Ah, a rebel in the ranks?"

"Something like that," he murmured.

She paused. "Well, think of me as one of those who deserves to escape."

He huffed a laugh. "I am no longer in the regiment. But if you are determined—" He stopped, took his hand from her. "Go on, then. Go, if you wish. If you manage to avoid Highland thieves and soldiers without morals, you might be lucky enough to find Sir Henry Campbell himself."

"Campbell?" She swiveled her glance around.

"Aye, he's out here searching for you, too. I saw him today, and I watched soldiers combing these hills. I'm sure Sir Henry would be delighted to offer you assistance."

"No doubt." She sounded uncertain.

"Perhaps he could help you obtain an annulment from your thief of a husband. Although you will have to appeal to Rome for that," he added. "It would take some weeks, but then you would be free to marry Sir Henry."

"You know I do not want to do that," she snapped.

"A dilemma, my lass—him, or me." He cocked a brow.

She drew a breath. "If I went to him, he would see that you were arrested for abduction."

"I'm sure he would relish that," he agreed affably. He watched her, his heart beating hard. It was a gamble to give a kestrel a chance to spread her wings. If she truly wanted to fly, perhaps he and her brother, too, had been wrong to hold her back.

He hoped not. If she took off, he would have to follow her all night just to ensure her safety. He waited, arms folded, heart pounding.

She did not reply, brow furrowed as she studied him warily.

Connor turned and began to walk. A moment later she fell into step with him, her skirts rustling softly. He slid her a glance, masking his vast relief.

"If you were going to try to escape, Sophie, you should have at least tried during the day. It's too dangerous out here just now for a lass alone," he explained quietly.

"I was too busy wandering around the castle, with

my guard and a pack of dogs at my heels," she snapped.

"Well, I'm glad you found something to do. Hush," he said then. "Hush!"

He stretched out his arm to stop her, silence her. His senses were alive, the hairs on his neck prickling with alarm. The rustle of old heather, the tranquil burble of a nearby burn, the snap of his shirtsleeves in the wind, the liquid trill of a curlew were normal sounds. But he had heard something more. Strands of his hair blew over his brow as he turned his head, watchful.

Within moments he heard them again—shouts muffled by distance and breezes. He heard cattle lowing, too. There were men and livestock on this same hill.

"This way." Taking Sophie's arm, Connor pulled her with him, turning with her toward the pine trees that fringed the hillside. "Hurry!" He began to run, and she hastened alongside him.

Ducking under the wide, low-hanging branches of a pine tree, Sophie fell to her knees when MacPherson pulled her downward. He grabbed her then, drawing her hard against him under the shelter of the tree. He knelt, and she half fell, half sat over his thighs. His arms wrapped quickly, tightly, around her.

"What is it?" she asked, and he lifted his hand to clap his palm over her mouth.

"Shh," he whispered in her ear. "Someone is out there."

She felt the tension in his body, taut as a drawn bowstring. She sensed the heavy thud of his heart against her back, felt it pulse in his hand over her mouth. Her own heart slammed, too, as she crouched with him, breathing through her nose.

Eyes wide, she peered through the thick branches of the tree that hid them. The Highlander kept perfectly still, and his restraining hold on her kept her frozen as well.

She heard the sound of men calling out, woven with the deep bellows of cattle and the heavy thudding of hooves on the hillside. Watching through the screen of pine branches, her breath nearly stopped in her throat, Sophie saw three Highland men and several cows in the same area where she and Connor had just been walking. Rising moonlight struck along the animals' horns and highlighted their huge heads and broad backs. The solid, shaggy, reddish creatures moved slowly across the incline, driven by the men who called and hooted.

"Caterans," Connor muttered soft in her ear. "*Cearnach,* we call them—cattle thieves. Those are Hamish MacDonell and his men, I think. A naughty bunch of lads. I think we'll wait here, you and I." His breath blew soft over her cheek, his voice resonating through her body.

Sophie squirmed a little in his arms, but he held her tightly, kept his hand over her mouth. Trapped in his arms, she waited silently with him, her breathing in tandem with his. The only other sound beneath the ancient pine tree was the sigh of wind through the branches.

She caught the pungent scent of sappy branches and old pine needles. Connor shifted slightly, adjusting his arms around her. His arms crossed her bodice, one at her waist, the other over her upper chest, so that one hand rested on her bare skin. She could feel the heel of his hand pressing against her upper breast. With each breath, her skin met his, gathering warmth and a subtle awareness.

She stayed perfectly still, only her eyes moving as she peered ahead, watching the group of men and animals wander over the hill. MacDonell's men called out, laughed, seemed to feel no urgency. The cattle lowed, snorted, turned in wayward directions. One ran so close to the cluster of pines that Sophie could hear the heavy breaths of the great shaggy beast. A man ran across its path, swearing as he tried to drive it where he wanted.

Hooves thundering, the animal headed directly for their tree. Gasping, Sophie stiffened.

"Easy," Connor murmured. "Shh."

At the last instant the cow veered in response to its drover, and Sophie blew out the breath she held.

Moments later the men and their clandestine herd disappeared over the side of the hill. Sophie sat up, but Connor MacPherson held her back.

"Not just yet," he murmured, holding her against him. "They could come back. Relax, lass."

His hands were warm and strong, one over her mouth, the other resting over her breastbone. His breath tickled her cheek, his voice vibrated through her. She closed her eyes, leaned back. She did not feel trapped any longer—she felt safe. She felt good, though she knew she should not.

He was a cattle thief himself, and worse. He knew those men, and probably stole cattle of a night himself.

"That's it, love," he whispered. "Easy. Keep still."

She tilted her head, and his breath flowed over her face, his warm, deep voice filling her. She sighed under his hand, loving the comfort and safety she felt in his arms—though she did not want to love it at all. Earlier that evening she had made up her mind, however conflicted she felt, to get away from him. And now she sat with him, wanting only to be in his arms.

"Aye then," he whispered, as if he understood somehow. "Aye, lass—be still." His lips touched her ear, traced the lobe, lingered.

A sensation rippled through her, delighting, exciting. She caught her breath, arched her head against his shoulder.

His lips touched her ear again, the warmth of his breath penetrating, and a feeling shot through her like lightning, flashing deep into her body. She turned in his arms like a lodestone, seeking more, her undefined hunger quick and surprising.

His hand slid away from her mouth, and when she began to speak—to ask what he meant to do, or perhaps to beg for it—he covered her lips with his own, taking the sound from her.

Allowing him to kiss her, she stilled her lips beneath his, tasting, waiting, not sure she should allow this again. Yet excitement built within her like a storm.

She was not afraid. What pulsed through her was passion without a touch of fear, she realized. Kissing him back, she tested the feeling, her lips softening under his, flexing.

His hand moved lightly over her upper breast, his fingers cupping the rounded flesh, and each tracing touch sent shivers down into her body. She gasped again, under the cover of his mouth, and felt his other hand cup her head. Twisting in his embrace, she brought her arms up to loop around his neck, her body demanding more, pulsing for more.

Like last night, she thought. She had wanted more then, too. And in the morning, learning more about her, he had rejected her.

Remembering that, she turned her head away, and froze.

"Aye," he said gruffly. "Enough of this." He pushed her out of his lap, half stood. She heard the thunk as his head hit one of the branches. "Come along—they're gone."

He took her hand to lead her out from under the tree. As she stood in the open, Sophie found that her knees were weak, her body trembling as she emerged into the open beside him.

This time she did not protest as she walked beside him, her hand clasped in his. Sobered by the thought of what might have happened had she encountered the cattle thieves or the regimental soldiers on her own, she said little to Connor as they went.

Just as he had on the night he snatched her and married her, he assisted her in crossing runnels and climbing the steepest slopes. And now and then as they walked along, she felt his fingers tighten on hers for no reason—and it felt good to her, so good.

"I am glad that you came along tonight, since the caterans were out," she ventured.

"It's one of the reasons that I wanted you at Glendoon," he said gruffly. "Neill and I saw MacDonell and his bunch in the glen earlier and wondered what they were about. I was keeping watch for them—and the soldiers, too—as I made my way back to the ruin."

"I found a chance to get away, and could not ignore it," she said, defending herself. He shrugged his understanding. "But I am grateful. You might have saved my life, appearing when you did."

He grunted acknowledgment and did not look at her. His mood seemed somber and thoughtful. Clearly he was displeased and in a hurry to get her back to Glendoon.

"I still mean to go to Duncrieff," she said. "I thought you would not much care if I left Glendoon. After all," she added, "I'm not the one you wanted."

"But you're the one I married," he said, and the teasing tone in his rich, velvety voice was surprisingly affectionate, unless she mistook it in her fatigue. "We'll go to Duncrieff as soon as we can manage, Sophie. You have my word on it."

She felt strangely reassured, and realized suddenly that had any other man stolen her, she would have fought more desperately for freedom, claimed any chance to get away. But some deep part of her wanted to go back with Connor MacPherson.

As they walked along, she squeezed his hand with her own. A small gesture of peace and gratitude, she thought, as his fingers answered hers.

He broke the grip to point ahead. "Look there, Mrs. MacPherson. Here's Roderick, come to find his wayward charge."

The young Highlander raced toward them down the slope that fronted Glendoon. Lifting his hand to wave, Connor pulled Sophie along with him.

Like it or not, she was back in the keeping of the laird of Glendoon.

Once they were inside the castle, Connor took the lantern from the kitchen table and led Sophie up the stairs. She moved ahead of him, her fire-colored dress whispering on the stones. He climbed just behind her, holding the light.

"Be careful on the steps," he cautioned. "If you walk around the castle in the dark, keep to only the chambers in use. A wrong step in the dark and you could fall to your death."

When they reached the landing leading to his bed-chamber, he opened the door, stepping back to allow her to enter.

"Good night, madam."

"Where will you sleep?" She turned to look at him.

"I doubt I will," he said, "after all this adventure."

"But . . ." She hesitated.

"If you are worried about the ghosts, they will not bother you. If you hear rattling and moaning, just go back to sleep."

"Connor—"

"Good night," he said firmly.

"Where will you be, if I should need anything?" Her eyes were wide and expressive, conveying a different message than her words. He thought she pleaded with those beautiful eyes for him to stay with her. Or was that wishful thinking?

But he would not, until he knew his own mind with this lady. He had kissed her under the pine tree when he had meant to keep his distance from her. But whenever he saw her, he felt challenged to resist her natural allure—and he meant to find out more about their marriage agreement before he waded any deeper into Duncrieff's possible trap.

He shrugged, though he wanted very much to come inside and share the bed with her. "I'll be about the place."

"If you sleep elsewhere, you will freeze. It's chill at night here, and in the mornings."

He tilted his head. "Do you care so much about my welfare?"

She brushed at her skirts, standing in the threshold. "I care about anyone's welfare."

"Saintly Sophia." He watched her, feeling tender suddenly. "Sleeping on a cold floor will do me no harm. I see you learned your manners well in your wee convent."

She lifted her chin high—he loved the line of her throat, long and delicate. "I learned decent behavior in the bosom of a caring family. I hope that same privilege was accorded to you."

"I dimly remember lessons in etiquette and morality. And I remember kindness." The urge to tell her about his family was very strong, but he smothered it. "Good night, madam."

He stood close to her, and she did not back away. With one hand he reached out to brush her hair back from her face where a wave had slipped out of its knot. He swept his hand over the side of her cheek, cupping her face. Aching to touch her more fully, he would not let himself.

"This is your bedchamber, not mine," she said. "If you do not wish to share it, then I do not wish to take it from you. I can sleep elsewhere. There are other bedchambers."

"You could have a private room to yourself, I suppose," he said. "The other bedchambers are unfurnished, and some are open to the elements. But we have straw pallets and extra blankets stored away. We could scare up a brazier for heat. I wouldn't trust the fireplaces in those rooms—they'll be full of birds' nests and debris. But if you do not mind sharing an empty chamber with mice and squirrels, then please yourself."

She sent him a sour glare. "An entire castle," she said, "and just one bed, scarcely used."

He watched her evenly. "I told you this was not my home."

"Where is your home, Mr. MacPherson? You never said."

"Under God's lovely stars, madam. Anywhere I will it, and nowhere at all."

"You could settle here at Castle Glendoon," she said, glancing around. "It was once a lovely place, so I've heard, a grand place filled with happiness and celebration."

"That was long ago," he said. "There was some tragedy here, from what I remember of the old legend. All the MacCarrans in residence packed up and deserted Glendoon like rats leaving a ship. All they left behind was this smashed fortress in the care of a couple of ghosts. Tragic lovers, or so it is said."

She shivered. "I remember something from family lore . . . and you mentioned a curse on this place."

"Aye, I've heard so. She leaped to her death, they say, trying to warn him—and he could not save her." He leaned forward. "Keep to your room at night, madam, and do not wander the ruins, should some harm come to you. Good night, lass," he finished quietly. Unable to stop himself, he reached out, brushed his fingers down the softness of her cheek. Then he turned on his heel and headed for the stairs.

"No harm will come to me," she said. "Not here at Glendoon."

He smiled to himself, a little, as he rounded the curve in the stair.

Chapter 15

"**O**h! Blast! Be damned, ye filthy, nithering cur!"

Sophie tentatively came down the corridor. She had not seen Connor that morning, and after dressing again in the amber gown—a sad ruin of a thing at this point, after last night's escape attempt—she had decided to go to the kitchen in search of some breakfast when she heard the woman cursing. As she rounded the corner, she heard the slap of a broom.

The woman stood by the outer kitchen door, wielding a straw broom. "Be gone, ye great keekie!" With a sound of disgust, she turned back toward the kitchen. "Oh! Mistress!" She stopped.

She hurried toward Sophie, her cheeks pink, tendrils of dark hair escaping from a lace-edged cap.

The woman had a sturdy, voluptuous build and wore a blue-gray dress with a wrinkled apron. A lightweight plaid was tossed over her shoulders.

"Mrs. Murray?" Sophie asked, coming forward. "I'm—"

"Aye, mistress—I know. Connor's wee bride! Took ye off in the night, how exciting!" Her sparkling blue eyes reminded Sophie of someone—Roderick, she realized.

"I . . . suppose it was exciting," Sophie said hesitantly.

"*Och*, some Highland brides begin their married life that way. Not me, I met my Neill in a market square when I was selling rags and trinkets with my father. I'm Mary Murray." She extended her hand, her grip warm and sure. "And I do apologize for the blathering on! Those damnable crows made me so angry!"

"Crows?" Sophie asked.

"Aye, taking the wee seeds out of the kitchen garden again. I planted a few seeds the other day—peas and slips of marigold and lavender, as I did at home. But they willna grow here, even if the crows would leave them be. Nothing grows in this accursed place. Nothing at all." She set aside the broom and beckoned Sophie out of the dark corridor and into the bright kitchen.

Mary Murray was a handsome woman, Sophie noted, despite her flustered, rumpled appearance. Her oval face had a serene beauty, with translucent skin and clear blue eyes. Her hair, slightly visible beneath her cap, showed silver threads among the dark waves. Though she had a grown son, Mary's lovely skin showed hardly a crease. Sophie could see that

Roderick had inherited his mother's pink-cheeked, black-haired sort of beauty.

"I'm so sorry ye heard me ranting on," Mrs. Murray said. "My folk were Travelers, and my grandmother swore like a fishwife when her Romany temper was up. I'm afraid she taught me, and so it slips out now and then." She grinned.

"I do not mind," Sophie said. After years in the convent, a woman who spoke as freely as she pleased was refreshing to hear.

"Roderick said you were exploring the castle. It's a sad place now, but was once very fine. There's a ghost or two here . . . well, ye'd know, it's yer own family that owns Glendoon!" Mary opened the wall cupboard, took out some potatoes and carrots and brought them to the table, where she began to slice into them with a small knife. "I've food to prepare, but there's porridge in the small kettle if you're hungry," she said.

Sophie thanked her and helped herself to the porridge, which was very good—steaming and thick, a bit salty, a bit sweet, with a trace of cream in it. After she ate, she joined Mary in her task, choosing a knife and setting to work to chop some carrots.

Mary Murray did not seem to find it odd that Sophie helped her in the kitchen. Nor did she seem to think it out of place for the laird to steal himself a bride. Sophie glanced at her.

"I heard ye've been away from Scotland for a bit," Mary said. "My lad Roderick said ye've been in France. I remember when the MacCarran chief was exiled. A fine man, loyal to the Jacobites. As is yer brother, may Heaven protect him."

"Thank you, Mrs. Murray."

"Mary. Did ye like France?" she prodded.

"I did. We lived in France for a little while, and then Rome, and I spent the last six years in Bruges. I was educated in the English Convent there."

"Broozh? Where is that?"

"Flanders. The Netherlands," she added.

"Oh! That's where the laces and wee flower bulbs come from!"

Sophie nodded. "Bruges is a lovely place, a little jewel of a medieval town, with canals and swans, so peaceful. There are women who sit in their doorways all day tatting lace. In the spring you could see whole fields of tulips and daffodils, just beautiful, miles of yellow and red and orange. At the English Convent, we had a garden in the front that was a mass of tulips and daffodils and hyacinths. The colors and the scents were wonderful." She smiled.

"Oh, ye had gardens! I do enjoy my wee garden at home—our house is at Balnaven, about two leagues from here—though I grow mostly vegetables. I have some flowers, daffodils and marigolds to protect the vegetables—the deer and rabbits won't come near those. I even have a few roses in my wee yard. Someday I would like to have some Dutch bulbs, which they sell at the markets in Crieff and Perth, but they are dear to buy."

"I brought some bulbs from Bruges," Sophie said. "Some of them are already started. I would be happy to give some to you."

"Oh, thank you!" Mary beamed.

"My things are at Duncrieff," Sophie said, frowning. "I . . . came here with nothing at all."

"Stolen away, aye. Well, there was no choice in the matter, from what I've heard."

"I do not agree."

"*Och*, ye'll understand in time. Though I'm sorry for the trouble the laird put ye through, and I'm sure he is, too."

"He is not sorry," Sophie said, chopping fiercely into the next potato she chose.

"He is," Mary said. "Though he's not likely to say it." She glanced at Sophie. "Tell him ye want yer things here, now."

"He means to fetch them . . . when he wants."

"I heard ye tried to walk home last night. Roderick told me. That's fine spirit, lass, but the hills are full o' rogues."

"So I learned. I hope Roderick did not have too much trouble with the laird."

"Not really." Mary chuckled. "Dinna let Connor MacPherson frighten ye with his grumphs and crabbit ways. He's a good man, though he doesna like others to know it."

"What do you mean?"

"He has a good heart, and he watches out for his tenants. They show him their loyalty in turn, too."

"Steals cattle for them, does he?" Sophie dropped the potato pieces into a bowl.

"Only if he must. He makes certain they have what they need. He seems a rogue for snatching ye, but he saved yer clan by marrying ye, so Neill and Roderick say. Yer own chief, God bless him, thought of yer welfare and sent the laird after ye."

"Saved my clan?" Sophie looked at her in wonder.

"Aye, that cold fish, Sir Henry, canna take control o' Clan Carran if he isna married to the chief's sister. My Neill says so. Ye must be glad to have Connor MacPherson for a husband, I am thinking." Mary smiled.

Sophie chopped the next potato so hard that the knife stuck in the wood of the table. She pried it loose and continued to cut vegetables in silence. Caught up in the immediate events of her abduction and marriage, she had not spared a direct thought about what Sir Henry might have wanted from their proposed marriage.

Oh God, she thought. Mary's remarks could be right. Clan Carran was indeed safer with Sir Henry not included in the inner circle of the chief's family members.

Mary chattered about the supper she intended to prepare with the potatoes, carrots, onions, and the oats and barley that were on hand, while Sophie murmured politely, scarcely listening.

Connor MacPherson might indeed have saved her in more ways than one. Later tonight, Sophie thought, he would return from whatever raid he had been running that day. For a moment she remembered the tenderness he had shown her last night, and the night before. Her body shivered pleasantly with the recollection.

Would he return, expecting to resume that, or would he act distant again? What would become of this impulsive marriage if the laird had changed his mind?

She was glad to be free of Sir Henry's hold over her and her clan, that was for certain. But she did not know where she stood with Connor MacPherson— or what she wanted herself from this marriage. He had cooled, that seemed clear to her. But she felt herself just beginning to heat up to the depth of her passion. His touch, his kisses, had set her fairy blood to sparking, and he had awakened her foolish heart, so eager to love.

Snatching up an onion, she chopped it with a vengeance.

" 'Twas not so difficult to bring this bridge down," Neill grunted as Connor walked toward him. The older man lay on his back on the bank, torso tucked partly beneath the bridge, his hammer in hand as he pounded nails into a wooden plank to patch the bridge. "But it is a devil of a thing to right it again."

"Aye, well," Connor said, reaching down to give Neill an assist to his feet. "It's time well spent, so that drovers and their herds can cross these bridges again. You'd best set the work aside for now. I saw the red soldiers as I came down the Benachallie Mor," he said, pointing toward a large hill in the distance.

"I saw them, too—searching the hills, stopping to ask at every house. They may very well head up to Glendoon."

"Not so far. They do not like that hill, nor the ghosts who haunt that castle." Connor grinned fleetingly. "And they seem to be more interested in Mac-Carrans than MacPhersons just now." He frowned. "I do not want the bride-stealing blamed on MacCarrans. I mean to speak with those lads, but if I must get word to Campbell, I'll do that, too."

"Now there's a risk." Neill brushed dirt from his plaid and bent to put his hammer and nails into a leather pound, which he then hoisted to his shoulder. "But you do not want to raise Campbell's suspicions."

"If I must, I will," Connor said. "Come ahead. We've been out all of today and long into the night, and I will not sleep in the heather when I could sleep in a bed."

"Eager to return to Glendoon and your bride, hey?"

Connor frowned. "I do want the chance to talk to her further about some of this."

"Ah." Neill was blessedly silent.

"And I want to spend some time taking care of my livestock," Connor said. "Fiona is not pregnant yet this season. She may never take again."

"Not so long as she grazes on Glendoon grass, perhaps," Neill said. "Barren place."

"So it seems, but I've little choice but to stay there."

"Women are particular about their homes, and your Sophie may not want a haunted place to raise her bairns."

"Bairns? The lass would prefer an annulment."

"After all that trouble to snatch her? *Tcha*," Neill said in disgust. "We'll finish these bridges in the next few days," he went on. "Though Hamish Mac-Donell says he'll drive his herd to the Crieff market next week, and he'll take this track. I wish no harm to his cattle, but I would not mind if Hamish himself got a bath." Neill grinned, quick and mischievous.

Connor smiled, aware of the longstanding rivalry between Neill and Hamish, who was a true rapscallion, save for a kinsman or two among the MacPhersons in his own line.

"Whose cows will he sell at the Crieff market this time?" Connor asked. He glanced about as they went, continually looking for soldiers, Highlanders, any sort of danger. After years of living as a renegade, it was second nature to him.

"*Ach!*" Neill shook his head. "None of his own, I'll wager. Hamish and his lads cut three reds from Allan MacCarran's fold last night, and two black ky-loes from Campbell's herd last week."

"I saw Hamish with those reds myself."

"And I told Hamish that if he takes Sir Henry's cows, he steals from Connor MacPherson himself. Hamish says you have no legal claim to Kinnoull herds now, and if cows wander in open pastures at night, he can borrow them as he pleases."

"He's only doing what we do ourselves, borrow-ing good cattle by dark of night." Connor hastened, half running toward the cover of the low hills. Neill, a shorter man but sinewy and strong, easily kept up.

"I reminded Hamish you do have a legal claim to cattle on Kinnoull lands." Neill was not one to drop a subject quickly, Connor knew. He glanced at his friend.

"My father's fate changed that. And my second petition for reinstatement is lost in the bowels of the London courts. When I was in Edinburgh a month past, my advocate had no answer at all."

"Useless long-robes. A Scottish advocate will have little influence in a London court. Lawyers," Neill snarled. "Smoke Campbell out and take Kinnoull back yourself."

"This is not the Middle Ages," Connor replied calmly. "Lawyers and documents, suing for rights, submitting petitions to London, waiting for a reply—that is my only course now."

"If the English king can still draw and quarter Scottish rebels, then his Highland subjects can still use smoke and axes to gain back our homes, and our rights."

"For now, stealing and harassing will have to do," Connor replied dryly.

"Campbell has no right to sit at Kinnoull." Neill spat.

"He has the deed."

"All the same, someday you will hold Kinnoull as your kin did before you."

Connor's throat tightened. When he and his father were arrested together, his father had whispered to him that he would have Kinnoull, no matter what happened. His father had been proven wrong, Connor thought. He had the title and some furniture, but nothing else.

His family had held Kinnoull for two centuries, but Connor had lost hope that he would ever gain it back. He was the last of his kin, the son and only child of his dispossessed father. His mother had died two years ago, and he felt estranged from most of his kin now. Most of his household had left Kinnoull House. And Cluny MacPherson, chief of the clan, had not been quick to offer help when he and his father sat in prison, or in the days surrounding his father's execution. Ultimately, it had been Robert MacCarran of Duncrieff who obtained his release.

Connor felt he owed Duncrieff more than he could repay. He did not know for sure that Duncrieff was dead, but he had no proof otherwise. And the legacy of the MacPhersons of Kinnoull would die with him. His descendants, he thought—if he ever had any—would only be the lairds of Glendoon, though blood heirs to a viscount's title that was no longer attached to its land.

Sighing, Connor rubbed his brow. He was tired, and he had yet to solve the more immediate problem of his bride. The little nun was by far the most distracting element in his life just now. She had set him—mind, body, and heart, as well—into turmoil.

As he and Neill climbed over the rocky slope, Connor paused, propping one foot on a rock to look around from the higher vantage point. In the distance he glimpsed red jackets and the flash of steel weapons as men rode on horses.

"*Saighdearean ruadh,*" Connor said quietly. Red soldiers.

Neill looked where Connor gazed. Riders came across the moor from the northern end, their red coats and white stockings highly visible in the murky light. As they followed the curve of the hills where they met the moorland, Connor noticed that three men rode with them who were not soldiers—one in a brown jacket, the others in Highland dress. He narrowed his eyes.

Connor stood waiting, hand resting casually on the handle of his dirk, one foot lifted to the rock. His shirt and his hair whipped in the breeze, but he did not move. Neill stood just behind him, a guard at his back.

Watching carefully, Connor noted every detail he could—faces, clothing, horses, weapons. Whenever he had occasion to speak to soldiers, he took care to learn names and regiments. He wanted to know who his foes were.

"Sir Henry is in the lead," Neill said. "I'd recognize the horse faster than I'd know the man."

Connor saw a fine bay mount and its nonmilitary rider. "Aye, Campbell."

As he came closer, Connor studied the magistrate. Sir Henry had a strangely forgettable appearance, average at best, with features that seemed blurred and poorly defined—small eyes of an indistinct color, a blunt nose, a weak jawline, a thin mouth, and, though of wiry build, a slight pudge about the middle. He favored brown suits and gray wigs, increasing the odd air of invisibility about him. In fact, the only thing truly memorable about the magistrate, Connor thought, was his cold grasp over the property of Kinnoull.

"You Highlanders!" Campbell called out, seeing them. "Stop!"

Considering that Connor stood motionless on the side of the hill and had for several minutes, he could have laughed. Instead, he fixed a flat stare on Campbell and waited.

"MacPherson!" Campbell called. "What are you and your man doing out here?"

"Neill Murray is my cousin and my ghillie," Connor corrected. "He is not a servant. Good day to you, too, Sir Henry." He inclined his head. "What business are you about?"

"By God, if you had stayed in the regiment, MacPherson, you would be about this damned business with us," Campbell said.

"I'm content to be a farmer now," Connor said.

Campbell grunted. "You weren't farming on this moor a little while ago. What were you both doing at that bridge?"

"Repairing it," Neill said.

"On whose authority? Duncrieff owns this land, and he is . . . unable to order repairs to his estate just now."

"So I hear," Connor ground out. "Since Highland drovers must guide their cattle over these bridges, we decided to fix them ourselves."

"Commendable," Campbell drawled.

Connor let his contempt for Campbell glitter through his narrowed glance. Thinking of Sophie, he wondered if she had enjoyed the magistrate's company at Kinnoull House. Had she smiled at him, thanked him for his hospitality? Had he kissed her hand, touched her in any way? He felt a burst of raw anger at the very thought, and fisted the hand at his side.

Campbell leaned away from the saddle. "How did those bridges come to be damaged?"

"Rain, I am thinking," Neill offered.

"Flood damage? I doubt that. Those bridges came down when those two dragoons there," Sir Henry nodded over his shoulder to the men behind him, "were escorting Miss MacCarran of Duncrieff and her maid over the moors at night. Two Highland men were with them. There was a disaster, and the bridges collapsed. Brought down by deliberate means."

"Nah," Neill said, wide-eyed. "Who would do such a thing?"

"I will find out," Campbell said, staring hard at Connor. "It is the work of Highland rogues. One of the ladies disappeared that night."

"Disappeared!" Neill said with gusto. Connor stood still and expressionless.

"Miss Sophie MacCarran is missing. She was abducted by some Highland rascals. What do you know of this Highland Ghost who plagues the road crews working under General Wade?"

Neill shrugged. "We've heard of him, and his deeds. So long as he leaves my cattle be, I will leave him be."

Campbell grunted. "And you, MacPherson?"

"He leaves my livestock alone, and that is all I care about."

"The fellow is more interested in tearing down the roads as they come up than stealing cattle or brides," Campbell said. "Frankly, I suspect the girl was taken by the MacCarrans who were with her."

"Her own kinsmen?" Neill burst out. "They were there to protect the lass. I'm sure," he added hastily.

"You have no proof of that," Connor said. "It's absurd, sir. Allan and Donald MacCarran are good men—farmers and herdsmen."

"Rebels," Campbell said, "like their chief. Who has lately been made to pay for his offenses against the crown."

"What do you know of him?" Connor asked warily.

"Not much, to be sure," Campbell said. "He was taken to Perth. I hear he did not do well due to his wounds."

"How does he fare now?" Connor asked.

"I do not know, but I intend to send a messenger to inquire. I promised Miss MacCarran to get word of her brother. Let us pray the news is not tragic. But we've got to find the girl first."

"If there was a commotion, her horse likely ran off with her," Neill suggested.

"We've been searching ever since she went missing. She is not lost, I think, but clearly stolen away. We could have used your expert knowledge of the area today, MacPherson."

"I'm sure the red soldiers know this glen well enough."

"Perhaps. Tell me—have you seen anything amiss? Odd behavior? Highland treachery?"

"Nothing like that," Connor answered mildly.

"I will count on that, sir," Campbell said. "Anyone with your history would be suspect, though after your family's comeuppance at the hands of the government . . . I will wager you would not dare to step out of line, as they say."

"Indeed," Connor growled.

"You've kept admirably clear of the law, too. Content to be a small laird with a bit of run-down property, eh? I understand you trade in some cattle stock, too."

"Some," Connor replied.

"A smart man watches his step carefully, sir, and avoids trouble. As a former regimental officer, do not forget your loyalty and obligation."

"I am aware of my loyalties," Connor said.

"Connor MacPherson was such a fine soldier that the general himself asked that he return to service with the Am Freiceadan Dubh," Neill added with pride.

Connor shot Neill a sharp look to silence him.

"I am aware of your fine record with the Black Watch, sir," Campbell said to Connor. "I am also aware of your family's history. I keep both in mind. You are fortunate to have the good opinion of General Wade. You may need it someday."

Connor inclined his head. "Perhaps so."

Campbell gathered his reins. "If I do not find the lady soon, I intend to interrogate the MacCarrans who were with her. It seems clear to me that they must have had a hand in this."

"Why should they?" Neill asked.

"It's possible they do not approve of the match between Miss MacCarran and myself." Campbell preened a little as he sat in the saddle. Connor stared. It was like watching a sparrow attempt to puff himself up. It was hardly noticeable.

But there was something in the man's eyes, Connor realized, that he did not like—a darkness, a cold flatness. He was suddenly reminded of a snake, able to blend with its environment, yet carrying a killing sting if it pleased.

"If you interrogate the MacCarrans, what then?"

"They may just join their chief in the Tolbooth. And I'll tear apart every house in this glen—burn them, if I must—to find where the girl is hidden."

"I see." Connor would not allow others to take the blame for what he had done. "The MacCarrans are not responsible for their cousin's disappearance. I took her that night."

"You!" Campbell sat straight in his saddle, glowering.

"I assure you she is fine. I have her." Though his heart pounded hard, he kept his casual stance. From the corner of his eye he saw Neill step up beside him.

Connor rested his hand on the handle of the long dirk that he had tucked beneath a fold of his plaid. He felt the whip of the wind, the heavy thud of his heart.

"I have her," he repeated. "She is now my wife."

"Stealing a bride," Campbell growled, "will earn the groom a hanging."

"They had a previous arrangement . . . to elope," Neill said. "They wanted it done quickly, once she returned from France."

"Flanders," Connor clarified, as Campbell gaped at him.

"Married!" the magistrate barked. "I won't believe it!"

"It's done," Connor affirmed. "According to her brother's wishes, done by a priest."

"You bastard—" Campbell sputtered. "She dined with me that night and gave no hint of it! You stole her away, MacPherson, and you'll pay for it!"

"From what she told me, she never intended to marry you."

"Stole her away, and fool enough to admit it!" Campbell motioned the soldiers forward again. They hesitated, looking at one another.

"You have your culprit, sir," Connor said. "Though taking her is no crime if the lady was promised to me."

"She was promised to me, sir," Campbell said. "What proof do you have of your claim?"

"I have Duncrieff's written permission for the marriage." Connor reached into his sporran and drew out the folded note to display it. "He is chief now, so that should supercede any claim you might have made with his father."

"I assure you, it becomes a legal matter where the lady is promised twice, on paper."

"Not after she is married. The reality, Sir Henry, is that she is my wife."

"Let me see that," Campbell snapped, holding out his hand. "I doubt it is genuine."

Connor handed the note to Neill, who walked down the slope toward Campbell. Although Murray opened the note to display it, he would not let Campbell lay a hand on it, but held it flapping in the wind.

"Give me that," Campbell said, trying to snatch it, but Neill turned and went back to join Connor, who slid the page into his sporran.

"Ask Duncrieff about it," Connor said, "if you see him."

"I will," Campbell snapped.

That quick response gave Connor an unexpected hope that Rob might be alive after all.

"Where is the lady now?"

"Safe. Settling in as a laird's wife," Connor said, wondering if she actually was.

"I intend to speak to her and judge this for myself. Bring her to Kinnoull House."

"You can talk to her in my presence at Duncrieff Castle," Connor said. "At a time of my choosing. She is my wife."

Campbell growled something under his breath. "Why would a clan chief give his sister to a small laird from a disgraced family? You're lying."

"Love," Connor said, shrugging, "is inexplicable."

"And if I ask about her wedding, she will not cry foul."

"Certainly not," Connor answered.

"They eloped by choice," Neill said. "Not much to be done about it. Love, that's a wild thing that cannot be tamed."

"Was the bride so eager as to run off? Or was it the groom?" The sneer was evident in Campbell's voice. "The priest can produce the banns, I suppose."

"Father Henderson of the Small Glen," Connor said easily.

"You'd better hope the details agree, MacPherson, or you will be looking through a hangman's noose."

"It will not be the first time. But as you said, I am a smart man, and will not risk that again."

"If all this is true, MacPherson, I'm cuckolded and

should call you out for it," Campbell said, raising his voice in a shrill, anxious tone.

"Highlanders are not permitted to use weapons," Connor said. "But I'll take you on if you like. Swords, pistols. Fists."

Campbell turned suddenly, snapping out an order for the dragoons to follow him. He whirled on his mount, sending up clods of mud and turf as he rode away without another word to Connor or Neill. The dragoons rode after him.

"*Tcha,*" Neill said. "Where are his manners? He did not even congratulate you."

Connor shot him a sour look, then turned to stride up the hill with his ghillie following.

The sky was deep black and star-sprinkled hours later, when Connor crossed the bailey and entered the castle by the kitchen door. Roderick was asleep on a pallet beside the warm hearth as Connor moved quietly past.

Roderick stirred, looked up. "Kinnoull? It must be very late. All is well here. And with you?"

"All is well." Connor headed toward the stairs.

All was hardly well, he thought as he climbed through the darkness. He wondered how long he could keep Sophie here before Campbell sent men to the ruin, or came after her himself.

After confronting Campbell earlier, and sensing the threat the man could wield, Connor had returned to Glendoon feeling a strong urge to see Sophie again, to know for himself that she was safe. To hold her, and more.

Yet he had sworn to himself to keep his distance

from her until he learned what Duncrieff had wanted with this marriage arrangement. Something was hidden. Connor sensed that with every part of him—and he had to find out what it was. His senses also told him that Sophie did not know much more than he did about Duncrieff's reasoning.

Reaching the third floor, he stood at his bedchamber door in silence, leaning his hand on the doorjamb. He desperately wanted to go in, yet he paused.

Suddenly he knew why. Weeks ago he had agreed to steal a bride to answer a friend's frantic request. But he had never planned to let the marriage affect him. He had never planned to fall in love.

But as every hour passed, every day, he felt that danger mounting. Now he knew that his heart was well and truly caught—he just did not know how deep yet. Nor did he know if he could extricate his heart and avoid an emotional commitment for which he was not ready—not until he was rightfully Kinnoull again.

He tried to tell himself all that, tried to use logic. Then he summoned a shield of reserve as he pushed open the door.

Chapter 16

Parting the heavy drapes to peer out the window, Sophie saw only darkness and mist swathing the view. She yawned, telling herself that it was past time to get back into bed. She had been asleep for a while, but something had woken her—not ghostly music this time, but something else, an uneasy sense, as if somehow the fabric of her world had changed. She wondered if something had happened, wondered where Connor was, for he had not yet returned.

Startled, she jumped a little as the door opened behind her. Whirling, she turned to see him standing there, just when she had been thinking of him—but he was never far from her thoughts.

"Oh, Mr. MacPherson!" she said softly, hiding her relief. She wrapped her arms around herself, shuddering with cold. She wore only her thin chemise with a plaid draped over her shoulders, her feet bare. The room was chilly, particularly by the window.

"Keep the drapes closed, lass," he said sternly, coming toward her. "You might be seen. And it's freezing in here. You're shivering. Get into bed, then." He touched her shoulder.

He stood so close, smelled so good, like pine and winds, like strength and freedom. Sophie tilted her head, felt his breath soft upon her cheek.

"I did not expect to see you tonight," she said.

"But I wanted to see you," he answered. "I just . . . wanted to see you." His grip tightened on her shoulder and he leaned down.

She drew her brows together. "What is it?" But her heart quickened.

"Sophie, I . . ." He leaned closer still, lifted a hand to brush his fingertips softly over her cheek.

Then he was kissing her, quick and fierce and with such richness that she gasped in surprise. Leaning into his embrace, she slipped her arms around him. The kiss renewed itself, one following another. Sophie felt her heart slamming now, felt herself turn to warm honey in his arms.

Drawing back suddenly, he slid his hand from her shoulder to the small of her back, where her hips snugged against his. With only chemise and plaid between them, she could feel how quickly, how surely, he wanted her.

But he let go and stepped back. "Lie down, lass." He turned her toward the bed.

She blinked up at him, startled, felt as if she was emerging from fog—his kiss had that much power. But when she realized what he was telling her, how cold his order was, she found her wits.

"I will not be taken advantage of, just because I—because . . ." Breath heaving, she stopped, glaring at him.

He frowned. "What?"

"Because I cannot seem to resist whenever you touch me," she whispered. "But that does not mean that you should take—"

"*Tcha*," he said, a sound of weary disgust. "You must be tired. It's late. And I told you to get in the bed because you are shivering from the chill." He lifted his hands as if to show her that he would not touch her.

Mortified by her impulsive, vulnerable statement moments earlier, she did not answer.

"And I'm that weary myself," he went on. "It has been a while since I rested peacefully. But until you move your feet from that spot, I've nowhere for a bed."

Surprised, she sat on the bed, tucked her feet up. "Where will you sleep?"

"On the floor," he said.

"Not—with me?" she whispered. "Because . . . I am not Kate?"

"That," he said, as he loosened the upper part of his plaid, "is not the reason." He knelt, then lay down, pulling part of his plaid over his shoulders like a blanket. Sophie lay back and heard him shift about, seeking comfort on the cold stone floor.

"You said you wanted to annul the marriage," he said then. "I will respect that decision."

She felt a sharp disappointment. Had she decided that or had he? Sliding under the blankets, she lay staring at the embroidered canopy. "Good night, Mr. MacPherson," she finally ventured.

"Good night," came a muffled growl.

"I was wrong," she added softly. "I apologize."

He was silent for a moment, then huffed acceptance. "Go to sleep, lass."

In that moment she felt different, as if her heart had turned within her, opened somehow. Sympathy flooded her, and something inexplicable. She cared deeply about him, she realized. Knowing him only briefly, she felt as if she understood him intimately, as no one else could.

Yet all she really knew was that he was a rogue and a thief, and hid in a ruined castle. He kept his secrets close. But she glimpsed the inner man now and then, and he fascinated her.

Connor valued home and family so much that he kept his family's things in safekeeping, yet refused to consider the ruin his home. His friends respected and loved him, and when he gave his word, he kept it no matter what it asked of him. He was intelligent, well-mannered, confident, and educated. And while he preferred to appear gruff and unfeeling, he was not. She was sure of that.

And when he could have done otherwise, he had not disgraced her. He had shown her kindness and patience, and had taken her into his arms to let her taste true passion. Not so long ago, she had feared that would never be part of her life.

Snuggling down, she punched the plump pillows in their soft linen cases. After a moment she sat up and flung one pillow out of the bed. She heard Connor's surprised grunt.

"Always the lady, Mrs. MacPherson," he said in the darkness.

She smiled. Closing her eyes, she felt safe—truly safe—with Connor nearby.

He sighed, shifted on the floor, punched the pillow she had given him. Turning also, she could not settle to sleep, aware of every sound and movement he made.

Finally she rolled over. "Connor MacPherson."

"Aye."

"Come into the bed."

"That would not be such a good thing," he said, "if you want to annul this marriage."

"*Tcha*," she said. Lifting to an elbow, she peered down at him. "Did I say you were to touch me? You are a tired man, and I am weary, too. Come into the bed, Connor MacPherson, and we will sleep."

Silence. In the darkness, she saw that he bent an arm over his eyes.

"And besides," she said, "I heard the ghostly music again just a little while ago. It frightened me." She had not felt so afraid, but she would let him believe so, if it brought him off the cold stone floor where he lay for her benefit.

After a moment he rose to his feet, and she felt his weight press the bed. Sliding over to make room, she opened the covers.

Connor lay beside her carefully, resting on his back, feet crossed, arms folded. Sophie lay on her side and regarded him in the shadows.

"You do not look very comfortable," she whispered.

"Much better than the floor," he answered.

She leaned close, feeling drawn to him like iron to a magnet. A thrilling excitement fluttered through her. "Are you cold?" she asked, tugging at the blanket.

"I have my plaid."

"It's chill in this room," she ventured, shifting closer.

Without reply, he opened his arm, inviting her in,

and she settled against him, resting her head on his shoulder. He felt so warm, so strong, so gentle with his arm encircling her. She tilted her head in the darkness, and his whiskers rasped along her brow.

Closing her eyes, now she could not rest for the heavy beating of her heart, the pulsing that grew in her body. Stretching her palm over his chest, she sensed his heart thumping as hard as her own. "Connor—" she whispered.

"Hush you," he said, turning his head. "Just hush." His fingers traced her jaw, tipped her chin upward, and he began to kiss her gently, slowly. Yet the tenderness impacted through her like lightning.

He turned toward her, kissing her, his hand stroking her shoulder and tracing down, pulling on the thin shift, the warmth of his fingers penetrating the cotton. She loved the sensation of all of his fingertips upon her at once, for he had one arm beneath her, splaying a hand on her back, while the other hand scooped over her cheek, his fingers brushing over her hair. His lips kneaded hers in one kiss after another. She felt enveloped in his big, muscular hands, felt cherished by his carefulness, his consideration, the way he held back when she knew—oh, she knew, for she felt it sing in him somehow—that he wanted her fiercely.

Rolling toward him, she returned the next kiss with new fervor, growing boldness. Tonight there was no whiskey to fire her courage, and she needed none, for she wanted this, had invited this, she realized. When she had lain in his arms before, head whirling from whiskey, still stunned by her abduction and marriage, she had hardly known what was happening—though she remembered that she had wanted it keenly, the craving deep and indescribable.

But she did not fully recall what had happened, and for that she felt deprived in her body and in her heart, for she had missed a moment that she had wanted to experience and treasure.

She gasped to herself, realizing that she wanted this—whether she stayed with him or left him, she desperately wanted to know more of passion, of him, of what love could be like. Her desire for adventure in her life grew pallid compared to what she desired now.

Opening her lips, feeling his tongue trace her, enter her, she tasted him in return. Pressing her body against him under the shared coverlet, she felt the prickle of tartan wool against her skin, felt the hard shape of him against her hip as he turned.

"Sophie—" he whispered.

"Hush, you," she said, and silenced his protest with her mouth. She moved against him, and heard the groan that rippled through him, and she smiled to herself, feeling a gentle power unlike anything she had ever imagined.

As his fingers slipped downward over her hip and her leg to bunch up the cloth of her chemise, she pulled in a quick breath. His fingers, warm and strong, moved upward, grazing over her inner thigh, stopping her breath, grazing past the nested place between her legs, tracing over her belly and upward. She could scarcely breathe for the anticipation of where he might touch her next. Waiting, she felt on fire; splendid, delicate fire. His fingers caged her breast gently, and she felt herself pearl against his palm, and her breath returned in a rush. She moaned, writhed for him, invited more of his touch with her body, her breath, her hands upon his shoulders, his back.

He kissed her deeply, then drew away when she wanted more and traced his mouth down her throat, shoving aside the low neck of her chemise, the cloth caught between his tracing kisses and his caressing hand. She lay back then, arched her throat, opened herself to him in a way that seemed wanton to her, and yet she did not care. The feel of his mouth upon her breast, now, was too wonderful, and the desire that churned in her was far too powerful.

His fingertips danced over her ribs, light and warm, tracked over her belly, arousing an irresistible sensation, a delicate fluttering, a deep need. Leaning her head against the pillows, she pushed her hips toward his hand, letting her body take on a delicious will of its own.

"Connor," she whispered, sinking her fingers into his thick, silky, wavy hair.

He lifted his head to kiss her and drew back. "This is not what I intended." He drew his hands away from her. "Not until—"

"No," she said, capturing his hand in both of hers, pulling it against her chest, where her heart pounded. "I need to know . . ."

"What?" he whispered.

"That first night," she said, "I had taken too much of Mary's whiskey—I remember little of what we did." She shrugged. "The next day, I felt . . . cheated, somehow. I truly wanted to know what that is like. But I do not remember." She gasped, a half laugh. "And I am sorry for that."

He brushed back her hair. "There is no need to apologize."

"If I . . . invite you to do this now, if I want it, too, then no one is forcing anyone, and you are not . . . a cad. A rogue and a bride stealer, aye," she added crisply, so that he chuckled. "But not a cad. Do you know what I am saying?" Her heartbeat drummed with the boldness she felt.

"Aye," he breathed, and kissed her again, and cupped his hand upon her breast, grazing over the nipple until she sighed, tilted back her head, arched. He lowered his head to touch his tongue to the nipple so that it grew taut, sending shivers through her, easing a deep sigh from her.

The pleasure she reaped from even his simplest touch made her want desperately to share it and return it to him. She pulled at his plaid, skimmed her hand over his strong bare thigh, heavy with muscle, yet soft, his buttock a smooth curve beneath her palm, and she boldly rounded on the path to find his hip, his lower belly, the hair there thick and soft to touch, so soft.

He moved against her hand, and his fingers caressed her further, found the cleft in her, separated it gently. She gasped aloud, and he tilted his head to kiss her mouth. As his tongue touched her lips, his finger eased into her slowly, and she gasped again, and moved against him. Heat stoked in her lower body and her legs melted open, her body arched, and she felt her breath take on a new rhythm. Her body rocked, pleaded.

God, she wanted to share the feeling—generosity was her nature, her impulse in so many things. She sought him, took hold of him boldly. Warm velvet over steel, he was, and she a glove for him. She stroked along the lovely length, and he groaned, deep and earthy, in her ear. That low sound, and the warmth of his breath there, shot through her like the wick of a flame.

"Sophie," he whispered, "leave me be." He moved away from her hand. "Let me touch you, just you. I owe you that, I think. And if you continue to touch me like that, I will not be able to stop myself from—hush now," he said, as she began to speak. "And just let me . . ."

He moved his fingers, circling delicately, coaxing further, and she felt herself turn to flame where his fingertips teased and loved her. She felt her body melt into honey and fire, and she began to move as a rhythm pulsed through her. He kissed her, held her, and murmured something against her hair that she could not hear. She wanted to hear—but she began to soar then, crying out with the power of what he was doing to her with that exquisite touch. Sinking back into his arms, she felt the embers catch fire in her again, and she lifted again with its force.

And suddenly she knew, in that moment, how much she trusted him. She had to trust him to let him touch her as he did now, so intimately. And to know that he loved her this way for her, only for her, and not for himself, brought her an even deeper thrill. His generosity was tender and profound. She realized that she could trust this man with her body's secrets, and with her life. Perhaps she could even trust him with her heart, her very soul.

As she sank again into his arms, she hid her face against him, and he kissed her, then rolled away from her with a low murmur, a pat on the shoulder. A gentle reminder to sleep.

The fairy crystal rolled, sparkled in the low light

on its chain. And she remembered that the small, bright stone would bring love to its wearer, but the wearer, it was said, must have the courage to face the sacrifices that would come.

Love makes its own magic. The words came to her again. And she wondered if it had begun to weave its inexorable force in her life, whether or not she wanted it.

Connor stared at the drafty, vaulted ceiling and thought about cattle.

Cattle, sheep, fiddles—anything to take his mind off the tantalizing girl beside him. His wife—she was perilously close to that role now. He had tried to hold back, but the searing hunger that she aroused in him was demanding, irresistible. He had forgotten resolve, or the dilemma.

The insistent feeling within him had grown too powerful to name. He told himself he was not ready for this. Not yet.

He gazed at the bed canopy and thought about anything he could to take his mind off of her. Lying next to his bride, his skin still sheened with the light sweat of the pleasure she had so unexpectedly, impulsively, brought to him, he sighed out. No, he told himself, do not think of that, do not let this continue, for he already waded far too deep.

He tried to consider instead what he wanted from life, beyond immediate urges. A fine herd to take to market, sheep grazing fat on his hills, a warm hearth in a cozy home—all those were important to him. He wanted to be a good laird for his tenants, wanted to see them secure.

And he craved someone to love who would love

him in return, someone to hold on cold nights, someone to watch the stars with him, listen to his music, laugh with him. He had grown too solitary in these last years, cutting himself off from all but a few friends, and breaking the hearts of the women who he knew had imagined themselves in love with the young heir to Kinnoull. He had even imagined himself in love with one or two of them, long ago, when his life had been peaceful and his future safe.

He was weary of living in a ruin, hiding, having no home of his own. He was weary of being alone, even among his friends. He had never intended to become a hero of the rebellion, yet somehow that had happened. He wanted to be a gentleman farmer, the viscount and laird he had been raised to be. All that had been taken from him.

But now, almost more than any of it, he wanted the girl who lay in his bed, and he would not let himself think about that. Not until questions were answered and the future was clear.

Standing, he adjusted his plaid and looked down at Sophie where she lay in the shadowed, curtained bed. He listened to the whisper of her breathing.

Then he leaned down, kissed her brow, traced his lips along her cheek. Just one stolen kiss. She sighed, nuzzled into the pillow.

Deciding to leave before he did more than he could accept in good conscience, he thought an hour or two of reading might soothe him. He left the bedchamber quietly, taking the stairs down to the small library where he kept both his papers and his father's, too, and where he tucked away all of his dreams.

All of his dreams, that is, until he had stolen Sophie MacCarran.

Chapter 17

With her heeled shoes sticking in fresh mud, Sophie turned in the castle yard. The morning rain had cleared and sun filtered through clouds, so that the pale stones of the old keep shone like mother-of-pearl.

Glendoon had once been a stout fortress, easily defensible. Few but the hardiest enemies would climb those treacherous slopes, Sophie thought, then or now. The castle was also defended by rumors of hauntings. She had heard the ghostly music herself, though it intrigued her more than frightened her.

She was glad to be outside in fresh air under the sun's warmth now that the showers had passed. For the past hour she had pulled weeds in the kitchen garden, though that was scarcely enough time to make a difference in the wilderness of that plot. It would take work, she knew, but she was sure that it would be possible to bring the little herb and vegetable garden to life.

If she stayed here long enough. She glanced around. Logic told her to take any chance and flee from this place. She belonged at Duncrieff. Yet part of her wanted desperately to stay with Connor MacPherson, for a little while at least, stay with him and savor more nights like the last nights. She glanced down with a little smile, sensing her own blush.

The Highlander had become as compelling as a lodestone to her. Unable to resist his charismatic touch, she no longer wanted to run from him—she only wanted to be with him. She knew that it made no sense, but her heart was not following a logical course.

But she was not so foolish as to think he was succumbing to any charm she might have. He seemed to find her attractive at night—she was a healthy young woman in his bedchamber, his wedded wife, and he was a very healthy male—but she would not disillusion herself. He wanted Katie Hell, not Saint Sophia. As soon as Kate came back, he might be more than eager to dissolve their hasty marriage.

She sighed, glancing up at the castle keep as she walked through the muddy yard.

Her MacCarran ancestors had deserted Castle Glendoon centuries ago, she recalled from family stories. The castle had been the site of a tragedy, a feud with another clan that had ended fatally for a MacCarran laird and his lady love. Their ghosts, with others, were said to inhabit the castle ruins as well as the old chapel. Later the MacCarrans had deserted Glendoon to build Duncrieff Castle deeper in the glen.

Looking over the curtain wall, she could see the tops of the hills and mountains on the opposite side of the glen, where Duncrieff Castle was located. Homesickness overwhelmed her in that moment, so strong that she felt dizzy with it.

Turning, she saw the front gate, and glanced about for Roderick Murray. Earlier, she had glimpsed him working at the back wall, digging or repairing there, and had not disturbed him. Only the dogs were guarding her now, following her every step as she wandered the courtyard, so that she sometimes tripped over them or skirted around them. They were more attentive sentinels than young Roderick, she thought.

The untended gate beckoned, despite what had happened the other night when she had slipped out. Walking toward it with the dogs trotting alongside, she listened for Roderick's hammer.

The bolt looked heavy but was not difficult to lift and set aside. Grabbing the iron latch next, she pushed it open, wincing at the creaking sound it made. She pulled open the smaller door cut inside the larger one and peeked out.

No, she told herself. No.

If she went out again, it would only cause problems for Connor. She realized now that Sir Henry would be after him in earnest if he discovered that she had been held at Glendoon. As Connor had explained, it was better for her to stay here—for now. Just for now.

But as she peered outside, still longing for a taste of freedom, she saw flowers scattered throughout the grass—a haze of golden buttercups and the delicate hue of bluebells. Pale snow crocus and dark violets clustered near the rocks.

If she dug up some of the flowers, she thought suddenly, she could plant them in the kitchen plot, where they might flourish and make a lovely carpet beside the door.

Surely she could just step out and get some flowers. Glancing over her shoulder, she set a foot outside the gate.

Shoving past her skirts, first one little terrier, then the other, leaped past her to burst through the gap. Ears and tails up, they raced away from the gate. Sophie gasped, while behind her Tam and Colla began barking furiously. A moment later the spaniel dashed past her and through the doorway like an arrow leaving its bow. Colla set up a loud, monotonous barking.

"No!" Sophie cried. "Tam! Come back! Una! Scota! Oh no, please come back!" Without waiting for Roderick, who would surely come running when he heard the noise, Sophie hurried after the dogs as they tore across the sunlit grass and down the hillside.

Picking up her skirts, she ran, then stopped suddenly, her heels slipping a little on the wet grass.

A man approached the castle, a kilted Highlander who came up the crest of the hill, having already crossed the gorge. The afternoon sunlight glinted on his brown hair, poured gold over his shoulders, turned his dark blue and green plaid brighter.

Connor MacPherson. Sophie stood frozen in the sunlight, her skirts billowing in a quick breeze. The dogs ran toward him, leaping up, barking ecstatically as he bent to greet them.

He had seen her. How could he not, she thought, for she stood in plain sight exactly where she should not be standing—just outside the castle gates.

He came toward her with the eager dogs at his heels. Sophie folded her hands to wait with dignity, knowing there was little else to do. Once more Connor stopped, murmuring to the dogs, patting their heads before resuming his approach.

"Leaving us again, Mrs. MacPherson?" he called.

"The dogs ran through the gate," she said, realizing immediately how foolish that sounded.

"Lifted the bolt and flipped the latch, did they? Tam, you rapscallion," he added, scratching the spaniel's head.

"I opened it," Sophie said tersely.

"I see." His eyes, she saw then, were a stormy green color.

"I wanted to pick some flowers. Truly," she added.

"Ah," he said. Clearly, he did not believe her. "Where is Roderick?"

"He is busy with something at the back of the bailey. The dogs were with me."

He quirked a brow. "This lot, guarding anyone?" He bent down as one of the terriers reared on her hind legs. "Aye, Una, you fierce wee doggie," he murmured. "You great beastie."

"I opened the gate, and the dogs went through. I thought they meant to run away, so I went after them."

"This bunch would come right back when they were ready. They must have seen me or sensed me coming, and came to meet me. Did you never have dogs?"

"We had several at Duncrieff when I was growing

up, but we did not have them when we stayed in France and at the Muti Palace in Rome with the rest of the court. The Mother Prioress at the English Convent had a lap dog, though. A nasty wee thing," she added. She looked down. The wolfhound had followed her and now nudged his gray head under her hand. She patted him.

"Ah, so Colla the Fierce likes you."

"He's not so fierce. They are all quite friendly."

"So much so, I fear they'd let red soldiers inside the gate . . . now that the dogs have the knack of the latch."

Seeing the twinkle in his eyes, their green gone from stormy to calm, Sophie laughed softly. He tilted his head, watching her. In the sunlight, his hair was dark brown, enriched with strands of gold. Sophie longed, for an instant, to sink her hands into that soft, gleaming thickness, as she had done last night.

"Now I'm back, Mrs. MacPherson, so you'd best change your plans and come with me." He took her arm and turned her to walk beside him. The dogs came, too, trotting in crazy circles as Sophie and Connor moved along.

"How is it that you have these dogs here?" she asked. "I would not think that a band of outlaws would keep so many."

"I brought them in with the furniture and plate."

"They were your dogs?"

"Still are," he clarified. "Where are the Murray lads?" he asked, looking toward the gate.

Did he mean both Roderick and Neill? "I saw only Roderick Murray today."

"His brother should be there, too. Perhaps you have not yet met him." The press of his hand and his quick stride gave her no choice but to keep up. Rather than resenting it, she felt only that same spiraling thrill that came whenever he touched her.

She shook her arm free of his grasp and walked ahead. Connor followed with the dogs running happy loops around him.

As they went through the gate, Roderick came toward them.

"You are supposed to watch the gate," Connor said.

"I am sorry, Kinnoull," Roderick said. "I was watching most of the morning. Mistress Sophie was poking about in the garden, and I thought she would be fine there."

"Garden?" Connor asked.

"I have been thinking about clearing out the kitchen garden and replanting," she said.

"Nothing will grow there, so it is a waste of time. You should have been watching the gate," he told Roderick impatiently.

"I was, but Fiona escaped over the back wall, where the rubble is lowest." The young man pointed toward the back of the bailey yard. "We chased her down the slope and dragged her home again. Padraig and I have been repairing the break in the wall."

Thinking of the rubbled, broken wall she herself had climbed, Sophie gulped.

"Clever lass, to get out again," Connor said.

"Fiona?" Sophie stared at Connor. "Did you have another prisoner in this place?"

"Fiona is a cow. She escapes whenever she finds the chance. Like my wife," he added wryly.

"I cannot blame her for that," Sophie replied,

glancing past him as another young man came toward them from the rear courtyard, leading a shaggy reddish cow on a rope. "I did not think that cows could climb."

Roderick hooted. "They cannot. But now and then they make their way into odd places."

"Aye. Fiona is a nimble wee thing with an adventurous soul. Like you," Connor murmured.

Feeling herself blush, Sophie laughed softly when she saw the sparkle in Connor's moss-green eyes.

"She's learned to step over parts of the back wall where the stones have collapsed," Roderick explained to Sophie. "We've repaired it several times, even used stones and mortar, but the goat strikes it down as soon as it goes up."

"Goat?" Sophie asked.

Connor looked at her. "You could have saved yourself the trouble of opening the front gate, and just gone over the back wall with Fiona." He chuckled as Roderick laughed out loud.

Sophie sent him a withering look.

"Roderick, where is your mother?" Connor asked.

"She is tending things at home. She'll be here soon."

The second young man came closer, and Fiona butted her great shaggy reddish head into the cluster of people to shove at Connor's arm. Sophie stepped back in surprise, unable to see Roderick's brother over the cow's massive back.

"Hey, my lassie, easy now." Connor fondled the cow's muzzle. He murmured to her, and the cow licked his arm with a great lolling tongue. Astonished, Sophie gaped.

"*Ach*, the lass loves her laird," Roderick crooned. "She'll be jealous now he's wed."

Connor ran his hand over the cow's bony shoulders and the great protruding curves of the rib cage, "She's still thin from the winter, but let's hope she fattens better this year. Fiona, meet Mrs. MacPherson," Connor told the cow. "Next time you flee, lassie, I think she'll flee with you," he whispered to the cow, rubbing her furry head. "Say hello, lass."

"Hello," Sophie said, then realized that Connor addressed the cow. Huge, gentle brown eyes looked at her from under the thick fringe that covered much of Fiona's enormous head. The cow snuffled, blowing warm air outward through wide, brownish-pink nostrils. Sophie leaned away.

"Go on, pet her," Roderick said. "She loves it."

Tentatively, Sophie reached out and patted the tufted spot between Fiona's ears. Her fingers grazed past Connor's as he caressed her head, too. Sophie murmured softly to the cow, feeling awkward, but soon warming to the calm, enormous animal.

Roderick's brother, still holding Fiona's rope, laughed. "There, see, not so bad," he said.

Sophie glanced at him over the cow's broad back and her eyes widened—Padraig had bright blue eyes, black hair, pink-stained cheeks, and a dazzling smile. "You're—Roderick's twin!"

"*Ach*, he's mine," he answered. "I was born first. Padraig Murray, mistress."

"I'm Sophie MacCarran," she said, then glanced at Connor.

While the twins chatted with Connor about the repairs to the back curtain wall, Sophie listened, her hand resting on Fiona's big head. She felt part of the relaxed camaraderie between the men, and when they told her the amusing tale of Fiona's first escape attempt, she laughed with them—for that moment felt like the laird's true wife rather than his stolen bride.

Watching as Connor smiled and laughed easily, she had a glimpse of the true man, rather than the outlaw or the renegade. Curious to find she was even more attracted to him in this simple role as farmer and friend, she tipped her head, watching him.

"Fiona is a shaggy Highland cow, sturdy and hardy, bred for centuries in Scotland," Padraig told Sophie.

She looked at Connor. "My father had cows like this one. He had a fair-sized herd on his estate when I was younger." Giving her twinned smiles, the Murray brothers turned and crossed the bailey.

"Duncrieff's herds are good stock, the best of their breed. At one time your father had a brindle bull, as I recall, a fine animal," Connor said. "Fiona is his granddaughter."

She lifted her brows. "You've seen my father's herds?"

"Aye." He rubbed Fiona's muzzle.

"I used to sit on the hill outside Duncrieff and watch the herds as they wandered the slopes and moors," she said. "They even waded into our lochan on hot days. Ours were a range of colors—red like Fiona, and golden, black, brindled brown, silver gray. I never went near them, though. My father did not think it seemly for his daughters. He wanted us to be educated women, not dairy maids, so that we would make the best marriages."

The words were out before she could take them back. Blushing fiercely, she rubbed Fiona's huge snout, the pink nostrils moving gently with the cow's warm, slightly odiferous breath. Sophie wrinkled her nose, and saw Connor frowning down at her.

She need not wonder at his thoughts, after her remark.

"And you? Did you want to be dairy maid, or a fine lady . . . or a nun?" He lifted a brow, and seemed to take no offense.

"Actually, I wanted to be a gardener. My mother hired a garden designer who came to Duncrieff from France when I was a girl. He created beautiful terrace gardens, a maze, and rose gardens. I loved watching the gardeners tend to the beds and the rosebushes. I was given a corner of my own to plant seeds—pansies and nasturtiums, pinks and carnations, and I raised marigolds and columbine under glass until they were ready to be put in the soil, and so on. I loved it, and my wee flowers grew so well that the gardener set a fountain at the center and made it a set piece in the Duncrieff gardens. But my father did not want me to dig about in the soil as much as I pleased. Tending roses was ladylike enough, but the rest was not to be allowed."

"Sounds as if you have a gift for it, though. I do appreciate your intention to clear the kitchen garden, but there's not much point, lass."

She shrugged, touched the crystal at her throat. "I like digging about in the dirt. I have a little knack for growing things, I suppose. But when my father was exiled, he sent all of us to schools on the Continent, and I went off to the convent school. After Father died, my mother remarried and Kate and Robert returned to Scotland to live at Duncrieff with relatives. I stayed in the English Convent to finish my education there."

"Are you a bookish lass?" He smiled a little. "Latin and Greek, poetry and sums? History and philosophy?"

She laughed. "Not in the least, though I love poetry and stories. I worked in the gardens alongside one elderly sister who spent her life growing flowers. Despite what my father wanted, I ended up just where I wanted to be—in a paradise of flowers."

He tipped his head. "Ah. You did mention that you brought some potted tulips back with you." He paused. "I understand that your father died in France while he was in exile. I was sorry to hear it."

"He was forced to leave Scotland because of his sympathies with the rebellion, and died before he could return. He refused to disarm, and did not collect arms from his tenants."

"I know," Connor murmured.

She looked at him in surprise. "Did you know him?"

"Not myself, but my father did. Like your father, mine also refused to disarm. But he went further, and hid weapons for the rebels during the 'fifteen."

Sophie stopped, looked up at him. "Was your father exiled also?"

"He was executed three years ago," he said. "For treason." Tugging on Fiona's lead, he walked ahead.

Chapter 18

$\sim$ ∞ $\sim$

Though his back was to her, Connor felt her gaze like the touch of a hand. Her sympathy was there, too, as a gentleness around him. When he heard her footsteps, he did not turn.

"Connor MacPherson," she said. "I am sorry."

He nodded without looking at her. "Go back inside. It will rain again soon. See those clouds?" He pointed. Sunlight poured gold over the slopes, and distant clouds swept a veil of rain over the far mountains.

Sophie shaded her eyes with one hand. "That storm seems very far off," she observed.

Connor stopped, and Fiona butted his shoulder. He ruffled the fringe over her brow, rubbed her ears. Her rosy tongue protruded, then licked Sophie's hand.

Sophie jumped a little, but rubbed Fiona's ear while she studied Connor thoughtfully. He noticed, really noticed this time, the pretty little crystal at her throat, set in silver on a silver chain, winking like a star between her slim, delicate collarbones. Fairy magic, he thought. He wished fairy magic was real and that the stone could restore what all of them had lost from this damnable rebellion. But such things were not possible.

"Kinnoull—Roderick called you Kinnoull!" she said suddenly. "My brother wrote it in his note, too, but scratched it out. You said you are sometimes called that, and your friends use it, too. Why? Was your family—Oh! The MacPhersons of Kinnoull!"

Connor turned. She would have to be told sooner or later. "My father was Lord Kinnoull. He owned the estate on the other side of Glen Carran. But the property was forfeit to the crown when my father was . . . sentenced for treason."

"Truly, I am so sorry. I did not know."

He shrugged. "You need not be sorry."

"For your losses, I am. So you grew up near this glen? I never knew you. I met Lord Kinnoull, and Lady Kinnoull, when I was a girl. I remember they were a handsome couple, and kind to a shy wee lass. But I do not remember you. And I would have," she added.

"We never met. I would not have forgotten you, either," he said softly, gazing at her. In the late afternoon sun, she glowed as softly as candlelight.

She looked at him curiously. "I remember your parents quite clearly, now that I think about it. Your father was a tall man with a deep voice . . . he was strong and kind. He came to see my father one day, and fetched my sister's kitten out of a tree in the garden."

Connor smiled a little. "Aye, he would have done something like that, setting all else aside to help someone."

"And your mother—you look like her," she said, tipping her head to one side. "She had dark hair and green eyes, too. And I see her in your eyes, your mouth."

He glanced away, touched more than he could say that she remembered them, and fondly. He had almost no kin left after the ravages of one rebellion after another in the Highlands. For the past two years he had felt very alone. Now, in Sophie's company, he felt that cloud begin to lift.

"She would have liked you," he said quietly. "My mother passed away—of a broken heart, I suppose—when my father was executed. Her constitution was not strong by then, and she failed sharply. She died months after he did."

"Oh, Connor," she breathed.

He shrugged, the quickest way to show her that he appreciated her thoughts but had recovered as well as he could. "I was my father's heir, but I lost the rights when the lands were proscripted."

She frowned. "Sir Henry Campbell owns Kinnoull House now."

"Rents it," he corrected. "The English king owns it. But he wasted no time in taking over the property."

"So the furnishings, the spinet, the books—" She glanced toward the castle.

"The carpets, the plate, the dogs," he continued. "The kitchen kettle. All of it came from Kinnoull House. I brought whatever I could out of there before

Sir Henry took the place over nearly two years ago. Castle Glendoon does not have space for all of it, and those steep slopes made transporting some pieces impossible. But what is here is mine."

She watched him. "Fiona, too?"

"Ah, clever lass to work that out." He glanced at Sophie with admiration. "Fiona was my father's prize, a perfect one-year-old red Highland with an impeccable breeding line—from your father's herd. My father hoped she would breed new generations of the best cattle in Perthshire." He smiled bitterly. "I stole her from under Sir Henry's very nose one night, while he sat in my house, drinking his fill of the wine stores."

She nodded, frowning. As Connor led Fiona toward the byre at the back of the bailey, he was glad when Sophie walked alongside, despite mud, puddles, drizzle, and their combined effect on her bedraggled gown and shoes.

She did not seem to mind. She had an amazing tolerance for poor conditions, and for shocking news, which she listened to without serious complaint or dithering. He glanced at her in admiration.

"Did Sir Henry take Kinnoull from your father?" she asked.

"Only as the local magistrate carrying out the crown's orders. Though it would not surprise me if he had a hand in it. The proscription was an act of the crown."

"Did your father lose his title as Lord Kinnoull, too?"

"The title is fixed in the blood, and has been in our family for two hundred years. My father was a viscount, and so I am Lord Kinnoull, regardless of my estate. And that makes you, my lass, Lady Kinnoull." He inclined his head, then glanced at her over Fiona's bony back, where a pair of flies buzzed.

She tipped her head. "Lord Kinnoull." She had the carriage of a queen, he thought, and the dignity of an angel. And she stood in the mud with him and his cow and did not seem to mind.

"We are lord and lady over nothing much, you and I."

"Over something, Kinnoull." She waved her hand. "Castle Glendoon has a proud history. If the stones are broken here and there, they can be repaired, and the yard and the outbuildings can be renewed, too. The gardens can be cleared and replanted, and the castle rooms are filled with treasures that you love. You have loyal tenants, healthy livestock, a fine title and heritage. You have . . . a wife."

"Do I?" he murmured.

"Though we shall see which one you decide upon . . . and which one will have you."

He looked at her steadily. He knew which of them he wanted, and his heartbeat quickened with the realization.

"Despite all, you have a home here, Kinnoull," she insisted.

He huffed. "You have a pretty way of putting a shine to gloomy matters, madam. Be careful not to polish away the truth."

"What is the truth, then?"

"I have no home," he said soberly. "You need not chirp on about what a marvelous place this is for my benefit."

She hastened to keep up with him. "I am only trying to be cheerful, given such gloominess on your part. And if Highland thieves had not snatched me away, I would be of a more pleasant temperament. Glendoon truly is a marvelous place, I like ruins. They are picturesque and grand, filled with history. And ghosts," she added quickly.

He wanted to laugh suddenly. He so rarely wanted to throw back his head and truly laugh that it felt strange, and he suppressed it. Looking up at the sky, he saw an odd blend of sunlight and drizzle.

"Sunshine and storm, Lady Kinnoull," he murmured. "Turnabout with the winds, my lass, hey? Now go inside. It will downpour at any moment. You will ruin your dress."

"It's ruined already. And the rain might stain the fabric darker. This amber color is too bright for me. I am . . . the same color as your cow," she said in dismay.

He did laugh then. And he wanted to kiss her. The urge pulsed through him with such power that he almost moved. He wanted to push the cow aside and take Sophie the nun, with her whimsical and wanton ways, into his arms.

He wanted to stand with her in the mud and the rain and the sunshine, and cover her with kisses. He imagined stripping the satin gown from her shoulders and draping her in pearls and silk and deep kisses, and doing all he wanted to do to her.

He only smiled slightly. "The color suits you, just as it does Fiona. Though you two lassies are only truly alike in your fiery garments . . . and your determination to claim your freedom."

"I was not trying to escape through the gate, though I ought to do that. I still might."

He smiled again. "Fire and sunlight and fancy

satin. And now you are a viscountess. Your father would have wanted that for you."

She returned his gaze. "He wanted the same for Kate."

"Aye, well," he said. "There is that."

He saw the storminess enter her eyes, which went from blue to gray, like a dark cloud sweeping through. "I think I will go inside now, Kinnoull. It is beginning to rain in earnest."

She turned, lifting her gown as she ran.

Connor watched her cross the yard and enter the kitchen door. When she disappeared into the shadows, he felt as if a lantern light had gone out.

Connor left Glendoon later in the day with scarcely a word to her, and Sophie shared a quiet supper with Mary and Roderick and his twin, Padraig. Although she gently questioned them all, hoping to learn more about Connor and his intriguing past, the Murrays seemed unwilling to speak in much detail about how he had come to stay at Glendoon, although they did not hold back their praise for Connor in other areas.

"He's a good laird," Mary said. "So concerned with the welfare of his tenants—only us just now on Glendoon lands, but the tenants on the properties of Kinnoull still view him as their rightful laird, and they bring their rents to him every year regardless."

"But do they not pay that to Sir Henry?" Sophie asked.

Mary nodded. "Aye, to him, too. They collect double rents, y'see, and that is why the laird doesna want them to do it, for it is a hardship for them. But they revere him, and he does not realize how much." She smiled and glanced at her son.

"Kinnoull has a strong sense of principle," Roderick said. "Even in this time of so much injustice, he upholds freedom, and so he must support rebellion to keep that right. He has no qualms about acting on his beliefs. And he honors his word, once given."

Sophie nodded. "I know," she said quietly. "What my brother asked of him was a great deal, but he has done it."

"And without complaint," Padraig said. "He keeps most of his thoughts to himself, does Kinnoull. But he will not do what he does not feel is right." He looked evenly at Sophie.

The MacPhersons, she then learned, came from a long mixed line of noblemen and rogues. Sophie suspected which line had birthed Connor. According to the Murrays, he did not hesitate to borrow cattle or sheep from pastures if need arose, or to protect livestock in other pastures from caterans. He had a Highlander's fierce devotion to the Stuart cause, and took risks to defend it. Like many Scotsmen, he held the conviction that James Stuart had the only true claim to the throne of Scotland, and his son Charles after him. If a chubby German prince sat on the English throne now, Mary and Roderick explained, that should not affect Scotland and its people—yet it had, deeply and irrevocably. Connor MacPherson was one of those who had the courage to protest. His family had shared those loyalties, but had suffered greatly for them.

How Connor himself had suffered, Sophie could not fully discover. "He keeps most things to himself," Mary said. "He will not discuss them—may never talk about them in his lifetime. And we respect that."

Padraig walked his mother home after supper, and Roderick promised to watch the castle through the night. Sophie retired, deeply tired.

Sleeping a little, she awoke to find herself still alone. Connor had not returned. She lay in the darkness, sensing the hours creep past, while she dozed and woke again, and wondered if he was safe, worried if he was injured. Had he run afoul of the men who were looking for her?

Rolling to her side, curling under the blankets, she realized that she felt lonely in the big bed without him there. She missed his strength, his wit, his unexpected kindnesses, even his gruffness. Surprised with herself, she had to admit that she anxiously awaited his return.

Ridiculous, she told herself, punching the pillow. Foolishness and fancies. She would be better off without him.

Later, drifting to sleep, she realized that she had not heard the beautiful ghostly music. She almost missed that, too.

Almost, for she did not relish the idea of being alone in the old tower with a ghost who played tunes poignant enough to break the heart.

Chapter 19

Bending down, Sophie pushed aside a tangled clump of weeds. The pathway that led to the kitchen door was edged by unkempt rows of old leaves and new weeds entwined with exhausted ivy. She found remnants of the flowers and herbs that had once flourished here—grayish clusters of dry lavender, the sword leaves of iris, a few crisp marigold heads from another year. Stroking the plants, easing aside the mass of ivy, she saw curled rosemary leaves, knots of thyme, mint leaves, other herbs. She crushed a few leaves, finding traces of their delightful scents.

Connor had told her that nothing would grow at Glendoon, but she saw growth everywhere, in the kitchen garden and elsewhere in the yard. However, it was sparse, lacking will and vitality.

Pausing for a moment, she made her decision. Then she bent her head and slid off the little silver necklace that she always wore. Holding the delicate chain in her right hand so its sparkling crystal hung suspended and perfectly balanced, she waved it gently over the patch of garden in front of her, where Mary's marigold and lavender shoots had already wilted. Winking and sparking in the light, the pendant swung back and forth and then took on a circular path.

Closing her eyes, she put out her left hand and moved it slowly over the tiny, weak plants, over the patch where the crows had pecked at the seeds, over the brownish tangle of old plants and the bare spots where the soil was weakest. Sweeping her hand slowly and letting the delicate fairy stone dangle, twinkling in its circular path, Sophie closed her eyes and let the fairy magic pour through her.

This she knew, this she understood, the use of the Fairy's Gift to heal and encourage flowers and other plants. Inside, she sometimes felt a power that she could not quite explain, a subtle feeling that swirled through her. Over the years of working with plants and flowers, she had learned to summon it when she wanted.

And she had learned, too, that the pretty little pendant gave her a stronger sense of the power. Growing up, she had thought of the necklace as just a symbol of the fairy ancestry of which her family was so proud, and she was pleased to wear it for that reason. But she began to realize that sometimes it shimmered and sparkled almost unnaturally, and grew warm or cold, as if it held a force within it. One day she discovered, by waving it over a bed of tulips, that the pendant itself seemed to increase her gift for making things grow.

At the convent, she had used it secretly, almost guiltily, sure that the nuns would never have understood. As she waved her hands over the plants one day with the silver chain draped around her fingers, she looked up to see old Sister Berthe standing nearby, watching her.

"Good," the genial little nun had said. "You're praying over the plants. I do that, too. It helps them grow, just like magic." She had winked before walking past her. "It's just love, after all. Only love, and all living things need that."

Only love, after all. Sophie let out her breath, finishing her private ritual, and slipped the fine silver necklace back over her head. Perhaps some love and magic would help the sadly neglected garden patches at Glendoon.

She stood, brushing her hands. But much of Glendoon was in a state of neglect, she told herself. The castle was a temporary thieves' den, not a home—or so Connor insisted, even though the rooms were filled with his family's legacy.

Turning, she heard a shout, and looked past the curtain wall to the hills beyond. She could see Connor and another Highlander—Neill or Andrew, she thought—walking toward Glendoon. Tam the spaniel trotted beside them, and the terriers scampered ahead. In the distance, chasing before them in a haphazard way, were several sheep.

She had not seen Connor yet this morning, and she felt a thrill of excitement to see him approaching unexpectedly in the middle of the day. He had not come to her last night, and she awoke yearning for him, remembering how he had explored her body, rousing her passions to a fever peak—and she had missed him so much then that she ached.

But she tried to tell herself that it was nonsense.

Drawing a quick breath, she turned away to see the old wolfhound, who ambled toward her and sat on his haunches, lifting his head in a series of throaty barks.

"Hey, Colla. Do you sense your master coming home?" she asked. Walking over to the old dog, she patted his head, and he shifted his cool nose under her hand to beg for more.

Another glimpse over the curtain wall revealed that Connor and his companion had reached a hill-crest and were wading through a cluster of sheep. She would have known him anywhere, she realized, even at a distance—that proud posture, that easy swinging carriage, the dark plaid he favored draped over his shoulder. She knew the turn of his head, the familiar sweep of dark brown hair gilded by sunlight, the habit he had of setting a fist to his hip. Stopping, he surveyed the area and then looked toward Glendoon.

Even from where she stood, she felt his gaze, as if he saw her in the bailey yard. A shiver slipped along her spine—anticipation, pleasure, remembered ecstasy.

She put a hand to the flexible rim of the wide straw hat she wore, which she found in the trunk that had belonged to Connor's mother. This morning she had finally relented, borrowing a plain, comfortable everyday dress from the trunk as well. Of blue flowered cotton, the simply cut gown fit like a roomy coat, buttoning only at the waist, its bodice and skirt panels open to show a linen chemise and underskirt.

She had found sturdy leather shoes, too, only a bit too big for her, and white woolen stockings as well. Clean garments were a relief after too long in the torn, grimy satin dress.

Since the day was sunny and warm, she was grateful for the shade of the wide-brimmed straw hat. She had found leather gloves in the chest, too, and steel shears in a sewing box. Though she hesitated to use the things, she sensed Connor would not mind. As she handled his mother's possessions, Sophie felt peace and calmness, as if the owner's spirit lingered easily in objects she had once touched.

"Mistress!"

Sophie whirled. "Oh, Roderick! I thought you were out with the laird," she said as he came toward her.

"Oh, not me, I do not herd cows or sheep," he said disdainfully. "I am here to guard you." He puffed with pride, his quick smile and youthful charm dazzling. She smiled back.

"Good," she said. "I have some work for you today."

He lifted his brows. "Work?"

"Aye. Do you have a shovel and an axe?"

"For what?" He looked at her suspiciously.

"Gardening. We'll need a rake, too, and a trowel. I want to clean up the kitchen garden. I've done some weeding, but it needs heavier work."

"*Ach*, mistress," he said in dismay. "The herb garden is women's work."

"Not at all. I need a pair of strong arms and a strong back to clear the weeds and trim all that ivy, and cut back the plants worth saving. I think we can encourage healthy growth over the summer." She tipped her head. "Would you rather chase me away from the front gate, or see that I am kept busy?"

"Busy," he said grudgingly. "Since you've tried to leave the place twice—aye, very busy."

"Well then." She smiled. "I also want to look at the larger garden—I saw it from the library window." She began to cross the bailey yard briskly, and Roderick fell into step beside her.

"That big garden, the old one? Mistress, do not ask me to dig that out for you. It would take an eternity. You'd need several men to do that."

She headed toward the rough pile of stones that marked the interior garden wall with the collapsed gate at its center. "It's not the old garden I want to clear out today, it's just the kitchen plot. I'll help you, if you have a rake to spare for me."

"Aye, then. I'll not turn down the offer. What do you want me to do, mistress?"

"The undergrowth must be cleared, and the overgrowth cut back—especially the ivy and the strawberry tendrils, which are wrapped around nearly everything. The kitchen path must be made wider for walking. I think we can fit beds of about four feet in width to either side, two of them on each side, with alleys of about two feet between them."

"*Ach*, I can do that in a couple of days. I'll ask Padraig to help when he comes back from herding the cows—he likes farming and such work, does Padraig."

Sophie nodded. As they crossed the bailey, six or seven chickens trotted past in a neat line. Sophie laughed outright to see the way they traveled through the yard. When Colla woofed and strode toward them, so that the chickens panicked and scattered, Roderick waved the dog away.

"*Ach*, when the silly birds come out and about, the

dogs do not like it," Roderick grumbled. "Kinnoull has trained his dogs to leave the chickens alone, but the birds do not know that. I'll be back with the shovels and things," he said, and took off, shooing the chickens toward the ramshackle buildings at the back of the yard.

Colla walked beside her as Sophie continued toward the larger garden. Reaching the sagging interior gate, she stepped inside. Surveying as she turned, she saw a once lovely garden gone wild. Mingled plants of several varieties verged on walls, stones, the natural slope of the garden floor. Stone and plant and wood intertwined, in places supporting, in other places crushing each other. Vines twisted around stone features, and thick snarls of brambles and ferns encroached upon pathways and tree trunks. Grass feathered through bushes, and tough ivy, miles of it, swallowed everything it touched. Wide stone steps, heading up the incline, peeked through the vegetation like the bones of a skeleton.

This would be a place to try using her fairy touch, Sophie thought, touching her crystal pendant—and no doubt would challenge her modest inherent ability to bring lushness and growth to plants.

She saw a small pool obscured in the chaos, with a stone bench nearby, hopelessly wound in ivy beneath the shade of the trees. At the back, Sophie recognized apple trees as well as cherry and pear, and a few delicate hawthorn trees. The garden tangle was so great that any fruit would fall unpicked to rot among the undergrowth.

Near the sunny curve of the outer curtain wall, she saw briar rose vines. Bare and thorny, they ran all along the wall, arcing and drooping in crazy patterns.

"The roses here must have been beautiful once," he said.

She whirled. Connor stood behind her, his brogans crushing ivy and a clump of small purple flowers just beginning to bloom.

"You are stepping on the violets," she said.

"Oh." He shifted his stance, and they sprang up, unharmed, around his left shoe. "That's a fine hat, Lady Kinnoull."

She felt herself blush, and touched the wide brim where the sunlight speckled through. "I hope you do not mind—I borrowed it from your mother's things. She was truly Lady Kinnoull," she added.

"It suits you." He smiled a little. "The hat does, too."

In response, she found herself smiling, too, a feeling that rose suddenly from her heart like a gentle glow.

"I saw Roderick," Connor said. "He is in the kitchen garden, working like the hounds of hell will be after him if he does not. He said he must clear out the old ivy and strawberry vines. I think you've taken command over your own guard, madam." His tone was teasing and he lifted a brow.

She laughed. "There is a good deal of work to do there, and I'm glad to have such a willing sentinel."

He glanced around. "I know it must distress you to see how sadly this place has been neglected over the years—over centuries, really. But not much can be done to change things here. Plants don't flourish at Glendoon as they do elsewhere. The soil is thin and rocky."

"They could grow here as well as anywhere, with help and encouragement. There is lots of growth here, but the plants are smothering and choking each other, and in other places they do not thrive for lack of light and air. Aye, the soil is weak, but it can be nourished. Mary Murray said she sowed seeds in the kitchen plot. I thought that if I cleared out some garden space, I could do that, too."

"The birds took most of Mary's seeds, and the rest did not sprout."

"She planted marigolds and a few herbs. Perhaps the marigolds should be planted in hot beds first, for better protection. I thought to add other flowers and herbs—Mary says she has some seeds and seedlings to spare. Marjoram, mint, chamomile all do best when added as slips or seedlings. I can sow sorrel, thyme, fennel, and some others directly into the ground. I'd like to add lavender and rosemary, too, from shoots. Mary would have done it, but she has no time to tend another garden, with her own home and family to see to. But I have some time—for a while at least."

"And the knowledge, I think," he said. "It's a far better pastime than trying to find your way out of here." He watched her evenly. "Do what you will in the garden. Castle Glendoon belongs to the MacCarrans, after all."

"Glendoon could be lovely with some effort." She turned to stroll along the vine-cluttered path toward the collapsed wall. He turned with her, taking her elbow as they stepped over clumps of tangled plants and negotiated around fallen stones.

"That would be a miracle of transformation," he said wryly.

"Not so much. Plants need some basics, of course, but they thrive best with some love and encouragement."

"As you wish. But I warn you not to be disappointed."

She almost laughed. "You may be surprised, Kinnoull. I am not confident about many things, but I am about gardening."

"Not confident?" He stopped, his hand on her arm. "The fire in you, lass, begs to differ."

She glanced up at him. "I have some fire, I suppose, when I need it."

"You make very good use of it," he murmured.

Her heart bounded, for she thought he meant to kiss her, for he leaned close—so close—and she inclined toward him, welcoming, waiting. Then he straightened away and resumed walking beside her. Her yearning lingered, but Sophie moved on. She tried to remind herself that he was just a brigand. But she knew differently now, and the more she learned about him, she only wanted to know more.

"Well," he went on, "if you can actually convince these gardens to flourish, I will plant your wee tulips myself."

She laughed. Her shoulder bumped his arm as they made their way along the nearly obscured path. "I would like to see that."

"You just might." He guided her around a stone.

"This garden was lovingly tended, long ago, and well designed," she said. "There's a paradise to be reclaimed underneath all this chaos. It only needs some attention."

His arm came over her shoulders, and he turned her toward him. "Sophie, this is not a wee hobby, or a few idle days' work. It would take a lifetime's dedication to maintain this garden in the way you imagine it could be."

A lifetime, she thought. I would like that. But she only nodded. "I've always wanted a garden of my own to muck about in."

He glanced up, where clouds swept over the sun. His arm stayed about her, both a comfort and a thrill. "If you start mucking about in the gardens just now, you'll be up to your elbows in mud before long. We'll see rain soon, I think."

"It will be good for the plants," she answered, looking up as well. The tilt of her head brought her closer to him. Connor lifted a hand to brush back her hair, cup her cheek.

"You think more about what is good for others, even plants, than your own welfare," he said. "It is admirable."

"It is not so bad to be trained by nuns," she said lightly.

"I am getting very fond of nuns," he whispered, lowering his head. His mouth settled softly upon hers, his fingers slipping along her cheek, into her hair.

The force that went through her then was like a gentle surrender, so that her knees buckled and her heart soared, and she had to hold onto his arms or fall.

He kissed her again, thoroughly, and she let him angle her head while she arched toward him in complement. All else vanished but the warm press of his mouth on hers, the hard strength of his body, the power of that strong, beautiful kiss. Only desire, and willingness, and exquisite tenderness remained.

When he drew back, she held to his forearms for support, her heart beating madly, her breath quick. She glanced up.

"Thank you," Connor said.

She blinked. "Thank me—for what?" For falling in love with the Highland rogue who had snatched her away from all that was familiar? She could hardly think, only stared at him.

He glanced around. "For finding something of worth here in this ruin of a place."

"There is something to rescue here," she said breathlessly. "I want to do that. Let me do that."

He let her go then, stepped back, turned to walk again, and she went along beside him.

"There is an old curse over this place," he remarked. "They say nothing will flourish at Glendoon until the magic returns."

"Magic?"

He shrugged. "I think it was your ancestors' way of saying that Glendoon is full of rocks and ghosts, and its hill is too blasted steep to bother with."

She looked around at the overgrown garden and beyond it to the old keep with its broken walls. "Glendoon needs love and hard work to restore it, but it needs to be a home again." She glanced at him. "Then the magic would return."

"It's too remote to ever become a home."

"Anyplace can be a happy home. The hearts within make it so, not the condition of its walls, or the steepness of its hill, or the health of its fields."

He glanced at her thoughtfully as they neared the gate. Opening it, he waited for her to pass through.

"Sophie," he said. "You are a wonder. Now you'd best go see to your wee garden. Your faithful servant has been rather zealous." He gestured toward the keep, where Roderick toiled beside a huge mound of plant debris.

She walked past Connor and made her way across the yard. Roderick straightened to look at her, rake in hand, sweat dampening his black hair.

"There, mistress, I've cleared the path and torn out all the ivy," he said, indicating the torn-up plants.

"*All* the ivy?" she asked in dismay, realizing she should have been more specific in her instructions. "And the strawberries?"

"Aye, and I'll finish it by today or tomorrow, so you can plant your wee seeds if you like."

"Oh, thank you, Roderick. Tomorrow I'll want a trench laid at one end, too, and filled with about six inches of dung. Horse is better, but cow or sheep will do," she said.

"Dung?" Roderick gaped. "Dung? *Ach,* mistress, I'm a guard, not a—"

"Do as she says, lad," Connor said casually, approaching behind Sophie. "It's part of your duty here. Lady Kinnoull knows what she wants and what she needs."

"I do," she said, looking at him. "I think I do."

"We'll have acres of tulips in these old gardens before long, if she has her way." Connor gave her a quick smile before sauntering past them toward the kitchen door. "Oh, Roderick—there is plenty of sheep dung in the hills if you want to go fetch it." Winking at Sophie, Connor walked away.

Roderick muttered under his breath, while Sophie pinched her lips together to hide her smile and picked up a rake herself, setting to work, too.

"Glen Carran," Connor remarked, "will never be a peaceful valley again." He lay prone on a heathery hillside, peering down at the moorland where the river sliced past.

"Someday the return of Lord Kinnoull to his rightful station will bring happiness back to this place," Neill said.

Connor huffed softly. "Better to return the chief of the MacCarrans to Duncrieff Castle and his people than to bother with a small laird. But too late for that."

Nearby, Neill and Andrew lay supine, their plaidwrapped forms hidden in deep heather tufts, still brown with winter, though pale green tips showed here and there among the drab.

Connor was glad to see that greening up in the hills, for it meant an end to a long, bleak winter and a bleaker year, studded with misfortunes like stones in a field. With the arrival of spring, life could begin again and he would have hope.

Concentrating his gaze on the moor below, he watched a large crew of soldiers apply themselves to various tasks—some at the foot of the very hill where Connor and the others lay watching. The men worked steadily to apply gravel to a nearly finished part of the road. A half mile or so ahead, another large crew used shovels and pickaxes to dig a fresh track and break up any stones that were in the ground. The sound of chisels and axes and shovels rang in the air, echoing against the hills.

"I am thinking," Andrew said, "that these roads may be a good thing."

"And why is that?" Connor trained his gaze on the soldiers.

"They're fair roads," Andrew said. "Sixteen feet across, some of them, twelve at least, straight and smooth as an arrow. We can drive a lot of cattle and sheep along such roads."

"Their hooves would suffer on the gravel topping," Neill pointed out. "On the old drover's tracks, it's soft earth and packed grass, worn smooth with use. Better for cattle, that."

"The driving takes longer. We could shoe the herds for the journey and get them to market faster. They'd be healthier, not so thin from the extra miles. You could sell them for a higher price." Andrew glanced at him. "You could buy a gig."

"A gig," Connor repeated.

"For your lady," Andrew explained. "So you could drive her through the glen on fine straight roads, and take her to Crieff and to Perth, to the merchants there, and she'd spend your fine cattle earnings as only a wife can do." His eyes twinkled.

"Shall I buy her a parasol as well," Connor drawled, "so she can tour the countryside as the stolen bride of Glendoon?"

"Not Glendoon," Neill said. "Lady Kinnoull is a viscountess, and will need a gig in high style. A sleek pony, and a driver, too." He grinned, getting into the spirit of the teasing. Connor rolled his eyes.

"I'll drive," Andrew said. "I'll want livery, though."

"Hush it," Connor hissed. "Both of you, hold your nonsense." He turned his gaze back to the hill. A stiff breeze blew through, fluttering the heather tufts, billowing shirts and plaids and whipping at their hair.

After a moment Neill shook his head. "I tell you, lads, I am tired of the cold and ready for spring. And I am heartily sick of brown everywhere. The heather in bloom is a softer bed after hunting red soldiers."

"The heather does not bloom until July," Connor

pointed out pragmatically. "The gorse blooms earlier, but you wouldn't want to lay in that."

"*Ach*, he's tough enough for it," Andrew drawled.

"I must be getting old," Neill said. "I'm wanting warm weather and some green and color in these hills. And let's hope there will be some growth in our fields this year," he added. "If we have another year like the last one, we will have no food in our larders, nor hay in our byres, and our cattle will starve next winter. Without the Duncrieff's generosity last year, I do not know where we would be now."

"A sad loss, that," Andrew muttered.

"His death has not been confirmed," Connor said. "I will not mourn him until I know he is gone."

"If he is not, you had best find him," Neill said.

Connor nodded in silence.

"You've had bad luck ever since you rented that old ruin from Duncrieff," Andrew said. "The curse on those walls is sucking the fortune away from all of us."

"I don't much believe in curses, or ghosts, or fairies or bogles. I believe in luck, the good and the bad of it, and I believe we make of life what we can," Connor said.

"Maybe your bonny bride will bring you some luck," Neill said. "They say MacCarrans have fairy blood. She has the look of that ilk."

Connor frowned. "I've heard of the fairy legends of the MacCarrans, but I know little about them. Duncrieff himself never mentioned the subject. It's likely nonsense—pretty tales."

"My old granny says that Duncrieff's sisters bear the fairy blood and its gifts," Andrew said.

Connor looked surprised. "Both of them?"

"So I've heard. So Granny said." Andrew shrugged. "If your bride could turn stones into gold, or give you back your lands, that would be useful."

"Wake up, lad. There are few lambs in my flocks, and none of my cows have calved for two years. Glendoon's fields have scarcely produced in that time, either. My lands are gone, and my rented castle is falling about my ears. A bit of fairy blood will not fix all that."

"If it is a true fairy's gift—" Andrew began.

"Hey, look there." Neill pointed. "Those are Mac-Carrans."

"Aye," Connor said, looking down the hill at two men who climbed the slopes. "I sent Padraig with word that I would be in these hills until evening and that I would speak with them."

As the Highlanders loped closer, Connor rose to his feet and lifted a hand, waiting, while the wind blew his hair, the sleeves of his shirt.

"We'll have a word with you, Kinnoull," Allan MacCarran said as they came near. He set his hand to the dirk half concealed in his belt.

Chapter 20

"**W**here is our cousin?" Donald MacCarran glowered at Connor.

"She is fine, and safe," Connor said bluntly. "I have her. And you should know that I've married her."

Donald, the shorter and darker of the two men, touched his dirk handle. "You dumped us into the water while you were at it!"

"Stop," Allan said, putting a hand to Donald's shoulder. Connor looked at him in surprise, and Allan nodded. He had the golden coloring of his cousins, though in a ruddy way. "Duncrieff himself said this might come about. But we did not expect it to happen quite that way," he added.

"So he told you," Connor murmured.

"Not long ago," Allan said, "he said he would prefer Sophie to marry you rather than Campbell. He thought it a better match."

"He did mean Sophie, and not her sister Kate?"

"Aye, of course. He did not want Sophie to marry Campbell, though the old chief arranged it years ago," Donald said. "But now we disagree with the MacCarran's choice, MacPherson. He thought you a friend, but you showed yourself a poor comrade."

"Have I?" Connor narrowed his eyes.

"The night of the raid, weeks ago, when Duncrieff was taken," Allan said. "Tell us the truth of that, MacPherson. We were there, Donald and myself, and your lads, too." He nodded to Neill and Andrew. "We went ahead of you and Duncrieff, that night he was shot." His gaze was bitter. "He said it was not serious, and we left him with you."

"He fooled us all," Connor said. "He had a slight wound to the arm, but he was pistol-shot in the back, which he concealed until he collapsed."

"Did you leave him to die?" Donald demanded.

"I left him." Connor hated himself for saying the words.

"Why?" Allan gripped the handle of his dirk.

"They say he was betrayed by a friend that night," Donald said. "The red soldiers say they caught him because someone shouted out where he was and fled. We knew it was you."

"If you think I'm guilty, why did you not come after me before this?"

"We did not want to believe it," Donald said. "We went to Glendoon, and Mrs. Murray said you had gone to Perth."

"Aye, to see Duncrieff. The guards said he was ill

and could have no visitors. I returned again and again, but never saw him."

"We went there as well," Allan said. "They would not admit us, either, his kinsmen. We've had no word since if he is alive or dead."

The last time Connor went to Perth, the guards had told him that Duncrieff had been transferred and died en route. But he would not say that now until he knew it was true.

"Tell us why you left the lad," Donald snarled.

"Wounded as he was, I could not save him," Connor explained. "I had to gamble that the government would respect a clan chief, even a Jacobite rebel. General Wade has some decency in him," he admitted. "Duncrieff would have died that night had he stayed with me. I followed to make sure that the soldiers took him to a physician, which they did."

Allan and Donald watched him warily, then spoke in muted tones, their hands still on their weapons. Connor waited, tense and expressionless, knowing they had reason to despise him.

He would not tell them how he had done his best to stem the bleeding, while Rob demanded that Connor leave him and flee. Nor would he recount how bitterly they had argued, harsh words that burned in his memory.

"Leave me here," Rob had said. "Go—but make me one promise. I want you to marry my sister. She will return to Duncrieff next week—I must have your promise on it before I die."

"You will not die," Connor had insisted. "You will not."

"Conn, do this for me . . . marry her—she is

named on this page, and I've set my seal to it. You can save her, and Clan Carran, too, from threat—if I am not here to watch out for them."

Seeing how pale and weak his friend grew, Connor had given his word quickly, not thinking of marriage, thinking only of his friend. He owed Duncrieff so much, and loved him and his clan. "I trust only you to do this, Conn," he said. "But you must go—"

"Trust me to stay with a wounded comrade," Connor had growled.

MacCarran of Duncrieff had shouted out then, bringing the soldiers toward them. Connor refused to leave, but Rob had shoved him into a screen of bushes with the last of his strength as the dragoons came near. He had sacrificed his own freedom to save Connor's life.

Realizing that the red soldiers would take Duncrieff directly to a military physician, Connor had let them go.

"I did leave him there," he said now. "It was the only way I could help him. And I gave him my word and kept it."

"Duncrieff told me he trusted you," Allan replied. "He said only you were good enough to marry our cousin Sophie, and he would see to it."

Connor felt his throat tighten. He felt the presence of Neill and Andrew at his back, silent and strong, men who trusted him without question. He took Duncrieff's paper from his sporran and handed it to Allan, who read it and passed it to Donald.

"You had no choice, I see," Allan said.

Connor nodded. "I beg your pardon if you got a soaking the night we took the bridges down. It was the fastest way to take her away before Campbell could interfere."

"If our chief wanted this, we'll accept it," Allan said, handing back the note. "You'd best treat her well, Kinnoull." His hand had not yet left the ballock handle of his dirk.

"I would never harm her," Connor growled.

"Sophie is a treasure," Donald said. "She has the gift."

"The gift?" Connor frowned.

Allan nodded. "The Fairy's Gift of the MacCarrans. And more than that, she is the finest treasure of our clan."

Connor looked from one man to the other. A suspicion began to dawn in him. "Why did Duncrieff insist that I marry her?"

"Surely you know why," Allan said.

"There was no time for him to explain." Not even time enough to make clear which sister, he thought.

"She's the heiress of Duncrieff," Donald said. "The 'Maiden of Duncrieff,' as we call a female heiress—before she's wed."

Connor stared at him. "Heiress?"

"Duncrieff is not yet married, and has no child. Sophie is the older sister. She inherits if anything should happen to him."

"Inherits the estate," Connor clarified, hoping that was what they meant. But he feared there was more.

"The estate, aye, but that is divided with her sister. Sophie is head of Clan Carran should her brother die without an heir of his own," Allan replied.

Chief. The hills, the sky, seemed to tilt on its axis. Connor summoned his wits. "Sophie inherits the chiefship? Why not a male kinsmen—one of you two, perhaps."

"Some clans name a cousin or kinsman when there is no close heir, particularly to protect the clan," Donald said. "But MacCarran tradition says the heir must come from the chief's closest kin, regardless of gender. No matter—Duncrieff has only been arrested. We'll petition for his release, and all will be well."

"Why would he choose me to marry Sophie?" Connor asked, still stunned and trying to puzzle it out. His bride was the chief of a Highland clan—and she did not even know it.

"Duncrieff trusts you implicitly," Allan replied. "And your title as Lord Kinnoull could help our clan. Our chief currently has no title. He is a chief and a laird, but not a peer. In such times, with England ruling Scotland—for now—we need the advantage of those who are born and bred to power and position."

"My title is of no use to anyone now."

"You'll be reinstated one day. Duncrieff was sure of it, and I am sure of it, too," Allan said. "And you can help protect our clan from someone like Campbell, who has been hungry to take control of the clan. He would have more say in government as a Whig with influence over an entire Highland clan."

"Or so he thinks," Connor growled.

"Exactly. We suspect that is why he wanted to marry Sophie in the first place. Otherwise he would not bother with her."

Connor let out a bitter laugh. "So Campbell knows about Sophie's status?"

"He is the magistrate for this region. He knows."

"Does she know about this herself?" Connor asked quietly.

Allan shook his head. "She never wanted to be the heiress, and suggested Kate instead—but Kate is involved in the rebellion, which could go badly for her and the clan if she were ever to become chief. Duncrieff meant to talk to Sophie about this when she returned home to Scotland, but he had no chance. He had decided to ask if you would marry her—but not so soon."

Connor nodded. Much of it made sense to him now, but raised new challenges. "I had best tell her about this."

"Tell her, or not." Donald shrugged. "It does not matter. Duncrieff will be released, and all will be well for our clan."

"Kinnoull, you must keep Sophie safe," Allan said.

"You and your clan have my word on it." Connor extended his hand first to Allan and then Donald.

"We'd best move on," Allan said. "Whenever the military sees Highland men in conversation, they become suspicious."

"Good day to you," Donald said. "Cousin."

Connor nodded grimly, and the MacCarrans turned to leave.

"Hey, one thing more," Donald said, turning back. "You do know about Sophie's gift."

"The legend of the Fairy's Gift? I've heard of it," Connor said in surprise. "But I know little about your clan's lore."

"Ask her about it," Donald said. "She was born with fairy blood, and the gift as well—so was Kate, come to that. Ask her." He grinned, and waved as the two men left.

Frowning, bewildered, Connor turned toward Neill and Andrew, who had stood silently to one side throughout the meeting.

"No wonder Duncrieff did not tell you the truth of this," Neill commented.

"Aye," Connor muttered as he walked ahead.

Marrying the female head of a clan was far more to ask of a man than marrying a troublesome hellion, Connor thought. Had Duncrieff presented his request under civilized circumstances, he would have hesitated, probably refused altogether. All his adult life, he had longed only for a peaceful, simple life. Now he wanted only to reclaim his home and his future, and continue to seek that simple lifestyle.

But the marriage was made, and he would accept his role. If he could help Sophie and her clan, then so be it. He had given his word to Duncrieff.

And he suspected that he had already given his heart to the man's sister.

Much later, returning to a sleeping household at Glendoon, Connor walked quietly past the door to his bedchamber, where his wife lay sleeping. He was not prepared yet to face her with this revelation. Should he tell her outright that she was chief? If so, he would have to tell her what he knew of her brother.

Neither of them were ready for that yet. The hour was late, and his need to be alone to think burned in him. He took the stairs up toward the ruined corner guard tower with its shelter and solitude.

Beneath a canopy of stars, he opened the fiddle case and removed the instrument. Tightening the bow, tuning the strings, he set the fiddle to his shoulder, closed his eyes, and let the melody come to him.

A slow down bow, a quick bowing up, and the sound created itself without his conscious effort. He pressed callused fingertips against the fingerboard, slid up, danced down, while his fingers and the bow coaxed the melody from the strings.

For this brief time only the music filled his mind. He felt himself begin to relax, felt his tensions ease as the tune poured through him, flowing as naturally as breathing.

At first he played a steadily repeating tune, more rhythm than melody, and when its droning magic had calmed him, a new melody began to form, soft and slow, with a lilting quality. He had never played it before; it simply emerged.

The tune had a golden sweetness, he thought, like Sophie, a gentleness and a bright spirit. He saw golden hair like sunshine, eyes like blue-green crystal, a beautiful smile that warmed his heart. The cadence of the song reminded him of the fluid grace of her walk, the lilt of her voice.

He repeated the melody to fasten it into his memory, reminding himself to jot it down in musical notation later. Perhaps he would title it "Mrs. MacPherson," or even "Lady Kinnoull," according to her married title.

Perhaps, he thought then, he ought to call it "The Bonny Chief of the MacCarrans."

He raised the bow and played a different tune, and when the song ended, he looked down the steep hill that led to the glen. The waterfall foamed white in the darkness and sounded like distant thunder.

That roar distorted the fiddle's music, turned it ghostlike, adding to Glendoon's mysteries. Whenever he could, Connor kept watch from this spot like an eagle in an aerie.

But when all was peaceful, when the sky bloomed pale at dawn or burned to embers at sunset, he stood alone, and heard music in the water, in the wind, in his own heart. Somehow Sophie had entered into his music, too, stirring him to express his feelings through his fiddle and bow.

Furrowing his brow, he tipped the instrument to his shoulder again and played the new, exquisite little air just for her.

The music slipped down cold corridors, through cracks in stone walls. Sophie stood by the bedchamber door, listening. As before, the tune was plaintive and slow, but this time it had a strong but delicate beauty to it. This time she was not frightened—she only wanted to hear more.

Opening the door carefully, she paused. The music was faint but definite, emanating from somewhere inside the stone ruins.

Achingly beautiful, the air expressed poignant emotion in its lovely notes, lifting, falling, soaring pure. Sophie placed a hand over her heart and felt tears starting in her eyes.

Then the music stopped as mysteriously as it had begun. After a moment she closed the door. Going back to the bed, shivering, she slid under the covers.

In a while, as she began to slide into sleep, the little melody played through her mind again, and she sensed once more the tenderness in its notes—as if love itself had turned to sound, she thought.

Chapter 21

❦

"**M**ary Murray makes a fine stew," Andrew remarked as he scraped his spoon across his pewter plate.

Murmuring agreement, Connor reached for another crisp oatcake, breaking it to offer half to Sophie, who sat beside him and across from Andrew. Alike as twin halves of an apple, Roderick and Padraig sat facing each other.

The long, polished table in the great hall gleamed with candlelight as Connor looked around at his comrades and his wife. The room, even with cracked and crumbling walls, seemed grand somehow, nicer than he had ever realized, warm with firelight and camaraderie.

In that moment, he almost felt content—he almost felt at home. These people were as dear to him as family, and he felt at ease in their company. He smiled a little to himself.

Sophie accepted the oatcake from him and ate it with a small wedge of cheese. Slathering his own piece with butter from a crock, he glanced over at her.

"You've eaten little tonight, and you've had none of Mary's good stew, lass."

"I'm fine. You all were hungry and needed a good meal."

Connor paused, buttered oatcake nearly to his mouth. He and the others had eaten their fill of the meal in the kettle, while Sophie had eaten only hot porridge with cream and a slice or two of cheese. The lass did not eat much; he'd noticed that already. In fact, he'd scarcely seen her eat much at all since she had been at Glendoon.

"Here." He slid his half-empty plate toward her. "I've had enough. Will you finish the rest?"

Her eyes grew wide, as if in dismay rather than hunger. "No, thank you. I'm truly not hungry."

"I'll give it to the dogs, then." He bent to offer the plate to Tam and Colla, while the two terriers, who had been content with a small bowl of scraps in the corner, trotted over.

"Hey! That's good stew. I'd have eaten it," Andrew groaned.

Connor leaned toward Sophie. "Is our plain food not fine enough for you?" he asked softly. "You've not eaten much all the time you've been here—soup and porridge and suchlike."

"I'm fine," she repeated with a wan smile.

"Does captivity not agree with you?" he murmured.

She sent him a frown. "Mary Murray makes wonderful vegetable and barley soups that are delicious and filling. I can hardly eat much else, really. And I'm not hungry just now. But thank you for your concern." Her frown brightened to a fresh, warm smile.

Connor melted inside, even as he felt impatient. He marveled at the ease with which she showed sweet politeness. He could marvel at her influence at Glendoon, too, he thought, for his comrades behaved with better manners and politeness in her presence, though it sometimes sat awkwardly on them.

"Perhaps the mistress prefers French fare to Scottish," Roderick suggested. "Wheat bread and snails and so on, I think they eat there."

"I fondly remember Scottish dishes from my childhood at Duncrieff," Sophie said.

"What did you eat in Bruges?" Andrew asked. "What do nuns eat—bread and water?"

"We ate very well there, and had a big, busy kitchen and bakery. Fresh breads and puddings, cheeses, soups, eggs, and cooked vegetables were on the menu most every week. We had fresh fish often, and chicken, and sometimes there was bacon or ham, though I . . . do not care for that."

"Now I'm hungry again," Andrew said, and Padraig shoved his unfinished serving toward him.

"Here we have fine Highland beef," Roderick said. "You'll have missed that over there, I'm sure. And venison and rabbit, of course. Pheasant, grouse, and capercaillie when we can get them. Fish, too, though most Highlanders are not so fond of fish."

"It's our Highland beef you must have," Andrew said. "It will restore you, lass. You're a bit thin."

"And mutton and lamb, of course," Padraig said. "We should ask our mother to roast a lamb, and we'll have a celebration."

The girl went pale, Connor noticed. "I am just so happy to have good Scots oats again," she said quickly, and took another spoonful of porridge, though it had congealed in her dish.

"Aye," Connor said. "We'll roast a wee lamb or two in honor of our wedding. And we shall have a side of beef—bloody rare, with the juices running. For our health," he added.

Just as he thought. She went white as bleached linen and her fingers clutched the spoon. "Oh no, that is not necessary. Thank you." She swallowed hard.

"You do not eat lamb or beef," he guessed, watching her. "Or meat of any kind, I suspect."

Sophie shrugged. "I eat no flesh foods, but for eggs and sometimes fish."

"No meat?" Andrew sputtered. "Did you take a convent vow?"

"It's not a religious vow. I just stopped eating it because I wanted to do so. It was not a difficult habit to break." She shrugged. "That was why I got sick the night we . . . married. I could not avoid all the rich foods and meats offered on Sir Henry's table."

Connor nodded. "Rara avis," he murmured thoughtfully.

"What?" Andrew asked, his mouth full.

"Rare bird," Sophie translated, returning Connor's glance. "So the outlaw knows Latin."

"As does his bride," he acknowledged.

"The outlaw knows a good deal more than Latin," Roderick said. "He knows French and Italian and Greek, too. He's got a room full of books, and he's read them all. Why, he even plays—"

"Enough," Connor said.

"Your lass does have a finicky stomach, so I'll eat this," Andrew commented, snatching up the last of the cheese. "She sicked up the night of their wedding—all over his brogans," he told Roderick and Padraig, who chuckled.

"I do have a touchy stomach, and I do not understand," Sophie said, looking hard at Connor, "how you can care for the wee lambs and take joy in their sweet natures, and then slaughter and eat them. And I do not know how you can watch over Fiona with such love as you do," she went on, "and then eat her."

"I am not going to eat Fiona," Connor said. "She's a milk cow. As for the rest of it," he went on, "we raise some cattle for market, some sheep for their fleeces, so that we have some income. We take a few livestock for their meat through the year, but not so many as you'd think."

"We have the chickens, too, and we catch fish in the lochs and rivers," Roderick said. "We hunt deer and birds and other creatures. There's nothing wrong with it—'tis heaven's plan for feeding all of mankind."

Sophie lifted her chin. "I feel for the animals, and find that I cannot eat them so easily."

"Well, she can live on oats and cheese, kale and eggs, now that she is back in Scotland," Padraig said. "Such simple fare is not unusual in the Highlands."

"Aye, but you hardly need concern yourselves. I may not be here for long. If your laird has his way, he'll send me back." Sophie sent Connor a sharp look. "It was another he was wanting anyway, one who is not so finicky in her ways and can better keep up with a rogue."

"Aha," Andrew crowed, and cocked a brow. "Not after what happened yesterday—"

Connor sent him a fast glare. Roderick applied himself diligently to eating, and Padraig cleared his throat.

"Yesterday?" Sophie looked from Andrew to Connor.

"I saw your kinsmen—Allan and Donald."

"Oh!" She sat forward, hands pressed on the table. "How are they? What did they say when you told them—you did tell them about the marriage?"

"We spoke about it, and I assured them that you are fine. As for the rest—I saw Sir Henry, too," he went on, with a quick look at Andrew.

"And what did he say?" Her voice was subdued, wary.

"We'll talk later," Connor said, standing. He collected his empty plate, accustomed to doing for himself at Glendoon. "For now, Padraig and I must go out to the byre to see to the evening milking, if we can collect any at all. Roderick," he said, as the twins stood, and Andrew as well, "stay with the lady. Andrew, I believe you and Neill have an errand this evening."

"Aye, Kinnoull, we do."

"Go, then, all of you," Sophie said. "I'll collect the dishes and such. We will meet later, you and I, Kinnoull?"

His name had a pleasant cadence on her lips, though Connor sensed a curious tension. She was displeased, or anxious about what he meant to say to her. He could not blame her. As the other men filed out of the great hall, he leaned toward Sophie.

"Meet me in the study later, lass." He preferred a quiet and neutral place for this discussion, not the great hall with its vaulted spaces, or the kitchen with its open doors—and certainly not the bedchamber, where the bed would distract him with its possibilities. "Just across the corridor."

"I know where it is," she said crisply. "I know every inch of this place by now. There's not much to do at Glendoon but wander, or garden, while I wait to see how long I will be kept here like a prisoner."

"The guard is for your own good, lass, though you might not believe it." He turned and headed for the door.

"There's always the front gate," she called after him. "I could always explore that."

"Ask Fiona to show you the back wall," he suggested as he pulled the door shut after him.

He should not have replied sharply, he told himself as he pounded down the steps. But she sparked him like a fire at times. And what he had to tell her later made him tense as a drum now.

He strode into the bailey yard, noticing quickly as he passed that the kitchen garden was neater and sprouted a thick fringe of green leaves and tiny flower heads almost ready to open, their green buds touched with color.

Odd, he thought. Perhaps Sophie's efforts to clear the garden plot had uncovered some plants pushing up—although he was sure nothing had been ready to bloom there. Nothing at all.

Milton was unfashionable these days, as was Spenser, Sophie thought, looking at the contents of the library bookshelves by the light of the candle she held. She loved their poetry nonetheless. Connor liked them, too, she saw, for his copies of *Paradise Lost* and *The Faerie Queene* were well-thumbed.

She traced a finger over leather spines as she studied the books on the shelves: Clarendon's *History* and Rowe's *The Works of Mr. William Shakespeare*, with slips of torn paper tucked among the pages, as if someone had marked favorite passages; a new copy of Swift's *Tales of a Tub*; works by Defoe; and Pope's translation of *The Iliad*.

Connor MacPherson was far more than an outlaw and a gentleman farmer, she thought. He was obviously well-educated, with a diverse mind. Nor was he a particularly tidy man, she thought, smiling. Books and papers were stacked everywhere, on shelves, on the desk, even on the floor. Wooden boxes containing books and portfolios filled the corners of the room.

An elegant mahogany desk and an upholstered armchair took up the center of the room. The writing surface was cluttered with books, quills, an ink pot, and more papers. As her skirt brushed the desk edge, a sheaf of papers spilled down. Sophie picked them up, noticing that they were maplike drawings, indicating boundaries, fences and buildings, wells, trees, and watercourses. She set them aside, puzzled.

The pile of books on the desk concerned farming, agriculture, husbandry. Frowning, her interest caught again, she examined the spines: Walton's *Compleat Angler*, Cooke's *Complete English Farmer*, a slim book called *The Gentleman's Pocket Farrier*.

The largest book on the desk surface, *Systema Agriculturae*, had a worn cover and foxed pages. The date, she saw on the flyleaf, was 1669, and an ink inscription read, "Duncan MacPherson, Lord Kinnoull, 1702—his boke." Another beside it was in French, D'Argenville's *La Théorie et la Pratique du Jardinage*.

Days ago she would never have guessed that Connor had any such interests. But she had seen him with his sheep and his favorite cow, his adoring dogs. He seemed comfortable in that role. Now, as she explored his study, she realized he was much more a farmer than an outlaw.

She lifted another book and opened it. "Van Oosten," she read aloud. "*The Dutch Gardener, or the Complete Florist.*"

"Recently translated," Connor said behind her.

She whirled. He stood in the doorway, a shoulder leaned to the jamb, his arms crossed. He looked as if he had been watching her for a while.

"I was looking at your books. I hope you do not mind."

"Not at all." He walked toward her and picked up one of the books stacked on the desk. "*A New System of Agriculture,*" he said. "John Laurence. I picked it up from Allan Ramsay's bookshop in Edinburgh. Have you ever been there?"

She shook her head.

"We will remedy that one day. A fine bookshop, and a fine city to visit." He set the book down and glanced around. "This is my favorite room at Glendoon. It feels . . . like home."

"It must remind you of the library at Kinnoull House."

"Somewhat, though Kinnoull's library is huge, and bright with windows and bookshelves fronted in brass mesh. A wonderful place. Those shelves hold five thousand volumes. I made off with a few hundred books in crates and sacks, along with some furniture. My father's armchair," he said, resting a hand on its high back. "This room does remind me of my father's private study." He shrugged.

"And the other rooms? The great hall, the . . . bedchamber?"

"The bedroom furniture came out of one of the guest rooms at Kinnoull—it proved easiest to cart away in the night," he said. "And it's a good enough bed." He looked at her.

Sophie felt herself blush. "Do you still have some things at Kinnoull House?"

He nodded. "Sir Henry is sleeping in my own bed, I imagine." He picked up another book.

"I was there, the night you . . . stole me away."

He looked up at her quickly, keenly. "I know. How did the place look to you?"

"It is a beautiful house, elegant yet spare. And the gardens, by the sitting terrace, must be lovely in late spring and summer. I strolled there with Sir Henry," she explained.

"My mother was particular about her flowers. Even raised them in stone pots all along the terrace. You and she would have had much to talk about." He set the book down. "Had you married Sir Henry, you would have been mistress of Kinnoull, with gardens to dig about in ad nauseum." His voice had an edge to it that she did not like.

"Sir Henry would probably disapprove of a wife who digs."

"I would not mind it," Connor said, opening *Systema Agriculturae*.

"If I had married him, I would not have been Lady Kinnoull," she said quietly.

Connor traced his long fingers over the items on the desk, fanning some papers. "Does that matter to you?"

"That would depend on who was Lord Kinnoull." Her heart beat faster suddenly.

He glanced at her, then turned to shelve the large book.

"Did the gardening books belong to your mother?" she asked.

"They're mine," he said. "I always thought to be more or less a farmer, and I hoped to expand the gardens at Kinnoull one day. While I was at university— I spent two years at Edinburgh, but did not complete it because of my father's situation—I studied botany, agriculture, and husbandry. All I really wanted was to look after my estate, my tenants, and so on. Instead, well . . ." He shrugged.

"You're a cateran?" she supplied.

"And a herdsmen and a shepherd, by turns."

"A rogue as well." She turned to shelve a couple of books. Connor took a volume from her hand and shelved it high. "I suppose you did not expect an outlaw to have a full library."

"You're clearly an intelligent and educated man. What surprises me most is that you plan your attacks so carefully."

He laughed. "My what?"

"Your cattle raids. They are all planned out with maps and drawings." She indicated the papers. "Fences and pastures, and so forth. I could not help but notice."

Connor laughed, the sound bubbling up from a deep well. He shook his head. "I am not planning cattle raids, lass. Those are some projects, some ideas

I had in mind for Glendoon's lands. A few crops, a good garden, livestock. But none of it was meant to be." He lifted a shoulder.

"Oh! I am sorry. I . . . never thought that you might have . . . dreams for the future."

"Everyone has dreams," he murmured.

"Aye," she answered, folding her hands in front of her.

He drew a breath. "Well, you won't do much gardening at Glendoon, with its shallow, stony peat soil. Only tough heather and gorse thrive here."

She tilted her head. "I can make something grow here, if there was time enough to try."

"Take all the time you want," he said quietly.

Her heart thrilled at that, so casually spoken in that beautiful voice. "Connor, what did you want to tell me . . . about what my kinsmen had to say?"

He sucked in a breath, went to the window, leaning his forearm there as he gazed out. Sophie joined him. In the twilight, the yard was shadowed, the hills beyond dark and lovely with a scattering of stars above them.

"Do you have any idea why Duncrieff wanted us to marry?" he asked.

"Only that I wrote to him saying I could not marry Sir Henry," she said. "Campbell seemed so cold and unfeeling. He did not even extend financial or legal help to my father when he requested it, although my father had promised him my hand. Perhaps Robert thought our marriage would be a solution."

"Aye. But there is another reason." He paused. "You are Duncrieff's heiress."

Sophie stared at him. "I'm . . . what?"

"According to your cousins, as the older sister,

you inherit Duncrieff should your brother die. That includes the title of chief of the clan."

"That's not possible," she said quickly. "I asked him to give that privilege to Kate."

"He never did," Connor said.

"I—" Sophie looked down, puzzling it through in her mind. She remembered the discussion, over months by mail, in which she had begged her brother to change the inheritance once he became chief. "And that is why he chose . . . you to be my husband?"

"He told Allan what he intended. Said I was his most trusted friend. Part of his plan was to prevent Sir Henry from marrying you—Duncrieff told me that himself. But he must have been thinking, as well, that he could stop Campbell from having any say in the clan, should Rob come to harm. Campbell would not wish your clan well," he went on. "Believe me—look what he wrought for Kinnoull with his greed. He took the place as soon as it was forfeited, while my father and I were still in prison."

She gasped. "You?"

"I spent seven months in the Edinburgh dungeons, waiting for the hangman's noose. Your brother obtained my release. With your father's blessing, he went to the Courts of Session and pleaded for my father and I, and paid what coin he could. Only I was freed. My crimes were only by association," he said, "or so the government thought."

"Would Sir Henry want to marry me just to—Oh, I think he would," Sophie said, answering her own question. She put a hand to her brow.

"Of course he would." Connor watched her calmly.

Sophie paced away, turned, still pacing, thinking, her thoughts tumbling. "I suppose my brother believed that your title, as Lord Kinnoull, might be of help to the clan, should we fall into some difficulty. And I expect Robert thought that you, of all men he knew, would be most capable of protecting me—and most willing, if I should ever become chief."

"Willing, aye," he said quietly. "I owe a great deal to Duncrieff."

She nodded. "So that is what our wedding was all about."

"Apparently so. You and your brother think alike. I am not surprised he wanted your good practical sense at the head of his clan. Your sister is a bit of a hothead, I suspect."

"She would be a fine chief. Stronger willed and braver by far than me."

He quirked a brow. "You do not know much about yourself, do you? But even as Lord Kinnoull, I can be of no use to your clan. My title might look impressive on documents, but otherwise it is hollow. I do not even possess my own lands now."

"It will not be an issue, since I will not become clan chief. Robert will be released soon enough, I'm sure." She looked up at him quickly, thoughts racing. "Connor, could you or your friends help me in any way to get him free? Talk to others—even help him escape?"

He frowned at her, then glanced away. "Sophie, there is more to this. I have some recent news . . . of your brother."

She heard the knell in his voice. "No—do not say it." She stepped back.

He took her upper arm, turned her toward him.

"Sophie, listen to me. It is just a rumor, but I was told last time that I went to Perth . . . that Robert had been moved out of the Tolbooth, and that he later died of his wounds."

"No! That is not true." She wrenched away. "His family would have been told!"

"The government might want to keep the death of a chief, a young and vital hero to the rebellion, quiet as long as they could. I got a hint of it from one of the guards when I bribed him with some of Mary's whiskey. Otherwise, no one outside the prison would know yet, I think."

"No, he cannot be . . . dear God. I should have felt it, but I did not. But we were so—close." She swallowed a rising sob. "How long—have you known?"

"I learned it a day or so before we met."

"We met?" She heard herself go shrill with anger and distress. "You snatched me! And you knew my brother was . . . gone"—she poured her grief into sudden fury—"so you must have been thinking you could take control of the clan this way!"

"I thought only of my promise to Duncrieff. I did not want a wife. Not yet."

"And not this one," she returned. "The nun. You set your sights on the hellion!"

"At first." His eyes, stormy green, were piercing. "That is no longer an issue, Sophie."

"Surely you knew," she went on, hardly listening. "You at least suspected that marrying the heiress to Duncrieff and Clan Carran could improve your circumstances!" She swept her arm wide.

"Enough," he said. "I gave my word, I kept it, and that is the whole of it."

"Why did you not tell me about my brother, then?"

"How could I?" he demanded, taking her shoulder. "How could I tell you when I had just wedded you, bedded you? I am not so cruel as that, though you may think it. I did not know myself if it was true. It is a rumor," he growled. "And I mean to prove it one way or the other."

She looked up at him, breath heaving, tears blurring her vision. "Then prove it wrong! You put my brother in that prison, from what I've heard—then prove this wrong, Connor MacPherson, and bring him home again!" She yanked out of his hold and went to the door, flinging it open, catching back a sob as she ran down the corridor.

She did not even know where to go—Glendoon was not her home, with familiar places for her to find peace.

Racing down the steps, she ran toward the great, wild garden, to seek comfort there.

Chapter 22

In the dusky purple twilight, he saw the sheen of her flaxen hair as she walked in the old garden. Stepping over the broken stones of the low garden wall, he approached her along paths newly cleared. Even in the gloaming he could see fresh green shoots pushing up through the soil.

Sophie turned, and he saw streaks of tears on her cheeks, saw that her eyes were large and troubled. Connor came within an arm's length and paused, wanting desperately to take her into his arms and comfort her.

But wisdom told him to keep a little distance, give her some time just now. Sophie was strength and grace, he knew, and strong enough to bear this, to bear anything. But she needed to realize that for herself.

"For a while, I did not want to tell you about Duncrieff," he said. "But you had to know."

She nodded, arms folded, and turned away. "He is not gone."

"I sincerely hope so," he said, "but we must be prepared for the other possibility. I understand what it is to lose someone close, Sophie. You have been through it before, too. It hurts," he said, drawing a breath, "it hurts for a long while, and then one day you realize that the burden feels a little lighter, just a little. Finally the lead weights begin to break away, bit by bit. We move on. We still carry the burden, but we find a wee place for it, and though it is still inside us, the pain is not so sharp."

She nodded again, looking down. "I know. But this . . . I do not want this burden." He heard a catch in her voice, and sensed her inner strength.

"We both feel this one, Sophie. You are not alone with it. He was near enough a brother to me, and it cuts me like a blade." He took her arm gently.

She did not pull away, though he felt her tension. "Tell me, then," she said in a quiet voice, her head turned away from him.

"The night that he was taken," he began, "we were out spying over the military road that General Wade is laying through this glen—Robert wanted maps. He wanted to see the plan the general had in mind. He had asked your sister to fetch them for him, but she had not been able to find them. He came to me and asked for help, and we went out, a few of us. But it went wrong—too much moonlight, bad luck, whatever it was. We were sighted and pursued by dragoons."

As simply as he could, he told her the rest—how Robert had been shot and concealed the extent of his injury; how her brother had sent the others ahead and given him the note, pleading for his promise to marry Katherine Sophia.

But he did not tell her that Duncrieff had summoned the guards himself. He would not beg out of his responsibility in his friend's capture.

"So I had to keep my word," he finished. "I had to."

She nodded, arms folded, golden hair shining like moonlight. "We never know what we will be asked to bear."

"But bear it we will," he murmured. "And besides—I am not certain of the truth. Let me find out if it is true. He may yet be alive."

"I feel that he is," she said. "I cannot believe that he could be gone. I think I would know it, somehow."

"I have the same sense . . . or else I do not want to accept it." He stroked his hand over her soft hair. "I am sorry, Sophie," he whispered.

She nodded, her head bowed. "I wish I knew."

"Perhaps your Fairy's Gift can tell you." He touched the shining crystal at her throat.

She looked up in surprise. "You know about that?"

"Some, not much. Truly, I don't believe in Fairy's Gifts and fairy curses, ghosts, and the like."

"There's a ghost here," she said quietly. "I've heard it moan at night. But it is most beautiful. Haunting. It sounds like violin music."

He gave her a long look. "Tell me about the fairy of Duncrieff."

She nodded, glanced around the dark garden. "A long time ago," she said, "in the time of the mists, a

MacCarran laird rescued a fairy woman from drowning. They fell in love, and married—she was of the most ancient race of her kind, the sort who are said to be very beautiful, and of a size with humans."

"Aye?" he asked softly, looking down at her. He reached out and brushed back a lock of her hair. "And what happened to this happy couple?"

"They had three sons. Each one inherited a bit of the power from their mother, the Sight, the gift of healing, the gift of conjuring up whatever is desired. She showed them how to use their talents. Then one day she had to return to her people. But she left behind a cup of hammered gold, shaped by the fairies and set with small crystal stones. Whenever a MacCarran child inherits the Fairy's Gift—it is not always recognized immediately," she clarified, "then he or she is given one of the stones to wear."

Connor reached out and took the small crystal between his thumb and finger. "What sort of magic did you inherit?"

"I have a version of conjuring, I suppose. I can make things grow—just flowers, vegetables, that sort of thing. It is a strange gift, and not very remarkable compared to the fairy magic that has occurred in my family. Most plants will grow on their own anyway—they just seem to bloom faster if I am their gardener. Sometimes they grow quite fast," she added.

"An important gift for a lady who loves to garden . . . and who is married to a farmer."

She stared up at him. "Oh, thank you," she breathed.

He lifted a brow, once again puzzled by her unexpected show of gratitude. But this time he understood her better, knew this was just another wonderful aspect of the woman he had begun to care for so deeply. "For . . . ?"

"For finding a little sense in my fairy blood. I've never thought that it was very useful, other than for growing flowers. In my family there are such remarkable tales of how the Fairy's Gift has manifested—true healing abilities, the Sight, gifts of charm magic, even conjuring. My ability felt . . . small and unimportant, as if it was not quite there. Even inconvenient, as if the blood had not taken hold in me properly, as it had in others in generations of MacCarrans."

"Sophie," he said, "sometimes I think there is magic all around you—I just did not know there was an explanation for it." He smiled a little. "And how is it inconvenient? Gardens bloom easily for you. Flowers, fruit trees—"

"You should see the weeds," she said dryly.

He laughed quietly, drew her closer, slipped his arm around her waist. "I think we could clear those out."

She melted toward him, and he took her shoulders to kiss her gently, a strand of simple kisses as pleasing, in that moment, as any others he had tasted of her. Wrapping her in his arms, he drew her close, resting his head on hers for a moment, drawing comfort from the embrace even as he sought to comfort her and ease the hurtful blow of her brother's death.

"How did you first know," he said, "that you had this gift?"

"My parents knew it by my eyes. MacCarrans who

are born with the fairy's touch in their blood have eyes that are very light in color, sometimes green or blue or gray, but large and a bit unusual."

He tipped her chin up to look at her beautiful eyes, with the changeable color of bright sea and sky in them. "Extraordinary," he said, "not simply unusual. I noticed your eyes immediately, and wondered."

"My sister has similar eyes," she said, "so it is no wonder you made a mistake in taking me."

"Not a mistake," he mused, "quite. What of the wee crystal you always wear? Does it bestow that magical talent you have for growing things?"

"Not exactly." She touched it. "But according to the legend, those who have the ability must wear one of the stones that come from the Fairy Cup of Duncrieff. If we wear the stone, we will be able to use our talents, and the stone itself can sometimes give one further gift—a true miracle." She looked up at him.

"A miracle?" He frowned. "Has that happened in your life?"

She shook her head. "I have waited—but no. Perhaps it never will. There is a condition, and a price."

"Go on." He waited.

"The miracle, if it comes, happens only once . . . and only for the sake of love. True love," she added.

"Nothing ordinary," he murmured. "The sort of love that is destined."

"So the legend says."

"Could you not help your family with this magic? You love them. Your brother could benefit." He watched her. "I do believe he is still alive, Sophie."

She nodded. "The gift will not work for family, as much as I love them. It depends on the sort of crystal one is given to wear when it is taken from the Duncrieff cup. Mine is the sort that brings true love," she said, touching it gently. "I always thought that this crystal was wasted on me. Kate makes better use of the power in the one she has."

"Oh," he said, "you use your power quite well. And you never know what life will bring."

She gazed at him for a moment. A feeling stirred in his heart, and words formed in his mind—beautiful, private words—but he did not speak them.

Feeling suddenly like a coward, and suddenly skeptical, he moved back and crossed his arms.

"So how do you use that wee crystal?" He waved a hand. "Can you fling it about and place James Stuart on the throne of Scotland? Or make this ruinous castle whole again, in the blink of an eye?"

"That would be wizardry, not fairy magic. Our fairy blood gives us a sort of natural magic," she explained. "Like healing power, or seeing the future, even creating beautiful music, art, poetry . . . charming others in some way that can seem normal but is actually quite extraordinary. A fairy touch as we go through our lives, if you can understand that."

"I can," he said, knowing the truth of it. "Go on."

"If true love is sought, and found, then that magic can create miracles. Or so it is said."

Looking at her, he could easily believe in fairy magic. Again he wanted desperately to express his heart—but that was followed by a strong urge to silence those thoughts. "Your fairy touch could create a real miracle in the Glendoon gardens," he said lightly, distracting himself from dangerous thoughts of true love.

Too fast, he told himself, too deep, too unexpected. He had not planned for this—he was not ready.

"I am doing my best," she said. "I wish I could use this gift to help my brother, and my clan. Then it would be truly useful. I wish I could wave some wand and get Kinnoull House back for you—and restore your family to you," she added softly.

He caught his breath, watching her.

She touched her pendant crystal again. "But the power of our Fairy's Gift does not always affect history, though it has in the past. Most of the time it is limited to . . . love. Simply finding love, and honoring the passions of the heart."

"Is that not enough?" he murmured, but caught himself before he could go further with that thought. Love—when had he ever given it so much thought?

"I think it could be," she said, watching him.

"So that is why you can make plants grow," he said as it became clear to him. "You have a passion for that work. You love gardening. So for you, that is the fairy's touch. It is wherever you put your love, I think."

Her eyes brightened. "Perhaps so." She smiled.

That beautiful, impish smile, just for him. His heart warmed. "Ah, but true love . . . that is a rare thing indeed," he murmured, feeling enchanted himself, standing with her in the twilight. He wanted to kiss her, wanted to say what rose from his heart to his lips, but he bit back the words.

"But it does exist," she said, turning away.

Skeptical as he was—fairies and spells and the bestowing of a miracle for love seemed beyond fanciful to him—Connor stopped. Something in her voice, in her luminous eyes, in the sincere lilt of her words, left him stunned.

Love. He had nothing to offer a bride, and should

not let himself fall in love. Now he knew that love had found him regardless, never asking him if the time was right.

"I would do anything to save my own true love, Connor MacPherson," she said quietly. "Anything. And I would not need a Fairy's Gift to help me act upon it. Good night, sir." She pushed past him, then turned. "I'll sleep alone tonight. I have much to think about."

He stood in silence as she left the garden and crossed the yard. The rising moonlight caught her, set a glow all about her. The petals of flowers that had not been there, even a day before, brushed at the hem of her gown.

Watching her, Connor felt as if his heart danced a little, and changed somehow.

"Sophie."

About to enter through the kitchen door, she turned to see Connor standing in the yard. "Aye?" she asked.

"Go get your cloak and come with me," he said.

"Where?" she asked, puzzled.

He whistled softly, and Sophie heard a gruff bark behind her as Tam, the brown spaniel, left his post by the warm kitchen hearth and pushed past her to trot toward Connor. A moment later Una and Scota followed out of the kitchen shadows to stand with Connor and Tam.

"Come with us," Connor said. "We'll wait while you fetch your cloak."

Tipping her head, curious, she walked out into the yard. "It's not so cold out here. I'll be fine." What could he want?

"As you wish." He took her hand and led her across the yard, around the massive tower keep, toward the front gate. Without comment, he lifted the bolt and shoved open the creaking gate, standing back in invitation.

She nearly laughed. "You want me to leave?"

"I want you to come with me on an adventure," he replied. His eyes seemed to twinkle. Again he whistled to the dogs, who leaped through the portal and ran out onto the meadow that fronted the castle. Connor ushered Sophie outside, and she stopped, looking up.

"I'm not going," she said stubbornly.

He looked down at her with a quizzical expression.

"I've had quite enough adventuring for a while," she explained. "If you mean to go chasing caterans or spying on soldiers, you will have to do that without me. I do not care to walk for miles over the hills in the dark."

"It's not so far this time. Just up there." He indicated the peaks of the hills that rose behind the castle.

"What's up there?" she asked.

"Stars overhead," he answered. "Mountain air, sweet winds. You need to get out, Sophie lass. I've kept you confined too long. It's beautiful up there—you will enjoy it."

"Well . . ." she said. "Well . . ." She stepped forward.

"But you must promise to stay with me."

She was beginning to think she would go with him anywhere. "What's this about?" she asked as she fell into step beside him. The three dogs scampered ahead, barking.

"I need to take the dogs into the hills tonight, and I'll be gone for a while. I thought you might like to come along." He glanced at her. "You like lambs, don't you?"

"Not to eat," she said.

He chuckled. "I'm taking the dogs out tonight to look for fox dens. It's lambing time for the hill sheep now, and we run the dogs out into the hills often at night, to frighten the foxes away from the new lambs and the flocks. Roderick and Padraig usually do this, but now and then I take a turn."

"Hunting foxes? Oh no," she said, slowing. "I do not want to see that." She glanced at him. "You did not bring your pistol."

He clapped a hand to his belt. "I have my dirk hidden here—I always have that. But there's no need for pistols tonight. There are only hill sheep and mountain goats—and foxes up here. And we're not hunting them. The dogs have a job to do."

"Killing foxes? No," she said, pulling back.

"You're a tender wee thing, Saint Sophie," he said, and his hand rested on her shoulder. "Do not worry. The dogs will just guard the flock, and put up such a commotion with their barking that no foxes will dare come near. They are good, loyal wee warriors, these dogs," he said. "The terriers are what we used to call earth dogs in the Highlands—they follow the trails of the foxes down into the dens if they must, to make certain the wee beasties will not come out to harm the lambs or any in the fold."

"The foxes have cubs at this time, too," she pointed out.

"Aye, they do, which is why they want to feed their little ones. And I want to protect my wee ones, too."

Her heart stirred unaccountably. "The lambs?"

He nodded. "At lambing time, the newborns are tiny, and make a tempting meal for foxes. We bring the dogs out regularly at night at this time of year. Foxes are smart—they learn to keep away. And if they do not, well—that task is up to the dogs."

"Oh," she said in dismay.

"It's just Nature at work, lass."

"I know," she said. The shadows were long now, and deep, as they climbed the slope through long heather that in sunlight would show greening tips. Somewhere nearby she heard the burble of a rushing burn, like music in the fading light. Looking up, she saw three deer silhouetted on a far hillcrest.

She drew her breath, taking in the sweet, peaceful air. Turning, she looked down into the glen far below, where a loch and the river reflected the sky and the moon, and behind the hills the last violet glow of the twilight faded.

"This is nothing like the last time we were out walking the hills together," she said, and gave a sigh of contentment.

Connor laughed softly and set his hand at her waist as they mounted the incline. The dogs caught a trail and ran off, barking. After a moment Connor left her side and followed the dogs, ascending the hill ahead of her.

His dark hair fluttered in the breeze, his shirtsleeves showed pale, and his dark plaid rippled as he walked. She admired the length of his stride, the strength and grace of it. And she found herself smiling a little, private, glad smile.

The sheep were scattered all along this hill and the next, milky blurs in the darkness, the adults stodgy and darker, their fuzzy-coated lambs small and sweet where they leaped about here and there. Sophie stood watching them for a while, laughing at their antics. Looking up, she saw Connor standing on the ridge of the hill, watching the dogs who had disappeared down the other side.

He was right, she thought. She needed to be out here on this beautiful night in the open, with the long bowl of the glen below, water shining like sheened steel, the hills dark and majestic. The sky was wide and beautiful, sparkling with stars above the lavender haze left by the setting sun.

She turned again, realizing that Connor had stepped out of sight. The dogs barked in the distance now, the sound muted and earnest.

He had given her a perfect chance to flee, she thought. She could easily run in any direction from here, and he might never see the path she took.

Yet she realized that ever since he disappeared over the hill, she had missed him. She felt strangely out of sorts without him near her now.

Resting against a large boulder on the hillside, she watched the sweet lambs and their truculent parents, and felt a sense of freedom such as she had never known before—for she made a choice in that moment for herself, perhaps the first in many years.

Chapter 23

Striding over the hilltop, Connor looked down and felt a sharp sense of relief to find Sophie still there, waiting. He had half expected her to be gone. The slight breeze ruffled her hair, blowing golden strands free. His heart beat hard, fast, with deep excitement as he descended the slope. Somewhere behind him the dogs barked, busy with their task.

Three rams watched the scene from up above, lined along the hillcrest like an honor guard. The rest of the sheep grazed here and there along the slope. Some of the ewes watched their lambs, and others stood patiently while their newborns nuzzled at them.

Connor felt his heart swell with feeling. As it swept him along in its course, he walked toward Sophie purposefully, passionately. When he reached her side, he took her hand and pulled her to her feet.

The night had a quiet beauty, never silent—the wind shushed and the burn bubbled; he heard the liquid trill of a curlew and the soft bleating of the lambs. But he was utterly silent as he drew Sophie toward him, bent and kissed her.

Pulling her hard against him, he gave in to the yearning that had grown so strong in him. He wanted to feel her body answer his, craved it hungrily, as he had craved the air of the high hills and the stars overhead tonight. Out here, away from the ruined castle he rented, away from the life he lived and the life he had lost, he was just a shepherd, a farmer. He was not a brigand or a rebel with something to prove, something to pursue. He was more purely himself here than anywhere.

And when he was with her, he felt more completely himself. He captured her mouth with his own, cupping her face with his hands. As she returned his kiss fervently, he slid an arm around her and pulled her to him at the waist.

Her arms looped around his neck and she pressed herself tightly against him, and he pressed back in some instinctual effort to express the fierceness of the demand he felt, though that only increased its force. He kissed her more avidly, exploring, compelled, seeking satisfaction, striving to give the same to her. She arched her hips against him now, opened her mouth beneath his, and he tasted the sweet, moist tip of her tongue, while his body throbbed and pulsed against her.

Keeping a hand at her waist, he eased the other hand down her back, her arm, let his fingertips tease along her upper breast, letting her know the direction of his desire. As he moved his fingertips, every fiber of his body responded to touching hers. She leaned back her head and accepted his kiss again, deeper this time, a slow massage of the lips, a sweeping of tongues, pressing bodies so close, yet not close enough, never close enough.

He felt no hesitation in her, only the heat of her own passion heightening his own. Sensing the rapid drumming of her heart, he felt his own heartbeat increase.

No words were uttered between them—there were no words for this, and none needed. She angled herself to allow his touch, to welcome it, and she soothed her own hands over him.

As he swept his hand over her breast, he felt her nipple tighten, even beneath the stiffness of her undergarments. He felt himself shudder and burn, and he had to have more, much more, if she would let him.

Dropping down with her to the heather-clad hillside, he felt the slide of her body along his own. He came to his knees with her and sank lower, falling gently to lie with her just where the grass was thick and greening, heather clumps surrounding them. Far off, sheep bleated, the dogs barked, the wind shushed past. He thought about none of it.

Lightning struck through his body as he pulled her against him where they lay on the cushion of the earth. Her palms flattened over him, sliding along his back and down, tucking under the plaid, her hands warm and soft and bold, and he sucked in a fast breath and angled away—not yet. Not yet.

The fervent need to feel her, taste her, plunge deeply into her and release his passion and her own now overwhelmed him. Desire felt like a living ember within him, and he was compelled to burn to its will. Her lips beneath his were urgent, needful, glorious and willing.

The dark cotton gown she wore closed simply at the front, and his fingers worked the buttons, while her fingers, too, pulled at the laces of her undergarments, so that soon—faster than he knew—fabric parted and her body emerged, pale and smooth and beautiful in the purple light. She lay beside him clad in chemise and stays, and soon those, too, came away.

Within moments he unpinned his plaid and unwound it to wrap both of them in its folds. He cradled her there against him, the kiss of skin to skin warm and miraculous. He closed his eyes, savoring, grateful—truly grateful—that she was here with him, and that they were not in the castle where he had kept her confined, or in the bed that had belonged to his family.

Out here, in the hills, they were truly alone, and truly themselves, and choices could be made, passions unleashed, that might never find expression in the ruined castle, with its broken dreams and trapped hopes.

His need to take her, to make her his own, was powerful now, irresistible, for she did not protest. She had shown him with silent kisses and caresses that she wanted this, too. She wanted this as much as he did, and his heart soared. He wanted to give her back a little of what she had given him, tender pleasure and unexpected delight—and something more that he still could not name.

And he wanted to say that he was sorry for so much—for causing the loss of her brother and the threat to her clan, for bringing her fear and pain and grief, when all he had wanted to do was protect her, keep her safe, and keep his word.

He touched his tongue to her lips and she opened for him there, and he yearned for her, with the cool wind upon him and the hard earth beneath him. He slipped his hands over her naked body freely, marveling, savoring the smooth sheen of her skin and the lush grace of her curves, the weight and feel of her breasts, so perfect for his hands. And he felt the longing within her like a match for his own.

He drew back, rested his brow against hers, his breathing as ragged as hers, and forced himself to speak, knowing there was something that must be said, though her heart beat fast beneath his hand and her hips surged against his and he knew the answer.

"If we are to ensure the sanctity of this marriage," he said, "and if we . . ." He paused, slid his hand beneath her breast, the softness there a fascinating distraction. ". . . if we are to secure your inheritance and the welfare of your clan—"

"Then we should go on," she whispered.

"If you like." He could scarcely think for the pulsing of his body and blood, for the drumming of his heart.

"Connor," she whispered, and it was all the permission he needed. He slid his hand to cup her breast, and she inhaled quickly and closed her eyes, leaning her head back, opening her throat to his kiss. And he knew that she was still able to trust him utterly—in this, at least.

Dipping his head, he traced his lips along her throat, drew downward and lightly teased her nipple with his tongue. She arched suddenly, gasping. Licking lightly, he slipped his hands down.

She was so delicate, so smooth, so small at the waist and taut and firm across the belly, and as he glided his touch over her skin, he felt the ridges of her rib cage, then up again to cage her breast in his fingers. Her nipple was tight and pliable as he encircled it with his fingers, found it again with his lips, and she pulled in her breath and pleaded against him with her hips. Her arms came up his back, down again to cup the mound of his buttocks, her fingers rucking under the enveloping plaid. Then they skimmed, cool and questing, over his thigh until she discovered him, touched him.

He caught his breath, felt himself fill further, harden, the feeling in his groin hot and heavy and insistent. Kissing her breast, he nuzzled, traced and teased and warmed his breath over one, then both. With one hand, she sank her fingers deeply into his hair, and he felt shivers all through him.

She let her knee slide inward, pressing against his groin, kneading, drawing out, a sort of pleading rhythm that her fingers echoed, sweeping over his taut member, stoking the fire in him until he could not think.

Then he slipped downward, tracing his mouth in a heated path along her flat abdomen, and he found her, clefted and warm, and so moist that when he eased his fingers into her, he closed his eyes and groaned against her. She moaned a breathy answer and arched, so that his fingertip slid easily over her delicate folds, circling, teasing, until he knew she burned with him.

Gasping, she trembled as he touched her, and her fingers clenched in his hair. He lifted his head and touched his lips to her breast, drew in the nipple, and felt her quiver in his hands now, opening, writhing, seeking.

He felt her heart race, sensed the strong rhythm of the passion within her, and she moved against him like a wave of the sea, and he knew she was ready, knew it from the slickness he felt, from the sweet arch of her back and the quickening of her breath.

And he could bear it no longer, holding back to let her soar first. Shifting, he set his weight upon his hands, palms flat upon the earth, upon the hills from which he so often drew strength. A fierce need swept through, threatening to overtake reason and being. He was starved for her, and yet he waited, paused above her, looked at her.

She was so beautiful, the loveliest creature he could ever imagine, and her passion enflamed his own. When she parted her legs and rocked toward him—her need as desperate now as his—when she wrapped her hand around the hard, ready length of him and guided him within her, she made the choice herself.

He had waited for that, though it nearly slayed him to do so, and he gazed down into her beautiful eyes, their clarity bright even in the dimness. He squeezed his eyes shut then, shifted, felt her move in perfect agreement. She slipped over him, gloved him within her moist heated sheath, and he felt the force inside him build, then flare through him like the release of lightning.

The power overtook him, and he lost all thought, thundering through that magnificent need, that joyful force of being. He grabbed her hard against him and felt her move with him, teasing even more power out of him in a crashing wave of passion. Her soft cries fell into rhythm with his own breathing, and the feeling pounded through him like a dark storm.

Then the force abated and peacefulness replaced it, sweeping in like sweet air after the thunder. He sank upon her, sheened with sweat, the plaid wrapped around them both like a cocoon. Her arms were about his waist, her head tucked against his shoulder, her kisses tender upon his lips, and he kissed her with the remaining hunger he had—and found it was not waning lust, but something different, enduring, cherishing.

He rolled with her in his arms, inside the plaid, and just held her. She held him, too, and he had never felt so good, so complete, wanting for nothing, wrapped in love. She belonged in his arms. She felt like home.

Closing his eyes, he tucked her against him, treasuring the silence and the peace that had been created between them. And he slept.

Connor awoke, shivering, to the bleating of a sheep and the insistent press of a nose. Raising his head, he realized that it was hours later, for dawn glowed pale behind the hilltops. Raising his head, he glanced around, taking care not to disturb Sophie, who lay with her head tucked on his outstretched arm.

Nearby, one of the ewes pushed at his foot as she grazed at the grasses, two lambs beside her. Connor propped his knee to allow her to reach the tender new grasses covered by the plaid.

The dogs lay asleep, curled together, Una's back warm against his leg. God, he was cold, he thought, shivering again.

Sophie slept close beside him, but he realized then that she had rolled in her sleep, taking much of the plaid with her. Naked, much of his back and shoulder exposed, Connor shuddered in the dawn chill and tugged at the plaid. Still sleeping, she did not relinquish it.

He smiled to himself and shifted, tucking her against him, the two of them like spoons, and eased the plaid around to cover both of them. As her body's heat restored warmth to him, and the dogs nestled closer and snuffled in their sleep, he heard the bubbling cry of a cuckoo far off.

He closed his eyes to sleep a little more, just a bit, for this moment was the greatest contentment he had ever known.

Chapter 24

"**O**ver a dozen eggs this morning when I checked the nests!" Mary told Sophie the next morning. "Ye willna think it odd—but believe me, lass, those three hens hardly lay an egg a day between them. I was thinking they'd make good soup if they didna start earning their keep."

"Eggs! That's wonderful," Sophie said, peering at the bowl. "What will you do with so many eggs?"

"*Och*, I have a bonny dish to put them in," Mary said. "Kinnoull loves it, but we never have the eggs for it. 'Tis an oatmeal pudding—oats and thick cream, a little salt, some sugar, cinnamon and spices, and several eggs. A thick and hardy baked pudding that cuts like a cake. He'll be that pleased to see it on the table."

Sophie smiled. She still felt the effects of her secret

adventure with Connor the night before, a little stiff from the chill and a bit sore from the loving, but she did not regret a moment of it. That sort of glorious ecstasy could never be regretted, no matter what might happen later. After what he had told her about her brother, she wanted to be alone—yet he was right to bring her out into the hills with him, where the sense of freedom, and the abandonment of loving, had been far more conforting than an evening alone with her thoughts and her grief and worry. She had needed his arms around her last night.

She needed him now, she thought wistfully.

"It sounds delicious," she told Mary. "But what about the cream? Connor says the cows do not give much milk."

"We have cream, too!" Mary beamed. "Fiona gave generously this morning. It's like a wee miracle here at Glendoon! And did ye see how bonny yer flowers are looking already? 'Tis a wonder." As she spoke, she went to the cupboard to fetch oats and sugar, salt and cinnamon, setting them on the table with the eggs. "So I hear you met our Fiona."

"I did. Kinnoull seems very fond of her," Sophie commented.

"He's very protective of her, too."

"Is he afraid she'll be stolen in retaliation for the cattle he has stolen from others?"

"No one would dare take from Glendoon's fold. He treats her well, she's nearer a pet than a milk cow. He's tried unsuccessfully to breed her, but she hasna fared well with it in the past. She should not be bred at all, I say, and Kinnoull agrees now. But now and then she goes over the wee wall to meet her bull in another field—it's not our own bull, but another she's enamored of."

"Isn't that good? You want more cows or bulls, I presume?"

"Any farmer wants more, and it's better to make them than steal them, aye," Mary said. "But Fiona loses her calves. It is a sad thing to see her labor so long and for naught, though Kinnoull does his best to save the dearlings each time. He takes it hard, the loss of the calf."

Sophie listened thoughtfully. "He raises them with care."

"Aye. He prefers to raise them, not steal them. He takes only from Kinnoull lands, and those livestock are his own. Oh, my oatcakes, they'll burn!" Mary whirled away to take the cakes from the oven using a wide wooden spatula. "I suppose you're accustomed to fine wheat bread," Mary said, "but we've precious little flour here. Oats are plentiful enough, and so we have a steady supply of them. At times, when other foodstuffs are low, we have the oats to see us through."

"I like oatcakes very much. Especially yours." Sophie took a folded towel from a stack of cloths on the table and covered the steaming oatcakes to keep them fresh.

"I think I have heard your castle ghost," Sophie mentioned as she worked. "I heard some music, quite sad and lovely. I've heard it either very late or near dawn." She glanced at Mary.

"*Och, that* ghost. Ye must ask Kinnoull about that one."

"Has he seen that ghost? He's never said."

"That one keeps the soldiers away. They willna climb the hill with the haunts making their eerie music about the place." Mary's eyes twinkled, and when she laughed, Sophie saw the twins' bright smiles there.

"So this really is a haunted castle."

"If it is, a wee oatmeal pudding will brighten our laird's home a bit. Crack the eggs in that bowl, dearie."

"I wish oatmeal pudding could fix his troubles," Sophie said, beginning her task.

"So do I. He has no fine life in this ruin, like he once had. Kinnoull keeps his family's things about him, but what he wants most is to have a true home again."

"He thinks Glendoon is no home at all."

"Aye." Mary sighed. "I know he does."

Later in the day, Sophie found Roderick, who was always somewhere close by in the castle or the yard. He would have guarded her every step if she had let him.

"Come with me," she said. "We have work to do. We'll need the shovel and rake."

"*Ach*, not again!" He pushed a hand through his hair. "I thought we were done with the kitchen garden."

"We are, for now. It's time to start clearing the big garden." She smiled. "And I will need your help."

"But that place is a mad tangle—it cannot be undone. The ivy alone would take a year to pull up and trim out."

"We'll do it faster. Though we must apologize to it first."

"Apologize?"

"Of course. It will thrive and grow just the way we want, if we treat it with respect."

"Mistress," Roderick said, "you have been wandering around this old place too long."

She laughed. "Bring a scythe, too, if you will."

"A scythe?" He blinked. "I am not cutting grass. Padraig does not mind that task, but I am not doing it."

"Then ask Padraig to come as well."

"Padraig is out in the fields."

"When he's done, then." As she spoke, she led him toward the garden. When she reached the low wall, she lifted her skirts and climbed over, while Roderick held out a hand to assist her.

"Oh, and we could use an axe and a sharp kitchen knife. There are branches and vines that need trimming."

"Mistress, this is a hopeless task."

"You helped me rescue the small garden," she reminded him. "And it is doing very well now. You are more of a gardener than you think." She gave him her brightest smile.

Roderick nodded truculently and walked off to fetch the tools. Sophie picked her way through the overgrown garden, pushing through a section where flowers had once been bedded and ivy now covered a curving flagstone walk. Making her way toward the apple trees at the back, she pushed through brambles that snagged at her clothing. On the other side of the apple trees, she was delighted to find blackberry and raspberry bushes, alongside a rowan tree that reached bare branches upward. Desperately in need of trimming and thinning, the bushes had already started to produce a little. Once they could breathe again and had space to grow, she was sure they would burst with berries by summer.

She wondered if she would be at Glendoon then, to see it.

Shoving through a thicket of lilacs, finding the flowers already fragrant and blooming, if thin and hidden from sight, she moved past, toward another part of the old garden.

Here, roses had once thrived. Climbing and shrub, vine roses and briar roses, they were bare yet, tracing in thorny arcs along the wall. The stems were long and leggy, so that the flowers would be few, if any. But with careful pruning and nurturing, Sophie thought she could bring them back.

Would she be here to see them flourish?

By the time she made her way back around to the low entrance wall, Roderick had arrived with the shovel, a rake, and a pickaxe. Though he complained a little, he waded into the chaos of the garden with her, and together they began to pull at the ivy and the weeds, and shred out delicate but stubborn runnels of strawberry plants. Cutting and trimming back, they created piles of debris that Roderick carted off in an old wheelbarrow.

Much later, Sophie stood up, rubbing her lower back. The garden beds were neater, parterres of soil and slate forming the hub of the old garden design, which had a circular layout. The strawberries and ivy vines had been tamed, the rosebushes and climbers trimmed, the walkways and benches exposed. Though there was much more to do, the beginning was promising.

That was reward enough for a long day's work, she thought. She looked forward to preparing beds and seeding them, and made plans in her head to create hotbeds to protect the seeds. She would start some seeds inside, too, in boxes set in sunny windows.

Glancing at the sky, she saw the sun sinking. She wiped at her cheek, realizing in dismay that her fingernails were grimy and her hair, coming loose from its braiding, was as much a tangle as any vines. She was dirty, aching, exhausted, and happy.

Truly happy, for the stresses had lifted from her for a while, and honest physical aches had replaced the elusive ones in her heart. Cutting, trimming, and putting the garden right again helped her to sort things in her mind and make them clear.

Looking around the garden, she imagined what it could be someday, with flowers spilling down the hill, fragrant and colorful, with a fountain burbling and birds chirping in the branches of blossoming fruit trees. Closing her eyes, she could see it, almost smell it.

And she realized then, without a doubt, that when the flowers bloomed in wild abandon and the berries hung fat on the vines, when the apples and pears grew sweet on the branches, she wanted to be here with Connor to see it all.

Chapter 25

"Saighdearean ruadh," Connor said—red soldiers—glancing at Neill and the others with them. "Get down!"

Connor and Neill stood with Andrew and his younger brother, Thomas, on a hill crest a hundred feet above the valley floor, their perch hidden by the steep incline. In quick reaction, the four men dropped to their knees and bellies in a deep, rough carpet of brownish heather.

Peering through the thicket, Connor swore. "The time has come to do something about their wee road," he said, gazing down through the twilight to watch Wade's latest effort.

The road itself was enough of a threat, he thought. But the bridge, swiftly being erected not a half mile from where the road crews now worked, was the greater hazard.

"If there is a way to stop this, then let us act on it," Andrew MacPherson said. He had met with Connor and Neill while crossing Glen Carran with his youngest brother, Thomas, a gangly lad with a wispy beard, a tendency to sullen silence, and an unerring aim with any weapon to hand. Connor noted with chagrin that the lad carried a firelock, imperfectly hidden.

Now, Connor leaned his chin on his folded hands, looking downward. Wade's road ran straight as a ruler through the pass into Kinnoull lands, where the men now crouched. The stone road ran over the moorland to follow the river toward Kinnoull House in the distance. The road met the riverbank in parts, while elsewhere it barely changed course even as the river curved.

More than a hundred men, mostly soldiers along with Highland men in need of paying work, were divided into several crews. Toiling at various sections of the road, they used axes and shovels, and moved earth and stones in wheelbarrows. They dug the foundation of the roadway and placed stones in successive layers, placing larger stones at the bottom of the cleared area, followed by a layer of smaller stones, and a final topping of gravel.

"The good general is quite the engineer," Connor observed. "And his approach is highly organized. But he's no architect with the design. He has a mathematical brain for making roadways. He sees the world in terms of geometry, lines and intersections, angles and perfect curves. The Highlands are not geometrical—

these mountains and glens are supremely organic in design, and every natural flow and turn of the land should be respected even by an engineer."

Neill and Thomas looked at him as if he was daft, while Andrew ignored him altogether.

"Aye, that road is straight," Neill allowed.

"Wade has no feel at all for the curves and hollows of the land," Andrew said, surprising Connor. "The earth and the hills are like a woman's body—follow those sweet curves and honor them, and you'll have pleasure and peace. Plow through them without regard and she will make your life hell."

Neill grunted agreement. Thomas gaped.

"Absolutely," Connor said. "Though the general is cutting military roads. If a straight line gets his troops from Fort William to Fort George, or from the Great Glen to Perthshire, he'll not waste time curving the track to fit the land."

"Whatever is in his way, stone, hillside, or bog," Neill said, "he blows it to hell and moves through it. Look at the wagon over there—it carries kegs of black powder."

"Either that or whiskey," Thomas observed.

"A little whiskey might do them good," Andrew mused. "If they were all drunk, we could sneak down there and take that black powder and blow their wee road to hell." He glanced at Connor. "We've done that before. Though it was at night, when we could not be seen, when there were no soldiers around in force. And in the Great Glen, there were trees to hide us."

"They'll be taking those kegs to the magazine at Wade's camp north of here," Neill said. "They're hitching the ox to it again, see. It is time to decide, I am thinking."

"Well, then," Connor said. "I think we should blow the wee bridge, not the road."

"The bridge? Aye!" Andrew nodded. "So that is why you sent me out to fetch Neill and meet you here on this hilltop."

"I could take that powder keg," Thomas said, drawing his pistol. "I could blow those red soldiers apart." He aimed the barrel.

Connor laid a hand on the boy's wrist before he could cock the gun. "Thomas MacPherson, I know your mother raised no fools."

"Exactly." Andrew slid the gun from his brother's grasp.

"I could get that black powder for you," Thomas insisted. "Let me go down and snatch it away. You could blow the bridge at night, when the red soldiers are gone."

Connor exchanged glances with Neill. "We could."

"But the lad will not be getting the powder by himself," Neill said.

"We should not wait long to do it," Thomas said.

"We'll wait long enough to borrow that powder in a safer way than walking down this hill in plain sight," Connor said.

"I am thinking, if we blow the foundation, they'll just rebuild it." Neill pointed to the bridge.

From his vantage point high on the hill, Connor could clearly see the structure, which did not yet span the river. Two abutments had been constructed, curving into piers. The skeleton was there, and the keystone would be set in place soon, he thought. But the paving of the bridge was not in place, and at this point, only wooden planks served for the workmen to move back and forth.

The watercourse narrowed at that place to a width of thirty feet or so, he knew. A single arch stone bridge would suffice. In peaceful times, he thought, a stone bridge would be useful, and in fact more than one bridge had gone up in that very spot—but flooding had taken them down again. Very likely, General Wade was unaware of that history. The bridge would go up quickly enough, but before it could be washed away, thousands of troops might cross it to further invade the Highlands.

"That's true," Connor agreed. "Destroying a bridge that is more complete would send them in search of a place to start over."

"And not so near Kinnoull." Neill grinned.

"That would be my hope," Connor said. "We will wait to blow it when the keystone is set in place."

"That will be soon, by the look if it," Andrew observed. "But how will you do it?"

"Late at night, by stealth," Thomas said. "I'll do it."

"You'll not," Andrew said. "We would have to plug the powder into the stones somehow—between the crevices. But how? Break the mortar and pack it in there?"

"It would not stay," Thomas said. "I know about gunpowder. You'll have to put it in something to pack it or it will trickle out."

Connor nodded. "He's right. Something to contain and concentrate it. Parchment would not work, nor leather. A cup might do."

"I am thinking," Neill said, "that the pewter tankards you have at Glendoon would be just the thing."

"My mother's set of German tankards?" Connor huffed. "They might."

"We'll dig into the mortar between the stones," Neill said. "We'll need chisels. Thomas, you can help, lad, if you can keep a cool head."

"I can," Thomas said.

"Fuses," Connor said. "We'll need those, too, do not forget—good string will do, but we'll have to wax it well, or it could get damp near the river. Long lengths. We want everyone to be away from this thing when it goes down."

"I'll ask Mary to help us with that," Neill said.

Looking around as they talked, Connor sighted three redcoats climbing another hill. One of them carried a surveying tool, another a tripod for the instrument. Setting it up quickly, they took turns peering through it, one of them jotting notes.

"What's that, small cannon?" Thomas whispered.

Neill shook his head. "They're measuring the lay of the land with their geometry and all."

"What will they use the black powder for?" Thomas asked. "It's all flat down there."

Connor pointed. "Look far ahead, past where they are setting up the bridge. A hill juts up where the river curves sharply. They'll blow through that to continue their road."

"Soldiers," Andrew growled, gesturing to the left, where another party of redcoats climbed an adjacent hill. They were fitted in full gear, Connor noted—red jackets, black tricorns, boots and gaitered shoes, and some carried muskets and bayonets. One man stopped, called to the others, and conferred. Another soldier pointed, the men turned, and muskets were shouldered.

Connor felt a cold chill. "We're seen—quick! Down the other side and away!" He shoved at Thomas, urging his young cousin down the back of the slope. Andrew tumbled after him, followed by Neill.

Sliding after them, rising to his feet to run, Connor followed the dip and rise of the rumpled hill, purposefully lagging behind his comrades. When he was sure they would be safe, he turned and made his way into a shadowed gap formed by the close, steep sides of twin hills. Keeping close to the rocky incline in the gathering darkness, he leaned there to watch.

Two soldiers worked at reloading the wagon that held black powder and other supplies, and hitched the ox into its harness. They would take it away for the night. The laborers were also preparing to leave, laying down their tools and stopping work due to the increasing twilight. Wanting to see where they might take the supply wagon, Connor stayed still, hidden in shadows.

Startled, he turned to see Thomas running toward him. Pausing in the gap, Thomas then launched ahead, toward the road in the glen, before Connor could stop him. Pounding down the hillside, Thomas rolled partway and slid behind a boulder.

Andrew came flying just behind him, and Connor grabbed him fiercely. "I'll see to this," he hissed, and went through the gap, streaming down the hill at a low crouch. As he neared Thomas, his young cousin looked around wildly, then careened down the hill again.

Connor swore as he glanced around to look for the red soldiers. Their attention was still focused on the other side of the hill, where the group that had sighted them still searched. None of the laborers or their supervising officers glanced directly above them to see the Highlanders there. Yet, Connor thought.

"Thomas," he hissed, his voice blending with the wind, lost in the noises of carts, stones being stacked, and men calling to one another. "Thomas!"

The boy ignored him, intent on his reckless mission, running and sliding farther down the hillside, using rocks and gorse to hide his progress. Connor followed, desperately wishing for a rope to loop over the lad to haul him back to sense and safety.

Somehow, within a few moments' time, Thomas made his way down to the level of the road. The darkness was descending rapidly, and the soldiers were busy packing up tools and equipment. Connor knew from experience that they never left anything out to use the next day, for it was too likely to be stolen or destroyed by Highlanders disapproving of English roads. And they customarily posted guards to discourage sabotage.

That had not kept Connor and his comrades from wreaking havoc where they could, upending stones, tipping wagons and carts into gorges. More than once they had acquired some of Wade's supply of gunpowder or black powder, using it judiciously to destroy whole sections of roadway. On one occasion they had blown apart the side of a hill already ravaged by the construction. Tons of earth had collapsed onto the newly built road, closing the pass.

"Thomas!" Connor called softly, crouched behind a rock just above the boy. "Come back!" He glanced over his shoulder then, to see Andrew making his way down the hill as well, silently and quickly. Connor motioned him to go back.

At the same time, heart pounding, Connor drew his own firelock pistol, its single shot primed and ready. He swore again, but prepared to aim to protect the lad.

With speed and stealth, Thomas came near the ox-drawn supply wagon and jumped on the rear axle. He snatched a keg from the cart, dropped back, turned. Then he ran up the hillside as if the dogs of hell were after him.

Soon enough they were. Soldiers spotted him, shouting out. A few of them began to run, but none drew near enough to catch Thomas as he pounded up the hill carrying the compact wooden keg.

One of the soldiers aimed his musket. Connor knew that if the shot missed the boy and caught the keg, his foolish young cousin would be blown to bits.

He stood tall, cocked his own firelock, and took aim. A shot cracked the air—not from his pistol—and the soldier fell.

Connor glanced back and saw Andrew with a smoking pistol. Thomas was still running uphill, reaching the highest part of the slope. Connor followed, breath tearing in his throat, heart pounding near out of his chest. He twisted to look behind him, his firelock ready to discharge.

More soldiers were running now, shouting upward. Another redcoat aimed a musket. Nearing Thomas now, Connor dove at an angle to protect the lad's retreating back.

The musket ball screamed free, and Connor felt the piercing sting of it in his side. The impact dropped him to one knee, but he regained his footing to run toward the tight gap between the hills where his cousins had disappeared.

Neill waited there, extending a strong hand to pull Connor into the shadows.

Chapter 26

"Ach, I've corrupted you, lass," Roderick said. "Connor will have my head for it. You're thoroughly ruined now."

Sophie laughed and tossed down her last hand of cards. "I believe I am."

"You're a natural for winning." Roderick shook his head in wonder. "You trounced me soundly three games in a row at Ombre, and before that, twice at Primero."

"Three times at Primero," she pointed out. "Why would Connor be upset with you?"

"I've spoiled his bonny innocent bride." Roderick grinned.

"I wonder if he would care," she said sourly. "He's hardly even here."

"He would care," the young man murmured.

"And it serves him right for not coming back for supper again. We were forced to amuse ourselves." He tilted an eyebrow.

Laughing, Sophie glanced over his shoulder toward the door of the great hall where they sat playing cards by candlelight. She had glanced there repeatedly all evening, waiting for Connor to appear. An uneasy feeling pecked at her. She could not shake the sense that he was not safe, that he might even have come to harm.

"I thought he would return by now," she said. "Do you think something has happened? Did he go to meet Neill, or Andrew?"

"He's fine," Roderick said. "Conn is always fine. He'll be here when he's here."

"Did he go raiding, or hunting perhaps?" But Roderick only shrugged evasively. She frowned. Perhaps her uneasy feeling was ungrounded and Connor had simply decided not to return to his bride, she thought.

Roderick shuffled the cards. "Have you truly never played cards before?"

"We were not permitted to use playing cards at the convent. My parents enjoyed games of cards, but they never taught their children—said it wasn't seemly until we were older. But I do love playing cards. Thank you for teaching me."

"*Ach*, what else could I do, I was told to guard you, and it's miserable standing in the rain making sure you do not go too near the front gate." He wiggled his eyebrows.

Sophie smiled, and swept a small pile of chipped stone pieces toward her. "I have a wealth of pebbles now. I wonder what I should do with them."

"Patch one of the drafty holes in this castle," Roderick suggested. Sophie laughed in delight, while he chuckled.

"I'll save them for our next lesson in social corruption and unseemliness," she said.

"Oh, the laird can teach you that far better than I can," Roderick replied with a wicked twinkle in his eyes. "But I'd be glad to play cards anytime. If I had any coin, you would have emptied my pockets. I'll be more careful next time. How did you manage to win so often?"

"Fairy blood," she replied lightly, without thinking.

Roderick lifted his eyebrows. "They do say the MacCarrans have true fairy blood in them. Is that why you have such winning luck? I can well believe there's some magic in you, mistress." He winked. "You look like a fairy queen. Delicate, like."

"Thank you." She touched her crystal necklace out of habit. "There is some fairy blood in my family, or so they say."

"Did you inherit the MacCarran magic? I've heard the stories, though I do not know much about it."

"I . . . may have a touch of it," she said.

"They say each MacCarran who inherits it has a certain sort of magical skill. What's yours? Card games, I'll wager, or gambling. I'll take you to London to make my fortune."

"Nothing so grand. Sometimes I can make things grow."

"Aye? Can you make me taller? Or better yet, for the sake of the lassies . . ." He grinned mischievously.

"Oh, stop!" She tried not to laugh. Roderick reminded her of her brother, she realized with a twist of sadness, even while she smiled. "No, it's flowers, plants, vegetables, that sort of thing." She shrugged. "Nature grows anyway, so it's not much of a magical skill. I tried to explain it to Kinnoull, and he did his best to understand."

"He is not much for fairies and ghosties and such."

"He's seen the ghost that's here."

"Has he?" Roderick looked puzzled. "Oh, that one, aye." He laughed. "So, tell me—is this why you like to go digging in the dirt, mistress? We've tried to tell you, little grows or flourishes at Glendoon." He shook his head.

"So I've heard. Why?"

"There is a barren curse on this place. Long ago, when one of the early lairds of Glendoon died, and his love with him, a terrible curse befell this old place. Nothing shall flourish here, they say, nothing at all, until . . ."

"Until what?" She took the shuffled cards he handed her and fanned through them.

He shrugged. "Until the magic returns. But no one knows what that means."

She glanced at him quickly.

"Connor says it is all nonsense, that nothing grows because the castle sits on solid rock, and we can expect only weeds and bleakness for our efforts."

Hearing the door open at the far end of the great hall, Sophie started and looked up. Immediately, foolishly, she hoped to see Connor. But he was not there, and Mary smiled at them.

"I've filled a tub for ye, mistress," Mrs. Murray said. Her face was flushed. " 'Tis not much, a wee hip bath, I thought ye might like it, having been working hard in the gardens all day. I have a bit of my good soap here, which I make with lavender and rose petals," she added proudly.

"Oh! Thank you, Mary." Sophie smiled. She glanced at her hands, which she had scrubbed in the kitchen, but she felt as if a film of garden mud still clung to her like a pall.

"Since ye were raised in this glen, I thought ye might have the Highland habit o' keeping clean, as we like to do, rather than the Frenchie habit o' living with yerself," Mary said.

"Ah . . . thank you," Sophie repeated, trying not to laugh.

"Ye can fetch clean linen and clothing from the wardrobe in the laird's bedchamber. The tub is down in the kitchen, where it's warmest for bathing," Mary went on as Sophie joined her.

"I'll be down directly. Roderick, thank you for the card lessons," Sophie said, looking at him over her shoulder.

He smiled and waved her out of the room. Sophie headed upstairs to collect clean linens and something fresh to wear. She did indeed have the Highland habit, as Mary called it, of preferring cleanliness. Her back ached mildly and her shoulders were stiff from the day's work, and the thought of a hot, fragrant bath was deliciously tempting.

He nearly had to fight Neill off at the front gate, with his concern and his offers of help. "I'm fine," Connor growled. "By the devil, Neill, leave me be."

Finally he convinced Neill that he could make it inside by himself. "It's nothing," he insisted, though he kept his hand pressed to the cloth-covered gash.

"Damn fool," Neill growled. "I saw a fair amount of blood."

"A wee scratch," Connor said.

Mary and Roderick came running toward the gate, as did the four dogs. While Connor patted Colla's head and the terriers and spaniel jumped about, Neill explained to his wife and son what had happened. Mary insisted on tending to Connor's wound, but he refused.

"I'm fine." He urged them all through the gate, urged them home, promising to go inside and to bed. "Go home. It's late. Sleep will heal this faster than bandages and possets and well-meaning Murrays."

"Let yer bride tend to ye," Mary said. Although she understood the Gaelic that the others spoke, she generally used her native Scots. "She's waiting for ye. Make sure to go in by the kitchen door."

"Ma—" Roderick began. Mary elbowed her son.

"There's bandages and healing salve in the kitchen cupboard," she went on. "And whiskey on the shelf as well. Yer bonny lady will take care of ye."

"Very well," Connor grumbled, though he did not plan to reveal his injury to his bride. He did not want to alarm her. And he did not want any anxious feminine fidgeting over his person. If she cared to do anything else to his person—well, he could find the strength for that. Perhaps by morning, he amended.

He shut the gate on the Murrays while they were still talking. Then he bolted it and turned. He felt relieved, but he hurt like hell.

God, how he hated attention, hated fussing over him. He always had, from infancy to manhood. In particular, he loathed having to admit that he needed help, that he was hurt or weak, that a damned Sassenach bullet had caught him.

The dogs wanted to fuss over him, too. They gathered around him, licking his hand, nudging at him as he walked. He realized that the wolfhound was offering his shoulder for support. Connor leaned on the old dog as much as he dared and tried not to trip on the terriers.

Clutching at his side and taking slow breaths, he crossed the yard in the darkness. God only knew how he had made it up that beastly hill outside the castle, but his bed was only a bit farther, up the turning steps. Or he might just sleep on the warm kitchen floor, he thought.

Reaching the back of the yard, he headed for the rectangle of light thrown by the kitchen door, staggering as he entered.

Low flames glowed in the hearth, and Connor saw that the room was empty. The wooden hip tub sat before the huge hearth, filled with steaming water. A floral smell wafted toward him.

Bless Mary for leaving him a full, hot bath, he thought, even a flowery one. Normally he bathed quickly in a cold loch or a river or washed at the burnside—like many Highlanders, he preferred cleanliness and did not consider it unhealthy. The tub was hauled out for cold winter nights, but Mary must have prepared one for his bride that day. She had been kind to leave it full for him afterward. It was just what he needed to soak away grime, blood, and exhaustion.

First he went to the cupboard for the bandages and salve, and poured a whiskey dram into a pewter tankard from the small keg that Mary kept on the shelf. Taking a fortifying sip, he carried the supplies to the tubside.

Testing the water, he found it not as hot as he liked, but Mary had left a bucket of steaming water by the hearth. He poured it in, wincing again as he lifted the bucket.

Then he stripped slowly, grimacing in pain as he bent over to remove his shoes and woolen stockings and as he eased out of his plaid and the bloodstained shirt. Standing nude in the firelight, he took away the cloth stuck to his wound to look at the gash. The pistol ball had nicked his side, grazing through skin and flesh, but had not embedded itself.

Stepping into the tub, he sank down into the heated water with a deep groan. The tub was not large, a washtub really, but he could submerge to his chest if he bent his legs, knees high. The warm water stung his wound at first, then blissfully soothed.

Sliding deeper, he closed his eyes.

She had forgotten her fairy crystal. Coming toward the kitchen, lantern in hand, Sophie remembered leaving the fine silver chain and pendant beside the tub when she had bathed not long ago. Now she hurried through the corridor, wearing a voluminous dressing gown of rose silk damask, long and full-sleeved, over a cotton shift. Her feet were bare, the old stones cool and hard beneath her soles. She had borrowed the garments from Connor's mother's trunk, having nothing clean to wear until Connor went to Duncrieff to fetch her belongings— or until she left Castle Glendoon altogether. And that, she knew, could well happen.

Entering the dim glow of the kitchen, she moved toward the tub, her gaze searching the floor for the glimmer of the necklace. Hearing a splash, she looked up to see a dark head and shoulders just beside her, and met Connor's gaze.

"Oh!" She stared for a moment, long enough to see that he sat naked in the wooden tub—her gaze caught the lean folds of his belly, the dark hair that arrowed downward. Water glistened on his broad, well-muscled shoulders and arms. His knees and thighs, partly visible, were well-shaped, too. Soaked to blackness, his hair curled and touched his shoulders.

"Ah, Mrs. MacPherson," he said, brow lifted. Cupping water in the palm of his hand, he dribbled it back into the water. "Come down to join me?"

"I've had my bath," she said a bit stiffly. She wanted to turn, spin away like a shocked girl, but she made herself stand there, returning the bold gaze he gave her.

"Your hair is wet. It looks like dark gold." He tilted his head. The compliment, his attention, was unexpected and touching, and the deep, warm tone of his voice resonated through her body.

She touched her hair without reply. Her heart pounded as she looked at him. He was a stunning vision, all raw power and rugged beauty. Suddenly realizing how intently she regarded him, she glanced away.

"I—I left my necklace. I came back to find it." She trained her gaze on the floor, then dropped to her knees to search for the silver chain. "I left it just here," she said, on her hands and knees. "But I do not see it."

Connor stretched his arm over the side of the tub,

fingers grazing the floor, to assist in the search. His hand brushed the hem of her gown, touched her bare foot. Even that slight, accidental grazing felt like fire to her. Then he rested his hand briefly on her back, almost a caress. His hand was warm through the silk damask before he lifted it away.

"Where are Mary and Roderick?" She glanced around.

"I sent them home."

"Ah." Her heartbeat doubled. They were alone, then. The awareness plunged through her body like lightning. Alone, and he was nude, and near, and she could not keep her gaze from him. In the deep golden light of the fire, he was all muscle, sinew, smooth gleam, with a sweep of dark hair over his chest, dark whiskers smudging his jaw. His face had a hard beauty, his cheekbones flushed and prominent, eyes bright, his lips gently curved. Remembering the tenderness and the power of his kisses, she caught her breath.

He opened his eyes and looked at her in silence. His eyes were very green in the firelight. She wondered at the thoughts there, what made his gaze burn so.

"You were gone a long while," she said. "I—was concerned. For some reason I had a strange feeling . . . that you might be hurt. But you are fine," she finished with relief.

"All in one piece," he murmured. He sank in the water, leaned his head back, and closed his eyes. She heard his sigh, heard a grind in it, a weariness.

"Is anything wrong?" she asked.

Eyes closed, he waved his fingers at her. "Tired."

Sophie looked to the floor again. Seeing a quick

sparkle on the slate, she found her necklace, then knelt back while she fastened the clasp. But her fingers trembled and the clasp was very small. She huffed impatiently.

"Turn around," Connor said, and reached out.

She obeyed, pivoting on her knees, bending her head down. She felt his fingers at the back of her neck, warm and featherlike as they closed the clasp. When that was done, his fingers cupped the back of her neck, rubbed there, soothed.

That simple caress felt like heaven. Sophie closed her eyes, let him touch her, easing the tension from her. Shivers cascaded through her. His fingers were warm and damp from the bath, and he smelled divine—clean and masculine. He slid his hand down to rub along the small bones of her neck and upper back, chasing away stiffness that she had not even known was there.

"Oh," she breathed.

"Nice?" he whispered.

"Aye," she murmured. Realizing where this could go, these tracing touches, she felt a frisson of nervousness. Would she give in to him so willingly again?

Oh yes, she would, and it scared her to know it. Her defiant inner craving now asked more than exciting adventures—she wanted more of his touch, so much more. She wanted to feel his hands upon her and his body within her. She wanted to discover the tender, noble-spirited man that she sensed inside him. The man hidden behind those closed lids, within those silences.

"Sophie." He took her forearm, his fingers warm and wet.

Caressed by that rough velvet voice, her name felt intimate, almost beloved. His simple touch compelled her to stop.

"Sophie," he repeated, and looked up at her. "I . . . need you."

Her heart leaped. "Aye?" she whispered.

Releasing her arm, he sat forward with a low groan. Then she saw the dark swirl in the water, saw the gash along his side, beneath his ribs. "Oh, Connor!"

"It's nothing. But just now, it hurts like hell." He glanced at her. "I meant to tend to it myself, but now that you are here . . . I could use your help. The bandages and salve are there."

She knelt. "Let me see it." She lifted his arm to look.

The gash was not deep, but ugly enough to make her wince. Uglier still in contrast to the hard perfection of his lean, muscled torso. The wound split his skin just beneath his ribs. Sophie rested her hand above the wound, his skin warm and slick with water.

The more she peered at it, the less frightening it became. Her silken sleeve trailed in the water. She did not care. Resting her hand on his shoulder, she loved the firm strength in his body, though her thoughts were focused elsewhere. "I knew . . . I felt you were hurt."

"And you were right, Mrs. MacPherson." He watched her.

"How did it happen?"

"Pistol," he said.

A thousand replies occurred to her then—questions, comments, reprimands. Some wise inner voice told her to be still. She only looked at him.

"Splendid lass," he murmured after a moment.

She moved closer, her hair falling over her shoulder. "Let me see again," she ordered.

He moved his arm, resting it on the edge of the tub, while she leaned over to peer at the wound in the low light. Her robe, loosely draped, sagged into the water, soaked through to her chemise.

"That gash needs stitching. I do not know if I can do that."

"Have you done much embroidery? No? Then I'd prefer you did not attempt any on me," he drawled. "It is a clean slice. The bullet grazed past, rather than going into me."

"So lucky." She lowered her head. "God and the angels have saved you for something." *For me.* The words came unbidden, unspoken.

"At least I wasn't punished for bedding a nun," he said. "Look here, my lass—the edges of the skin nearly meet. If this is tightly bandaged, and I behave myself for a day or two, it will knit on its own."

Her eyes sparkled. "Can you behave yourself, Connor MacPherson?"

Chapter 27

❦〜∞∞〜∞

"**N**ot sitting here like this with you," he murmured. Reaching out, he combed his fingers through her hair, sweeping the damp strands away from her brow. She closed her eyes, sighed, and he shifted his hand to cradle her face. Then her eyes opened.

"No, we should not. You need tending. You're bleeding. I'll get the bandages. And you'll need a fresh shirt—"

"Hush," he said, and drew her closer while he slid toward her. A feeling overcame him that he could not resist, however foolish it might be. He wanted her in his arms, had to touch her. "Hush, and come here."

He tilted his head, touched his nose to hers, slanted her chin so his lips met hers in a kiss that began gently, mouths easing together, and strengthened to a chain of kisses, each one hungrier than the last.

His mouth moved over hers, under hers, his fingers sank into the rich thickness of her hair, still damp. He kneaded his fingertips along her head and felt shivers run through him. She moaned, arched into him, nearly fell into the water.

He caught her under the arms and slid her over the side of the tub and into his lap. His muscles and the cut in his side protested, but the warmth of the water eased that. Water enveloped her as she came against him, sloshed over the sides of the tub. He cradled her across his body, her bottom nestled enticingly between his opened legs.

Sophie looped her arms around his neck and kissed him, and his hunger increased. He felt her mouth opening for him, and slipped his tongue inside. He had never known such urgent need, so strong that it tossed all reason aside, letting passion pour in to replace thought. He wanted this, here and now, though it made no sense, and he thought she wanted this, too—though that made little sense, either.

His hands slipped through the water, over wet silk, under soaked cotton, to find her skin and the incredible softness of her breast. She moaned again as his fingertips skimmed over the nipple, ruched for him. She felt exquisite, wet, delicate, wild. His lips moved on hers, his tongue gently probed. The water lapped around them, saturated her clothing, but she did not seem to notice, or care. To him, the tangle of fabric was only in the way, and he pushed at it.

A moment later he stripped the robe from her shoulders, pushed it over the side to slap to the floor. His hands skimmed down the wet chemise, dragged it over her thighs, her abdomen, to free her breasts. He slipped the saturated cloth over her head and flung it away.

The sensation of her bare breasts molding against his torso, her nipples like tender pearls against his chest, took his breath away. He rounded his hand over the delicate softness of her breast, and the throbbing that began between his legs was demanding. She arched, moaned against him, and already he could hardly bear the exquisite pressure building within.

All the while, she touched him as he touched her, tracing her soft hands over his shoulders. Dropping her hand below the surface of the water, she slid her fingers along his uninjured side to find the curve of his hip, the flat valley beneath her own hip. He felt himself fill and harden to push against her, and when her fingers found him, he nearly jumped.

With her mouth sweet against his own, she shifted in his lap, and his heart nearly bounded from his chest. He uttered a low, raspy groan.

Cold water would not have stopped her faster. She straightened, pulled away.

"Oh, dear, I am so sorry—oh dear God, I am sorry." She clambered out of the tub, water sloshing, her hip scraping over the edge. Naked, beautifully naked, she grabbed for the wet chemise, covering herself and kneeling beside him. "Please—forgive me."

"For what?" He leaned against the tub, one arm resting casually, the other cupping his side. He pressed away the pain there, but could do little for the other throbbing discomfort that his earnest bride had roused in him. He was fully aroused and cresting the water.

Gasping, Sophie tossed the chemise into the tub. Connor laughed. "Enough, I know," he said. He regarded her, smiled. "My God," he murmured, reaching out to touch her face, skim his hand to her shoulder, the top of her breast. "You are so fine to me, lass, like whiskey and cream and honey all at once. I cannot resist. I cannot get enough. I am the one who should apologize." He sat up, taking her hand, which rested on the tub rim. Bringing it to his lips, he kissed her knuckles, then turned her hand and traced his mouth over her palm. She shuddered, and he felt himself surge.

"I cannot get enough," he murmured. He stood then, in a rush, pulling her to her feet at the same time. She was magnificently shaped, curving here and full there, both lean and luscious. Stepping over the edge of the tub and onto the floor beside her, keeping hold of her hand, he pulled her to him, wrapped his arms around her, flattened his body to hers. He felt himself slip between her inner thighs, his core brushing against that soft, nested, feminine place. He stirred deep and quick, and felt himself beginning to melt, catch molten inside.

"Your wound . . ." she breathed. "It will open. . . ." She stepped back, pushed him away a little, tossed the chemise, so damnably cold and wet, against him where he supposed he needed some covering—and some relief.

She would make him wait, then. Well, one of them had some common sense, he thought, for he looked down and saw blood dripping down his side. He placed his palm over the wound, which he knew was not deep or serious, but was painful and bothersome—particularly now.

"Grab the linen, then, and we'll see to this," he said. But he pulled her tightly against him again, for his body was made to fit hers like no other he had ever sampled. She matched him in proportion, nestled perfectly. He throbbed like a drum.

Then she tilted her head just so, and he leaned down to touch his lips to hers, opening her mouth easily with the pressure of a single melting kiss. He did not know how much more of this he could bear.

"This is mad—what are we doing?" she whispered.

"If you do not know—"

"I know you need bandaging just now," she said primly.

"I need more than bandaging, woman," he growled, "now."

She stepped away. He loved her nudity, and she did not seem to mind that he watched her. The kitchen was warm, the fire casting its glow over her skin. His gaze moved over her as hungrily as his mouth, his body, yearned to do. She was graceful and beautiful, and the power and allure of the moment astonished him.

But she snatched up a linen sheet and wrapped it around her. She moved here and there, gathering the wad of bandaging cloth, the potted ointment, the tankard of whiskey. Connor stood waiting, still aching hard for her.

"Lift your arms and keep still," she said.

He did so, but let his gaze go decidedly wicked. She slid him a glance that was coy and lovely but did not abandon her task or toss away her towel, as he hoped she would.

She tore off a piece of the bandaging cloth to dab the wound. He winced. She handed him the tankard without a word, and he swallowed, glad of the distracting burn of the drink. She took the tankard from him and swallowed deep herself. Then she dabbed the cloth into the whiskey.

"Hey!" he protested, but she pressed the poultice to his wound swiftly. Connor hissed in a breath, turned his head, fought the wild sting of it.

Sophie dabbed ointment over the gash. He smelled of almond oil, basil, lavender. Taking the longest piece of the cloth, she wrapped his midsection, circling him until the bandage was a thick, snug band about him. She tied and tucked the ends.

"There," she said. Standing close to him, the linen sheet that wrapped around her draped him as well. She looked up at him. "And now you must behave yourself."

"Later," he said gruffly, and took her by the shoulders to kiss her, so that her head went back and her throat arched, her breasts rising against him. Scooping her to him, he dipped his head, traced kisses along her jaw, her throat, dipped farther. Easing the sheet away from her, he dropped it at their feet.

As he bent lower and took her nipple into his mouth, he felt her weakening, melting like butter, while he heightened like a flame. Pushing at him gently, firmly, she urged him toward the wooden bench beside the fire. She meant for him to sit and rest. He was not going to rest.

Leaning his back against the stone wall, which was warm from the fire, he drew her down with him. Coaxing her, he seated her on his lap, facing him, so that her beautiful, lean legs straddled him. He splayed his hands around her waist, traced his palms over her back, her creamy smooth skin, the delectable curves of her hips. She sat just high enough that he could kiss and tease her breasts, touching his tongue upon first one nipple and then the other, so that she arched and gasped, and pressed herself against him.

God, she felt good, soft and smooth, damp and warm. She smelled good, too, lavender soap and woman, and he felt himself urging hard against her, felt that fire within that stoked him so that he could scarcely think. She shifted so he teased at the hidden cleft, and she gasped again. He was silent, but his breath caught, his body burned.

But she was not ready yet, he knew, for what he knew would happen, his certainty that of heart and soul, and he knew she felt the same need. The course was set, and neither had resisted. He was more than ready, but she was not quite, and he swelled further at the thought of making her so.

Slipping his fingers downward, he found her, warm and slippery and delicate, and he eased his fingers inside, swirled and teased and pressed until she arched and cried out, bucking against him. Her hands clutched at his shoulders, her fingers dipped through his hair. He felt her knead his scalp, sending shivers all through him, crown to sole.

When she arched again, he captured a nipple in his mouth, tugged, swept his tongue, heard her sharply indrawn breath. She shuddered and moved against him, opening her legs, inviting him, pleading, slick and sweet as warmed honey.

And he eased himself between her legs then, placed his hands on her hips and glided upward. She pressed down over him, welcoming, enveloping, and he lost himself in her.

Lost himself utterly, felt passion sear through him like wildfire. He rocked with her, felt the force thundering, sweeping him along with it. He plunged, trembling and hot, deep into her, pulled back, moved deeper still.

She gasped, soft and willing, a glorious and breathy sound. Looping her arms around his neck, wrapping her legs around his waist, she arched and drove forward with him. Her breath came fast and sweet as her spirit shuddered through her.

As his crashing need poured through him, he felt passion explode, felt his own soul move into the depth of him, move with him in an ancient, magnificent rhythm. Stunned by the ecstasy he felt, he could have stayed with her, his love, forever.

And suddenly he was back where he began, on the bench with his shoulders to the stone wall and his beautiful wife in his arms, still gloved around him, warm and snug and pulsing. But he would never be the same again.

Leaning his head to hers, brow to brow, he sat with her, spent and silent. And he knew that he could not go back, could never go back, to the way he had been not so long ago. Nor did he want to return to that bitter, solitary existence.

He had moved on, and the pain had lessened, and she was the gentle, shining force that had nurtured and teased and loved him out of the shadows.

The quaver of the bow upon the string soothed him, released him. He felt the music rise up in him, flow through him. As he played, he blended with the music more than thought about it, created it more than played it. When the melody took him like this, it was as if the music had its own soul, expressing its joyful existence through his hands and his bow upon the fiddle. When he played like that, he felt washed clean, forgiven. The past faded, the present brightened, the future became possible—its path spun out before him like the music.

Eyes closed, he saw her face, saw her smile, laugh, weep. He felt the sense that often came to him when he played slow, plaintive airs and laments. He felt loved, and loving.

The music swayed through him, the tones resonating in his hands, his chest, and he played without thinking of the notes, his mind free. The music's poignant beauty was the sound of the wind, its rises and falls like the mountains and the glens.

He played, listening to the slow rise and sweet fall of the melody, the exquisite touch of grace notes, creating a poignancy that tugged at his heart. His thoughts turned to Sophie then, to the beautiful curves and planes of her body, the long smooth path of her thigh, the sweet arch of her back, the gentle swell of her breast, the hollow of her throat like a grace note upon the melody. He stroked with the bow as he would stroke her, and the lure of the music intensified, so that he was lost in it, and glad for that.

When the last note faded, Connor set the fiddle on its side, set the bow upon the upper edge, and turned.

She stood in the throat of the stairwell, her eyes wide. The wind feathered her hair, feathered his. She wore a chemise and the damask robe, rumpled from its soaking. She flattened her hand to her chest.

"So it's you," she said. "The ghost of Glendoon."

He nodded. While she came toward him, he

waited beside the parapet, wind filling the sleeves of his shirt, rippling his plaid, lifting his dark hair along his shoulders.

"That was beautiful," she said. "There is such heart in the melody when you play it."

He shrugged. "I come up here now and then to keep intruders away. That's all."

"Mary said that the ghost who haunts this place keeps the soldiers away from here. But your music is so lovely—it would lure visitors who would be curious to hear more."

"It sounds like a dreadful caterwauling from down the slopes, according to Neill and Andrew," he said wryly. "The sound of the falls masks it, makes it sound like a haunting."

"It is haunting. I could not keep away. It's not frightening from within the castle—just inexpressively beautiful. Each time I've heard it, I was drawn to come up here, but I did not dare to climb the steps all the way. It was the thought of meeting a ghost, not the ghostly music itself, that sent me running back to the bed."

He smiled. "So you found a little courage at last. But you always had it." He reached out to slip his hand along her cheek. She tilted her face into his palm for a moment. Turning away, he picked up the fiddle to put it away.

"Oh, please not yet," she said. "I want to hear more. Do you play reels and jigs, too, as well as airs? Do you play for ceilidhs?"

"I can and I have, but not for a long while. It's a solitary thing for me, this fiddling, I suppose." He set the violin in place, tipped his chin and lifted the bow. Then he paused, tapped his foot a bit as he waited for the tune to come to him. He chose a jig for her, one with a constant, joyful, simple rhythm. Sophie began to clap, swaying, smiling. He walked about a bit, stepping over the broken stones in the collapsed room, turning to look out through the collapsed wall at the pewter sky above the mountains just before dawn. When the song was done, he lowered his instrument and looked at her.

She was smiling, her arms wrapped around herself, the damask robe billowing in the breeze. "Where did you learn to play? In Paris, when you went to school there? Or did you have a music master at home?"

He shook his head. "I learned by ear, mostly, and from an older cousin, who learned from his father—the notorious James MacPherson, who was my great-uncle. Have you heard of him? No? Well, he was a fiddler with Gypsy blood in him, and famous for his misdeeds as a thief and a rogue. Have you ever heard 'MacPherson's Lament'?"

He played a little of it for her, the lilt and sadness in it that always touched him. He lowered the bow again. "Jamie MacPherson was caught for his rascal ways and sentenced to hang. Before his execution day he wrote that tune, and fiddled it for the crowd who came to watch him die. He moved them all to tears. Then he offered to give his fiddle to anyone brave enough to take it from him, and no one would. He broke it in half moments before the noose was set round his neck. The irony of it is, there was a pardon on its way for him. But he had an enemy in the sheriff, who saw the rider approaching and set the town clock ahead a few minutes, so that MacPherson was dead before his pardon arrived."

She gasped. "So you come from a long line of rascals."

"On one side of the family," he said. "The rest of them were rather dull." He winked at her, and she laughed. "My father had that sort of boldness in him, though he was a titled laird. I suppose I have some of it as well."

"I would say so!"

He began to play again, this time the melody he had written for her, only for her. She moved in a gentle dance, closing her eyes. He smiled to himself as he played, and the music made him feel loving and fulfilled, as music played from the heart could do.

Usually when he played, it was a solitary thing, but now Sophie was here to listen, to feel the music as he did. She brought brightness into his life, with her smiles and her temper, her penchant for honesty and her touch for growing things. His rented ruin felt more like a home now, as if Sophie had opened windows into his soul.

She was a balm for loneliness, bringing comfort and fire into his bed, and she had taken hold in his heart. He had not meant for it to happen, but it had, and there was no further resisting. All he had to do now was keep her.

He played, eyes closed, the music weaving into the fabric of his being. When he set the instrument down, he felt the chill wind of morning.

"Look." Sophie pointed toward the distant mountains. "You played the sun awake." Beyond the castle, over the mountains, dawn bloomed pale in the sky.

"Supper is ready," Mary said, hurrying into the large garden toward Sophie, "and Kinnoull and

Neill are nearly here, and likely hungry. Unless ye need me, mistress, I will go back to Balnaven with Neill. Or shall I stay to serve the food? Though I canna find all the pewter tankards—odd. And we canna use the pretty wineglasses that Connor's mother owned—ye've planted those in the gardens." Mary looked bewildered, gazing at a neat row of upended green glass goblets, their rims sunk into fresh earth.

"I'm using them for cloches," Sophie said. She stood, wiping her hands on the apron she wore while working in the garden. "They'll protect the seedlings and keep them warm until the weather improves. I hope you do not mind."

"Hinny, what's in this castle belongs to ye now," Mary said, "not me. Though I wonder what has become of the pewter tankards. Perhaps Kinnoull and the rest drank ale in them and left them somewhere. Well, I'll go then, if ye dinna need me further tonight."

"Thank you, Mary. And do go home, please." Sophie picked up her skirts to walk with her toward the garden gate. "I will see to everything here."

"Thank ye, mistress. I'll be back in a day or two. I've chores to see to at home."

"Come back when you like. I can manage the kitchen and the household on my own."

"Ye'll make this old place the home that the laird wants. He needs ye here, does Kinnoull."

Sophie caught her breath at that, felt a swirl of happiness. "Thank you." Just days ago she would not have thanked anyone for saying that the rogue needed her. Now she realized that she needed him as well.

"*Och*, aye. And Neill needs me more than he will admit. We've not been together much lately." Sophie saw the pretty flush in Mary's cheeks, the sparkle in her eyes.

After years of marriage, Mary still felt a love so strong and true that the return of her man brought fresh excitement. No matter how long or short the separation, no matter how many years they had been together, the Murrays' love for one another still burned bright.

Sophie wanted that feeling in her life, too. She knew love already budded within her, but she did not know if her hasty marriage could weather the turmoil of its beginnings to flow into years of happiness and contentment.

Fingering the crystal at her throat, she turned toward the kitchen door as Mary headed for the front gate. Then she stopped and turned again. Walking past the new sprouts in the kitchen garden, she walked round the edge of the tower.

Connor and Neill came through the gate, and Mary went to her husband. Connor looked up and stopped, watching Sophie as if he was as unsure of the moment as she was.

With trembling fingers Sophie tucked a stray lock of hair behind her ear and smoothed her skirts. Then she hurried toward him.

Chapter 28

❦❦❧

"**K**innoull, what do you think of the good news?" Padraig called as he came through the yard, tugging on Fiona's rope.

Connor, crossing the yard after supper, stopped to look around. "News?" He was concerned that Andrew and Neill had not yet returned from a mission that evening to watch what the soldiers were about and report back to him. Since the theft of the powder keg, he knew they must all keep a wary guard.

"The chickens," Padraig said, coming closer. "They are laying again. My mother collected over a dozen eggs, and made that fine oatmeal pudding for us. And I just found six more eggs."

"Mary mentioned that and I did think it odd," Connor said. "I wonder what set the chickens to laying again."

"And there are shoots coming up in the garden already where Mistress Sophie planted her seeds, have you seen?"

"Weeds," Connor said. "Grasses. It is April."

"No, beans and sweet peas, I'm sure of it, coming up already, and getting tall fast. And there are daffodils and buttercups sprouting in the front, more than I've ever seen. There are some little purple flowers, too. The yard is thick with them. Have you noticed?"

"I have," Connor murmured. "Perhaps it's all the rain we've had. And it is spring—plants are bound to grow." Nonetheless, he glanced over his shoulder toward the kitchen garden, where he had seen Sophie last.

"Maybe the old curse of Glendoon has lifted." Padraig grinned.

Connor frowned. "This old ruin has been a barren place for years, long before I came up here. My small crops of oats and barley have failed, most everything has failed. Last summer was a bleak season." He shrugged. "Much as I'd like to believe the curse is broken, I would not be so quick to say so just because we have a few flowers and some eggs. Take Fiona back to her stall, if you will. Have you persuaded her to give any milk at all?"

"That's the other strange thing. She filled the large bucket today, so Mother said."

"The entire bucket?" Connor raised his brows in surprise. "She's given scarcely more than a half bucket since her calf died. Bonny lass," he told Fiona, patting her wide rump as Padraig led her away.

Turning, he saw Andrew MacPherson and his brother Thomas running around the side of the keep at a fast trot, with Roderick loping past them to wave frantically to Connor. Noticing that the MacPhersons were out of breath and agitated, Connor ran toward them.

"What's happened?" he asked curtly.

"Campbell!" Andrew said breathlessly. "At the bridge! Red soldiers came there when we were setting the powder—"

"We were going to wait until later tonight," Connor said.

"It was my fault, Kinnoull," Thomas said. "I went ahead with it, and Andrew and Neill Murray came after me."

"He's already set the charges in the stone," Andrew said.

"It's done?" Connor demanded.

"Set, but not blown. The lad did a fine job," Andrew said, "and we helped him. But we were going to fetch you for the rest of it tonight. As we were leaving," he said, gasping for breath, "Campbell and three dragoons came by, with a prisoner between them. They were about to cross the new bridge—it is not finished yet, but good enough for crossing. The soldiers caught Neill and Thomas and took them down."

"Caught Thomas?" Connor asked, looking at the lad.

Thomas turned his face to show a purpling bruise. "Campbell let me go," he said, sounding humiliated, "and told me to bring a message to you."

Connor reached to brush his thumb over the boy's cheek, feeling a rising dark fury. "What message?" he growled.

"You are to meet him at the bridge now if you want

Neill to live," Thomas reported. "You are to bring your bride with you."

"Did he say what he wants?"

"He wants Mistress Sophie," Andrew said. "He is serious, Connor. I've never seen the wee man in such a rage. Cold anger. I would heed him."

Connor narrowed his eyes. "And if I do not?"

"He will be killing Neill Murray and the other prisoner."

"Who is that? One of the MacCarrans?"

"Duncrieff himself."

Stunned, Connor stared at him. "You saw him?"

"We both saw him," Thomas said. "Campbell has Neill and Duncrieff, too, and he wants your bride in exchange . . . for Neill. Not for her brother."

"I'll go with you," Roderick said.

"We will, too," Andrew added. "Conn—he says he has an arrest warrant for you, for stealing the MacCarran lass. And he is intent on arresting her MacCarran kinsmen for conspiring with you to take her. He says she is his rightfully betrothed fiancée."

"Campbell was cuckolded, and I feel for the man in that regard," Connor said, "but this goes far beyond that complaint. He has something else in mind."

"He has Duncrieff," Andrew pointed out. "He wants you as well, and he wants the lass. Which one of you can he control best, and which ones are disposable for his ends?"

"He wants Sophie." Connor nodded. "If he does away with us and marries her, he will control a Highland clan."

"And the fairy magic of Duncrieff," Sophie said.

Connor turned.

She stood a few feet behind him. She must have come around the corner while he and the others were talking. He forgot all else for a moment. She was pale, her hands clenched.

"I'm going with you," she said.

"No," he replied.

"My brother is alive." She twisted her fingers together. "I have to go to him."

"I'll bring him to you," Connor said.

"I want to see him now," she said stubbornly. "With you. And I want to know where he has been all this time."

"I expect we must ask Sir Henry about that," Connor drawled.

"Sir Henry has wanted something from the Mac-Carrans from the beginning," she said. "It was his suggestion, this match with me years ago, and my father relented, gave his promise in return for assistance—which he never got. If Campbell will go to these ends now to gain me and to gain some hold over the clan, he must want the Fairy Cup, and its magic."

Connor huffed. "Absurd. He wants something more than wishes and fantasies. He wants a political hold in Perthshire, and he can get that through marrying you—if your brother, and now your husband"—he inclined his head—"are eliminated first."

"And perhaps he thinks that if he can harness fairy magic, he will have even more power. He asked several questions about our legends the night we had dinner. He was very curious about it, and kept examining my crystal pendant."

"Perhaps he just liked being close to you, madam," Connor said. "Come, lads. We're going down there."

"I'm coming with you," Sophie insisted again.

"No," he said sharply, and took her arm to guide her back to the kitchen. He strode so fast that she shuffled to keep up with him. It reminded him of the night he had taken her, dragged her over the mountains, forced her to find her courage. Now he would have to ask even more of her, if he were taken, if this went badly for all of them.

"This is partly because of me," she insisted.

"It's also due to what I did. And I will solve it. You," he said, leading her through the doorway, "will wait here."

"Not while Sir Henry kills you and my brother!"

"My love, he will not have the chance. We will fix this."

"How? Highlanders are not even allowed to carry weapons!"

"That has not stopped us before. And when did you become a militant wee nun? Go inside, please."

"You are still healing from your injury. Let me go with you. I'll plead with Sir Henry myself."

He laughed harshly. "And what will you tell him?"

"That I never intended to marry him. That I wanted you to take me," she said simply.

"Aye?" he murmured. "Unfortunately you will not have the chance to tell him that. Stay here and out of sight."

"He wants me there, or he means to harm all of you." She looked up at him, her eyes clouding like a stormy sea.

"I'll be fine. And you will wait for me." He lifted her chin with a finger. "Will you?"

"Do you still intend to keep me shut away here, when there is no reason for it?" He sensed her anger mounting.

"If you prefer to be with Sir Henry Campbell," he said in a bitter tone, "I can take you to him later. Not now." He let his voice go cold, while his heart pounded.

"Since you intended to marry my sister, not me, why should you care what I do?"

His heart gave an odd flip. She was all he wanted, and he had not yet told her. The feeling burned in him, though he fisted his hands. "I'll go, and you'll stay, and that is that."

"Do not risk your life for me. I have to help my brother—my clan. Connor, please understand," she added in a whisper.

He took her hands. God, she felt so good to touch—so good and comforting—and though there was no time for even a thought of it, he desired her. Her fingers gripped his.

"I want you to stay here," he said firmly. "We have much to do, the lads and I."

"I heard. What bridge?" she said, still persistent.

"The bridge to my heart," he said. "I think it has been breached."

"Connor, I must come with you," she whispered.

"No, love." He bent his head to kiss her. He thought she might refuse, but she inclined her head in complement to his, her mouth gentling beneath his own. He forgot all else—the urgency, the pistol pressing into his side, the lads waiting by the door.

All the while his heart slammed hard in the cage of his ribs, and something deep inside him opened that he once thought would always be closed.

"Padraig will stay here with you. Keep inside the castle," he added. "Do not come out for any reason, do you hear?"

"I cannot promise anything."

"Did you learn no obedience in that nunnery?"

"I need not obey you in this or any matter, but what I feel is right."

"I never expected obedience—just common sense. Your brother wants you in my keeping, and we all want you safe. All will be well. I promise."

She looked at him, her eyes limpid, beautiful. "And you always keep your word, Kinnoull."

"By God," he said. "I do."

He turned and went through the door, where the others waited in the kitchen garden, with its pale green sprouts and flowering buds out of nowhere.

Connor and the others moved quickly, their legs accustomed to Highland miles. The healing wound in his side still smarted, but the snug bandaging helped as he moved. And he would not have cared about serious pain had it been there.

As they descended the slope that led away from Glendoon, Connor kept scanning the hills. The skies dimmed toward twilight, and he saw no red soldiers anywhere. Andrew, Thomas, and Roderick ran along with him.

He motioned them along a high drover's track, rarely used now, that followed the tops of the hills without dipping into the glen to follow the river. This way was shortest to Kinnoull, and they ran at a steady pace. Up here there would be no question of horses or carts. Only strong legs and strong hearts could take them where they needed to go.

Far off, he saw a few red soldiers, easily visible in scarlet and white as they moved through the glen on some mission. Connor knew where he was going and did not stop, nor did his three companions. Soon they reached the pass between the hills and ran along the high shoulder of a hill above the river's winding course until they were in Kinnoull territory. The river was in spate, brimming with spring rains and melting snows from the mountains, and flowed fast and full between its banks. In the hills above, Connor and the other Highlanders ran fast and hard along their course as well.

Through the gathering darkness, now, he could see the bridge spanning the river. No one was near it, but men were on the gentle slope that led from the riverbank between the bridge and the house.

Kinnoull House, glowing pristine in rosy sandstone, sat proud and high on its green lawns against a backdrop of dark pines, set among lush gardens like a jewel. And he had no time to look there, no time to yearn for what was lost.

Neill sat upon the hill, his hands bound behind him. Three guards with muskets stood about, and Connor saw Campbell, too, in gray, so that he looked like a man turned to stone.

At his feet sat another captive in ropes, tall and lean, fair-haired and handsome. *Duncrieff.*

Connor ran ahead, motioning the others onward.

Sophie lost repeatedly at cards that evening, disappointing Padraig, whose twin had told him tales of her gambling magic. Pleading headache, she retired early to climb the stairs to her bedchamber.

Every fiber of her being felt alert to some danger she could not name.

She stopped in the dark stairwell, her lantern casting bright patterns. Her brother was alive, thank God, and she had to see him. She could not wait.

And she realized that she had to be with Connor, together with him, and her brother and the others, in this. Danger or none, whether he lived or died, whether she stayed here or left entirely, she would never be the same again.

He was the most exciting, dangerous, beautiful man she had ever known, could ever imagine. She could not easily walk away from the spell he had cast over her.

Nor could she stay here while men were in danger for her sake, and while Connor placed himself at risk for her, her kin, and his friends.

Touching the crystal pendant, she sensed its quiet power. The magic of the stone, and the fairy blood within her, seemed to call to her in a way she had never felt before. Holding it, she felt filled with a longing for love, for Connor, and a sense of incompleteness without him.

In that moment she made up her mind.

Connor had given her his word, but she had made no promise to him. If anything went awry for them tonight, only she could right it. Only she had a hope of convincing Sir Henry Campbell that it was pointless to covet her or any hold over Clan Carran—if that was possible. She had to try.

Hastening to the bedchamber, she raced to the wooden chest beneath the window. Setting the lantern down, she opened the chest and rifled carefully through its contents—folded garments of all sorts, she noted, an array of colors and fabrics, undergarments, gowns, kerchiefs, stockings, shoes, cloaks, shawls. There was no time to examine them all.

She had already borrowed an everyday gown of dark blue, which fit her well enough, if a bit long in the hem and wide at the waist. What she needed were the sturdy shoes she had worn earlier to replace her tattered heeled slippers. She found them and grabbed, too, a dark shawl in soft, lightweight tartan wool.

When she dragged the shawl from the chest it came in a lump, and she discovered that it had been wrapped around a small wooden box, latched in brass, which fell to the floor. The latches broke loose and papers and jewels—necklaces, earrings—scattered over the rug.

"Oh!" she muttered as she gathered the items and crammed them into the box again. A phrase on one page caught her eye. *Connor MacPherson*, it said, and *Lord Kinnoull*.

Perhaps it was Connor's box, then, and not his mother's. Hastily adding the pages to the box and latching it shut, she set it aside. Throwing the tartan shawl over her head and shoulders, she went to the door.

Tiptoeing down the stairs, Sophie passed the great hall, where she heard Padraig talking softly to the dogs, who were so familiar with her step that none of them barked, though they no doubt heard her. She made her way carefully to the kitchen door and slipped outside into the gathering darkness.

Crossing the bailey, she realized that the gate would make noise, so she turned and hurried through the back, searching the wall for Fiona's escape route.

Passing the byre, she heard the cows lowing and a chicken make a nervous chuckling sound. Ahead she saw the patch of wooden planks set in the broken stone wall. She could not break through the repaired planks as Fiona might, but she could scramble up and over to the other side.

Perched on the wall ready to swing her feet over, she heard the dogs barking. Turning her head, she saw Tam and one of the terriers scurrying toward her.

"Shoo," she hissed, lying on the upper rim of the wall. "Off with you, now!" She rested precariously on the top of the wall, one leg and skirts dangling over the edge as Tam barked at her. Then Una, or was it Scota, leaped so high on her hind legs that Sophie feared the little dog would flip backward in her excitement.

"Go away," she pleaded. *"Truis!"*

"There you are, mistress," Padraig said. He strolled toward her while Sophie looked around to see him. "I was warned you might try something like this."

"Padraig! You must let me go. Please!"

"Kinnoull would have my head if I did."

"He does not care what I do."

"Of course he does. He made me promise to watch over you, and I must keep my word."

"Padraig, I must be sure that my brother is safe."

"Do you not trust Kinnoull to see to that?"

"It is Sir Henry I do not trust."

"Well," Padraig said, "neither do I. And I did not want to be left here while they all went off without me. I'll come with you, then." He began to scale the wall.

"Bless you, Padraig Murray." She smiled as he joined her at the top. In return, his beautiful grin was dazzling in the twilight. Then he swung himself to the ground on the other side and held up his arms to her.

"Mistress, promise me that you will not get yourself into any trouble tonight."

"I'll try not to get you into trouble, either," she said, and dropped over the edge. Padraig caught her by the waist and lowered her to the ground.

"I know which way the lads went. Hurry, mistress." He took her arm.

"It's Sophie," she said, rushing along beside him.

Chapter 29

"**W**e cannot just walk down there and tell them to give us back the lads," Andrew observed. Thomas grunted agreement.

Connor propped up on his elbows on the hill overlooking the scene. Campbell, in gray, and his red soldiers paced the hillside. "They are waiting for me, and for Sophie. But we'll let them wait a bit longer." He turned to Thomas. "The gunpowder is already plugged into the bridge—where did you put it?"

"It's packed into three pewter tankards," Thomas said. "We dug them into the underside of the stone bases, there, on the banks, two on the side of the river nearest the red soldiers, see, and one on the other side."

"Did you embed the fuses?" Connor asked.

Thomas nodded.

"What are you thinking, Kinnoull?" Andrew asked. "You cannot blow the bridge with the men so close—it's too much of a risk for Duncrieff and Neill."

"We cannot walk out and grab them," Connor explained. "And I have no intention of walking in the open to meet Campbell. We must catch their attention first."

"Ah," Roderick said. "Once we are ready to snatch the lads, we light the fuses."

"Exactly," Connor said. "Listen now. We'll go along to the bridge below the riverbank, where we won't be seen. Andrew and Roderick, can you run in the direction of the house?"

"Aye. That will lead them away from the prisoners," Andrew said.

"What about me?" Thomas asked.

"You'll be with me under the bridge. Do you have your firearm? Aye. Few men are as keen with that as you, Thomas, and you'll have your chance to prove it."

Thomas nodded. "I know where the fuses are, too."

"Aye so." Connor rose to his knees, watching the group of men on the hillside, and watching, as well, the sky above. It was dark enough now that they would not be seen easily if they kept close to the riverbank.

Drawing a deep breath, Connor knew he was placing all of his loyal friends at risk, but he also knew that they would have it no other way. And he was deeply glad that Sophie had stayed at Glendoon, where Padraig would keep watch over her.

The time had come, and they had to act. "Lads," he murmured.

One by one they rose to a crouch and moved like

wraiths down the side of the hill toward the river-bank, dropping swiftly over the side.

"Get down!" Padraig pulled Sophie back behind a cluster of large rocks. She fell to her knees beside him, stumbling on the hem of the overlong dress.

If she leaned just so, away from the rock, she could see the house, the river, the stone bridge that arched over the water. A group of men stood on a hillside, with two seated on the grass.

And she could see Connor and the others running forward, crouching low, then dropping to their knees and bellies in the heather. She could only pray that the soldiers had not seen them.

"Campbell cannot go through with this," Padraig said. "If he does, he will have more trouble than he could imagine. He has to prove that Connor has done some crime. Connor is Lord Kinnoull, and he is known to the military."

"He was in the Am Freiceadan Dubh," she said. "He told me."

"Aye, as a former Black Watch captain. The military will treat him with respect—or so we can hope. Campbell cannot eliminate him so easily—or Duncrieff, either."

Inching to the left, Sophie glimpsed Sir Henry and another guard walking up the hill and out of sight, leaving the seated men still guarded.

As they shifted positions, she saw Robert.

She knew the set of his shoulders, the ash blond hair. She caught her breath, and tears started in her eyes. He was alive, and seemed strong enough to sit upright, though his hands were bound.

She watched in silence for several minutes, until

she leaned so far that Padraig yanked her back. "I should never have let you come out here," he said.

"Well, you could not stop me, then or now," she hissed.

"Perhaps I could, then," a voice said politely behind her.

Sophie whirled. Padraig leaped to his feet beside her, only to be knocked to the ground by the heavy thunk of a pistol butt.

"So nice to see you again, Miss MacCarran," Sir Henry said, stepping aside as Padraig slipped to the ground.

"Oh!" she cried, falling to her knees. At a growl from Campbell, the red-coated soldier grabbed her by the arms and pulled her to her feet, holding her firmly in place while she writhed.

"Miss MacCarran," Sir Henry said. "Finally we find you! It is so good to know you are safe at last."

"Am I?" she asked coldly. She wrenched back, dodging his outstretched hand. He stepped closer and extended his hand again, taking her chin in his fingers, turning her face back and forth as she was held in the unyielding grip of the burly redcoat.

"So lovely," he murmured. "There's fairy blood in you, and no doubt. Delicate features, that hair like spun gold—and those eyes, such a remarkable color."

She squeezed her eyes shut so he could not look into them, for his were hard and flat, of indeterminate gray or brown. His mild features had gone cruel.

Before she had ever met Sir Henry, she felt repulsed by him because of the way he had manipulated her kind father in his time of need, when he had to beg favors from friends in his exile. And then when she met him, over a candlelight dinner, he seemed pleasant enough, if overly eager to be near her, touch her, stake a claim upon her.

In fact, Sir Henry Campbell was very nearly a stranger to her, and yet he had created deep turbulence in her life.

She opened her eyes. He was smiling, his lower teeth jagged and yellowed. "What do you want of me?" she asked. "Let us all go—you have no reason to keep any of us." She looked frantically at Padraig, who lay on the ground, still and handsome and looking so young and vulnerable. Blood ran down his cheek from a cut on his head.

"I want my promise fulfilled, that is all," Sir Henry said. "We were to marry."

"I never wanted to marry you," she replied. "And that is my choice in the matter. There. It is over. You have no need to do anything more to any of my family, or my friends, or my—"

"Your husband? Or so he claims to be. Come along." He motioned to the soldier, who urged her to walk between him and Campbell. Sophie glanced back to see Padraig stir groggily, but the men led her around the back of the hill, so that she could not stop to help him. And she knew that if Connor looked in that direction, he would not be able to see her in Campbell's company.

"Connor MacPherson is my husband," she agreed. "And that was my choice, too. No one forced me to say my vows." Well, that was true in part.

"He stole you away like the thief he is."

"I am glad to be his wife," she replied firmly. "I love him." When she said that aloud, it felt good—so right. "I love him," she repeated. "There is no crime here. Leave us be, Sir Henry. The only wrongdoing is on your part."

"I am owed my rights," he said. He stopped, took her arm, pulled her to him, growled something to the soldier, who stepped back.

Campbell bent his head and placed his mouth on hers, cold lips, thin and moist. Sophie twisted, turned her head, tried to scream. He clapped his hand over her mouth—he smelled of tobacco and foulness—and dragged her against him. He was not a tall man, but wiry and strong, and she could not break free.

"I said," he intoned in her ear, "I want my rights, and I will have them."

She breathed hard, breasts heaving in the dark cotton dress, her stays snug against her ribs where he held her against him.

Campbell released his hand from her mouth, dragged her head around to look at him. "And you will please me in this, or you will see your brother die today, and your husband hang for his crimes."

She shoved, stomping on his foot with the heel of her shoe. He staggered back but did not let go. She whirled to look at the red soldier behind her, and saw that he was very young.

"Will you not help? Will you watch this, knowing that it is wrong?" she demanded.

The soldier stared at her, and his eyes shifted uncertainly toward Campbell.

"Go on," Campbell barked. "Guard the prisoners. It is your duty. I'll take care of my fiancée—she ran from me in a fright about marriage, but I will treat her kindly," he said, pulling her against him again.

"So kindly. Go!" he snapped. "You are here, soldier, to guard the prisoners in the magistrate's keeping. Do it."

The young soldier hesitated, glancing at Sophie. Then he turned and ran off, disappearing over the hillside.

Campbell turned her in his arms and kissed her, his fingers tight on her jaw. Sophie shoved at him, wrenched away only to be pulled back. She bit his lip and he let her go abruptly, swearing, though he kept one hand clawlike on her arm.

"I only mean to please you," he said raggedly. "You had no cause to run from me. I intend to help your clan. They are risking all by their Jacobite sympathies. I can restore the reputation of Clan Carran, in return for—"

"For what?" she asked breathlessly, heart pounding. "You think to murder my brother and marry me, to be husband to the clan chief? Did you think I would do your will because I had been in a convent?"

"I am sure you know how to obey," he said, and twisted her arm behind her, walking her forward. "I am sure we can come to a reconciliation. Your brother and your groom will have to pay for their crimes, of course, but the rest of your clan need not pay a price for rebellion," he snarled.

"The rest—" She stopped, turned to look at him over her shoulder.

"I can ruin all of them unless you consent to be mine," he said. "All of them, Sophie, for they are as bad a pack of rebels as has ever walked Highland ground. I will have your kinsmen arrested, their homes burned. I will have Duncrieff Castle forfeited to me. I will make certain," he growled, "that your sister is arrested. Do you know what happens to women in prison? No? I am certain that you can guess . . . now that you have been in MacPherson's bed."

"My sister—" Oh God. Not just Rob and Connor, but all of them, Kate and her cousins, all of Clan Carran would suffer if she did not do this man's bidding.

"Why—Why do you want this?" she gasped as he marched her forward.

"There is no clan in the Highlands like the Mac-Carrans," he said. "There is power in their blood, and they say there is fairy gold in that castle. Untold wealth, a king's ransom."

"That is just a legend," she said. "There is one cup. One gold cup. Would you wreak all this damage for one old goblet?"

"If it held the key to the wealth of an ancient realm, I would," he said.

"You're mad. Will you risk your eternal soul for power over one small clan?"

"If it led me to paradise on earth," he said, "I might."

He dragged her forward, over the peak of the low hill, so that she saw Kinnoull House, majestic against the trees to her right, and the river flowing calmly at the base of the hill, crossed by the nearly finished bridge.

Connor and the others were nowhere in sight; Sophie glanced about wildly, hoping to glimpse them again.

She saw her brother then, and cried out. He turned, his golden head, darker than her own, glinting in the sunlight.

* * *

Connor and Thomas slipped along the riverbank, keeping just above the level of the water, and Roderick and Andrew followed. The river was high, but it was not overflowing its banks, and there was room enough to move along, though the way was damp and mucky. Darkness hid them. All seemed in their favor, and Connor sent up a few silent, desperate prayers as he went—not for himself but for the others involved.

Reaching the underside of the bridge, he relied on Thomas to show him the tankards filled with black powder, crammed into crevices in mortar and rock. He saw the fuses, tucked along the rough edges of the stones so they would not dangle. They were long and coated with wax, he saw, and would take several minutes to burn away, until the black powder was reached and the coal within it set off an explosion, shattering the bridge to Kinnoull.

Once the strings were lit, there would be just enough time, and no more, for him to do what he must.

He had taken chances before, faced danger many times. And he had used explosives before, breaking apart sections of roadways, irritating Sassenach troops and making their progress difficult. But he had never taken a risk of this magnitude. This time it seemed worth the price of his life, if it came to that.

The irony struck him then, as he waited in the shadows of the bridge. He had finally opened his heart and found love—and now he was willing to give up his life to protect that love.

He huddled with the cold water lapping at his feet. Moments later, craning his head out just enough, he looked toward the slope and could see Neill and Duncrieff and the two redcoats guarding them.

Duncrieff looked well enough, though pale and gaunt, his hair long and his jaw covered in unshaven scruff. His plaid and shirt were filthy, and Connor wondered where he had been kept all this time. He suspected that Campbell could answer that.

Where the devil had Campbell gone? he thought then. The magistrate had disappeared from sight.

Neill appeared to be unharmed, though his hands were tied behind him and his feet were roped together. If the Highlander could have gotten away, he would have outrun them all, Connor knew.

But Neill's son could do the same. Connor turned and motioned to Roderick and to Andrew.

"Go," he whispered. "Run toward Kinnoull House, and past it to the trees on the hill—you'll find shelter there. The guards will see you and chase after you—and that is the idea, my friends—but keep to the riverbank until you have put enough distance between you and them that their shots will not find you. I've a flint here," he said, patting his sporran, "and I'll light the fuses when you are a certain distance away. Aye?"

"Aye," the two men murmured in tandem.

"God go with," Connor murmured, and Thomas, beside him, repeated it in farewell. At Connor's signal, Thomas raised his pistol to guard them.

Connor watched as Andrew and Roderick crouched along below the line of the riverbank and ran. After a moments they swarmed up to the level of the moor and began to run, their steps pounding the turf.

One of the guards noticed, and called the alarm. Campbell, who Connor could not see from his vantage point, shouted out an order. Two red soldiers went off in pursuit, shouting to the Highlanders to halt.

Duncrieff and Neill came to their feet then, exchanging glances, as the two redcoats raced away. A shot was fired, and Connor looked toward the runners, relieved to see both of them still on their feet.

Grabbing the end of the longest fuse, Connor took the flint from his sporran, flicked it a few times until he got a spark, then lit the wick. It sizzled, smoked, and began to burn.

He gestured for Thomas to follow as he made his way along the riverbank. Waiting while Andrew and Roderick slipped out of sight, and waiting for the fuse to burn closer to the black powder, Connor readied himself to run toward the men on the slope.

Turning, he saw Sophie on the hillside then, with Campbell. They were moving toward Duncrieff.

"Robert," she sobbed against his shoulder. "We heard you were dead—" She hugged him with one arm, but he could not hug her back. Then Campbell dragged her back a step.

"What the devil—" Rob said. Sophie shook her head to discourage him from saying more or endangering himself.

"Neill," she said. "Are you harmed?" She looked toward him.

The older Highlander shook his head. "And you, lass? Are you in need?" He glowered at Campbell.

"I'm fine," she said, though Campbell held her fast. She looked at Robert. "Kinnoull and I were married."

"Aye?" His light blue eyes gleamed. "I'm glad to hear that." His face turned hard quickly and he looked at the magistrate. "Campbell, let her go."

"That does not suit." Campbell pulled on Sophie's arm.

She twisted in his grip. "You have no right to hold my brother or threaten my husband," she said. "No right at all."

Campbell slid a pistol from inside his frock coat, out of its belt sheath. Rob leaped to his feet, hands tied behind him, and snarled. Campbell let go of Sophie, then grabbed Rob's arm and held the pistol to his side.

Neill leaped to his feet, too, and Campbell snapped an order to the guard, who lifted a long musket, pointing it toward Neill. "Stay here with him," he said, then turned to Sophie.

"You'll come with me," he said. "And if you don't, Duncrieff will not make it through this day alive, though I kept him alive for the past three weeks."

"Kept him alive?" she asked, stunned.

"He has been holding me at Kinnoull House," Rob said. "I was ill at first—and not sure of my surroundings. He took me out of the Tolbooth and brought me here. Allowed me to recover, for which I must thank him," he added, nodding to Campbell, "but that is all the gratitude he deserves."

"Just so," Campbell said. "Both of you—this way." He began to walk. "A little stroll, and we'll discuss this."

Sophie hurried along beside them as Campbell dragged Rob with him, under threat of the pistol, and headed toward the bridge. Its span was unfinished, she saw, but complete enough to walk upon, lacking a top finishing layer of cobbled stone. The parapet that jutted up on either side was incomplete as well.

With the two men, she mounted the bridge and came to the peak of its arch. From there she looked down at the winding course of the river as she leaned out a bit.

Connor was there, as she had hoped he might be, for she had glimpsed him and his friends earlier. He crouched at the side of the river, out of sight of those on the bridge. Then he glanced up and met her gaze.

He appeared shocked at first, then angry, brusquely motioning for her to get off the bridge.

She shook her head and calmly turned away.

Campbell moved toward the parapet with her, and she angled in front of him, blocking his view.

"What is it you want, Campbell?" Rob asked. "Leave my sister be—you have no quarrel with her!"

"I should let the lady go, shouldn't I? But she is my fiancée, as you no doubt recall, Duncrieff. We've had a falling out, but that will be righted soon enough." He kept his pistol trained on Robert.

"You have Kinnoull House," Robert said. "You took it from the MacPhersons. Do you intend the same for the MacCarrans?"

"I had a chance once," Campbell said, "to head a clan. A rare opportunity, and something that your father and I agreed upon—but he died, and you, Duncrieff, filled his shoes. Unfortunately, you proved even more a rebel than your father. Many Highlanders are flocking to the Stuart cause, and the MacCarrans are solidly among them. They have some influence among their Highland peers. I wish to guide them toward better political wisdom."

"That's madness," Robert snarled. "You could never influence or lead my clan."

"Once Sophie is chief," Campbell went on, "I will

make decisions on my wife's behalf. I can sway this clan away from supporting Stuart's foolish claim to the throne."

"You did all this," Robert growled, "to further the political cause of the Whigs and fat King George? You're a Scotsman yourself. Where is your loyalty?"

"I have loyalties that you cannot possibly understand. Weeks ago it seemed necessary to move you aside quickly, possibly have you killed outright. But luck was with me when you were arrested. Your brother was staying at Kinnoull House, my dear," Campbell said, "when you were there, not so long ago."

She gasped. "You were there that night? Oh, God." She reached out for her brother, but Campbell pushed the pistol into his throat.

"Rob—he has a mad thought to claim the gold of Duncrieff. I've told him it's but a legend. We've only got a cup."

"One cup," Rob agreed. "And a lot of legends. That is hardly worth this madness, Campbell."

"I will judge that for myself, once I hold Duncrieff Castle. I had a bit of bad luck," Campbell mused, "when MacPherson stole Sophie away and married her. But I've been after that lad for a few years now. He's no innocent. I've watched him for a while—I suspected he and his lot have been doing the damage to the military roads."

Campbell leaned over the parapet.

"MacPherson!" he called. "Show yourself! I know you're down there somewhere. If you want your wife to live, you had best come out."

* * *

Clinging to the underside of the bridge, Connor swore. He watched the fuse shorten, inch by inch, and he had heard some of the conversation on the bridge. The fuse had burned too far now. He could not reach it to cut the sizzling end away from the rest.

The bridge would blow apart, and Sophie was there, standing on it, with Duncrieff. His heart slammed.

He had asked her to stay home—he had never really expected her to listen, but hoped that she might. If anyone had a chance of talking Campbell out of whatever mad scheme he had created, Sophie did— but not on the crest of that damned bridge.

He cast a glance at Thomas, who had worked his way downriver, following the muddy bank. He hoped the boy had sense enough to keep hidden as long as possible, until he could use that faithful aim where it was needed.

Casting an uneasy glance at the fuse, Connor came out from under the bridge, walked up the bank, and turned.

He spread his arms wide to show he was no threat, and walked toward the arched bridge.

"I suspect your true quarrel is with me, Sir Henry. Let them go, and you and I will settle this between us."

"No doubt you have some resentment toward me," Campbell said smugly. He pressed his pistol end to Rob's neck. Sophie looked alarmed, pale, turning to glance at Connor.

He did not look at her. He could not, for if he did, he might falter. She was his strength, and she was his weakness.

"I suppose so," Connor admitted. "My father was

dispossessed for his crimes. You took advantage of that."

"I did," Campbell said. "Any man might have done the same—a chance to own a fine estate. Two fine estates, and a clan in the offing, had you not interfered with my engagement to Miss MacCarran," he growled.

"Let them go," Connor repeated, thinking of the burning fuse, trying to count out the seconds in his mind. "Your quarrel is with me, not them." He stepped on the bridge.

Campbell stepped back, dragging Rob with him. Sophie stood stranded in the middle, eyeing Campbell warily.

Connor looked casually over the side of the bridge. The fuse was very short now. He was sure of it.

Below, he saw Thomas aim his pistol, saw him point it upward at Campbell's back as he edged along with Duncrieff trapped in his grip.

Connor gauged the distance between him and Sophie, and tried to judge the time that had passed. Glancing again toward Thomas, seeing his fervent gesture, he knew there was little time indeed.

Lately he had discovered a chance at happiness, and that chance stood on the stone bridge, staring at him with the most beautiful eyes he had ever seen.

He could not cause any harm to come to her now.

He saw the crystal stone winking on the chain around her neck, and he realized that he loved her in the way she wanted—truly. Passionately. He would do anything for her. Anything.

And if it took all he had, life and limb and soul, he would get her off that bridge, and her brother with her.

"Sophie," he murmured softly, taking a step nearer to her, nearer to Campbell. "Do you know that I love you?"

She stared at him, and he saw her catch her breath. She nodded, and touched the stone at her neck.

"It is too late now for whatever miracle you carry around in your fairy stone," Connor said. "But I want you to know that this is true love. It is."

She gasped again, tears filling her eyes.

"Can you swim?" Looking startled, she nodded.

He moved closer, looked at Campbell. "Let them go," he warned in a louder voice. "They have done nothing to you. It was all my doing—my crime. I took your bride away. Took your chances away for what you craved most. Let them go, and deal with me."

"I might," Campbell said, "if you were to die, sir." He took the pistol from Rob's neck and aimed it at Connor.

Connor was already moving in that instant. He rushed toward Sophie, grabbed her, and threw her over the side of the bridge into the river, where she had a chance to escape the explosion. Turning with a roar, Connor spun and knocked the pistol from Campbell's grip with a thrust of his elbow, then rushed into Duncrieff, tipping him off the bridge as well, into the water with his sister.

All of this in a moment, and in the next moment the bridge, the very air, shattered. The water split, tons of stones collapsed like so many pebbles, and Connor felt himself propelled outward as if blown from the barrel of a gun.

As the earth and river seemed to roar and crash apart, as water spewed skyward, the arched bridge fell apart as if it weighed nothing at all. Sophie screamed, and surged through the water. But Rob held her fast, where they crouched in the water at the side of the river, and now Padraig was there, his face still bloodied as he jumped down from the bank to join them. Another lad, golden-haired and armed with a long pistol, joined them also.

They all stared toward the bridge, and Sophie felt the impact of the explosion in her ears, so that sounds were muffled. And she felt the impact of the moment in her very heart.

For it broke the instant she saw Connor tossed into the air like a straw doll. He went down with the debris, with the rocks, sank and did not come up. The water heaved and sprayed, and she counted the seconds. He did not rise to the surface.

"Oh, God," she groaned, turning away, turning back. Her brother's hands were tight on her arms, or she would have thrown herself into the water, too. "Connor!" she screamed. "Connor!"

Then she remembered what he had said. *It is too late now for whatever miracle you carry around in your fairy stone. . . .*

This is true love. It is.

It was not too late—it could not be. Whatever sacrifice she would have to make, she would make it gladly, a thousandfold, if Connor could only be safe.

She touched the stone, and wished, and waited. Watched the surface of the river, where debris floated. She saw part of Campbell's gray coat, and did not want to see the bulk that lay beneath it. He was clearly gone, taken by the storm of explosives that had destroyed the bridge.

Watching, waiting, she could hardly breathe. Something constricted her heart, her sides. She squeezed the stone and prayed more fervently, more sincerely, than she ever had before.

She looked at the water, which had begun to grow calm again, despite the wreckage upon its surface and the wreckage of her life.

"Oh God," she sobbed, and turned to Robert. "Connor—he's gone—" She could hardly get the words out.

"He'll be fine," her brother said. "Conn is always fine."

She blinked up at him. Roderick had said the same thing once. She stared at him, wondering how he could be so callous, so casual, when her brother smiled at her.

"Conn is always fine," he repeated. "Look."

She whirled. He was crawling up the bank, drenched in mud and sopping, but he was moving.

Sophie plunged through the water, splashing, falling and sinking, climbing up again, until she reached the bank and began to run through mud and sloppy muck.

He sat there, waiting for her, and rubbed a hand over his face. Then he grinned, his smile flashing white amid the grime, his eyes impossibly green.

As she neared him, he reached down and grabbed her outstretched arm, half dragging her toward him.

She nearly threw herself at him, looping her arms around his neck, crying and laughing. Connor lowered his head, pressing his wet cheek to hers, the mud and water dripping from both of them.

"Mrs. MacPherson," he murmured, pulling back

to smile, sweeping his hand over her brow and her head, pulling the dripping tendrils away from her face. "Mrs. MacPherson, I love you."

"Aye, Connor MacPherson," she whispered, kissing his lips, kissing him again as she spoke. "And since this is true love, some sacrifice must be made now that the fairy crystal has brought you back to me."

"And what sacrifice is that?"

She pulled at his shirt, at the sopping plaid sliding from his shoulders. "When we get home, I think we will be sacrificing our clothing, both of us."

He laughed, a wonderful sound that made her heart leap and dance. There was music in it, and joy, and all the promises she could ever want, fulfilled in that one deep, mellow laugh.

"Oh," he said, "you do not believe in that fairy nonsense, do you, madam?"

"I might. Wait until you see your garden when you get home again." She smiled.

"Home," he said. "Home, aye." And he kissed her, deep and full and sticky with mud.

And she knew, as she tilted her face for another kiss, that his survival had been the miracle, and that the sacrifice had been his, not hers. He had been willing to give up his life for her. The Fairy's Gift had turned itself around and about, as such things would do.

Sophie kissed Connor once more, and helped him to stand, laughing as she realized something. "Love makes its own magic, Connor," she said, looking up at him.

"Aye, my lass," he murmured, pulling her close. "It does."

Epilogue

❦

"**C**ome here," Sophie said. She took Connor by the hand and pulled him with her across the length of the long room, their steps echoing on polished wooden floors, quieted by plush Turkish rugs in red, blue, and gold. "This is what I brought you here to see."

He laughed. "Oh? Not to have dinner with your brother, the chief of your clan, and your kinsmen? Not even to meet dear Mrs. Evans, who claims she nearly died of apoplexy the night I snatched you? Not even," he said, catching her close to him, so that she laughed breathlessly, "to see your childhood home, and the gardens you mucked about in as a child? Just to see this."

"Aye, this," she said, dragging him by the hand toward a sideboard of polished mahogany, with a gleaming glass dome set upon a wooden pedestal draped in red velvet.

Inside the protection of the glass stood a goblet. A simple thing, really, its golden bowl and stem of hammered gold, its base intricately etched with a band of engraved swirls and spirals that matched the border circling the rim of the cup. Set within that engraved upper border was a sparkling chain of small crystals, winking in the light that flooded through the windows of Duncrieff Castle's second-floor drawing room.

"And this is . . ." He was determined to tease her a little.

"The Fairy Cup of Duncrieff," she said. "Our castle's most precious treasure."

"I could argue that." He slipped his arm around her, snugging her close. He peered at the shining goblet. "So this is it. Looks a bit old. Well-used," he said.

"It's very old," she said. "It is said to be made from fairy gold, hammered by fairy goldsmiths. And the crystals were mined deep in the mountains of this glen, so they say, by the fairies themselves."

"Ah. And this treasure of yours was given to one of the lairds of Duncrieff? The one who deserted Castle Glendoon?"

"Oh, no, long before him, and he did not desert— I'm sure the story will be somewhere in our family records, which contain all the stories of the Duncrieff MacCarrans," she said. "Many of them were written by the hands of the MacCarrans who lived those very same adventures."

"I'd rather write music than tales of our adventures together, my love. You had better do that for us."

"I will," she said. "The first laird was called Malcolm MacCarran. His fairy wife gave him the cup—a very long time ago."

"You are determined to tell me the story of the legend, I think, though your kin are waiting for us out on the terrace."

"I told Robert that we would join them after I showed you the Fairy Cup. Now," she said, sliding her arm around his waist, "in the time of the mists, so the tale goes, this first MacCarran rescued a fairy woman whose horse had thrown her from a bridge into a river during a summer storm."

"I nearly did that," Connor said.

"But you made sure your fairy woman did not get wet. Hush it," she said, laughing. "He took her to his castle, a small tower in a remote setting, not this current castle. There they shared a warm hearth, a dram, a bowl of porridge, and more, so the story goes."

"Ah," he said. "This sounds familiar." He was genuinely intrigued, but he enjoyed teasing her just a bit longer.

"They fell in love, the laird and his fairy woman, and soon they were wed. I know," she said, when he drew a breath. "We did that part first."

He chuckled. "Go on."

"The MacCarran learned that his beloved was a princess of her ilk—the most ancient sort of fairy, beautiful and kind and of a size with humans, and possessed of powers of natural magic."

She paused as if expecting him to comment. He kissed her.

"And in their happiness," she went on, "MacCarran and his fairy bride had three sons, each more beautiful than the last. The sons inherited gifts from their mother—the Sight, the touch of healing, and the gift of charms and magic. When her children were grown, and although it broke her heart to do it, the fairy left her family and returned to her people, for that was her agreement with her own kind in exchange for those years of joy."

Connor listened intently now, fascinated, while he circled his arm around Sophie's shoulders.

"She left behind the legacy of her fairy blood, which now and then bestows the same abilities inherited by her sons, passed on through generations of the MacCarrans of Duncrieff. She left, as well, a golden cup smithed by her fairy kin."

"Aye," he said, looking at the goblet with heightened awe.

"It is shaped from what is said to be fairy gold," she said. "And its rim is set with a band of nine crystals."

"Some of them are missing," he said, tipping his head. "Two . . . no, there are four gone."

She nodded. "Kate and I each have one. According to family tradition, whenever a MacCarran child is born with the Fairy's Gift, a crystal is taken from the rim of this cup and set on a chain to be worn for that person's lifetime. Later it is returned to its original setting in the cup, and that person's tale is recorded by family members in the Book of Duncrieff, kept in a locked cabinet here, in the castle."

"And the crystal can create a miracle for its wearer," he said, "if conditions are met."

"Our tradition says that the Fairy's Gift some of us bear brings with it a singular burden. The crystal will grant its wearer one miracle—just one—for the sake of true love. If the privilege is misused, or summoned where true love does not exist, the Fairy Cup will lose its magical charm, and never again will a MacCarran inherit the Fairy's Gift."

"My God," he murmured. "I did not know about that risk. What of the empty settings, love? There are two. Is it just age, that two of them have been lost?"

"One crystal, they say, has never been returned. Mystery surrounds that certain tale, and I know little about it. But it is said that its power still holds true, for its love is still ongoing. Legend holds that the lost crystal is in the keeping of the castle's ghost, the Maiden of the Tower, who has not yet claimed her miracle."

"Duncrieff Castle?" he asked. She nodded. "Have you seen this maiden ghost?"

"I have not, but my grandmother did. You do not believe in ghosts, fairies, magic, and suchlike, remember?"

"I am learning. Go on. What about the other stone?"

"We do not know what happened to that stone. One tradition claims that it is still in the keeping of the fairy who bestowed the cup on her beloved family."

"What of the gold said to be hidden here?" he asked.

"No one has ever found it. I always heard that it was only a myth. How lovely if it were true, but—" She shrugged.

He nodded. "And the book you mentioned?"

"The Book of Duncrieff. An old manuscript that we keep here. Tales are added to it in every generation. The first part of the book is so old that we do not open it, do not handle it for fear it will crumble. And to be fair, we do not know if these tales are truth or fancy, history or just legend. But they are wonderful stories. My grandmother told me many of them as I was growing up." She smiled, turned into his arms, looked up.

"And our story?" He smiled, brushed his hand over her hair.

"I'll write it," she said, "when I have the time. I expect to be very busy for a while."

"Aye, with your garden projects at Glendoon, and here at Duncrieff."

"And Kinnoull House," she said.

He frowned. "Kinnoull? I wish I could say that was true. But even with Campbell dead now, my dear, I have not gained back Kinnoull House. I do not know if I ever will."

She slipped something out of her pocket. He saw that it was a packet of papers, folded, tied with a ribbon. "Connor," she said quietly. "I found this. I did not realize at first what it was—then when I looked at it again, just yesterday when we were up at Glendoon, I knew you must see it."

Looking at her quizzically, he took the packet and opened it. "A letter . . ." He peered closer. "No, it is—by God, it is the deed to Kinnoull. Where did you find this?" He stepped away from her, astonished, to peer closely at the document, its writing precise and ordered, the royal seal at the bottom of the page.

"I found it in a box in your mother's trunk."

"This . . . is the deed my father owned. It has his signature."

"There is a letter—aye, there. Your father wrote it."

He scanned the familiar hand, years since he had seen it. His heart pounded and his eyes seemed blurred with tears, suddenly. " 'I relinquish my title as Lord Kinnoull and my ownership of Kinnoull House and its environs to my son, Connor David MacPherson'—my God, Sophie," Connor breathed. "Father wrote this before he was arrested." He looked at her. "He gave it all to me, every part of it."

She nodded, smiled. "Kinnoull House is yours."

"But it's more than that," he said, looking from page to page, his mind whirling. "By signing it over to me before he was ever arrested or charged, it means the lands could not be taken from him by forfeit. It was never legal, that forfeiture. The property was always mine. We just never knew it. He never had a chance to tell me." He looked at her. "But he saved Kinnoull."

"So it never belonged to Campbell all those years."

He felt stunned. Simply, wholly stunned. He folded the pages, hands shaking, and slipped them inside the drape of his plaid, next to his heart. Then he reached out and pulled Sophie to him, clasping her close, holding her in silence for a moment.

He pulled back. "Thank you," he breathed. "Thank you."

She smiled through tears and kissed him, her mouth warm and delicious.

"Sophie love," he said. "I would never have known this without your help. I can never thank you enough—" He kissed her again, snugged her against him, deep in his embrace.

"You do not have to thank me for everything, Connor MacPherson," she said primly. "You are a polite thing for a great brigand."

He laughed. "Now I have something to offer my bride."

"You always did," she pointed out. "You just never knew. I would have fallen in love with you for the price of one fiddled song, played at the top of Castle Glendoon."

"That easy, was it? And all my struggle for naught." He sobered his smile. "Sophie, I've not said it enough. I love you."

"I know." She raised up to kiss him. "And I like to hear it often."

"I truly love you," he repeated, and pressed his cheek to her hair. "Come on. I'm glad to be shown your wee Fairy Cup, but I'm anxious to go home."

"Home," she said, and her voice broke. "Where, Connor? We've three homes now—Duncrieff, Glendoon, and Kinnoull."

"Glendoon is just my rented property, and I think I'll give it up. It has a beastly great hill."

"Oh no, you will not," she said as he led her out of the long, grand room with its polished floors and its golden cup, winking under glass. "My brother is giving us the property for a wedding gift. So I can finish the gardens, and we can refurbish the castle someday."

"Roderick will be pleased to hear that," he drawled, and she laughed.

"For a man who had no home, you have more than enough now."

He stopped, setting his hands upon her slender shoulders. "You," he said, "bring miracles in your wake, I think. Not just one, but many."

"A lifetime full of them," she whispered, and set her hand to her stomach. "There will be another a few months from now."

He looked at her, lifted a brow. "Is it so?"

She nodded, her skin blushing rosy. "I think so. We'll wait, and see."

He pulled her to him and closed his eyes in grateful silence, hardly knowing what to say, his throat tightening.

He led her out of the room and headed down the grand staircase in the old castle, rebuilt years ago. Through a bank of wide windows he saw the stone terrace and glimpsed the others waiting for them— his friends, her family.

And beyond, through the doors to the terrace, he saw a row of pots, each filled with blooming tulips, fresh and bright and lovely.

"Wait." He stopped, drew her near and kissed her.

Kissed her until her knees faltered beneath her, until she gripped his arms. Kissed her until he felt the fire within him stoke to a fever pitch. And then he drew back, drew in his breath. Her eyes were bright and beautiful, her cheeks flushed with love and with life.

Home. He was truly home, wherever she was.

*Bring on the spring thaw with these
hot hot hot March romances
from Avon Books!*

Just One Touch by Debra Mullins

An Avon Romantic Treasure

Caroline could not have imagined that her betrothed husband would be so tender, so warm, so . . . sensual. Rogan was expecting a meek and timid wife, but instead he finds her vibrant, charming and . . . passionate. Will this arranged marriage turn into something they have secretly hoped it would be? Something like a love match?

Special of the Day by Elaine Fox

An Avon Contemporary Romance

After a hideous break-up, Roxanne Rayeaux pitches the world of modeling, diets and philanderers and moves to Virginia to open a nice quiet restaurant. She wants some peace and tranquility, but instead she inherits the restaurant's contentious but sexy bartender, Steve Serrano. Steve is so totally *not* her type . . . so why is he so irresistible?

Lessons in Seduction by Sara Bennett

An Avon Romance

Normally prim and reserved, Miss Vivianna Greentree is beside herself. The heartless (but heartbreakingly handsome) Sir Oliver Montegomery is threatening to tear down her home for orphaned children! Vivianna is prepared to persuade Oliver to keep the orphanage by any means necessary, even if she needs lessons from a notorious courtesan to accomplish her task . . .

A Kiss in the Dark by Kimberly Logan

An Avon Romance

Two people from vastly different backgrounds are about to find out that their lives are entwined. Frantic to find his runaway sister, Lord Tristan Knight reluctantly turns to Deirdre Wilks, the most notorious woman in London, for help in tracking her down. But as Deirdre becomes a part of Tristan's life, she fights to conceal a secret that threatens to end the passion fast growing between them . . .

REL 0205